SKYLARK

Noel,

Always follow your dreams!

xo

Megan Michelle

SKYLARK

The SEAL Saga: Book 1

MEGAN MICHELLE

© 2024 by Bound Books, LLC

All rights reserved. This book or any portion thereof may not be reproduced or used in any manner whatsoever without the express written permission of the publisher except for the use of brief quotations in a book review.

The characters and events portrayed in this book are fictitious. Any similarities to real persons, living or dead, is purely coincidental and not intended by the author.

ISBN: 9798988886105

Printed in China

PART I:

DUTY

Chapter 1:
SEPTEMBER 2018

THE AIR WAS FULL of anticipation as they circled each other. Rachel was less patient, moving in with a quick uppercut to Christopher's stomach. She assumed he would see it coming. Hoped he'd be distracted by the taunting laughs coming from the other side of the gym.

No luck.

Christopher grabbed Rachel around the arms, restraining her.

"Life was easier when you didn't see that coming," Rachel teased.

"Still seems to work just fine on terrorists," Christopher said through gritted teeth.

Rachel gripped his forearms, her nails digging into his skin, and pulled his arms tighter around her. Then she threw the entire weight of her body into a somersault, flipping Christopher onto his back and allowing Rachel to free herself in the process.

"You and your fucking gymnastics moves!" Christopher yelled, though he was laughing.

He got to his feet, his own counterattack landing a thunderous strike to Rachel's ribs. She was momentarily winded by the impact, but she recovered quickly, launching a fierce barrage of punches at Christopher's abdomen. He ducked and weaved, his reflexes sharp. Rachel, lean and agile, matched his determination with unwavering confidence. The sound of their fists meeting flesh echoed through the gym, punctuated by their controlled grunts. Without warning, Christopher lunged forward, aiming a quick jab at Rachel's side. She swiftly sidestepped, countering with a low sweep kick that Christopher gracefully evaded. Their bodies moved in perfect synchrony—a dance of power and skill that was a testament to their nine years of training together as SEALs.

With a renewed burst of energy, Rachel threw a powerful punch aimed at Christopher's jaw. He grabbed a hold of her hand, spinning her and pinning her arm behind her back before forcing her to the ground. She shifted and rolled her body, sweeping her leg around his so that they were both on the floor, wrestling for control. Christopher climbed on top of her, holding her down. Rachel's heart raced. They were breathing deeply, drenched in sweat.

Rachel smiled up at him, her eyes sparkling. Christopher couldn't help but smile back.

They knew each other's strengths.

But she also knew his weaknesses.

As their eyes locked, Rachel used her hips and all her body weight to flip him onto his back, expertly pushing his own arms against his throat as he landed.

Christopher chuckled. "Why do I feel like you use that move in other sorts of situations too?"

Rachel winked and gave him a sultry pout as she pressed her thighs into his hips. "Imagining me in bed, are you?"

"Doesn't have to be a bed." Christopher flashed her a grin.

"Phone!" someone shouted from the other side of the gym. When neither Rachel nor Christopher broke their eye contact, the voice shouted again. "Commander Rachel Ryker!"

Sighing, Rachel glared over at their team's inter-agency liaison, Lieutenant Ryan *Raven* Rhodes.

Ryan held up her cell phone. "You've been summoned, Skylark. Admirals are here."

Rachel wrinkled her nose then looked down at Christopher. She was still straddling him on the ground. "Sort of in the middle of kicking Williams' ass," Rachel told Ryan.

"Looks like you already did." Ryan gave Christopher a once over. "Get up. Conference room three."

"For fuck's sake," Rachel muttered. The last thing she wanted to do was sit in a meeting. Ryan had mentioned Admirals, plural. That couldn't be good. "You're in charge." She pointed at Christopher. "Finish hand-to-hand combat training, then get the rest of the team up to speed on the situation in Afghanistan."

"Yes ma'am." He grinned before pushing her off him.

She fell onto the mat beside him and slapped him on the arm with the back of her hand. "Didn't you learn in kindergarten that it's not nice to push people?" They both burst out laughing.

"Have a fun meeting, Skylark," Christopher teased.

Rachel leaned back in her chair and stared at the ceiling, mentally preparing for what she was sure would be a long and arduous intelligence meeting. She closed her eyes and focused on her breathing, knowing she tended to run her mouth during these things. The thought of listening to a group of old men who hadn't stepped foot in the Middle East in over a decade was not a happy one.

The door to the conference room opened and her commanding officer, Admiral Paul Eastwood, Master Mission Commander for the Middle East Special Projects SEAL squadron, walked in. Rachel began to rise, but he gave her a quick wave with his hand, indicating she could remain seated.

"Ready?" Eastwood asked her.

"Maybe. Wanna clue me in a bit?" Rachel asked. She had no idea what they were going to discuss in this meeting other than time-sensitive intelligence. Something so time-sensitive that two admirals had flown from SEAL Command Headquarters in D.C. to Dam Neck Naval Base, just to see her.

"Emergency mission. Khost," Eastwood said.

"Covert?" Rachel asked, excited by the prospect of going undercover in Khost, Afghanistan.

"Why the fuck else would you be here?" Eastwood gave her a wink.

"Alright, well . . . who else is coming to this meeting?" Rachel noticed the second admiral had yet to arrive. She had no clue which agencies or branches of the military would be involved. She looked Eastwood in the eye, knowing he'd catch her meaning. "Who am I in this mission?"

"You are Rachel Ryker, U.S. Navy SEAL, commander of the Middle East special projects squadron and team leader."

"I know, but if we're going covert . . ." Rachel shut her mouth just as the door opened again. Both Rachel and Eastwood rose this time.

"Admiral Leftwich, sir," Rachel said seriously.

"Sit down," Leftwich barked. He took a seat at the head of the table as his chief of staff, Captain Simms, took up post, standing at attention to the side of him. Leftwich handed a file to Eastwood then an identical file to Rachel. She casually flipped it open with her right index finger and skimmed the first page.

"Indigo's deployment is getting pushed up," Leftwich stated.

"I see that." Rachel nodded, forcing her face to remain neutral. Her team—Indigo, the top covert ops team in the Middle East Special Projects squadron—was supposed to be at Dam Neck Naval Base in Virginia Beach, Virginia for training until November. Leaving in October instead wasn't horrible though. "So, the CIA lost a USB stick with some sort of malware code on it?" Rachel asked, feigning innocence. She'd pretend that she didn't understand the report, though still hoped Leftwich would notice her jab at the CIA.

"We're not even five minutes into the meeting, and you're starting with the attitude already?" Leftwich bellowed.

Rachel's eyes darted to Eastwood, wondering if he was going to intervene. He was busy reading the report. Or at least pretending to.

"You call yourself a SEAL, you may want to start acting like one. Show a smidgeon of dedication and loyalty to the Navy."

Rachel fingered the trident pinned to her collar and looked at Eastwood again. "If I recall correctly, I kicked everyone's ass all through BUD/S and got fast tracked through Green Team. Not to mention, I've deployed with my SEAL team for the past eight years."

Leftwich sized her up. "Yeah, I know what you really are though."

Rachel raised an eyebrow.

"There are a lot of secrets in this room." Leftwich pointed back and forth between Rachel and Eastwood. "Secrets and lies and cutting corners. Eastwood may tolerate you. He's all about keeping secrets too. You two and your joint operations, inter-agency bullshit."

Rachel blinked twice before looking back at the report. "Well, if you're so confident in this report, then I guess I'm taking my team to Khost. What does this code do?"

"That's need to know."

"It's a malware code stored on a green USB stick," Eastwood said. Leftwich glowered at him, but Eastwood continued. "It's programed to hit Iran's nuclear program. Their power plants."

"Don't worry your pretty little head about the code. All you need to do is bring in Saad Ayad. Alive and with the USB stick." Leftwich narrowed his eyes at Rachel. "So, you know Saad Ayad is personally responsible for funding at least fifteen terrorist cells and countless insurgent groups throughout the Middle East."

Rachel focused on controlling her face. She didn't know why Leftwich insisted on telling her information she already knew. She had Saad Ayad's entire resume memorized and knew everything there was to know about the man, other than where he currently was. She waited as patiently as she could before interjecting.

"Alive?" Rachel wrinkled her nose and turned to the last page of the report, unable to hide her displeasure.

"Skylark, you and Raven are gonna be busy," Eastwood teased.

"Busy? Saad's just one guy. Shouldn't take long at all." Rachel shrugged casually. "We'll get you what you need. Of course, it would help if I knew what information we were after." Rachel flashed Leftwich an innocent smile.

"It clones their servers so we can monitor and track everything they do. Every keystroke, every data point," Eastwood explained.

"For the nuclear weapons they allegedly don't have?" Rachel joked.

"For their nuclear reactors."

Rachel's eyebrows knitted together. Cyber and tech were far from her areas of expertise. "Are you talking, like, military installations or . . ."

"Their entire fucking power grid," Leftwich said, his lips curving upward.

Rachel pursed her lips and wrinkled her nose. "So whoever has that code essentially controls the light switches for all of Iran?"

"Or whatever country's servers that program gets installed on," Eastwood said, knowing she could connect the dots.

"Fuck." Rachel's eyes went wide. "So, Al-Qaeda now has a code with the potential to control *our* energy grid?"

Eastwood's head dipped slightly to confirm.

"And Saad Ayad has this code on a USB stick?"

"Correct," Leftwich said.

Rachel pressed her lips into a tight line and leaned back in her chair, contemplating the situation.

"Ryker." Leftwich held her gaze, unwavering. "Your team *will* succeed at this."

"Yes, sir." Rachel nodded and watched as Leftwich stood and marched out of the room without another word.

"Skylark." Eastwood gave Rachel a serious look once Leftwich was gone and the door slammed shut behind him. "He's on my ass to pull you from the field again. He wants you at HQ where he can keep an eye on you, assuming he's forced to keep you around at all."

"Fucking piece of shit, misogynistic jackass," Rachel muttered.

Eastwood ignored her comment. "If you don't succeed, if anything goes wrong on this mission, he's planning to use it against you."

"That's why it's a capture and not a kill, isn't it?" Rachel cringed, finally understanding why the mission was more complicated than it actually needed to be.

"Leftwich isn't an idiot." Eastwood looked straight into Rachel's eyes, and she saw the faintest flicker of fear cross his face. "He set this up for you to fail. As much as I'd love to have you working for me at HQ, I know that's not what you want, and I can't even promise that's where you'd end up if you fail this mission and Leftwich gets his way. You know he hates it when women are smarter than him. The fact that you're–"

"Young? Hot? Well-liked by everyone?"

"Something like that," Eastwood's shoulders shook with silent laughter until his tone turned serious again. "Watch your back, Skylark. On the mission and with the social politics."

Rachel bit the inside of her cheek, forcing her face to behave. She needed to shut down her emotions. Anger, sadness, rage. None of those were acceptable responses. Not now anyway. Right now, she was SEAL Commander Ryker—tough, badass, and untouchable. Not physically and not mentally either.

"Take a minute, get your head straight, then go brief your team." Eastwood closed the file in front of him, picked it up, and left.

Chapter 2:
SEPTEMBER 2018

"**WHERE ARE WE GOING,** Skylark?" Christopher's voice was as familiar as her own. It had been at her back, right behind her, for the past nine years.

Rachel turned from the bulletin board she'd been staring at and smiled brightly at him. "Your favorite place in the entire world, Hawk!" She gestured toward a large table covered in intelligence reports and maps.

Christopher moved over to the table, studying the map that Rachel had laid out for him. After a moment, she joined him.

"Khost again, huh?" He turned the map so that north was at the top from Rachel's viewpoint, because of course he knew she would have a hard time turning the map in her head. He could always predict what she needed, even before she knew herself.

It was a city map of Khost. They had both been there before, and Rachel was confident that Christopher had already memorized the streets, including where the safe roads would be. Even though the city had technically been under U.S. control since 2001, it was still a Taliban stronghold.

Rachel shrugged. "I guess they missed us." She dropped the intel report she'd received on the table in front of him.

Rachel handed him the intel report, the file peeled back to the first page, where the document outlined their mission to capture Saad Ayad. He looked up at Rachel, hopeful. "Please tell me I get to put a bullet in his head."

"You don't even care what Saad did this time to make him our target, do you?"

"No. He's a terrible human being and I really, really want to kill him." Christopher's eyes widened with excitement.

"Our official mission is to capture Saad and deliver him to the CIA for questioning." Christopher wrinkled his nose, clearly displeased. She chose to ignore him. "Leftwich assured me he knows where some stolen computer code is, but it doesn't seem like the sort of thing he usually gets up to."

"He's usually too busy blowing shit up to worry about stealing intel from us." Christopher's eyebrows knitted together as he contemplated what Rachel was saying.

"Exactly." It was the same suspicion she'd had when looking over the report with the admirals, but she was more at ease knowing that Christopher agreed with her.

Christopher clutched his lower back, which Rachel knew bothered him frequently thanks to an old injury. "In the spring and summer of 2008, when I was a Surface Warfare Officer, there were numerous car bombings in Kabul. We were looking for him, and not only did he almost kill us, but he kept getting away and planting more bombs, and then kept training more people to plant bombs . . ."

"Yes, I know. Can we please focus?" Rachel had heard the story of Christopher's adventures in Afghanistan more times than she could count. She was well aware that Saad Ayad was personally responsible for the bullet that had lodged itself in Christopher's lower back and that it bothered him more than he would ever admit. There was a fine line between documenting injuries in order to qualify for disability in the future and documenting too much and getting pulled from the team.

"Fine." He crossed his arms over his chest, trying not to pout at Rachel's lack of interest in his story. "What are you thinking?"

"Well, I know how badly you want Saad dead, so I decided not to disagree with Leftwich or his stupid report. So, for now, we pretend to do what the Navy says."

"I'd prefer if I got to kill him," Christopher noted.

Rachel shot him a sideways glance. "We will do our best to deliver him *alive* to the CIA, but, you know," she gave him a playful wink, "all sorts of things can happen."

Christopher looked at her, amused. She always made everything more fun. "What's our in?"

"I think I can work with his sister," Rachel said confidently. She turned toward the bulletin board she had been working on before Christopher joined her, turning it for him to see. Dozens of pink Post-its were pasted to the board along with a hierarchy of photos of Al-Qaeda's most radical criminals, thin lines of strings connecting between them. Saad Ayad was at the center, and from there, the strings branched out to the names and faces of his network.

Rachel tapped on the photo of Saad's younger sister, Amina Barech. "Amina is thirty-five years old. Married with five children. Three girls and two boys." The photo must have been taken before she'd become a wife and a mother—at least a decade old, if Rachel had to guess. It had been taken before Amina started wearing a burqa, opting instead for a bright blue headscarf, and it was the only photo Rachel had been able to find that showed Amina's face. She had perfectly plucked dark eyebrows that filled out her deep-set eyes and high cheekbones. Her hand was raised, as if trying to stifle the laugh that split her lips wide, a set of gold bracelets dangling from her slender wrist. She was beautiful. "She grew up in Saudi Arabia, but then moved to Afghanistan after her father and brother insisted she marry Imdad Barech, a rich businessman with ties to both the Taliban and Al-Qaeda."

Rachel couldn't help but sneer a little bit at the mention of her husband. Amina had been used as a bartering chip in her brother's grab for power as he tried to move his way up the Al-Qaeda hierarchy. Amina had no say in her life. No agency, no choices, no chance of escape. She was a victim, but Rachel was determined to change that.

"The mosque is probably your best bet to find her. More privacy. No men around," Christopher said.

Rachel nodded in agreement. They both knew that being female was secretly one of her greatest assets since it allowed her to speak more freely with women, who, given the current living situation for women in the Middle East, were more than a little reluctant to speak with men.

Christopher turned his attention back to the map, and Rachel cocked her head, struggling to read the lines that crossed and bisected through the city. He looked up and met her eyes, then traced his finger from the small star of their safe house down to the city center, showing her what he was planning. "The mosque is in the middle of the city. It should be a thirteen minute walk from the safe house."

"Specific as always." Rachel beamed as his bright cerulean eyes locked with hers, causing her to feel instantly calmer.

"What the hell does that mean?" Christopher sounded slightly offended.

"It means, obviously, that a normal person would say it's a ten-to-fifteen-minute walk."

"But it's not a ten-to-fifteen-minute walk. It's a thirteen minute walk." Christopher was obviously missing the point.

"Thirteen minutes and how many seconds?" Rachel teased.

"It depends on how crowded the sidewalk is," Christopher said seriously.

Rachel pressed her lips together to stifle the laughter and jokes she knew were about to fly out of her mouth.

"We can get there and get set up in the safe house. I think you should go to the mosque on day one, then go every day. That will be your best bet for making contact with his sister, or anyone for that matter," Christopher said. "Bring civilian clothes, and I'll walk with you through the city so you don't get lost or arrested or anything else."

Rachel rolled her eyes. She knew Christopher was convinced she couldn't follow basic navigational instructions. She had gotten lost once while on leave in Paris, and another time in Madrid. But to be fair, she had also been very drunk both times, and her cell phone battery had been too low for her to look up directions. The getting arrested part was an actual threat in Afghanistan though, since women currently couldn't go out without being escorted by a male family member. And the 'anything else' part . . . Well, they'd had a few close calls her first time over there. Since Rachel was the first, and to their knowledge only, female SEAL, no one was used to wandering around the Middle East with a woman. It took a while on their first deployment with the team to work out the rules. She'd been young and especially brazen back then. As a former intelligence officer tasked with collecting intel from human assets, she was used to jumping into chaos, making sense of the situation, and shooting her way out if things went poorly.

"Can you finish this?" Rachel asked, gesturing to the collection of documents scattered on the table. "We need to present it to the rest of the team in an hour."

He looked at her and forced himself to keep a straight face, noticing how restless she was. "Yeah, I've got this."

Christopher knew Rachel couldn't sit or stand still for too long and guessed her meeting with the admirals had been a severe test of her patience. As always, Rachel had already more or less memorized every single piece of information. She knew what they needed to do and how to do it. All Christopher had to do was work out what route to take between various locations and plan the timeline. He did his best to ignore her and focus on the intel report in front of him, but his eyes darted to the other side of the room more frequently than he wanted them to. She was very distracting.

"What are you doing?" Christopher watched her out of the corner of his eye as she sat on the floor, playing with the ten-inch tactical knife she always kept in her boot.

"Checking if my knife is sharp," she grumbled.

"Umm, I'm sure it is." He turned his head and furrowed his brow. "Stop using your hand to check if it's sharp. You're gonna cut yourself whether it's sharp enough or not. Just sharpen it before we leave." He studied her for a moment longer, noting her suddenly sour disposition. "Maybe take a breath and chill?"

"I thought you were working?" Rachel asked with a tinge of irritation in her voice.

Christopher sighed and tried to refocus. Fortunately, he didn't have much to figure out. The mission itself would be complicated once they got there, but the actual plan was simple: fly to Afghanistan, hang out, interact with the locals, gather intelligence, hunt down the target, capture the target, and extract the team.

Rachel had already outlined a very detailed plan for each step, leaving notes on pink Post-its throughout various pages in the mission report. He always found it interesting that she chose pink. Every single time. He had never seen a pack of pink Post-its anywhere on any military base except for Rachel's notes. It was one of the few girlish things about her.

Sure, Christopher had noticed how beautiful she was. Drop dead gorgeous, if he was being honest. Stunning actually, with a radiant smile and sparkling emerald eyes. He'd thought it the first day they had met on the bus to start SEAL training together. Of course, everyone had assumed she was a nurse or someone from human resources. But he didn't see her that way now. None of the men did. She was one of them, through and through. The only time they considered her sex was when it put her at extra risk during their deployment. Laws for women were strict in the Middle East, and Christopher, as well as the other SEALs, had gotten used to keeping her out of trouble.

Besides, Rachel knew about a hundred ways to kill someone with her bare hands. She was tough and smart and as respected as any military officer. Not only for her skills in combat or for her talent in military strategy and planning. Everyone respected Rachel because of who she was at her core. She had integrity, always the first one in and the last one out during any mission, and she would never ask anyone on the team to do an assignment she wasn't willing to do herself.

"What are you pouting about over there?" He couldn't keep his eyes off her.

"I am not pouting," she insisted. Her wrinkled nose and pursed lips sure looked like pouting.

"Plotting how you're going to dismantle the patriarchy?" Christopher teased.

Rachel raised both eyebrows and gave him a look indicating that he was correct. That's what she was always doing—plotting and scheming ways to liberate every woman in the world from every sort of oppression. Her definitions of patriarchy and oppression were fairly broad too, so it was going to take a considerable amount of time, persistence, and bloodshed to accomplish. He was certain Rachel would die trying to accomplish those goals, and he was entirely certain he'd be right by her side, dying next to her, when the time came.

"Well, the rest of the team will be here soon," Christopher said.

Rachel glanced at the clock on the wall. "Shit!" She jumped up and ran out of the room. Christopher shook his head, no idea where she had run off to or why.

Rachel returned a few minutes later with several pizza boxes in hand. "Morale boost," she said, motioning to the pizza.

Christopher nodded. It was so like Rachel to think of that. Small things that would make a big difference to everyone as they prepared to leave their friends and family behind for a highly dangerous mission.

"Pizza!" Ryan called out moments later as he came into the room with Lieutenant Matthew *Nightingale* Johnson, the team's medic. "Thank you, Skylark!" Ryan grinned as he reached for a slice from the box on top.

"You are very welcome, Raven," Rachel answered.

"If we're getting pizza," Matt started, "I can only assume this isn't going to be a fun mission."

"Patience, Nightingale. All will be revealed shortly." Rachel winked. Other than Christopher, Matt and Ryan were her two closest friends. The four of them were practically inseparable. Of course, being the only four officers on their team, as well as living on base together for such long periods of time, tended to help people bond.

Ryan quickly inhaled a slice of pizza. As a New Yorker, he couldn't get enough of the stuff, even if he constantly complained about how terrible all pizza was outside of Brooklyn.

"Have you not eaten today?" Rachel wrinkled her nose, staring at Ryan.

"Obviously I have, but this is good. Which place did you get this from?" Ryan asked, brushing his nearly black hair away from his forehead with his fingers.

"Umm, the one just off base so they'd deliver, and I didn't have to go get it," Rachel said. Ryan gave her a thumbs up, his dark green eyes meeting hers momentarily before he started inspecting the other pizza boxes, investigating what his other topping choices were.

Matt stood to the side, smiling politely as he waited for Ryan to move. As a native of rural Kentucky, his southern manners made him seem quiet and shy compared to the rest of them. He was never one to turn down free food but knew better than to get between Ryan and pizza. He tried to hide his amused smirk as he watched Ryan sift through the pizza boxes, portioning out slices onto more paper plates. Moments later, Ryan handed him a plate with two slices of cheese pizza and one slice of pepperoni.

Their communications expert, Petty Officer Second Class Aiden *Blackbird* Bennet, came in next. "Am I late?" He stared at Rachel with a concerned look on his face.

"If you're late, then everyone else is really late," Rachel said, gesturing to all the empty chairs.

"Right," Aiden said, looking around. He noticed the pizza and nudged Ryan out of the way to grab a slice before sitting down. Ryan slapped his hand away then handed him a plate with three slices of sausage and mushroom pizza.

"Which one's mine?" Rachel asked Ryan.

"You get whatever's left since you'll eat anything, and other people are more discerning," Ryan explained.

Christopher flashed Ryan an irritated look and grabbed two slices of pepperoni—one for him and one for Rachel.

The rest of the enlisted men on their team trickled in, one after another: Michael *Eagle* Winters, their sniper; David *Sparrow* Hail, their explosives expert; Daniel *Condor* Hart, their tech guy; and Nate *Crane* Barnes, their drone operator. Next came Jason *Vulture* Andrews, Brendon *Albatross* Hayes, and Aaron *Pelican* Axelson, all of whom were vital to the team but had not chosen a specialization. Ryan handed each of them their respective plate of pizza as they came in.

Once everyone was happily fed, Rachel got started. "Alright guys, we're headed back over to the sandbox." She looked around the room at everyone. "We've got another one of those highly exciting joint CIA missions ahead of us. Apparently, we have a target that needs to be dealt with in Khost." Everyone groaned, knowing where this was going.

"Not that I'm advocating for the spread of war," Michael started, "but do you think we could ever go somewhere other than Afghanistan? It would be nice to see other parts of the world." This elicited a lot of laughter from the group. They all knew the Navy was fond of telling people that joining up was their chance to see the world on Uncle Sam's dollar, but the most any of them had seen was Afghanistan and Iraq, with the occasional venture into Pakistan or Syria. That was the downside to being on one of the most elite teams belonging to the Middle East Special Projects Division.

"I'm afraid not this time, boys. As y'all know, Khost is a densely populated urban environment with a high potential for civilian casualties, which we obviously want to avoid." Rachel explained the extent of their mission—the malware code, the nuclear reactors, the bullshit capture-and-not-kill order. She pulled out her bulletin board and went through the hierarchy, ending on her and Christopher's plan to use Amina to track Saad. "To summarize, he hates the West, he hates women, and he hates anyone who disagrees with him. Now, what questions do y'all have?"

"What is our actual cover? I don't think *computers* is the answer," Daniel said, trying to stifle his irritation. "Hawk, maybe you can explain it since we all know Sky doesn't understand much past how to send a text or email."

Rachel rolled her eyes. "I'm not an idiot."

Christopher cut her off before she could go on a tirade explaining everything she knew about technology, even if Daniel was right and it wasn't much. "We're allegedly partnering with the university in Khost and researching IT network design and security," Christopher clarified.

"That makes more sense. Thank you." Daniel tried to hide his smile.

"If we're being covert and quiet, I'm guessing we won't need too many explosives. What should I pack?" David asked.

"You shouldn't need to bring too much. Like I said, the safe house should be stocked with what we need. If not, I'll get you what you need." She hated relying on the CIA for supplies, but they had the resources and manpower in the Khost. Not enough manpower to get Saad Ayad themselves, apparently, but that was a whole different issue. "Any other questions regarding the mission, or should we move on to Share and Care?" Rachel asked. Share and Care was one of Rachel's brilliant innovations that she implemented after taking over as team leader four years prior. She insisted that everyone have the opportunity to express their thoughts, feelings, and concerns in a supportive environment without being judged. "Okay then, just to recap. The rules of Share and Care are simple. We go around the room. Everyone has to say something about how they are feeling and what they are thinking. Let us know in advance if you just want to share, or if you would like feedback or help problem-solving from the group. No one comments on what anyone else says unless you have something positive and supportive to contribute. Before commenting, you must ask if it is okay with the person who shared that you comment. No one leaves or gets out of their seats until everyone has shared. No touching or trying to comfort anyone until we're done. You sit in your feelings and you feel them. Good?" Rachel looked around again, trying to assess everyone's state of mind.

"Good," they all echoed back.

"I can go first," Christopher started. "I, like Michael, am fucking sick of Afghanistan. Not that anywhere else in the Middle East is much better, but at least it would be a change of scenery. I hope we can pull this off quickly. It seems straightforward enough, if not slightly boring. And I would really prefer it if we could kill Saad Ayad instead of giving him to the CIA. In any case, I'm excited to get to work."

"I'm sad to leave Charlene again," Matt said, referring to his girlfriend of five years. "Everything's better when I'm with her, you know? But at least I have you guys."

"I personally enjoy wandering around and talking to people," Aiden said. "So, I'm looking forward to this mission. I promised my grandma we'd be back for Christmas though. Maybe I shouldn't have done that. Do you think I should call her?"

"Was that an actual question that you wanted someone to answer?" Rachel asked.

"Yes," Aiden confirmed.

"We'll be back for Christmas. Calm down," Christopher told him. "But yes, call your grandma again before we leave."

"Okay, I will. Like I said, I'm very much looking forward to making some new friends in Khost!"

"We aren't going there to make friends," Aaron said.

"Hey, what are the rules? Only nice supportive comments," Rachel reminded Aaron. "Besides, you know Aiden can make friends with anyone. He probably will have a new BFF after this mission."

"I'm just in a bad mood," Aaron continued. "I got season tickets to the Stealers, and now I can't use them, and Jen is mad that I spent so much on them."

They went around the room, taking turns until everyone but Rachel had shared. She paused, looking down at the floor. "I'm excited to go, and unlike most of you, I hope it takes all the way through New Year's so I don't have to go home and see my family for Christmas." They all knew Rachel lied to her family about her job. The fact that there was a female SEAL was so classified that even Rachel's father, who happened to be an admiral, was kept in the dark about it. She looked around the room. "Anyone else want to share something?" The room was silent. "Okay, then I hereby declare this meeting over. See y'all for hand-to-hand combat training tomorrow at 0600."

Chapter 3:
SEPTEMBER 2018

THAT FRIDAY AFTERNOON, CHRISTOPHER drove Rachel, Matt, Ryan, and Aiden up to Atlantic City to celebrate Rachel's birthday.

After checking in to their respective rooms and leaving their bags, the group made their way downstairs to a cocktail lounge. It was sleek and sophisticated, with high ceilings, elegant lighting fixtures, and comfortable seating areas. They all scanned the room as they went, knowing it was their best option for finding someone to entertain themselves with, someone to distract them from their upcoming deployment. Well, except for Matt of course. They ordered their first round of drinks and were standing by the bar when Ryan said "target acquired" and made a beeline for an attractive brunette across the room.

"Oh, he's never gonna get her!" Rachel laughed.

"He might," Aiden said.

"If he tells her he's deploying to combat tomorrow, and it's potentially his last night on earth, maybe. But if he does that, then I'll make sure it *is* his last night on earth," Rachel threatened.

"Why? It's true."

"He's not deploying tomorrow. It's a fairly low-risk mission, and it's manipulative to use that line."

"Oh, it just pisses you off when we do that since it never works for you," Christopher chimed in.

"No, it does not work for me, which should tell you something about the sexist indoctrination you're all playing off of."

"It's not our fault girls fall for that line." Aiden crossed his arms over his chest.

"It's taking advantage."

"They're doing their patriotic duty!" Aiden did his best to keep a straight face as he said it, though he knew it would piss off Rachel.

"Fix your attitude, or I'll make sure you can't use your dick ever again," she threatened, her eyes going dark.

"Yes, ma'am." Aiden instantly stood straighter and shifted his gaze to the floor, knowing Rachel was more than capable of following through on her threat.

They watched Ryan for another minute before he came back, defeated. "Boyfriend," he said sadly. "She talked to me for a while before she mentioned that though, so who knows?"

"A no is a no," Rachel reminded him.

"Obviously." Ryan glared at her.

"Oh, that's not about you," Matt assured him.

"Yeah, Aiden pissed her off right before you came over here," Christopher added.

"What the fuck did you do?" Ryan slapped Aiden on the back of the head.

"I didn't do anything!"

"He said something about girls doing their patriotic duty by sleeping with him before he deploys." Christopher smiled maliciously, knowing it would piss off Ryan almost as much as it pissed off Rachel.

"Are you fucking kidding me?" Ryan crossed his arms over his chest and stared Aiden down. "Dude, we've talked about this."

"She started it!" Aiden pointed at Rachel. "She said there was no way you could get that girl unless you told her you were deploying tomorrow. I was just standing up for you."

"Seriously, your mouth goes a million miles an hour faster than your brain!" Ryan shook his head.

"You too." Aiden raised his eyebrows, daring Ryan to disagree.

"No, I'm not at all as bad as you," Ryan disagreed.

"You both have similar issues," Matt chimed in, hoping that would settle the argument.

"Oh, shut up, Matt. You'd be in the exact same situation as us if it weren't for Charlene." Ryan gave him a playful nudge.

"No, I definitely wouldn't be, seeing as I know how to speak to other humans," Matt insisted.

"I can settle this." Rachel snickered and walked to a table with four girls, motioning for the guys to follow her. She looked them up and down before addressing the girls, "Hi, I was hoping y'all could help us settle a debate."

"Sure." All four girls smiled as they eyed the guys.

"So, of these four guys, who would you be most likely to go home with and why, assuming you and they were single?"

"Just based on looks?" A blonde in a dark blue dress asked, eyeing Christopher.

"I don't care," Rachel shrugged, ignoring that the girl's dress was the color of Christopher's eyes. "However you would normally decide."

"That's not a very realistic test, Rache," Christopher pointed out.

"Fine, say words or something."

"Okay, well, tell us something about them," the brunette requested.

"They're all in the Navy," Rachel told them.

"What do they do in the Navy?"

"That's classified, I'm afraid." Rachel winked.

"I'm a combat medic," Matt told them his usual white lie.

"Wow." The girls were all staring at him with stars in their eyes.

"Okay, we all have medic training, but yes, he's actually technically the team medic," Ryan clarified.

"I think that solves that debate pretty clearly." Rachel giggled. "Matt wins."

"Of course, I do," Matt chuckled.

"So, are you single?" the brunette asked again.

"No, I'm not, but these two were trying to say no girl would ever want to go home with me if I were single, so we sort of had to prove a point." Matt pointed to Ryan and Aiden.

"That's not being very supportive of your friend," girl number three said as she twirled her red curls around her finger and eyed Ryan.

"We're not trying to be supportive of him," Aiden told her. "Why would we be supportive of our competition? You know, best friend or not." He shrugged.

"Well, I think we proved the point, Aiden." Matt smiled.

"Yeah, but that's only because people know what medics do, and saving lives is hot," Aiden said. "That's why everyone loves doctors and firefighters. I save lives too, you know? If it weren't for me operating the radio and being on the satellite phone all the time, none of you would ever get evacuated from anywhere, and it wouldn't matter that you're the best damned medic in the entire U.S. Navy."

"And if I didn't explain to you where we were, then you wouldn't be able to tell the helicopter where to go to pick us up," Christopher told Aiden. "So really, I'm the one saving lives."

"You're usually the one whose life we're saving," Matt noted.

"No, that would be her." Christopher pointed at Rachel.

"Wait, you're in combat with them?" The fourth girl, a shorter blonde in tight jeans and a sequined tank top, flashed Rachel a crooked smile.

"Yes. I happen to be their commanding officer, actually," Rachel said, trying to hide her pride.

"Wow, *that's* hot!" the brunette said, wide eyed.

Rachel shrugged. "See guys. As usual, I win. Debate settled. And now, thanks to your bickering, none of these girls are interested in any of you at all." Rachel sighed.

"They are all hot," the red head noted.

"Thank you." Matt was practically blushing.

Aiden exhaled and stared up at the ceiling. "Oh, go back to your corner and text Charlene some more. I'm sure she'll be thrilled to hear about this."

"She'll probably find it funny." Matt chuckled and pulled out his phone to do just that.

"So now that we've taken him out of the equation . . ." Aiden pointed at Matt.

Rachel glanced over at him and pressed her index finger to the underside of his chin, simultaneously closing his mouth and raising his amber eyes to a more appropriate height. "Seriously? You excel at communicating with people. That's why you're in charge of the damned radio. How come when we get you around pretty girls your brain turns to mush?" Rachel hit him on the back of the head with her palm.

"Well, I'm around you all the time and my brain works fine, so what's that say about you?" Aiden teased. His eyes were locked on the blonde in the blue dress.

"Alright, that's enough." Rachel huffed, realizing Aiden had blown his chances with all four of the girls by implying she was ugly. She turned her attention to the girls. "Sorry to bother y'all." She nudged the guys away from their table and toward the other side of the room.

"Why did you make us walk over here so fast?" Aiden asked.

"Because that was fucking embarrassing." Rachel glared at him. "Do y'all remember when we had that training on this? What did I tell y'all then?"

"Ask their name, give them a compliment, and ask about their interests." Aiden stared at the floor.

"Is that difficult to do?" Rachel glared at him.

"No." Aiden slouched.

"Okay and another helpful tip, don't insult women in front of other women."

"When did I do that?" Aiden wrinkled his nose with confusion.

"You just called me ugly in front of them."

"Okay, yeah, I guess I sort of did." Aiden scratched his head through his cropped brown hair and looked at his feet. "Can we get another drink please?"

"Will it help you to be less stupid?" Rachel asked.

"Maybe."

"I know you are capable of behaving like a normal adult human being,

Aiden." Rachel stared at him.

"There's too many girls in here! I'm nervous."

"No, you aren't," Rachel insisted. "You're just in a mood about something."

"What are you nervous about?" Christopher asked.

"Picking wrong!" Aiden burst out laughing, and Rachel rolled her eyes.

"All of the girls in here are gorgeous. You cannot pick wrong," Rachel insisted. She knew he was just saying things to provoke her and get her attention, but she didn't know why.

"But it really could be my last night on earth!" Now Aiden was deliberately taking it to the next level, and she knew it.

"Not true, seeing as how we aren't leaving tomorrow," Rachel said calmly.

"Fine, my last night to hook up with a girl."

"We'll be here tomorrow too," Rachel reminded him. "Wanna try again?"

"No." Aiden puffed out his cheeks and made his way to the bar. Rachel followed after him.

"Seriously Aiden, what is going on?" Rachel asked, sliding in next to him and signaling the bartender to get her another whiskey.

"My grandma is really sick, and it sounds like we're gonna be gone a long time." He turned sideways to face her, leaning his elbow on the bar, forcing his sculpted bicep to flex.

"Then it makes sense you're nervous and acting out like a child." Rachel took a deep breath. "Aiden, if you'd told me sooner, I could have pulled in someone else and you could have sat this one out."

"Where the hell are you gonna get a communications specialist who's as good as me?"

"I didn't say I could get someone as good as you. I said I could get someone else, and then we'd have to make it work. It's too late now, though."

"I'd never let you guys go over there without me. You know that." Aiden stared straight into her eyes. His typical boyish innocence had morphed into a hardened defiance she rarely saw in him.

"Yeah, I know." Rachel sighed. "Why did you come with us this weekend instead of having more time at home with her?"

"Because it's your birthday," Aiden said, as though it should have been obvious.

"I'll have a birthday next year too," Rachel reminded him.

"Yeah, maybe."

"No one is dying on this fucking trip, Aiden," Rachel hissed.

"Atlantic City?" His eyebrows knit together.

She clenched her jaw. "No, I obviously meant Khost. No one is dying here either, though."

"Alright." Aiden didn't sound convinced.

"We will have a fun weekend, then you can fly back to Oklahoma and hang out with your grandma for a few days and have your mom make you a pie, okay?" They'd all been hearing about the best apple pie in the world for years.

"No, she only makes me a pie when I come home from deployment. Not from getting drunk in Atlantic City." He pouted.

"Do you already have a plane ticket?"

"No."

"Get out your phone and book one then."

Aiden puffed out his cheeks on a sigh then pulled out his phone to check flights. "These are all too expensive!"

Rachel grabbed his phone and looked at the screen. "This isn't that bad for a last-minute ticket."

"It's fucking expensive, Rachel. Not all of us are officers and get paid a million dollars a year." He squinted his eyes and looked away from her.

"Well, you could go to Officer Candidate School if you wanted to. Also, none of us get paid a million dollars a year."

"Whatever. You know what I mean." Aiden turned his face away from her.

Rachel gave him a sideways look and typed in her credit card information, booking him a ticket.

A few rounds in, Ryan went for a second attempt with a short blonde with shoulder-length hair and a pretty smile. He bought her a drink, and within thirty minutes, he was escorting her back to his room.

Matt and Rachel watched with amusement as Christopher and Aiden flirted with a group of girls who were there for a bachelorette party.

"I am so happy I'm not single," Matt said. "What are you thinking tonight?" he asked Rachel.

"I'm thinking we're about to deploy for an unknown amount of time, and I'd rather not waste my night being disappointed," she answered.

Matt laughed. "Your standards are too high, Sky."

"My standards are perfectly adequate. Why should men be the only ones who can know for certain that they'll have an orgasm when they hook up with someone? I mean, really, most of y'all are either too stupid or too lazy. Why should I bother? Seriously, this is what vibrators are for. But we'll see what the options are tonight."

"Well, I'm happy I'm not sharing a wall with you then!" Matt shook his head and pulled out his phone to text Charlene.

"What are you writing to her?" Rachel grabbed his phone so she could see.

> Nightingale to Charlie: *I wish you'd come with me!*
> Charlie to Nightingale: *What are you doing? Watching everyone flirt with random girls at a bar? Or people I guess...*

Rachel looked up from Matt's phone and handed it back to him. Well he wasn't going to be any fun tonight. She scanned the bar, looking for her own target. "He's hot." Rachel jutted her chin toward a guy about her age on the other side of the room.

"The tall guy with wavy brown hair?" Matt tilted his head, eyebrow raised questioningly at Rachel.

"Yeah." Rachel grinned right as Aiden walked up to them.

"Which guy with brown hair? Chris?" Aiden asked.

"Gross." Rachel grimaced, but her heart started racing.

"No, the one in the corner that looks remarkably similar to Chris!" Matt burst out laughing.

"There is something wrong with you two." Rachel cringed.

"Uh-huh. We're the problem." Matt scoffed. "You do realize at some point in your life you're gonna have to take the walls down and let someone in, right?"

"I let people in all the time," Rachel winked.

"Emotionally, Sky!" Matt clarified.

Rachel scrunched up her face, not at all pleased with the turn in the conversation. She noticed that Christopher had moved on to a brunette who looked like she could be a supermodel. He looked like he was about to close the deal, but not quite.

"What do you think, guys? Should I go help him?" Rachel asked, pointing to Christopher. She decided competing with Christopher was much more fun than listening to Matt ramble on about emotions.

"Be nice, Sky," Aiden pleaded on Christopher's behalf.

"I'm always nice," Rachel insisted.

"To Chris, not to the girl!" Aiden laughed. "Be nice to Chris!"

Rachel walked over to Christopher and introduced herself to the brunette. "Hi, I'm Rachel Ryker, Christopher's boss. And as his boss," she continued, ignoring Christopher's clenched jaw, "I can assure you that he's the best of the best at everything he does." She smiled salaciously. "The only person better qualified than Christopher is me, hence why I'm his boss and not the other way around. So, you're in very good hands."

The corner of Christopher's upper lip curled as he gave Rachel a sideways glance. Rachel refused to engage him and admit to what she was about to do.

The brunette turned to Rachel curiously. "Why are you trying to convince me to settle for second best then?" she flirted, looking at Rachel intensely before pulling out her room key. "What do you say?"

Rachel bit her bottom lip and cocked her head to the side. "What's your name?"

"Angela."

"Lead the way, Angela!"

"Well played, Rache." Christopher shook his head in disbelief as Rachel wrapped her arm around Angela's shoulders and headed toward the elevators.

★ ★ ★

Matt and Aiden walked over to Christopher, laughing uncontrollably. "Oh my god! Did she just steal another girl from you?" Aiden asked. This was not the first time this had happened, and it surely wouldn't be the last.

"I was so close!" Christopher complained.

"She went over there to help you," Matt mocked.

"Yeah, well, isn't that how it always starts? Damn it, I hate it when she does that!" He'd never seen Rachel get shot down before. It seemed she could have any man or woman she wanted. "Why doesn't she ever steal girls from the rest of you?"

"I wouldn't say she *never* steals girls from the rest of us . . ." Aiden said.

"Maybe it's because," Matt gave Aiden a sideways glance doing his best not to laugh, "you tend to get a higher caliber of girls than certain other people do." Matt tilted his head toward Aiden.

"What the fuck does that mean?" Aiden was outraged. "What is wrong with the girls I'm hooking up with?"

"Nothing, as long as we don't have to talk to them about anything above a fifth-grade reading level," Christopher teased.

"Well, I don't know if you realize this or not, Christopher, but I'm not exactly inviting them to a book club," Aiden pointed out.

"Oh, come on Aiden. You have to admit your standards aren't always that high." Matt was trying to be diplomatic about it.

"I have very high standards."

"Yeah, his standards have gotten higher in the past few years," Christopher teased. "He's evolved from ready and willing to hot and ready and willing."

"True," Matt conceded.

"Are you giving up Chris?" Aiden asked.

"Hell no! It's still early." Christopher's eyes locked on a tall blonde standing at the bar. "Watch," he said. He walked up to the girl just before she could pay for her beer and handed the bartender a twenty-dollar bill. The girl looked at him, shocked and somewhat displeased.

"I can buy my own drinks, thanks," she said to Christopher.

"I know," he answered. "But how else would I be able to get someone as intelligent and beautiful as you to talk to me?"

"How do you know I'm intelligent? You know nothing about me."

"Any girl who pays for her own drinks, and orders her beer in a bottle rather than a glass in a bar this crowded, is definitely intelligent," he said. She looked at him incredulously. "Let me guess," he continued, "you just got off work, and this is either the closest bar to work or home that isn't complete shit. You're clearly alone, so you ordered your Bud Light in a bottle even though they have it on tap because you know there's a smaller chance that someone could slip something in your drink. I'll bet that after you finish your beer, you're planning to drink one, if not two, glasses of water before walking back to your car with your keys between your fingers, just in case."

"And tell me," the girl said, leaning forward, "how did you figure all of that out by staring at my ass from across the room?"

Christopher leaned toward her. She did have a great ass. It was one of the first things he'd noticed about her. Probably not something she needed to know, though. "I'm a naval officer highly trained at reading body language." She looked impressed. "Plus, I have two sisters and a female boss who likes to keep me up to date on all the precautions women are forced to take because men are terrible."

The blonde smiled brightly at him now. "I'm Layla." She stuck out her hand to shake his.

"Lieutenant Commander Christopher Williams." He smiled back.

"So, are we going back to your place or mine?" Layla asked.

"Mine's closer," Christopher answered, pulling out his room key and holding it up for her to see.

Chapter 4:
SEPTEMBER 2018

AT 1130 THE NEXT morning, Rachel sat on the beach just steps away from their hotel, staring out at the waves as the blue water collided with the pale sand and changed to white foam. The waves and the seagulls overhead were the most relaxing sounds in the world. Rachel's hair was wet and tangled, and her skin was covered in salt and sand.

"Hey," Christopher said as he sat down next to her. "I figured I'd find you here. Did you get any sleep?"

"Four hours. You?"

"Eight, like a normal person." Christopher looked at her for a minute then brushed the sand off her face. "Were you rolling around out here or something?" He pointed to a dog doing exactly that—running and rolling around in the sand. "Close your eyes," he instructed.

"Leave me alone!" Rachel giggled, swatting his hands away from her face. He grabbed both of her wrists in one of his hands, and she closed her eyes to let him brush the sand off her forehead.

"How did you get sand all over your face?" Christopher asked.

Rachel raised an eyebrow, then popped up to flip into a few cartwheels down the beach. Christopher roared with laughter and fell over onto the sand. "I'm kidding, obviously. Sort of," Rachel said as she settled back down next to him. "I was doing yoga—headstands—you know?"

"That makes sense." Christopher nodded. "I was going to go for a swim. I know we're headed off to the desert and mountains . . ."

"Yeah, why do you think I'm out here getting as much ocean time as possible?" Rachel asked.

"One last swim then?" Christopher suggested as he pressed the button to waterproof his smartwatch.

As a response, Rachel took off sprinting toward the water. She giggled, which slowed her down enough that Christopher was able to catch up with her. He picked her up and effortlessly threw her over his shoulder, wrapping his arms around her legs and waist in a safe, warm embrace, and headed straight into the water.

"I'd close my mouth if I were you," Christopher teased seconds before tossing her into a wave. Moments later, her head popped up over the water, and she flashed him a bright smile and a thumbs up, then pointed away from the beach. They swam together, perfectly synchronized, diving under wave after wave for the next forty minutes.

"What was up with Aiden last night?" Christopher asked Rachel as they walked up the beach.

"His grandma is sick apparently, so he's worried."

"Makes sense."

"I bought him a plane ticket to go see her for a few days before we leave, so if we can drop him off at the airport, that would be great."

"How much was it?"

"Why?"

"Because I'm splitting that with you," Christopher insisted.

"You don't have to do that."

"I realize that, but I'm paying for half of it anyway and if you try to transfer the money back to me, then I'll just transfer it back to you and we'll keep doing that until one of us is dead."

Rachel groaned. She knew he was right. "You're incredibly annoying sometimes."

"Shut up. You know I'm your favorite person in entire the world." Christopher gave her a playful shove.

"Obviously." She wrapped her arm around his waist and leaned into him.

"Besides, in the who's dying first debate, you know it would be me," Christopher said seriously.

"Why would it be you?"

"Because you know we'd both do something stupid and be on the ground next to each other bleeding out, and Matt would save you first."

"Why the hell would he save me first?" Rachel's brow furrowed.

"Because I'd tell him to." Christopher smirked.

"Well, I outrank you, so he'd have to listen to me telling him to save you first."

"That's dumb."

"No, it's not." Rachel stopped walking. All of their shared humor left her face and was replaced by perfect stoicism. "Christopher, you know your life is more valuable than mine."

"How do you figure?" He put both hands on his hips and stared down at her, genuinely confused by what she meant.

"You like your family. Past drama aside, I know you've worked everything out, and you love your family, and they love you and you actually have friends. You have people who would care if you died. They'd probably care a lot. My family . . . I mean, if I die, it wouldn't really affect anything."

"That's the dumbest thing I've ever heard."

"I'm sure it's not," Rachel argued.

Christopher crossed his arms over his chest and stared straight into her eyes. "First of all, your family would care if you died. You just don't care that they would care. Second, if you died, it would affect everything. The world needs you, needs your compassion, your moral compass, and your leadership."

"And I need you backing me up," Rachel reminded him.

"Then we better do something dumb enough to kill us both instantly!" Christopher smiled brightly. He wrapped his arm around her shoulders, pulling her against his side as they walked. She circled her arm around his waist and leaned into him.

Chapter 5:
OCTOBER 2018

TEN DAYS LATER, TEAM Indigo landed at Khost Airport in Afghanistan at 0900 on October 2. Rachel looked around at her team, a jolt of pride warming her. Her team of covert ops experts played their parts so well. They were dressed in civilian clothing, with most of the men dressed in either lightweight chinos and a linen button-up shirt or cargo pants and a polo shirt with the Princeton crest stitched over the heart. Rachel was in long, loose pants and a long-sleeved blouse. Her hair was pinned up and covered with a black silk scarf. With the cover of being a research group going to visit nearby Shaikh Zayed University, they needed to look professional, but not too professional.

"What is going on with your face?" Rachel asked, poking Christopher in the cheek as they stood in line at passport control. He had grown out his facial hair just enough to disguise his identity.

"Umm, you know, blending in and what not," he replied quietly.

"It looks terrible, Christopher." Her lips pressed into a playful pout as she looked up at him.

"It does not!"

"Really terrible. I think you've misunderstood the Quran. Women are supposed to hide their beauty, not men."

"So now I'm beautiful?" he teased with a proud grin on his face.

"Other people tend to think so." Rachel shrugged. He was absolutely gorgeous, and everyone knew it.

Christopher looked at the line moving ahead of them. "Where's your ring?" He looked down at Rachel's hand, where her grandmother's wedding ring should be. The perfect cover so she could go out with them. "Looks like you have about a minute to choose a husband," he teased. She would need a solid cover story for who her male family members were in case any of the Taliban guards stopped her on the street.

Rachel smirked then leaned into him, wrapping her arm around his waist. She looked up at him with a bright smile and a twinkle in her eye. Christopher draped his arm across her shoulders and smiled back. They moved forward in the line and showed their passports and visas to the immigration agents, easily clearing the border since they had everything they needed to enter the country, including papers from Princeton University and Shaikh Zayed University documenting the purpose for their visit.

After clearing passport control, Rachel led her team of twelve, including herself, through the Khost Airport and out to the parking garage where two pickup trucks were waiting. She may not be an expert navigator like Christopher, but she knew how to get out of the Khost Airport. She'd been to Khost more times than she'd like to think about, and while it was far from the worst place she'd ever been, it was definitely not her favorite either.

Khost, to her, meant bombs. She'd been an Intelligence Officer for two years, collecting intel from human assets behind enemy lines, before becoming a SEAL. On her very first deployment, Khost had been under attack. She'd heard stories of war from her grandfather, who had been a paratrooper during WWII, and had thought she was prepared for what she'd see. But watching people get blown to bits was very different than hearing about it. She'd been tasked with confirming the locations of key targets and had spent months in Khost behind enemy lines, learning the ins and outs of how to survive in a combat zone with minimal supplies. The experience had hardened her in many ways. She wasn't horrified by bloody, dismembered, dead, or half-dead bodies anymore. She didn't take shit from anyone, even if they outranked her. Learning to stand her ground physically and mentally had been the biggest take away from that experience.

It had softened her too though. She had interacted with families, with the women and children living in Khost, and saw firsthand how culture and politics impacted their daily lives. Women weren't allowed outside without a male family member escorting them, and the war was killing off the men quickly, leaving women stuck at home with their children, dependent on the generosity of neighbors, friends, and extended family. That fact made it harder to kill her enemies, knowing she'd be putting the women and children in vulnerable positions. But if she killed enough of the men, the women would have no choice but to fight back and defy the fucking Taliban and Al-Qaeda, or whatever ridiculous group decided to assume control and strip women of their rights on any given day.

Rachel climbed into the truck with Christopher, Aiden, Matt, Michael, and Brendon. Ryan drove the second truck and followed close behind them as they pulled out onto the road that would take them to the city. Rachel played with the music as she sat in the front middle seat, between Christopher and Aiden. Beside her, Christopher navigated the city expertly, as always, weaving in and out of traffic.

The team drove around for two hours, checking out the area and driving past their safe house twice. Aiden chatted with everyone on their handheld walkie-talkies the entire time. Rachel listened to several people who had no business giving relationship advice attempted to advise Matt on whatever conundrum he was having with Charlene.

"You've been together for five years, Matt, and we all love Charlie!" Aiden gushed. "If you don't marry her, I will."

"No way in hell Charlie would go on a date with you, let alone marry you!" Matt protested. Rachel groaned at the absurd turn their conversation had taken.

"I have been on a date with her!"

"What?" Rachel heard Ryan laughing over the walkie-talkie.

"We had a lovely dinner," Aiden insisted. "In fact, if we count every time

I've been to dinner with Charlie, I've been on several dates with her."

"Those aren't dates!" Matt yelled. "Charlene's hanging out with you as friends, you fucking moron."

"Thank you. I'm well aware of that!" Aiden yelled back. "I was just saying, it's about time you lock that down."

"I think they're pretty committed to each other, married or not," Christopher chimed in. "But Nightingale, if you want to waste money on a fancy party, I'm more than happy to get drunk and eat some free food."

"For fuck's sake, Hawk, stop encouraging them," Rachel said. "They can decide if they want to get married. It's not a team decision. None of us get a vote."

She leaned her head on Christopher's shoulder as she stared out the windshield and observed their surroundings. Khost was bustling with people and energy. The mix of modern and traditional architecture, made necessary by the damage from the civil war in the '90s, always fascinated Rachel. The traditional mud-brick construction and intricate geometric patterns, particularly in the older parts of the city, were sand-colored, sometimes with brightly painted accents around the windows. Sadly, the modern architecture—large concrete buildings—seemed to be taking over.

It was the people, though, who drew her attention most—the women in particular. She counted how many wore the burqas and how many didn't. While it wasn't mandatory, more and more women were giving in to societal or familial pressure by covering themselves from head to toe. She noticed that more women seemed to be wearing black and white or other neutral colors. A fashion trend maybe, but likely considered more modest and proper than the vibrant purples and reds she was used to seeing in Afghanistan. Rachel didn't have any issues with burqas or body coverings, per say. She had an issue with men dictating how women dress, how they act, when they could speak. She watched and observed these women and thought about the difference between them and the women she saw in America. She had to admit that the West's hypersexualization of women may be taking things to the opposite extreme. She'd never been catcalled on the streets of Khost before. Of course, she always dressed conservatively and had someone from the team, usually Christopher, right by her side. She'd wandered all over the world with Christopher though, and his presence didn't always stop comments, but her knee to a guy's balls usually did.

On the third pass of the safe house, Christopher pulled their truck over to the side of the road and the men all got out. Rachel adjusted her headscarf then got out of the truck. Someone had already unloaded her bag from the back of the truck, so she grabbed it and led the men up a narrow flight of stairs, keys already in hand. She unlocked the door, reaching her left hand over to flick on the lights. It was a small three bedroom, one bathroom apartment in the middle of the city. Really too small for the twelve of them. Each bedroom had two double beds that they would share as they rotated in and out of the apartment for their patrol shifts. Khost was quiet at night due to the upswing in violence and car bombings over the past few months. The locals tended to stay home after dark, which meant the SEALs, for the most part, could too. Christopher and the others checked the bathroom and the three bedrooms as Rachel absently set up her laptop to check the latest intelligence reports.

An hour later, Rachel called out, "Team meeting. Kitchen." The men all joined her and stood around the kitchen table where she was sitting. Without taking her eyes off her computer screen, Rachel started giving orders. "I want everyone out in pairs. Partner up and get to exploring." She slid a city map across the table. It was the same map Christopher had drawn over when they'd been preparing Indigo for the mission, black ink marking a grid pattern over the streets to divide the city into six quadrants. "Each pair will pick a section to survey, and we'll rotate sections every couple of days so that everyone gets eyes on everything. That way we can more easily maintain our cover too. No weapons. Civilian clothing only. Be careful and be safe." Rachel typed on her computer as the men all stood around for a few minutes, waiting for her to continue. "What the hell are y'all doing?" she asked, confused. "Go!" she ordered, her voice seeping with irritation. Christopher took over assigning the pairs of men to their respective sections, and each pair headed out as soon as they received their assignment.

Rachel complained as soon as they were all gone. "Is it really so hard for them to just pick a section of town and go? Jesus Christ, we shouldn't have to do everything for them."

Christopher's mouth twitched as he tried to suppress his laughter. "Are you going to tell me what you found in that intel report that's triggered your temper?" Christopher asked her.

Rachel turned the laptop so it was facing Christopher before explaining. "Latest from the fucking CIA. Trouble in paradise, it seems."

Christopher skimmed the intelligence brief. "They've identified three targets for us?" he asked, dismayed. "I thought it was only one?"

"Yes, apparently on top of Saad Ayad, we need to find and capture Munir Omarkhil. He's barely twenty-five years old. He was radicalized as a teenager and is now going around to villages raping women and killing anyone who doesn't agree with his way of thinking, likely on behalf of Saad Ayad, even if his tactics are more akin to those used by ISIS than Al-Qaeda. We also need Saad Ayad's nephew, Ibrahim Ayad, who seems to be assisting the other two by providing cars, housing, cell phones—anything they need to stay hidden. He's married to a woman named Noor, so I guess that gives me one more person to try to befriend."

"Lovely," Christopher grumbled.

Rachel let out a sigh and typed for a moment before turning the laptop back toward Christopher so he could see a photo—not a good photo—of Noor. "Maybe we won't make it home for Christmas after all," she said playfully, trying to cover her irritation. She suspected Admiral Leftwich was trying to make things more difficult for her.

Christopher scoffed. "In your dreams Skylark. This is going to be a piece of cake. You'll see."

Rachel raised both eyebrows, contemplating how much to share. She was an excellent liar, but lying to Christopher was always difficult for some reason. She realized that it might be a good idea for her best friend to know that the fate of her career rested on this mission, then decided against it. It wasn't his burden to bear. She forced her face into an optimistic smile and asked, "Did you save any part of that map for us?"

Rachel and Christopher left the safe house and locked the door behind them, nodding and politely greeting the neighbors as they passed. Her degree in International Comparative Studies from Duke University had ensured she was fluent in Arabic and Pashto, which were more useful than her fluency in German or French. But studying a culture and living in one were two very different things. The laws could be rigid and unforgiving, even for foreign visitors and U.S. military personnel, which had shocked her the first time she'd been in the Middle East. Now, of course, everything was more or less second nature.

They wandered the crowded streets and made their way to Khost Central Mosque just in time for midday prayers, hoping to catch sight of anyone in Saad Ayad's network. It was a huge building with sand-colored walls, a robin's egg blue dome, and twin pillars on either side. Out front, a large reflection pool mirrored the mosque back to her. Despite having been to the mosque hundreds of times, Rachel was always impressed by the majestic façade adorned with intricate tilework and calligraphy. The grand arched doorway was framed by motifs of delicate florals and geometric patterns that paid homage to the rich Islamic architectural traditions.

Rachel adjusted her black headscarf, making sure to cover every strand of her hair before following Christopher into the mosque. She carefully stepped her right foot in first, which was the common way of entering and exiting buildings in the Islamic world. It represented a practice of mindfulness and reverence and was considered to be a way of drawing closer to God.

They slid off their shoes and placed them on the shoe rack next to the entrance. Rachel gave Christopher a knowing look before moving toward the small prayer room designated for women off to the side of the entryway. She focused her eyes on the patterned red carpet, careful not to run into any of the large pillars holding up the high ceiling. She wasn't free to wander at her leisure or stare at the tilework the way the men were. She joined the line of women entering the small chamber, knowing Christopher would be fine on his own praying with the men.

She took her place in the back of the room and knelt on a prayer matt she'd gotten from the corner of the room, mindful to ensure that her feet didn't point forward toward Mecca, showing respect and reverence for the holiest of places.

It was a little ironic that Rachel was so steadfast in her decision not to attend church, but she would pray in a mosque. Of course, being there to collect intelligence was different from going to church to have an old man lecture her about her supposed sins. Promiscuity, adultery, wearing a short skirt—whatever some dumb man presumed Jesus would be mad at her for that day. Not to mention murder. She'd never understood the justification that murder was fine if done in the context of war. Then there was the debate of what constituted war. Sure, shooting the enemy in the heat and chaos of an ongoing firefight was one thing. But killing someone during a covert-op, did that really count as war too? It seemed like a convenient excuse concocted by men who wanted to go to war and kill for their greed. Or make other people kill for their greed. But she excelled at it, and so she did it, always doing her best to atone for her sins one way or another.

The words left her lips as she prayed to Allah, to God, to the gods of every pagan pantheon she'd ever heard of, begging for someone to alleviate the world's suffering.

Allah. God. Whatever Being is out there listening. Please take care of the women in this room. Rachel opened an eye, looking around at the women. Not all of them had chosen to unwrap their burqas, a choice given to the women in the privacy of their segregated prayer room. But there were a few women who had pulled the cloth back from their faces. There was a woman to her right who was smiling as her lips moved in prayer. Another woman knelt beside her, her own headscarf pushed back to expose a bit of silver hair. Fine lines crisscrossed her face, the signs of decades of humor and worry.

This was how Rachel would find Saad Ayad's sister, Amina, or any woman in any of their targets' social networks. The cross-cultural communal nature of women never failed to supply her with the information she needed to complete her team's missions, even if it sometimes took a while to build up the trust and acceptance by the local women.

Rachel grit her teeth. *End their goddamn suffering—the violence, the inequality. With your help or not, I will fight for these women.* This was the war she was fighting. This was her mission. Sure, she took orders from SEAL Command HQ, but she never let those orders interfere with her efforts to win the real war.

When the prayer service had concluded, she waited for the other women to rise, ensuring she didn't make any mistakes that may offend them. She scanned their faces, taking mental snapshots of every woman who had removed her burqa so that she could go back to the house and study all the photographs on her bulletin board. It was always difficult since they often relied on old photos. People aged, but she knew that with time, she would find her targets.

Rachel found Christopher and followed him toward the exit, moving silently, glued to his side, but never touching. They were so practiced at this after so many years that neither of them had to speak. It was almost like there was an invisible energy between them, like magnets, drawing her body toward his. They moved in perfect sync with each other as they navigated to the entryway. They both stopped to put on their shoes before heading out of the mosque, remembering to exit left foot first.

Chapter 6:
OCTOBER 2018

INDIGO HAD BEEN IN Khost for ten days without any luck of finding their targets. Each morning, they would pile into their trucks and head to the university, making their cover story more believable to their neighbors who had already expressed an interest in the group of Americans. Though the Afghan people were used to Americans coming and going over the past two decades, there was always budding suspicion and unease among those who feared western ideas. But then of course, there were those who knew exactly how to take advantage of most Americans' needs for a translator or local guide. The team didn't need any of that, of course, but their neighbors didn't need to know just how well-versed they were in Afghan culture or how familiar they were with the city.

Even with the connections they'd made with the translators, the team was still no closer to finding any signs of Saad Ayad, Amina Barech, or anyone else in their network. This called for drastic, if not highly unpleasant, measures.

"I'm going to meet our CIA liaison to see if she has any updates for us," Rachel announced to the team after a quick round of Share and Care.

"Why can't we all go meet her?" Aiden asked.

"Because twelve people do not need to go to the CIA office."

"But we want to meet her too!"

"No, you want to talk to her and flirt with her and test your luck," Rachel corrected him.

"I mean . . . the CIA girls are usually hot . . ." Daniel noted.

"Do you know what?" Christopher furrowed his brow. "There's an even number of us. Ryan and Rachel will be meeting with the CIA liaison. Matt will be restocking medical supplies. I will be going with them in case anyone tries to show Sky a map. I do not want to get stuck in a situation where she thinks it takes fifteen minutes to get somewhere when it actually takes seventeen minutes because she thinks fifteen sounds better."

"That happened once." Rachel glared at him.

"Once was more than enough." Christopher glared back.

"No one died."

Christopher placed both hands on his hips. "No, we all just almost died. In any case, I'm going with them, which means the eight of you can divide yourselves into pairs however you'd like. I know you're all more than capable of that."

"But . . ." Aiden protested.

Ryan slapped him on the back of the head. "Stop complaining and go outside and make some friends."

Christopher drove Rachel, Ryan, and Matt to an inconspicuous office building in the middle of Khost so that they could meet their CIA liaison. In this case, it was a young junior analyst named Paige. They all shook her hand then took their seats around a conference table.

Christopher couldn't take his eyes off of Paige. She didn't look a day over twenty-five, and her long blonde hair flowed straight down her back. She had a wide, enthusiastic smile and seemed overly eager to meet them.

"Welcome to Khost! It's so great you're all here!" Paige gushed. "Or I guess you've been here for a bit, but welcome to the office in any case."

"We're happy to be here." Christopher flashed her a bright smile.

"Right. So, updated intel," Rachel redirected.

"Of course!" Paige's head moved up and down in an exaggerated, overly enthusiastic fashion. "So, you need to find a man named Saad Ayad."

"Correct."

"Well . . . I don't know where he is," Paige told them. "But we're hacked into the city's security system and scanning their camera footage for him. So if we see him, you'll be my first call." She bowed her head and looked up at Christopher through her long, dark eyelashes. He bit his bottom lip as the corners of his mouth curled.

Rachel noted the smirk on Christopher's face and the twinkle in his eye. Her stomach turned. "I'll be your first call," she corrected, raising a finger in the air.

"Right. That's what I meant." Paige nodded.

"We are also supposed to be finding Munir Omarkhil and Ibrahim Ayad," Rachel reminded her.

"Of course." Paige's eyes went wide, and Rachel guessed this was the first time she had heard those two names.

"Do you need me to write them down so you have the correct spelling?"

"Yes please."

Rachel grabbed a stack of Post-its off a table in the corner of the room and wrote down the names of all three of their targets. She was trying to be patient, but it seemed like Paige had no idea what their mission was. She decided to give Paige the benefit of the doubt and skipped lecturing her on who the men were and why they needed to be captured, hoping Paige would figure that out herself once she investigated them.

"Then you can continually update us on whatever is on the security camera footage and any other intel updates you have, and we can fill you in on anything we learn," Ryan told her.

"Sounds good."

Paige's eyes wandered back to Christopher, and Rachel bit the inside of her cheek, desperate to hide her irritation and disapproval. She was well aware that the men on her team were above average on the attractiveness scale, but

Paige seemed to be above average on the easily distracted scale. "Paige, do you have any insight into the political situation in Khost right now?"

"What do you mean?" Paige's eyes snapped back to Rachel, her cheeks flushing pink.

"I mean, how much influence and control does the Taliban actually have at this point? According to the Constitution of Afghanistan, women are allowed out, they are allowed to have jobs, there are even women serving in parliament. However, women are still attacked on the streets for going out alone, right?" Rachel needed to know how careful she should be while wandering around Khost and wanted to confirm if she would have to take one of the guys with her every time she wanted to go somewhere.

"Correct. The Taliban has control over about sixty percent of the country right now," Paige confirmed.

"Violence against women is still higher than in really any other country, right?"

"I guess . . ."

"And it's not prosecuted. Not really anyway."

"Not that I can tell," Paige agreed. "From what I know, it's much worse in rural areas. The cities are less conservative. So if you leave Khost and go out to the countryside, all of the women will be in burqas. But here, they just have to cover their hair . . . or it depends on the family, I guess? So, technically, legally, you can go out by yourself, but I don't."

Rachel nodded. It was like going back in time, this huge backslide on women's rights. She knew that the president of Afghanistan had issued a code of conduct for women back in 2012 that dictated women could not travel without a male guardian or mingle with men they didn't know. The president claimed that it was all in line with Islamic Law even though it went against the country's constitution. A lot of it was semantics and interpretations, but mostly it was the goddamned patriarchy back in action, preventing women like Amina Barech and Noor Ayad from being able to act autonomously and make decisions about their own lives. Rachel was pissed. She knew she needed to act more assertively if she was going to find her targets and help the women of Khost. She couldn't keep to the shadows anymore. It was time for her to do what she came here to do. "Christopher, take me to the mosque."

The older woman Rachel had seen her first day at the mosque was there every day during midday prayers. Rachel had noticed her because she was one of the only women, beside herself, that opted for a head scarf rather than the burqa. They would exchange warm smiles every time they passed each other, but today, Rachel decided she would test her luck with the woman. It was time to initiate a conversation.

As Rachel walked into the women's prayer room, she greeted the older woman in Pashto. "You are here every day, and you are always so friendly and welcoming! What is your name?"

"Zarah," the woman answered, smiling warmly. "And your name?"

"Rachel." She glanced around the room and said, "Not many women wear bright colors here."

Zarah's hand reached up to the ruby red scarf draped loosely over her hair. "What I wear and what I do should be between me and Allah, and maybe my husband. Not," Zarah waved an irritated hand in the air, motioning toward the outside world, "you know."

Rachel smiled at the floor.

"You are here quite often yourself," Zarah noted.

"I'm not sure where else to go for social interaction, honestly," Rachel said, trying to sound timid.

"I understand. Why are you in Khost?"

"Oh, I'm a guest researcher at the university. I'm with a whole group from Princeton University in the U.S."

"Research?" Zarah asked.

"Yes. IT network design and security." Rachel was proud she finally memorized what they were allegedly working on. She saw the confused look on Zarah's face and rephrased. "Computers. How to make computers and the internet safer." That was the best she understood from all of Daniel's ramblings while he tried relentlessly to explain it to her.

"Oh." Zarah's brow lifted. "And the man you come with? Who is he?"

Rachel flushed. Zarah had been watching her. Rachel eyed Zarah's red scarf again. Something about the woman—her defiance of the social norms, maybe—made Rachel lean in. "Can I trust you with the truth, or do I need to tell you the lie that keeps me from getting arrested?" Rachel asked.

"Both," Zarah insisted with a sly grin.

"He's a colleague, but if we get stopped by the Taliban or anyone, he lies and says he's my husband." A slight smile spread across Rachel lips at the lie or maybe at the idea of Christopher actually being her husband. Warmth spread over her. She shut it down promptly.

Zarah grabbed Rachel's left wrist to inspect her hand. She nodded, pleased to see a diamond ring on Rachel's finger. "Smart girl." She gestured toward the ring.

"It was my grandmother's." Rachel fingered the ring on her left hand, a gold band with a small round diamond in a square setting and two small round diamonds on either side.

Zarah raised an eyebrow, clearly wanting to hear more.

Rachel went on. "She was from France and part of the resistance during World War II. My grandfather was in the U.S. Army and met her there." Her Grandpa Jack had told her many stories about D-Day and her grandmother's part as an undercover spy, luring Nazi officers into her bed so she could kill them. It was an intimidating legacy to live up to but inspirational nonetheless.

"Strong women in your family." Zarah nodded. "Good. Be careful."

Chapter 7:
OCTOBER 2018

TWO WEEKS PASSED. RACHEL was getting restless. She knew being accepted by a new group of women was always difficult, even in the U.S. But this was going slower than she had hoped. She was in the women's prayer room, getting up to leave when Zarah approached her with a young woman in tow. Rachel recognized her from her first visit to the mosque. This was the young woman who had been praying with a bright smile on her face, looking so calm and hopeful and happy.

"Rachel? This is Yashfa. I think you are close in age," Zarah said, introducing them. "You said you didn't know what to do here when you were not working?"

"Yes. Pleasure to meet you, Yashfa." Rachel bowed her head.

"You as well, Rachel. Zarah tells me you are a researcher from America?"

"Yes, I am." Rachel smiled at the lie.

"We have a group. Some women, I mean. We meet and talk and work on embroidery and other projects. Mending clothes, weaving, that sort of thing. Maybe you would like to join us?" Yashfa asked.

"I would love to!" Rachel's eyes went wide with excitement and full of hope. She was doing her best to stand still rather than bounce up and down and decided to clasp her hands together in front of her chest as a reminder to control her emotions.

"Good. We meet at my younger sister Yamna's home. It is a bit of a walk from here. You know not to walk alone?" Fear washed across Yashfa's face at the thought.

"Yes. One of my colleagues can walk with me or drive me. Could you write down the address and directions?"

"A male colleague?" Yashfa checked. She sounded incredibly concerned.

"Yes, and he'll lie and say he's my husband if we get stopped." Rachel flashed her ring. "Don't worry. I know how to stay safe and out of trouble here. The university made us take several classes before we could come."

"Very good." Yashfa did her best not to giggle. "We don't let the men stay."

"Good! Yashfa, I've had enough of men. I'm sharing an apartment with eleven of my colleagues. All men."

"Oh. That sounds terrible. So much work!" Yashfa grimaced.

"Work?" Rachel asked.

"Cooking, cleaning . . ."

"Oh, they help out. It's alright." Rachel gave a casual wave of the hand, indicating it was no big deal.

Yashfa stared at her in shock. "The men help cook and clean?"

"Yup. I'm not their mother."

"Well done!" Yashfa sounded fascinated.

Chapter 8:
OCTOBER 2018

CHRISTOPHER AND MATT DROVE Rachel across the city the next day. Neither of them was pleased about the idea of Rachel hanging out with a group of women they had never met. They had no way of knowing who else would be in the house. Rachel kept insisting it was fine.

"We'll just park across the street and wait for you," Christopher told her.

"You most certainly will not!" Rachel argued.

"You have no idea who else is in that house or what is going on." Matt reiterated the point Christopher had been trying to make for the past two hours.

"I have my knife. It's fine," Rachel insisted. "Besides, you don't know who else is outside watching you watch the house. It's just as dangerous!"

"Your phone is charged?" Christopher checked.

"Yes." Rachel drew out the word, irritated at the implication. Christopher reached out his hand expectantly, palm up. Rachel rolled her eyes and handed him her phone so he could see that it was fully charged. She had accidentally let it die twice in the nine years she had known Christopher, and he would never let her live it down.

"You're just seeing if they know Amina, right?" Matt checked.

"I'm making friends, Matthew." Rachel's tone was more than a little patronizing.

"Rache, focus. You just need to see if they can lead you to Amina, or to any of our targets. That's why you're here."

"I'm here to network and see what the current status is for women living in Khost, see how we can help, *and* see if they can lead us to our targets. I have a lot to do. It's going to be a while, which is why you may not sit in the truck and wait across the street."

Fourteen minutes later, they dropped her off in a housing complex on the south side of the city. Christopher and Matt watched from the truck as Rachel approached the house. A young woman who much resembled Yashfa opened the door, a purple scarf tucked loosely around her head. She slid the scarf down, letting it hang around her neck when she saw Rachel was alone.

"Hi, I'm Rachel. Are you Yashfa's sister?" Rachel asked in Pashto, struggling to temper her enthusiasm.

The young woman dipped her head. "Yes, I am Yamna. Nice to meet you, Rachel. Welcome," Yamna greeted her and let her inside.

Yashfa was at her side the second she was through the door. "You found it, Rachel! Not the most proper for me to invite you to my sister's house, but her children are younger and her house is larger than mine. Much better for socializing." Yashfa grinned.

"Yes, I did! Your directions were great. Thank you for inviting me." Rachel had no idea about the directions. That was Christopher's department, but he'd gotten her there without a problem. She listened for the door to click shut behind her before reaching her hand to her head. She made eye contact quickly with Yashfa, who nodded to confirm there were no men present. Rachel slid her headscarf off of her head so it was hanging around her neck, just as Yamna had done. Yamna showed Rachel around the modest mud-brick home with thick walls to keep the temperature regulated. She introduced Rachel to two other friends, Veeda and Shabana. Shabana, Yamna, and Yashfa each had at least two children with them, all under the age of five. They explained that their older children were at school as they settled in the living room in low armchairs and Yamna poured Rachel a cup of tea.

"Shabana was showing us an embroidery pattern her grandmother taught her," Veeda said. She was curled up in her chair with her legs tucked under her, a bright red scarf balled up in her lap. The long, loose waves of her silky coffee colored hair flowed over her slim shoulders. It was so rare to see a woman's hair so free here that Rachel couldn't help but stare at the gorgeous woman. Veeda passed Rachel the section of fabric she had been embroidering, allowing Rachel to inspect it.

"It's beautiful!" Rachel marveled. She'd seen embroidered tapestries hanging in homes all over the Middle East and for sale in the markets, but she had never actually seen the work being done. She was impressed by the intricately sewn roses and daisies. Bright reds and pinks and oranges were stitched onto a perfect field of jet black, making the colors look even more vibrant than they would have on their own. One of the children, a young girl, teetered over to Rachel and reached her arms up. She instinctively moved the tapestry out of the way and lifted the child to her lap. "Sorry." She caught herself and looked to Yashfa and Yamna for guidance.

"It's fine. Borrow her all you want. Her name is Moska and she is eighteen months old," Yamna joked. "I have my hands full with my other two." She pointed to two young children, maybe three and five, in a corner of the room wrestling for possession of a blanket.

"It's nice we can send the older ones to school," Shabana said. "When they tried to take girls out of school . . . I told my husband then and there, no more children. I will not stay home with that many children all day, every day."

"How many children do you each have?" Rachel asked as casually as she could. She couldn't even imagine having one kid.

"Five," Yamna answered. "My oldest son is eleven years old. Yashfa currently has six children."

Yashfa pursed her lips and nodded, looking at the floor.

Rachel raised an eyebrow and cocked her head to the side. *Currently?* It was an odd thing to say.

Shabana saw Rachel's confused look and leaned over to whisper to her. "She lost two babies . . . the first two."

Rachel's eyes went wide with understanding. It didn't matter if Shabana meant miscarriages, stillbirths, or that Yashfa's children had died some other way. She imagined losing a child would be just as awful regardless of how the child died.

"I have none." Veeda looked overjoyed. Rachel studied each of their faces and quickly concluded that while Yashfa, Yamna, and Shabana all seemed close to Rachel's age, Veeda was likely much younger.

"How many children do you have, Shabana?" Rachel asked.

"Six. All girls."

"Oh, that would definitely be difficult if you kept them all at home." Rachel wrinkled her nose.

"Six girls is already plenty difficult," Shabana confirmed. "You have to worry so much more."

"Unfortunately, yes." Rachel pursed her lips.

"How many children do you have?" Yamna asked Rachel.

"Oh, none so far," Rachel said as she brushed a dark curl out of Moska's face. Moska giggled and grasped for Rachel's blonde hair. Veeda gave Rachel a curious look, so she explained. "In the U.S., we tend to get married and have children much later than here. So, I still have time to figure all of that out." Rachel had no intention of ever having children. She didn't want to abandon them and force them to worry each time she deployed. She knew firsthand how difficult it was to have a parent on active duty.

The women fell into easy conversation from there. The common complaints about husbands and kids were interspersed with embroidery lessons from Shabana, playful prayers of thanks to Allah that Veeda didn't have to deal with husbands and children yet, and breaking up arguments between the kids. Rachel did her best to get the hang of embroidery, but was much more interested in observing the women.

Her eye kept going back to Veeda. She was young, beautiful, and charming, and gossiped freely about everyone and everything. Rachel listened to the names she heard, committing them to memory. Veeda moved her arms as she spoke, drawing Rachel's attention to the sparkling gold bangle bracelets around her wrists. Something about the bracelets were familiar. Rachel knew better than to complement them, knowing that in Afghan culture, Veeda would feel compelled to offer them to her as a gift. She decided to try a different approach.

"Veeda, is there somewhere I can buy bracelets like yours? Or if you could recommend any jewelry stores? Maybe I can take a photo of them so I can show the shops what I'm looking for?" Rachel asked. Something about the bracelets tugged at her brain, but she wasn't sure why.

"Oh! Yes!" Veeda held up her wrists for Rachel to take a photo and proceeded to ramble off a list of no less than ten jewelry stores, along with their addresses, general directions, and a description of what sort of style selection each store would have. "These, though, I got from my mother. They are not Afghan."

"What do you mean?" Rachel feigned, pretending to not understand that Veeda was implying her mother was not from Afghanistan.

"Um, my mother is from Saudi Arabia." Veeda looked up at the ceiling. She was hiding something.

"Interesting." Rachel nodded. Saad Ayad and his sister were also from Saudi Arabia. Maybe it was just a coincidence. "How did she end up here married to your father then?"

"Oh, you know . . ." Veeda averted her eyes, trying to avoid answering.

"Our families decide who we marry," Shabana explained. Rachel knew that, of course, but furrowed her brow, hoping Shabana would say more. She didn't.

"Fathers. Our fathers decide," Yamna muttered through gritted teeth.

"Your families, or fathers, decide . . . how?" Rachel tested as innocently as she could manage. She already knew that arranged marriages were common in Afghanistan.

Yashfa pursed her lips and looked up at the ceiling. "Political alliances, who has money, who has power, who has influence. If your father wants to gain influence in some way, you are married to a man who can help make that happen, or to that man's son. If your father wants money for . . . something, then you are married into a family willing and able to support that, um, project." She gave a casual wave of the hand as though she were brushing aside the seriousness of her words and all that her explanation implied.

Yashfa was choosing her words carefully and was nearly succeeding at remaining casual and calm about it, but Rachel could read between the lines just fine. "So, Veeda, your mother is from Saudi Arabia and was married to an Afghan man?" Rachel asked.

"Yes."

"Because?"

"Because she was young and beautiful, and my father wanted her father's support with . . . something," Veeda said carefully.

"Money?" Rachel raised a quizzical eyebrow. She knew better than to flat out ask who they were married to. That revelation would take more time and more trust. She received a wink from Veeda in return. "Yeah. My mom keeps trying to marry me off to the highest bidder too." They all burst out laughing, knowing that was more or less the only criteria their fathers had when choosing their husbands.

After several hours, Rachel had managed to stitch the letter *R* into the corner of a white linen handkerchief in bright purple thread. She had explained the entire English alphabet and how to spell her name to the other women. It was far from perfect, and an excellent illustration of Rachel's lack of domestic skills, but it was good enough that the letter was unmistakable. Somehow embroidering cloth was more difficult than stitching skin together. That she could do. Stitches didn't need to be pretty, just functional.

She had been there for three hours when Yamna called them all into the kitchen and handed out bowls of lamb stew.

"This is absolutely delicious!" Rachel remarked after the first mouthful.

"I can write down the recipe if you'd like," Yamna offered.

"Yes please! I'm a terrible cook, but I'll make one of my colleagues figure it out." Rachel grinned and handed Yamna her phone so she could type the recipe in for her.

Christopher and Matt came back with the truck to pick Rachel up at 1500, knowing that her new friends' husbands or eldest sons would be there to escort them home soon since the other women needed to get home before their older children returned from school. Rachel haphazardly looped her scarf over her hair and rushed out to the truck with a spoonful of Yamna's stew.

"Can you make this?" Rachel asked Christopher, shoving the spoon in his mouth, then showing him her phone with the list of ingredients and instructions.

"Calm down," he said after swallowing. "First of all, that is fucking delicious." He reached his hand out the window of the truck to straighten her headscarf. She'd been too enthusiastic running out of the house. "Second, yes, I want to make this . . . Or make someone make it." He studied the instructions Yamna had typed into a note on Rachel's phone. "I don't know this word." He pointed at the screen. Rachel scrunched up her face and ran back to the house to ask Yamna for clarification.

"I will come, Rachel. One minute." Yamna couldn't help but laugh at Rachel's excitement. Yashfa had already put a considerable amount of the stew into a bowl to send home with Rachel.

"What is this word?" Rachel showed Yashfa her phone and pointed.

Yashfa nodded and grabbed a mortar and pestle off the kitchen counter. They both covered their hair quickly and went out to the truck.

Yashfa took Rachel's phone and pointed to the word Christopher hadn't understood. "This is this." She held up the mortar and pestle. "You take the spices and you–" Yashfa demonstrated how she would vigorously crush the fresh spices. "Like this, yes? That is this word."

"Thank you! We will definitely try to make this," Christopher told her. "The one bite Rachel ran out here with was delicious."

"Don't worry, we will send you home with more." Yamna's face list up as she handed him the bowl of leftovers. He passed it to Matt in the passenger seat.

Matt held the bowl to his nose and inhaled deeply. "Wow, I was right to be jealous I didn't get a bite! It smells amazing! Thank you so much. We'll be sure to return the bowl to you promptly."

"Come next week, Rachel, and bring it with you then," Yamna said.

Rachel smiled happily and got in the backseat of the truck, watching as Yamna and Yashfa made their way back inside. "What are these?" Rachel picked up a stack of envelopes off the seat beside her.

"Absentee ballots," Christopher told her. "Midterm election. Our CIA liaison was kind enough to get those for us from the embassy in Kabul so we didn't need to make the trip."

"Paige?" Rachel asked, assuming the young, perky blonde was who Christopher was referring to.

"Yeah." He grinned.

Rachel raised an eyebrow then glanced at Matt. "How long were y'all at the CIA office for?" she asked, trying to get an indication of exactly what Christopher's grin was implying.

"Maybe ten or fifteen minutes," Matt replied.

Rachel scrunched up her face. She knew Christopher preferred to take his time with flirting, and with other things, but ten to fifteen minutes was plenty of time to do plenty of things with Paige. She wrinkled her nose at the thought of them together. She'd met with Paige a few times since arriving in Khost, assembling and analyzing her bulletin board of terrorists, and hadn't been impressed with Paige's analytical skills so far, but she wasn't sure that was the cause of the current bitter taste in her mouth.

"Do not fuck her, Christopher," Rachel said harshly.

"Why not? She's not Navy. Since when are the CIA chicks off limits?" Christopher furrowed his brow and glanced at her in the rearview mirror.

"Because she is annoying, that's why." Rachel was sure to enunciate every word so he would understand she was serious.

"Maybe she'd be less annoying if I fucked her?" Christopher smirked.

"I think that would make her more annoying, actually." Rachel crossed her arms over her chest and slumped down in her seat.

"Come on, you have to admit, Paige is hot." Matt turned around to look at Rachel.

"Well, of course you think so! She's like a younger, more optimistic version of Charlene!" Rachel gave a dismissive wave of the hand.

"Funny, I thought she was like a younger, more optimistic version of you." Matt winked, and Rachel watched the corner of Christopher's upper lip curl.

Rachel let out a huff of frustration. "New rule. You have to wear sunglasses any time you're around Paige, even if you're inside," she told Christopher.

"Why?" Christopher wrinkled his nose.

"You know why. You and your fucking blue eyes that can get any girl to do whatever the hell you want."

"Not any girl." Christopher frowned.

"Oh, yeah?" Rachel raised an eyebrow. "Tell me, Christopher. What girl has that not worked on?"

"You." Christopher smirked, and both he and Matt burst out laughing.

"Fucking disgusting," Rachel muttered, but her heart skipped a beat thinking about all the times she'd nearly let herself get lost in his bright, sparkling eyes. She fingered the envelopes in her hand, realizing she may need to give Matt and Christopher a better reason for the sour look on her face. "What are we voting for?"

"Senate, House of Representatives, some state stuff. Governors for example." Christopher glanced in the side mirror and changed lanes.

"Texas things?" Rachel raised an eyebrow and waited for Christopher to meet her gaze in the rearview mirror. "Is Timothy Hendricks running for anything?"

"Yes, he's running for Governor of Texas," Christopher confirmed.

"Do not vote for him."

"Why?" Matt asked, as though the Texas election had anything to do with him.

"He's a terrible human being, that's why. Who do I not like in Kentucky?" Rachel turned her attention to Matt.

"Rache, people can vote for whomever they want, and you are not allowed to look at their ballots or ask them about it." Christopher's voice was stern.

"Like hell I can't."

"No, everyone gets to vote for who they want, and they don't have to discuss it with you because voting is a private thing. That's how it works in a democracy."

Rachel felt a long-winded political science lecture coming, so she pulled her earbuds out of her pocket, popped them in her ears, and stared out the window. At least he wasn't thinking about Paige anymore. But *she* was. She was definitely reacting to the idea of *Christopher* and Paige and spent the rest of the drive back to the safe house trying to convince herself she wasn't jealous.

Chapter 9:
NOVEMBER 2018

RACHEL WOKE RYAN UP in the middle of the night. She had been tossing and turning, after several sleepless nights, as she went over every detail of Yamna's home and every word that had been spoken. Veeda's bracelets kept flickering into her mind. She recognized them from somewhere, but the dots weren't connecting in her brain. The fact that she couldn't place them was grating her nerves.

"Why are you kicking me, Sky?" Ryan mumbled, half asleep.

"I need a ride." Rachel whispered, not wanting to wake Christopher or Matt, who were both asleep in the bed on the other side of the room.

"Where?"

"Where the fuck do you think?"

"Ugh," Ryan groaned. "You can't go bother the CIA tomorrow?"

"I need to get into their database. I can't access it from here, and I can't sleep thinking about everything. You know I'm not allowed out of the house by myself."

"Fine. Find my pants, and I'll drive you," Ryan muttered.

Rachel already knew that would be his answer, and she was prepared.

She dropped a pair of pants and a pair of socks on his face and quietly left the bedroom, careful not to wake Matt or Christopher. They snuck out of the safe house, and Ryan drove to the CIA office a few miles away. He pulled into an unmarked underground parking structure, and they both got out of the truck. Rachel scanned her ID at the door, and they both went inside.

"Hello!" Paige greeted them.

"Fuck off." Rachel held up her hand defensively, hoping Paige would get the hint. She was tired and frustrated and in no mood for Paige's perky optimism.

"What the fuck?" Paige furrowed her brow and looked at Ryan with concern.

Ryan shrugged. "Ignore her. She's in a mood."

Rachel glared at them from across the room as she logged onto a computer using her CIA credentials. "I promise you both, something else is happening here. I can feel it. Feel free to be helpful!"

"How do we help?" Paige asked, taking a seat at the computer next to her. Rachel listed off her new friends' names, and they got to searching. "I'm not finding anything," Paige said after mere minutes.

Rachel sighed. She knew it would take more digging than a quick database search to find what she was looking for. "Remind me, are you a field agent or an analyst?" Rachel asked Paige, doing her best to be patient but probably failing.

"I'm an analyst," Paige told her. "You and Ryan are the field agents."

"We're Navy SEALs," Rachel corrected her.

"Right, that's why you have CIA IDs and CIA login credentials." Paige smirked.

"Keep your fucking voice down and never say that out loud again." Rachel glared at her.

"Top secret . . . Right." Paige slid her fingers along her lips in the typical schoolyard gesture of zipping her lips and throwing away the key.

"Mmh," Rachel grumbled, not amused by Paige's careless statement or her playful gesture. She cocked her head to the side and raised both eyebrows. "Why are you always so enthusiastic?"

"Umm." Paige stared at the floor.

"Right, the CIA doesn't have those obnoxious no fraternization rules." Rachel chuckled to herself, wondering who Paige was sleeping with and hoping desperately that it wasn't Christopher or anyone else on her team. But certainly not Christopher. "Alright, well, can you please be helpful? And try not to fuck anyone on my team?"

"Yes, tell me how I can help, other than running the names you gave me through the database," Paige requested.

It didn't escape Rachel that Paige neglected to comment on the second half of her request. That weird stabbing pain in her gut was back along with the revolting thought of Paige and Christopher, which was odd. Usually, she helped him get girls. She'd even once requested that he do something—*anything*—to improve relations with the CIA, practically begging him to charm his way into their good grace's on the team's behalf. She didn't know what it was about Paige that she found so obnoxious. Then Matt's comment popped into her head. *She reminds me of a younger version of you.* Rachel shook her head vigorously, trying to make the thought go away. Maybe if she shook her head hard enough, fast enough, the thought would shatter somehow against her skull and never be able to materialize again. "Didn't we just establish that you're the analyst?" Rachel furrowed her brow.

"I've only been here for two months, and this is my first assignment," Paige explained.

"Are you being serious?" Rachel asked.

"Yes. Why would I lie about that?" Paige furrowed her brow.

Rachel rested her elbows on the desk, burying her face in her palms. "You're fresh out of spy school and they assigned you to Khost?"

"Correct," Paige told her with a confident nod of her head.

"For fuck's sake. No wonder you have no idea what's going on. I'm sorry I called you an idiot."

"When did you call me an idiot?" Paige asked, looking at Ryan to see if he knew what she'd missed.

"Just now in my head." Rachel's shoulders shook with silent laughter. She was happy she'd managed to keep the thought internal for once. "Can you pull all the photos you can find of my new friends and of any women in our targets' networks, specifically Amina Barech?"

"Who?" Paige asked.

Rachel rolled her eyes. "No wonder you morons need our help all the time. Seriously, what are y'all learning at CIA training? She's Saad Ayad's sister."

"What makes you think she's in Khost?" Paige asked.

"Umm, one of your highly informative CIA intel reports told me so." Rachel cocked her head to the side, reconsidering if Paige maybe was an idiot after all. "I am trying to figure out where I've seen these bracelets before." She pulled up the photo of Veeda's bracelets on her phone and showed it to Paige.

"Those are beautiful!" Paige's eyes lit up.

"Jesus fucking Christ," Rachel muttered. "Alright Paige, scan all the photos of these women for these bracelets. I'm guessing we don't have some sort of software that can scan images for these?"

"No, facial recognition only works on faces, Sky," Ryan teased.

Rachel gave him the finger. "Feel free to make yourself useful."

"What do you want me to do? Assign me a task," Ryan requested.

"Look for Zarah."

"Do you have a photo of Zarah so we can run facial recognition?" Ryan asked. He'd been listening to Rachel ramble on about Zarah for weeks.

"I do not," Rachel admitted. "I don't know her last name either or who she actually is other than a nice old lady who passed me off to Yashfa. I don't know any of their last names."

"Well, if you look closely at this photo, look past the bracelets, you can see another woman in the background." Paige zoomed in on the photo to a woman with a purple scarf around her neck.

"That's Yamna," Rachel told her.

"Well, we can run facial recognition on this," Paige pointed out. She quickly sent the photo to herself and uploaded it to the CIA database to start the facial recognition search. Rachel watched impatiently over Paige's shoulder while Ryan leaned back in his chair and put his feet up on the desk.

"Yashfa and Yamna Khan?" Rachel read aloud as the results appeared on the screen. "Their father is Khalid Khan?" She pointed at the family photo, where a man with a long greying beard stood rigidly between a younger version of Yashfa and Yamna.

"Sky, what are you getting at?" Ryan asked, though he didn't get out of his chair to look at the computer screen.

Rachel pointed at a large whiteboard to her left. "Khalid Khan and Saad Ayad are both members of Al-Qaeda."

"Yes, we can read," Paige said.

"Yashfa and Yamna are apparently Khalid Khan's daughters." Rachel reached down to her right leg and, out of habit, pulled her knife out of her boot and began to twirl it in her hand.

"Are you sure?" Paige asked, though she was staring at Rachel's knife like she was horrified.

"Yes?" Rachel wasn't sure. "I mean, they're both right here in a photo with him, assuming your computer software is accurate. But I agree, it looks like them, even if they're much younger in this photo. So, they're related to him somehow. This looks like it was taken at a wedding." Rachel switched her knife to her left hand and pointed at the photo on Paige's screen again. She put her knife down on the desk and went back to typing, looking for anyone named Zarah in Khalid Khan's social network. Nothing. She tried Veeda next. Nothing. Frustration was taking over. She knew she was getting close, but she wasn't close enough. "I need alcohol. Too much is happening in my brain, and my logical reasoning is blocking out my subconscious."

"Umm, we're in Afghanistan," Paige reminded her. "Sort of not a lot of alcohol here."

"I know where there's alcohol." Rachel popped out of her seat and made her way down a long hallway to Director Cruse's office. She tried the door. It was locked. "Someone get me something to pick this lock with, or the keys. Y'all have thirty seconds before I bust the lock with my gun."

"For fuck's sake." With a grumble, Ryan opened a desk drawer and pulled out a pouch with all the tools she needed to pick the lock. He threw it at her, and she was in Director Cruse's office within minutes. Next up was the filing cabinet. She picked that lock too. Just as she'd suspected, several bottles of whiskey were stashed in there.

"What do we want? Johnnie Walker? Jack Daniels?" She held up each bottle as she named them. "Or whatever the fuck this is?"

"That's tequila." Ryan laughed, pointing at the bottle.

Rachel grimaced and put it back. "Okay, not that one." She pulled the top off of each whiskey bottle and took a swig, trying to decide which she wanted. She settled on both and made her way back to the desk. Ryan stared at her, furrowing his brow and pursing his lips into a crooked pout. "You want some?" Rachel held up the bottle of Jack Daniels.

"No, I'm driving, remember?" Ryan shook his head. "Just keep drinking and thinking until something clicks in that fucked up mind of yours."

Rachel smiled proudly at him for a moment, then pouted. "I cannot find Amina because the only photo I've ever seen of her is at least a decade old. Not helpful."

"Focus on what you do have, Sky," Ryan suggested.

"What I *do* have?"

"Yeah, tell me what you do have." Ryan was right. She usually processed information better and faster when she spoke out loud to an audience.

"Okay, what I *do* have . . ." Rachel walked over to the whiteboard where she had outlined the Al-Qaeda hierarchy and flipped her knife in the air, trying to relieve some of her anxiety and frustration. Ryan and Paige couldn't see inside her head, so she picked up a red whiteboard marker and drew a circle.

"These assholes circled in red, that's who I'm talking about." Rachel tapped the marker where the first picture was hung up. "Saad Ayad was our original target. Munir Omarkhil and Ibrahim Ayad were added once we got here. *Now*, what I'm saying is that two of the women I've been hanging out with are potentially Khalid Khan's daughters. Khalid Khan is very good friends with Saad Ayad."

"Okay, and what's his deal?" Ryan asked. Rachel had every aspect of these people's lives memorized the way normal people kept up with celebrity gossip.

"Khalid Khan is overly friendly with the Taliban, and as you can see here, a ranking Al-Qaeda shithead." She pointed to his name with her knife.

Ryan nodded.

"His father, who is dead, was one of the geniuses who came up with the idea to kick all the girls out of their schools. Talk about following in your father's footsteps . . . Fortunately, girls are allowed to attend primary school again but—"

"Focus," Ryan urged.

"Right, well, Khalid Khan helped write a lot of laws, or doctrines—whatever we're calling them—that stripped women of their rights and was instrumental in getting them implemented. If my father did something like that, I would not be too pleased."

"You'd want revenge." Ryan pointed at her.

"I'd get revenge." Rachel walked back to the desk and took another swig of whiskey. "I think they want revenge."

"Just because you would want revenge doesn't mean they do," Ryan pointed out.

"No vagina, no opinion." Rachel pointed the tip of her knife right at his face. He gave her the finger in response.

"Women here aren't like us," Paige reminded her.

"No. Women are women. We're all human, all driven by the same emotions and desires. They don't have the agency, means, or opportunity to execute, but they *want* revenge. I am very sure about that."

"For their father joining the Taliban and Al-Qaeda?" Paige asked.

"Maybe?"

"No, it's not enough." Ryan shook his head. "Keep drinking and keep talking."

"Feel free to help!" Rachel glared at Ryan and Paige.

"How do we help?" Paige asked.

"I need to know everything about Yashfa and Yamna Khan's lives. I need to know how close they or their father are to Saad Ayad right now in present day." Rachel tried to tone down her frustration, but it was an effort.

"Okay, it's probably easier now that we have their maiden name, Khan, too. Let's get to work." Paige and Ryan both skimmed intel reports from the CIA, Navy and any other agency they had access to.

After a few hours of searching and reading, Ryan found something. "Um, Rache?"

Rachel walked over to his computer and began to read out loud. "November 2001, a woman was killed by Taliban guards while walking alone through an open-air market. She was carrying a sick infant in her arms, walking unescorted. No male relative had been available to walk with her to the child's doctor. Both the mother and infant were shot dead."

Rachel turned and threw her knife at the wall, instantly filled with rage. It flew past Paige and Ryan before effortlessly getting stuck in the wall. Furious tears began welling in her eyes. She tried to keep reading, but the words were like a lump in her throat. She paused, trying to get her eyes to focus through her tears. "Mother's name, Yasmoon Khan. Infant's name, Kaamil Khan. The deceased is remembered by her two daughters, Yashfa and Yamna Khan, ages fourteen and twelve, and her husband Khalid Khan."

Rachel shook with anger. That was all the information she needed to do the math. She double checked the date on Yashfa's marriage certificate. "Yashfa was fucking fifteen years old when her father forced her into marriage." Fury was taking over as Rachel paced back and forth in the CIA office. Her hands were shaking and the muscles in her arms were spasming. This wasn't just about the mission anymore. Maybe it never had been. This was about Yashfa and Yamna and all the other women this network had touched. She wanted to hurt someone badly.

"Rache?" Ryan started. "Rachel, try to breathe. You have to calm down. We aren't going into combat anytime soon."

"I could fucking murder the first man I see right now. I'm so pissed off."

"Okay, well, that doesn't sound too great for me."

"Not you! You know what I mean."

"Right, well, you need to relax and save all of this fury for when we do find all or any of the people on that list." Ryan pointed to the whiteboard.

"I *will* find them all, and I will kill every last one of them," Rachel vowed.

"Yeah, I know you will, and I'm fairly certain I'll be helping you with that," Ryan told her. "For now, you need to breathe, and we need to get back to the safe house before everyone else gets up."

"Fine, but I'm taking these with me," Rachel said, picking up the two bottles of whiskey. She needed to talk to Yashfa and Yamna. She needed to track down the bastards that had torn apart their lives. But first, she needed to calm down.

Christopher inhaled deeply, his eyes still closed. Something had woken him up. He wasn't sure what. Then he heard her voice and the corner of his mouth tugged up involuntarily.

"Good morning, sunshine," Rachel whispered in his ear.

"What the fuck do you want?" Christopher mumbled. Mornings really were the worst. Mornings with Rachel, however, were always slightly better.

"It's not about what I want. It's about what I have that *you* want," she said, slurring her words a bit.

"A hot girl to have sex with?" Christopher asked optimistically.

"No, next best thing."

Christopher opened one eye slightly. He saw a bottle in front of his face, smelled whiskey, and then smiled. "No work today?"

"Apparently not." Rachel giggled.

Christopher inched himself up so he was leaning on his elbow and took the bottle from her. "You've already had quite a bit it looks like," he said, eyeing the bottle.

"Some." Rachel giggled again as she sat on the edge of his bed and took off her boots.

Christopher's eyes crinkled and the corner of his upper lip curled as he took a long, slow sip from the bottle. "You're right. That is the second-best thing. Now leave and get to work on finding me the first-best thing." He pressed his palm between her shoulder blades, playfully nudging her off the bed.

"It's been three weeks. Suck it up," Rachel told him, slapping his hand away from her before she fell.

"No one is sucking anything," Christopher blurted out without thinking.

Rachel burst out laughing.

"I'm serious! I'm almost desperate enough to fuck you!" He really wasn't awake, and there seemed to be a direct—and poorly regulated—line of communication between his subconscious and his mouth.

"Okay, that's disgusting. I may need to revoke your drinking privileges for that!" Rachel grimaced.

Christopher ignored her, taking another deep gulp of the whiskey before screwing the top back on and rolling it across the floor, out of their room and into the living room. Next, he grabbed his boot off the floor and threw it at the door. His aim was still pretty damned good considering he hadn't played football in about thirteen years. The bedroom door slammed shut and he put his arm around Rachel, pulling her down onto the bed beside him. "Sleep," he mumbled, instantly burying his face in her hair.

"I'm not tired." Rachel squirmed, trying to get away.

"Don't care." He tightened his arm around her, pulling her closer against his chest. She had barely slept the past few nights, and there was no reason to get up if everyone was drinking. "I sleep better when you're here." He mumbled into the back of her head.

She rolled over to face him and snuggled into him, her nose cold on his bare chest. She shifted, and he slid his fingers down her spine until his palm was on her lower back, commanding her to move closer. She responded to his touch just like she always did and relaxed into him.

"Please don't fuck Paige," Rachel whispered into his chest.

"I won't."

"You won't, or you won't again?" Rachel asked.

"I won't. But tell me why not? You don't normally care who I sleep with." He combed his fingers through her hair, tucking it behind her ear before tipping her face up to his. There lips were barely an inch apart.

"I don't want you getting hurt."

"What the fuck does that mean?" Christopher pulled away slightly so he could look down at her.

"I saw how you looked at her. There was something . . . Not just lust, not just thinking she was hot."

"Hmm." Christopher considered her words for a moment then pulled her tight into his chest again. "I am not and will not fall in love with Paige, nor will I sleep with her or do anything with her," he said seriously.

"I've never seen you look at a girl like that before."

"Jealous?" Christopher teased.

"Worried about my best friend getting distracted by a girl and getting himself killed," Rachel corrected. She paused and tightened her arm around him. Her fingernails were digging into his back. "What is it about her?"

"She reminds me of someone," he admitted. His mouth really was betraying all of his thoughts and feelings today.

"Who?"

Christopher brushed his fingers through her hair, then ran the back of his hand along her cheek, down to her chin, tipping her face up to his again. He stared deep into her eyes, hoping she would understand and not make him say it. Not make him admit Matt had been right. "Just some girl." Christopher brushed his thumb over her lips.

Rachel furrowed her brow.

Christopher chuckled, unsure if it was the whiskey or if Rachel really was that clueless about her own emotions and his. "I thought you were supposed to be smart?" Christopher teased. "There's only ever been one girl."

"Okay, well, you've never mentioned this mysterious dream girl before."

"Don't worry about it. It'll never be anything more than a fantasy." Christopher silently scolded his subconscious. He'd been having the same damned fantasy for nearly a decade.

"Why the hell not? Just flash her a smile, and let your eyes do the work."

"It's a little more complicated than that, Rache."

"Shit, she's married?"

"Yeah, she is, actually." Christopher nodded, thinking of Rachel's high school sweetheart, Carter. Rachel had needed a legal next of kin who wasn't her father, since he didn't know she was deployed, in case something happened, and Carter had willingly gone down to city hall and signed some papers. Neither of them really considered themselves to be married to each other. Even if it was obvious Carter sometimes wanted it to be more than it was. Carter was waiting for Rachel to wake up one day, her restlessness and desire for blood and adventure magically resolved, and run back to him to settle down into some sort of happy life. Christopher had met Carter on several occasions. He was a nice guy, but not the right guy for Rachel. He couldn't navigate her mood swings, didn't understand why she couldn't sit still, and constantly complained that she chose danger over stability. Carter needed someone more like him. Someone calm and normal. Someone comfortable with routine and peace. Rachel was none of those things, and she probably never would be. Christopher knew she'd never be with him either though. Best friends would have to be enough.

"Kids?" Rachel asked.

"No. She's too focused on her career for kids."

"Well, most marriages end in divorce these days."

"Right." Christopher buried his face in her hair again, and his lips grazed the top of her head. His hand slid down, tracing the side of her body until it landed on her waist. "Why are you cold?" Instinct took over and his hand slid further down, grazing her hip until his hand was on the back of her thigh, pulling her leg around his waist.

"Christopher? Tell me more about this girl," Rachel insisted, instinctually tightening her leg around him.

"Shh. Go to sleep." He ran his thumb over her lips again.

"I told you, I'm not tired."

"Be quiet, or I'll make you be quiet."

"Make me how?" Rachel's tone was more flirtatious than it should have been.

"Shut up, or I'm going to kiss you so you can't talk anymore." Exhaustion and two gulps of whiskey were clearly a terrible combination.

Rachel slapped him on the arm and giggled. "Don't be gross!"

"Maybe I'll just kiss you so good you wouldn't be able to be quiet."

"Fine. I'll go to sleep," Rachel conceded.

"Too bad. I sort of liked my idea." He was only half-joking. He tightened his grasp on her, and she sunk into him.

"Of all the stupid ideas we've come up with, that's gotta be the dumbest one." Rachel giggled.

"What?" Christopher breathed in the scent of her hair.

"Us kissing." Rachel cringed. "Terrible idea." Her eyes darted up to his and she couldn't help but smile.

"I dunno. It would probably be pretty great. We both know what we're doing," Christopher pointed out.

"Skills and compatibility are not the issue." She grumbled and turned away from him, pulling his arm tight around her and clinging to his hand as she pressed her back into his chest. They stayed still and quiet for several minutes. "I can't sleep," Rachel complained.

"Why not? What are you thinking about?" Christopher asked. Rachel's guilty laughter told him everything he needed to know. He was happy to know she was thinking about sex and not some fucked up traumatic memories from one of their past missions. "Let me call Command HQ and tell them I'm retiring, then I can help you with that," Christopher teased. He let go of her hand and grazed his fingertips along her stomach, down to her hip.

"Goddamnit, Christopher!" Rachel jerked away from him and sat up, turning to look at him. "I forbid you from retiring. You are never allowed to leave me."

"I wouldn't dream of leaving you."

"I can't . . . I don't ever want to . . . You're my best friend."

"I know."

"So don't leave me, okay? Don't retire, don't make me do this without you. I need you." Her voice was pleading and desperate, and panicked tears flooded her eyes.

"You have me," he promised, pulling her closer.

"Good, because this shit just got more complicated."

"Hey, calm down." He sat up and ran his fingers through her hair, massaging the back of her head. "Breathe. You have me, now and forever. I swear. I'm not going anywhere." He kissed her forehead. He knew he shouldn't, but he needed to calm her down. She was panicked. He didn't know why, but he needed to make her feel safe again. It was rare that she let her emotions show like this, that she allowed herself to be vulnerable with anyone, even him. "How drunk are you?"

Rachel shrugged.

"Then what's up?"

"Yashfa and Yamna are probably Khalid Khan's daughters," Rachel mumbled.

"Oh, fuck. That definitely complicates things."

"Or it could be just the lead we need."

Chapter 10:
NOVEMBER 2018

"I NEED TO SPEAK with you and Yashfa. Alone," Rachel said the second Yamna opened her front door. It was the next Thursday, and Rachel was back at Yamna's house. She saw Yashfa over Yamna's shoulder, sitting in the living room. She had been turning over the story about Yashfa and Yamna's mother in her head for a week now, unable to let it go. She'd been digging deeper into Khalid Khan's involvement with Saad Ayad, but found nothing helpful. She was running out of time and out of patience. Her trips to the mosque showed no signs of Amina, and their rotations around the city yielded little information. The girls must know something, anything, that would help.

Rachel glanced over at the children playing in the living room. She knew some of the kids were old enough to understand, or partly understand, and thought the better of having this conversation in front of them. Confirming that Khalid Khan was Yashfa and Yamna's father was step one. Then she would need to connect the dots. There were so many dots. Her typically analytical, hyper-focused mind was turning into a jumbled up chaotic mess of disorganized tangential information.

Yamna led Rachel and Yashfa into one of the bedrooms, far enough away that the children wouldn't overhear, but the women could still keep them in eyesight. Rachel shut the door ajar and turned to them, looking each of them in the eyes. Veeda and Shabana would be there soon. She didn't have time to waste being polite, so she jumped right in.

"I may have discovered something, and I'd appreciate it if the two of you could confirm that your father is Khalid Khan," Rachel started. Yashfa and Yamna looked at each other, their faces awash with shock. Rachel continued. "He's working with the Taliban and Al-Qaeda to take away women's rights. I also believe that your mother, Yasmoon Khan, was killed by a Taliban guard while taking your baby brother Kaamil Khan to the doctor by herself, unescorted." Tears welled up in Yamna's eyes, and Yashfa clenched her jaw. "Now I know why you were so concerned about me trying to get here on my own, Yashfa." Rachel paused and looked back and forth between them. Both women stared at the floor. "Was anything I just said untrue?"

"No," Yashfa said quietly.

"How do you know all that?" Yamna asked.

"Not important. What is important is that your father is a horrible human being, and I'd very much like him dead." She knew it was bold to be so honest, and it was definitely a risk, but she didn't have much time before Shabana and Veeda would arrive.

Yamna nodded slowly, and Yashfa snickered.

"We've never known a world without extremism, without men controlling us. We were too young to understand, to appreciate it, before the Taliban took over, but Zarah has told us . . . about how things used to be," Yamna said.

"Our father is the reason why women and girls can't walk outside freely. Why we can't attend school as long as boys can. So many things we thought were normal until Zarah told us about how things *could* be," Yashfa added.

The corner of Rachel's upper lip curled as she watched them react to her words. "So, you both would prefer he were dead too?"

Yashfa gave her a noncommittal shrug, and Yamna kept her gaze securely fixed to the floor.

"If you tell me where he is, I can make that happen."

"We don't know where our father is. Neither of us has spoken to him in over ten years," Yamna said.

"Will you really avenge our mother's death?" Yashfa asked hopefully.

"You bet your ass I will." Rachel was grinning from ear to ear.

"Can you really though?" Yamna wasn't convinced.

The bedroom door opened abruptly. Veeda looked back and forth between Rachel and Yashfa, trying to figure out what was going on. "Why are you all hiding in here?"

"Just chatting," Rachel told her.

Yashfa glanced at Rachel then back at Veeda and slid her index finger along her throat with a wicked grin on her face.

"I don't know what that means, Yashfa!" Veeda yelled.

"Calm down, Veeda!" Shabana had come in right behind Veeda and witnessed the entire exchange.

Rachel paused and observed as the tension built between Veeda and Yashfa. They were staring each other down, waiting to see who would speak first. Shabana seemed confused as to what was going on, and Yamna couldn't take her eyes off the floor.

"We were talking about Zarah," Yashfa said quickly, trying to change the subject.

"Zarah?" Shabana asked.

"She's this nice older woman at the mosque I go to. She introduced me to Yashfa," Rachel explained.

"Oh, Zarahfshaan," Shabana nodded.

"Yes." Rachel nodded, happy to have the woman's full first name finally.

"She's very kind, yes," Shabana said.

"How did you all meet her?" Rachel asked.

"At the mosque. Same as you," Yashfa replied.

"Tell me more about Zarahfshaan," Rachel said casually.

"She's just a nosy old woman," Veeda said quickly.

"Old women are typically nosy for a reason," Rachel commented.

"She wants everyone to be safe," Shabana said. "She remembers how things were before and is a bit delusional thinking somehow we will get back to peace and equality."

"Is she just an idealistic dreamer, or is she doing something to bring back peace and equality?" Rachel asked curiously.

"That's up for interpretation, I think." Shabana winked.

"She introduced us to you," Yamna pointed out.

"I know that, but *why*?"

"Why do you think, Rachel?" Yashfa asked.

"She had her suspicions about you . . . which you sort of confirmed earlier." Yamna looked at the floor.

"What did she suspect me of?" Rachel asked.

"Most Americans who come here for work, or whatever they're doing, do not go to the mosque to pray every day," Yashfa explained. "They focus on their humanitarian aid, or whatever they are calling it. They may go to the mosque to meet people, or see it as a tourist attraction, but they do not pray. Certainly not like you do."

"What do you mean? How do I pray differently?" Rachel asked, genuinely confused by Yashfa's statement. As far as she knew—and she knew a lot—she prayed exactly how one was supposed to in a mosque. She was suddenly concerned there was some local custom she'd missed.

"Like you are desperate for your prayers to be answered," Yashfa said. "Like you've seen and experienced horrible things, and you are seeking relief, or maybe even redemption. You pray like you are begging Allah to save you. To save someone, anyway."

"Only war makes people pray that passionately," Veeda said quietly. "War and the things that go along with it."

Rachel nodded and pressed her lips into a tight line. She thought back to that first day in the mosque, how desperate she was for help from whichever divine entity was on duty that day. Help to liberate the women of Afghanistan. Help to crush the patriarchy. She knew exactly what Yashfa meant. "Rape, sexual assault, abuse, forced marriage," Rachel listed off. She watched the faces of the women around her, carefully noting the fear and sadness as it crossed each of their faces in brief flickers and flashes.

"The greed of men is the diminution of women," Shabana said.

"Their thirst for power reduces us to nothing," Yamna clarified.

"That is what Zarah says," Veeda added.

"And what are you all doing about that?" Rachel asked.

"Nothing. We can do nothing." Shabana said. "If I could . . . If I could do anything, I would help my sister. But there's nothing to be done about anything. We have no power, no say in anything."

"We could offer our lives, but it wouldn't make a difference. Wouldn't even be in the news. And if it were, we would be painted as the criminals," Yashfa stated sadly. "Zarah believes things can improve, though how, I don't know. She tells us stories from before, of how it was. But how to get from this to that? I don't know that it's possible. Not in our lifetime."

"Our lifetime is days if we disobey," Yamna said, looking around the room at the young girls playing with their brothers, cousins, and friends.

"Minutes," Yashfa corrected.

"So, why haven't you spoken with your father since meeting Zarah?" Rachel asked.

"She told us not to," Yamna said quietly.

"He chose our husbands for us," Yashfa said. "Some sort of alliance with the sons of people he wanted to work more closely with. Zarah said we should keep our distance so that our father could not bring us or our husbands into whatever they were doing. She said to think of our future children, what we would want for them. Our sons especially."

"We don't want to be involved. Don't want our children exposed to that sort of thinking, that violence is the solution. Suicide bombs, kidnapping, rape." Yamna stared at her feet as she spoke.

"What about your husbands?" Rachel asked. "If your father chose them, then I would assume they are already involved in whatever your father is doing?"

"We can't do much about that," Yashfa said. "They do what they want. So far, they are leaving our children out of it and treating us well enough."

"Let me help. I know people who can help," Rachel begged, suspecting that whatever Yashfa meant by 'well enough' was still pretty bad.

"Help how?" Veeda asked, sounding skeptical.

"I know important people. Politicians . . ."

"I think that's what started this mess," Shabana said cynically.

"True," Rachel agreed. "The U.S. wants the Taliban out of Afghanistan. Al-Qaeda too. If we could accomplish that, would things get better for the women here?"

"Maybe?" Yashfa said.

"Zarah thinks so," Yamna said quietly.

Thad lived with war, oppression, and tyranny since childhood. The idea of leaving their house on their own without prosecution was so foreign to them, it was incomprehensible. Especially given what had happened to Yashfa and Yamna's mother. There had been a few years where the Taliban had lost power, and the President had made strides to bring about equality, but it hadn't lasted. The next election had resulted in a much more conservative president. Even if women were technically allowed to work, and even if there were seats in parliament reserved for women, family and societal pressure, fear of the Taliban, and the belief that forcing women to cover themselves and stay home were in line with the Quran made it next to impossible for women to engage in public life. If a woman's parents or husband didn't want her going out, she didn't. If the woman fought back, she was beaten. If she complained about the abuse or requested a divorce, she lost custody of her children.

"Tell me how I can help," Rachel said quietly as she stared at the floor. She wanted to empower them, give them a sense of agency and control. Hopefully this was the first step. A tiny nudge in the right direction, but only time would tell if her new friends trusted her and were brave enough to fight back.

Chapter 11:
NOVEMBER 2018

IT WAS THE FOURTH Thursday in November: Thanksgiving. Rachel sat on the sofa, listening as Ryan, Aaron, Christopher, Matt, and Aiden all argued in the kitchen about how to make a pumpkin pie. The CIA had managed to get them all of the ingredients. Now they just needed to agree on whose recipe they were using.

"That's a disgusting amount of sugar, Chris!" Ryan yelled.

"That's what my mom said to do!" Christopher protested.

"No, that's way too much sugar," Aaron agreed.

"The crust dough doesn't look right," Aiden noted. "I'm gonna call my grandma."

Ryan checked the time on his phone. "It's 2200 there. Do not call your grandma!"

"Just make the pie this evening when your mothers and grandmothers are all awake," Rachel yelled to them from the living room.

"No, we're making this one for you to take with you," Christopher explained as he walked from the kitchen to the living room. "Yamna and Yashfa are always sending you home with food. You should reciprocate."

"With an experimental pumpkin pie?" Rachel furrowed her brow. She was highly skeptical of their plan.

"It's gonna be great!" Christopher assured her.

"Yeah, how badly could we actually fuck it up?" Ryan asked, walking into the living room to join them.

Rachel pinched the bridge of her nose and relaxed back on the couch, knowing they would either figure it out or give up and try again later after she'd left to go to Yamna's house. She listened as their bickering became more cooperative and was pleased as the scent of pumpkin pie baking in the oven wafted out of the kitchen forty minutes later.

"Now that y'all have that under control, does anyone have any updates on our mission?" Rachel asked from the couch.

"No. We haven't even gotten a glimpse of any of our targets," Nate yelled to her from the back bedroom. At least there was one perk about the apartment being so small. Everyone could hear each other regardless of what room they were in.

"Yeah, how do we know they're even still here?" Aaron asked.

"Because the CIA keeps showing me images of them taken off security cameras around the city, so we're just missing them. They're here somewhere." Rachel looked around the room. She could tell they were all close to the breaking point. They were willing to do just about anything to get this mission over and done with. "I promise, I am yelling at the CIA, and I am yelling at HQ every chance I get."

She was met with grumbles, groans, and eye rolling.

"Well, I think I'm making progress." Rachel was trying to be more optimistic. She knew everyone wanted to make it home for Christmas.

"Yeah, on finding Khalid Khan, not Saad Ayad," Matt noted. "Although I'm sure that's one of *your* top priorities, I'm not sure it's helping us with this specific mission."

"No, I just need to build more trust and then—" Rachel was interrupted by the sound of her cell phone ringing. "Where the fuck is my phone?" She looked around.

Christopher picked up her phone off the table in the entryway and accepted the call before handing it to her.

"Are you planning to come to San Diego anytime soon?" Admiral Tom Ryker asked as soon as Rachel said hi.

"No." She glared at Christopher, knowing he'd answered on purpose. She wouldn't have answered otherwise. He smirked in response.

"Why the hell not?" Tom yelled.

"Because I'm very busy, that's why."

"You do realize tomorrow is Thanksgiving," he pointed out.

"Thanksgiving is–" Rachel stopped herself before she said *today*, remembering the twelve and a half hour time difference between Afghanistan and California where her parents lived.

"It's been ten years. Not coming out here for over a decade is unacceptable."

"And yet everyone is still alive and well without me being there," Rachel noted.

"You realize I could bring you up on charges in court-martial?"

"Seriously? Let's not waste people's time with that." She rolled her eyes.

"Insubordination, conduct unbecoming . . ." Tom listed off potential charges.

"Daddy, don't be ridiculous. Not coming home for Christmas is hardly insubordination. I really don't have the time. I'm incredibly busy with work."

"Buy a plane ticket and get on a fucking plane, Rachel. You have plenty of leave. I know logistics officers get plenty of leave. I'm sure your department can spare you for a few days and you can fly out here for Christmas."

"Not gonna happen," Rachel said before hanging up. She bit the inside of her cheek and dug her fingernails into her palm, willing the tears away so no one would see her cry.

Christopher watched as Rachel paced back and forth in the living room, phone pressed to her ear. "What did your dad want?"

"You saw who it was and answered anyway?" Rachel yelled.

"Yeah, he's your dad. You need to talk to him and let him know you're alive occasionally."

Rachel sighed. She knew Christopher was right even if she didn't want to admit it. "He was wondering why I can't make it home for Thanksgiving or Christmas for the tenth year in a row. Apparently, as a logistics officer, I'm entitled to all this time off." Rachel waved her hand in the air dismissively.

Christopher couldn't help but laugh. He thought he saw something in her eyes. If it was an amused twinkle or a glistening tear, he wasn't sure. He knew Rachel told her father she had gotten a position as a senior logistics officer before starting SEAL training nine years ago. As a high-ranking admiral, he could access their mission reports, even if they were heavily redacted versions. He wouldn't approve of her taking part in such dangerous missions, and she worried he had enough influence to get her transferred to a desk, so she lied.

"Apparently, not going home for over a decade is unacceptable," she clarified, putting a humorously sharp emphasis on the word *unacceptable*.

Christopher shrugged. He had spent several years away from his family after his younger brother, Josh, was killed in action. He had been in a military hospital in Germany at the time, thanks to Saad Ayad and his fucking car bombs and bullets, and had been offered the chance to medically retire after being shot in the back mere inches from his spine. Up until that point, the worst day of his life was when the chaplain had told him that his brother was dead and his father was on the way from Texas to get him. But then the doctor told him that, due to the severity of his injury, he may never run again. Christopher wouldn't have any of it, of course. He had demanded to see the most senior officer and someone from human resources. Like hell he wasn't going to run again.

The Navy had been trying to talk him into becoming a SEAL ever since he'd joined up two years prior. He'd gone to Officer Candidate School instead. All he wanted to do was get paid to travel and drive a truck and shoot some bad guys. Another nice perk was how easy it was to pick up girls in his uniform.

All of that changed the second he found out Josh was dead. He'd never known, never understood why Josh had enlisted. Christopher had been deployed at the time and got an email from his dad letting him know Josh had decided to delay college and had enlisted instead. Something Christopher thought was stupid, but it was Josh's life. That decision had cut his life short though. Christopher wanted revenge. He wanted to destroy the people who had killed his brother, even if he wasn't sure exactly who those people were.

His rage and need for vengeance were only multiplied by his mother's blame. She believed that it had been entirely Christopher's fault that Josh joined the Navy. She'd kicked him out of the house, screamed at him that she wished it had been him instead, and told him he wasn't welcome back. Hours of therapy taught him it was just her grief and depression talking. His mother loved him. She'd simply gone crazy with despair. Besides, she had a point. Josh was the stable, responsible one. Christopher had always been impulsive and reckless. If his mother lost a child, it should have been him. Every argument, every bit of his own anger and sadness had fueled him forward. He'd told the Navy he was going to become a SEAL, and to save him a spot at Coronado. They'd been unsure. He could barely walk at the time. But they saw his determination, held a spot for him, and put him in contact with a retired SEAL in Georgia. Six months later, he had met Rachel on a white bus headed from San Diego International Airport to Coronado.

Eventually, his mother came out of her grief and depression, and they'd worked things out. Much thanks to his two younger sisters meddling in the situation. Things were good now, as long as no one mentioned Josh or the framed folded flag sitting on the shelf behind his parent's kitchen table. "You gonna go see your parents?" Christopher asked.

"Maybe. If we're back in time for Christmas. He threatened to court-martial me on charges, conduct unbecoming, if I didn't show up." Her eyes glinted with merriment, not taking her father's threat seriously at all. "I mean, I'm sure he wouldn't actually do it! But, yeah, I guess it's time to go home. I'll just have to come up with a clever way to get out of going to church."

Christopher laughed out loud at that, knowing how much Rachel despised organized religion and that her mother was as obsessed with church as his own mother was. "I'm sure you'll come up with something," he assured her.

Rachel climbed into the truck, pie in hand. Ryan drove while Aiden was in the backseat, headed for Yamna's house. Their second truck was having mechanical issues, so Christopher begrudgingly relinquished the keys and let Ryan drive while he tried to fix the truck.

Rachel handed the pie to Yamna the second she opened her front door and did her best to explain the meaning of pumpkin pie and Thanksgiving, leaving out the part about the pilgrims bringing smallpox to the supposed new world and instead focusing on the happy giving thanks and being grateful part. "I hope it's good. Everyone was sort of arguing about how to make it, wanting to use their own recipe . . . or their mothers' recipes, I guess." Rachel gave a half shrug. "You can have it plain or with ice cream or whipped cream on top. It's better if it's warm too."

"We also have turkey, mashed potatoes, gravy, and green beans." Ryan held up a stack of Tupperware containers full of food.

"When the hell did y'all make that?" Rachel asked.

"While you were on the phone with your father and then sulking about being on the phone with your father," Ryan teased, causing Yamna to giggle.

"Do you get along with your father, or are you also in the *we'd prefer not to speak to them* club?" Yamna asked Ryan.

"My father is dead," Ryan stated with a slight smile on his face.

"Lucky you." Yamna nodded. It was Ryan's turn to laugh.

"We'll be back to get you at 1500, Rache." Ryan handed the food to Yamna and turned to leave. "Oh fuck," he muttered in English. Rachel was barely inside and turned to see what was wrong.

"You have got to be fucking kidding me." Rachel stormed out of the house, leaving Yamna standing in the doorway, pie in hand.

"Veeda, what are you doing out here alone? Get in the house!" Rachel ordered, as though she had any sort of authority over Veeda.

"I'm just talking to your friend." Veeda smiled brightly at Aiden, who was leaning against the passenger side of the truck.

"How did you get here?" Rachel asked her.

"My brother walked with me, but he was in a hurry so he didn't wait for me to go inside. Then when I turned to wave goodbye to him, he was already running off, and I saw your friend here." Veeda's tone was flirtatious and playful.

Rachel locked eyes with Aiden. "What the fuck were you thinking?" she scolded him in English.

"What? She was telling me about how she wants to open a school for girls in this neighborhood," Aiden explained.

"Aiden . . ." Rachel's tone was stern and unforgiving.

"She's so pretty, Sky. And really smart and sweet!" Aiden beamed as Veeda's bright eyes fixated on him.

"Unless you're willing to marry her and take her back to the states, which I'm certain her family would not approve of . . ."

"I dunno, she's pretty great." Aiden's smile got wider as he glanced over at Veeda.

"I'll kick your ass later." Rachel glared at him. He'd known Veeda for all of a minute. She switched back to Pashto and turned her attention to Veeda. "I apologize for Aiden's behavior, Veeda."

"No apology necessary." Veeda winked at Aiden.

"Veeda, go inside now," Yashfa demanded. She came bustling down the steps, her hair wrapped back in her scarf, and pointed to a car coming down the street. Yashfa and Yamna ushered Veeda back inside. Rachel glared at Aiden.

"I'm sorry," Aiden said.

"Get the fuck out of here, both of you. Aiden, you are not allowed out of the house until I get back. Is that understood?" Rachel ordered.

'Yes, ma'am," Aiden mumbled, looking at the ground. Ryan glared at him, and they got in their truck and pulled away, just as the approaching vehicle came to a stop and Shabana got out.

"What happened?" Shabana asked instantly, noting Rachel's tense shoulders.

"Veeda and one of my colleagues may have been flirting a little bit out here."

Shabana's eyes went wide, and she looked around, terrified. "Out here? Where anyone could see her?"

"I'll deal with *him* when I get home," Rachel promised, her jaw clenched with anger.

When Rachel and Shabana finally came inside, Yamna poured each of them a cup of tea. The food Rachel brought was in elegant serving dishes on the dining table, ready to be eaten.

"What were you thinking?" Shabana scolded Veeda.

Veeda smirked. "I'm just having a little fun! He's nice and so tall, and very friendly. What is it you think is going to happen to me? No one cares what *I* do."

Yashfa's expression hardened. "No one cares who your family is if you're behaving like that. In fact, I would suspect you'd get an even harsher punishment just to save your father and your uncle the embarrassment."

Rachel's ears perked up at that tidbit of information. She still had quite a bit of digging to do. "Who *are* your father and uncle?" Rachel asked Veeda as casually as she could.

"Not important or interesting," Veeda stated plainly.

"I disagree." Rachel took a sip of her tea. "If they're even a fraction as important or interesting as Yashfa and Yamna's father . . ."

"Not important." Veeda insisted. "Just more dumb, controlling, uninteresting men. Unlike your friend . . ."

"Leave Aiden alone, Veeda. You both would have been in a lot of trouble if anyone other than us saw you two like that."

"You're going to get yourself killed, Veeda," Yashfa said seriously.

"They can't marry me off if I'm dead," Veeda pointed out. All four women stared at her in shock, but they couldn't disagree.

"You want to open a school for girls in this neighborhood?" Rachel asked, deciding a change in topic was necessary.

"Yes. Yamna's daughters have to walk forty minutes to get to their school. It's terrible."

"I'll let the U.S. State Department know. Maybe they can get an NGO into the area to do something about that," Rachel said NGO in English without thinking.

"A what?" Veeda asked.

"A non-government organization." She switched back to Pashto to clarify.

"Sort of like a charity or humanitarian organization."

"Interesting," Veeda nodded. "How do I find one of those?"

"Google?" Rachel's eyebrows knitted together as she considered whether Veeda was actually serious about this project.

"Stop daydreaming and eat your food," Shabana scolded Veeda.

Veeda rolled her eyes then took a bite of her pumpkin pie. "This is different. Delicious though. How do we make this?"

"Unfortunately, I don't think you can get the ingredients here. We got everything from the embassy," Rachel lied. Or she supposed the CIA may have gotten everything from the embassy, technically.

They ate the rest of the meal in silence. Once they were finished, Yamna and Veeda got started on the dishes while Yashfa broke up an argument between some of the children. Shabana pulled Rachel into one of the bedrooms.

"Can you get people out of Afghanistan?" Shabana sounded hesitant.

"Like, put them on a plane, or do you want them to be able to legally stay wherever they get off the plane?" Rachel asked.

"Preferably the second option," Shabana said.

"That's more difficult." Rachel looked at her quizzically. "Who?"

"My sister, Pari." She paused, uncertain, before the words spilled out of her. "My brother-in-law raped her. Then my husband forced her to marry him when he found out she was with child."

"Your *husband* forced her?"

"Our father died when we were children. He was her closest male family member," Shabana explained. "From his perspective, he was doing the right thing and protecting her. It's better this way, for her reputation, the family's reputation."

"That man is going to keep treating her terribly."

"Yes, I assure you that he is. He leaves her home sometimes for weeks on end, never with enough food . . ." Shabana took a steadying breath and stared straight into Rachel's eyes. "Can you help her get out of the country to someplace safe?"

"Is she being abused?" That small tidbit about being left without food was bad enough, but Rachel couldn't commandeer a plane whenever she wanted.

"Depends on who you ask," Shabana said sadly.

Rachel knew domestic violence was prevalent in Afghanistan and rarely, if ever, prosecuted. Some international reports indicated that as many as eighty to ninety percent of women in Afghanistan were the victims of physical abuse at the hands of their husbands and fathers. "He hits her if she doesn't do what he says?" Rachel tried.

"Yes." Shabana nodded. "Do you consider that abuse?" Her voice was shaking, and her arms were wrapped tightly around her stomach as though she were trying to hold herself together.

Every muscle in Rachel's body tensed. "What about her child? Or children?" Rachel asked.

"She has two young children. Girls, ages five and three," Shabana said.

Rachel nodded. "Are they in Khost?" A plan was slowly taking shape in her mind.

"Yes."

"I'll need her address and a date and time when I can pick her up."

"Her husband is traveling," Shabana said. "He's gone until Sunday."

"Call her now," Rachel said. "Ask her when I can come pick up her and her children. They'll need to pack bags, whatever they absolutely *need* to bring. They should take as few belongings as possible."

Yamna walked over to them, having overheard their conversation. "Use my telephone. We don't want it in the call log on your cell phone that you spoke with her right before she vanished," Yamna told Shabana. "Call her now."

"Are you sure?" Shabana asked. Her eyes were filling with tears as she looked back and forth between Yamna and Rachel.

"You will likely never see her again, Shabana." Rachel noted. "You'll have to say your goodbyes over the phone unless you're going with her."

Shabana nodded and a tear rolled down her cheek. She went to the kitchen to make the phone call.

"Anyone else want a flight out of here?" Rachel asked.

"No. We cannot leave," Yashfa said.

"Too many children relying on us," Yamna added. "Besides, our husbands and our lives aren't terrible. Not great, but not terrible. Much better you help those who truly need help."

After finishing her phone call to her sister, Shabana said, "She can be ready in one hour, and her husband will be home on Sunday in time to escort her to midday prayers." Her voice shook, though she seemed to be vacillating between grief at saying goodbye to her sister and joy at the hope of Pari's new life.

"One hour?" Rachel raised an eyebrow.

"That's when she can be ready. She's packing now."

Rachel nodded and pulled out her phone to text Ryan over their encrypted messaging app.

"What?" Shabana asked, staring at Rachel wide-eyed with hopeful desperation.

"I'm figuring it out," Rachel assured her. "So you know though, the newspapers will report that she and her children are dead. There will be some story about how she was a victim of the Taliban. It will be framed in such a way that will cause outrage from the international community and put pressure on the Afghan government to stand up to the Taliban and Al-Qaeda."

"But you're not a spy?" Yashfa sniffed.

"No, of course not! I'm obviously an academic researcher at Princeton University!" Rachel insisted. Her phone buzzed a minute later with Ryan's response.

Rachel looked up from her phone. "Shabana, call your sister back and tell her I'll be at her house in ninety minutes. Make sure she doesn't tell anyone."

Shabana nodded and ran back to the kitchen to use the phone again.

CHAPTER 12:
NOVEMBER 2018

THIRTY MINUTES LATER, RACHEL was in the truck with Christopher and Ryan. Christopher drove, weaving his way through the city in the same measured, confident way he had their first day in Khost. He made sure they blended in with surrounding traffic.

"Is the other truck fixed?" Rachel's heart started racing, and she tried to distract herself with conversation. She definitely needed prior authorization to get anyone extracted from the country on an asylum visa. It was something that almost never got approved, and she would certainly be fucked if any of her higher ups knew she was enacting this plan without official permission

"No, it is not. But everyone else was out, other than Aiden, and I was told he's in a time out," Christopher said, sounding slightly annoyed.

"Did he tell you why?" Rachel asked.

Christopher's jaw clenched. "Yes, I know why. That's why I'm here driving you, and the other truck will have to get fixed later."

"So, no one is there making sure Aiden stays home," Rachel asked. It was like having kids.

"He's sulking in his room." Ryan chuckled. "He's fine. He knows he fucked up."

They pulled up in front of Pari's house an hour later. It was a worn down mud-brick home on the northern outskirts of Khost's inner city. There weren't many houses in the area, and Rachel hoped they wouldn't be noticed by anyone. Rachel took a scan of the area, ensuring no one was watching, then jumped out of the backseat and took four long strides toward the front door. After knocking three times, a young woman with a slight build tentatively opened the door. She looked terrified, and even younger than Rachel had expected.

"What's your name?" Rachel asked.

"Parivan," the girl whispered.

"You are Shabana's sister?"

"You're here to save me?" Pari's eyebrows knitted together. She seemed hopeful but terrified.

"Yes. Where are your children?" Rachel asked. Pari let Rachel inside so she could help with the two children and their luggage. Rachel went through their belongings quickly.

"Do you have any warmer jackets than these?" Rachel asked, not knowing exactly where Pari and her daughters would end up.

Pari shook her head.

"Okay." Rachel went through the clothes and shoes, negotiating with Pari until they had as little to take with them as possible.

"Can I take this?" Pari asked Rachel as she took a photo off a shelf. It was a photo of Pari and Shabana.

"Yes. I was just with Shabana. She is very happy for you but very sad too," Rachel told her. She bit her bottom lip and looked Pari in the eye. "You understand you can never come back to Afghanistan?"

"I understand. The only thing here to miss is my sister."

Rachel nodded. "Where are your passports?"

"Passports?" Pari's face flushed.

"Yeah, I need passports or at least copies of your passports to get your asylum visas."

"We don't have passports." Pari's panicked voice was barely above a whisper.

Rachel froze. "Shit." She saw the fear on Pari's face. "I'll figure it out. Don't worry." Rachel had no clue how she was going to figure it out, but she knew she needed to. She needed to save Pari to get Shabana, Yashfa, Yamna, and Veeda to trust her. She had to follow through on this at all costs. She pulled out her phone and called Ryan. "Hey, we're ready. Are we clear to walk out to the truck?"

"Hold position," Ryan told her. "We've got a few cars passing on the road." A few minutes later, he gave her the all clear.

Rachel opened the door to Pari's house and grabbed her bags and house keys. "Get in the back seat and stay as low as you can." Pari bobbed her head, then tucked each child beneath an arm and took off across the street. Ryan opened the door for them just as they reached the car, offering his hand to help them up into the back seat. Rachel locked the front door of the house before running to catch up with Pari and the kids. She tossed the luggage into the bed of the truck and ran to get in the front passenger seat. Christopher took off, speeding through the city toward the CIA office as quickly as traffic would allow. Rachel pulled a satellite phone out of the glove compartment when they were four blocks away and dialed the CIA's emergency line.

Rachel didn't even give the operator a chance to speak when the line clicked through. "It's Skylark. I have an emergency evac. Someone competent better meet me at the damned door." She knew better than to get out her own CIA ID in front of Christopher. That was a secret that needed to be kept and a conversation she never wanted to have.

They pulled into a parking spot in the garage moments later. Rachel pulled a pistol out of the glove compartment.

"What are you doing?" Christopher asked, eyeing the gun.

"Asylum visas need State Department approval, which I don't have and am not waiting for," Rachel explained.

"Fuck," Ryan and Christopher both muttered under their breath.

"You could lose your job for this," Christopher pointed out.

"She could lose her life," Rachel countered, nodding toward Pari.

"Right, but you save lives every day. Saving her, ending your career, means you can't save the next person who needs you," Christopher reminded her.

Rachel thought for a minute. She knew he was right, and her mind flashed back to her meeting with Admiral Leftwich and how Eastwood had warned her to be careful. Her career depended on this mission being successful. She had to color inside the lines, so to speak. This was the exact opposite of that. It was too late though. She'd made her choice. "Let's go," Rachel said.

Christopher and Ryan grabbed Pari's luggage from the bed of the truck while Rachel and Pari each picked up one of the children. Rachel led the way into the building and through a maze of hallways to a back office on the fifth floor. She knew this was where the documents for the CIA operatives' fake identities were made, since she'd been there to pick up a fake passport for herself before.

She barged in, startling the man sitting at the front desk. "I need three Afghan passports with asylum visas," she demanded.

"Umm." The man stared at her, dumbfounded. "Who approved this?"

"I did." Rachel rifled through drawers and cabinets until she found what she was looking for—a box of blank Afghan passports. She pulled out three and handed them to the man at the desk, then pointed at Pari and her daughters, making it clear the passports were for them.

The man raised his hands defensively. "I need an official operation plan or authorization from Director Cruse, at least . . ."

"Take Pari and the girls down the hall for their photos," Rachel said, looking at Ryan. He'd been through this process to get falsified documents for himself and would know where to take them. Ryan gave her a thumbs up and a terse smile before leading everyone out into the hall, leaving Rachel alone with the desk agent.

Her desperation was starting to take over. She could not fail Pari. She could not fail her friends. Getting Pari and her daughters out of the country was crucial to getting the intel for this mission.

Rachel's jaw clenched and she pulled the pistol out of the back of her waistband, clicked off the safety, and aimed it at the desk agent's head. "Get to work," Rachel ordered. She proceeded to give the man the names and birth dates of Pari and her daughters, all of which she'd had Pari type into her phone earlier. The man typed frantically as Rachel read over his shoulder to make sure he did as she said without hesitation or mistake.

"You know you're a little crazy," the man said to Rachel as he typed.

"You have no fucking idea just how crazy I am." Rachel smirked. "I would do this for every woman in the Middle East if I could, but that might be pushing it."

The man at the desk nodded and clicked some buttons. "I have their passports right here. Can you please confirm which kid is which?"

Rachel supervised as he dragged and dropped the correct photo to the correct passport then pressed print. Rachel grabbed the three brand new passports out of his hand. "Don't make me threaten your life next time," she said playfully. She glanced through the passports and frowned. "Where are the asylum visas?"

The man shook his head "Not my department." He cringed back in his chair, as if protecting himself from Rachel's wrath.

Rachel sighed, convinced he was telling the truth. She tucked the gun back into her waistband and went to find Christopher, Pari, and the girls.

Pari's daughters were doing somersaults in the long hallway, too young to realize or care that tiled floors weren't the best surface for that. Rachel held up the passports for Pari and Christopher to see and nodded toward the elevator. She led them all back the way they had come, then got Pari and her children settled in a conference room with some tea and cookies. Once the girls were satisfied and stuffing their faces, Rachel marched down the hall to Director Cruse's office, full of determination. She really didn't have a plan, but she knew she wasn't leaving until Pari and her children were guaranteed asylum.

"Rachel Ryker," Director Cruse said when she walked in. "I hear you stole my whiskey the other night."

Rachel decided to ignore him and get straight to the point. "I need emergency asylum granted for a woman and her two daughters."

"Why?"

"Because I'm asking nicely, and I never ask you for anything."

"No, you just steal things out of my office."

"Whatever. Help me or get the fuck out of my way," Rachel demanded.

"Get out of my office before you do something stupid." He leaned back in his chair and pointed towards the door.

Too late. She pulled her gun and tossed the three passports onto his desk.

"You're not gonna shoot me, Ryker." Cruse stood, leaning forward with both palms on the desk.

She turned the gun on herself, pushing the barrel against her temple. The metal was cool against her skin, the feeling familiar and strangely calming. "You know who I am, right? What I do?"

Cruse nodded.

"Is the CIA willing to lose me over this? I will die to get that woman and her children asylum. What's more valuable? My life and all the things I do to help all of you, or a few stickers in a passport?"

"I don't believe you'd kill yourself, either." Cruse glared at her.

"I've already been informed that if I fail at this mission my Naval career is over. That is the only thing that matters to me. The only meaning in my life, the only thing that makes me happy. If I fail at this mission, that all goes away. If Pari and her daughters don't get asylum, I fail. Trust is broken with my assets. My mission is compromised."

"What about your career with the CIA?"

"*That* gilded cage?" Rachel scoffed. "Misguided notions of a delusional seventeen-year-old. I've done enough for the CIA, seen enough. A bullet to the brain is more or less the only way to relieve me of duty."

Cruse was frozen, a blank expression on his face, trying to determine how serious Rachel was being. He gave up after a few minutes and got several stamps out of his desk drawer. "You're lucky you're good at your job or you'd be in a fucking psychiatric facility, you sadistic bitch," Cruse muttered.

Rachel flashed him a ferocious grin. Clearly, he knew very well what she did for the Navy and the CIA. "How long will it take you to get all of that in order?" Rachel waved her pistol, gesturing toward the passports.

"Maybe fifteen minutes?"

Rachel pulled out her phone to make one more call.

"Lieutenant Stephanie Hertz, SEAL HQ Logistics," said the voice on the other end of the line.

"It's Skylark. I need transport from the CIA office in Khost to wherever in the U.S. we send asylum visa holders."

"Um, honestly not sure where that is," Stephanie replied. "Who am I transporting specifically?"

"A young woman and her two daughters whom I'm trying to liberate from subjugation."

"Right. Okay . . . are they flying alone? They probably shouldn't."

"I'll get someone to go with them. Just get them a ride out of here." Rachel heard Stephanie's computer clicking away on the other end of the line.

"If the CIA will let us use their helicopter–"

"They will," Rachel interrupted.

"Okay, then CIA helicopter to a private airfield and a charter plane to D.C. I'll get it all set up and text you the details."

"Thank you, Hertz," Rachel said before hanging up. There was a reason she always dialed Stephanie's direct line when she needed something from the logistics department.

Director Cruse handed her the three passports back, which now contained asylum visas and everything else Pari and her daughters would need to legally get settled in America.

"I'm taking your helicopter," Rachel told him.

"Of course you are." Cruse sighed. "Anything else?"

"Paige is going with them."

"I need Paige!" Cruse protested.

"She'll be back," Rachel assured him. She left, passports in hand, to find Paige and explain to her that she would be traveling to D.C. with Pari and her daughters. Paige was more than happy to help. She was always happy to help with anything. This time, however, Rachel found her perky optimism significantly less obnoxious.

A helicopter was waiting for them on the top of the building. Rachel called Shabana so that Pari could say goodbye one last time. She couldn't hear what they were saying over the raucous helicopter blades, but the look on Pari's face said everything. Sorrow, grief, joy, and excitement at the prospect of a new life. Tears flooded her eyes as she hung up with Shabana.

"Thank you. Praise be Allah for sending you to me," Pari said, giving Rachel one last hug and a kiss on the cheek.

Rachel double checked that Paige had their complete flight itinerary and Stephanie Hertz's contact information in case of any problems. "Y'all are gonna miss your next flight. Get going," Rachel ordered, pointing at the open door of the helicopter. Rachel waited until Paige, Pari, and her two daughters all got in and buckled their seatbelts, then she pulled the helicopter door closed and backed away to watch them lift off.

"What's wrong?" Christopher asked as soon as the helicopter was high enough that they could hear each other again.

"Thinking." Rachel frowned. "You know, the women here, from my perspective, are being treated horribly. Just something they were all saying today—how Pari was forced to marry because it was better for the family. It was best for the most people. All of this subjugation and oppression and abuse. It's not as black and white as I like to think it is."

Chapter 13:
NOVEMBER 2018

RACHEL, CHRISTOPHER, AND RYAN went back to the safe house. Christopher quickly recruited Ryan to help him with whatever mechanical issue was plaguing the team's second truck. Rachel went inside and quietly closed the door behind her. She needed to talk to Aiden and remind him of how dangerous things could get for women here. Remind him that Veeda could be whipped or stoned in the street for looking at him, let alone talking to him.

She was trying to come up with her opening line, trying to decide if she should speak with kindness and empathy, or use her tough tone of authority. What he had done was wrong and risky and dangerous, but he hadn't done it with ill intent. Aiden was one of the nicest, sweetest men she'd ever met. Even in the throes of battle, she'd heard him apologize to people as he killed them. She took a deep breath and headed for his room. His door was slightly ajar and she paused as she overheard a conversation she definitely wasn't meant to hear.

"I met this girl . . . No, I can't say where I am, but I'm not in America. Grandma, you know I'm gone!" Aiden laughed. "She's smart and funny and so pretty, but she lives here. I've never met a girl like her before. She has the most beautiful eyes. Like she knows everything and nothing at the same time. I don't know how to explain it. Some sort of depth to her soul, but at the same time, she's got no clue about how horrible things are, or could be, or she just doesn't care. Vivacious I think is the word . . ."

Rachel could tell Aiden was talking about Veeda and decided to let her lecture wait. She snuck back outside, resigning herself to the boring task of watching Ryan pretend to help Christopher with the truck.

"We don't have any food," Ryan commented as soon as she'd joined them.

"I thought you and Aaron were taking turns shopping?" Rachel wrinkled her nose.

"Yeah, but we're both out of money."

"How is that possible?" Rachel closed her eyes and took a deep inhale before letting it out slowly. What a clusterfuck of a day.

"I don't know. I asked Aaron if he could go since he's out, and he said he doesn't have money either."

"I gave both of you enough money to buy enough food for all of us for the whole time we're here. So between the two of you, that's twice as much money as what it should cost to feed all of us."

"I thought we'd been eating really well." Christopher bit his lip to suppress a smile.

"We've been eating a normal amount of food." Rachel stared at Christopher, trying to understand what he meant.

"You didn't notice the quality of the meat they've been bringing home?" Christopher asked. Rachel just stared at him, clearly having no idea what he was talking about. "Shit, you really would eat cardboard if we told you to, wouldn't you?" He shook his head, trying not to laugh. "They keep coming home with exceptionally nice cuts of meat. I assumed they were good at haggling and were getting a good price. I can't believe you didn't notice."

"No, because not all of us are obsessed with cows."

"Just because I live on a cattle ranch does not make me obsessed with cows. And for the record, we've been eating lamb mostly, not beef, but whatever," Christopher corrected her.

Rachel closed her eyes and let out an exasperated sigh. "Fine. Ryan and

Aiden are both grounded. You and I will go to the market and shop."

"Why am I grounded?" Ryan complained.

"Because you somehow spent three months' worth of grocery money in five weeks! Aaron will also be grounded when he gets home seeing as he's somehow managed to do the same."

"So, I'm going with you?" Christopher asked. Rachel's eyes were like daggers, so he declined to mention the fact that the truck still wasn't running properly.

Chapter 14:
NOVEMBER 2018

CHRISTOPHER LED RACHEL DOWN crowded streets and through narrow alleyways until they arrived at an open-air market where they could purchase everything they needed to stock the team's kitchen. His sisters would be so proud of him for shopping on Black Friday, even if it was just grocery shopping.

"See anyone of interest?" Christopher asked.

"No one I recognize. You?"

"Negative," Christopher replied. His head was on a swivel, checking out their surroundings, taking everything in. Rachel knew he was feeling anxious when she felt his hand on the small of her back. He wouldn't be touching her in public otherwise.

"All good," Rachel said calmly to Christopher, trying to reassure him. As far as she knew, nothing traumatic or terrible had ever happened to either of them here, or in any market, but they were both on high alert, their eyes scanning for weapons, bombs, anything that could indicate danger. The hypervigilance brought about by a decade of serving in combat was both a blessing and a curse. It made them both more aware of their surroundings, which allowed them to zoom in on details, notice patterns, and take in more stimulus than the average person could. Of course, their SEAL training reinforced all of these skills, but it was something that couldn't be turned off either.

It reminded Rachel of the farmer's market near her apartment in Clearwater Beach, Florida. This was bigger though—more vibrant, more energetic. She was immediately enveloped in the sights, sounds, and scents of the market. The zing of the rich aromatic spices mingled with that of freshly baked bread. The stalls were stocked full of fruits and vegetables spilling out of hand-woven baskets. All around them, there was a symphony of haggling customers, spontaneous laughter, and enthusiastic conversation that created an energetic ambiance.

Rachel followed Christopher from stall to stall as they shopped, quickly gathering more than they wanted to carry, but feeding twelve people required a lot of food. As they passed the food stalls, Rachel's eye caught on a stack of colorful fabrics and textiles that showcased intricate patterns and exquisite craftsmanship. She hated shopping, but somehow the markets in the Middle East always pulled her in. She was likely drawn to the vendors' friendliness and their competitive yet playful bartering. She ran her fingers over the layers of fine silk, carefully inspecting the scarves. The bright colors reminded her of her mother's watercolor paintings, bright and dense, but more translucent when held up, diluted by sunlight rather than water.

"You don't need a scarf," Christopher told her in English.

"Actually, if I'm forced to go home for Christmas, I should probably buy people presents," Rachel pointed out.

"They aren't supposed to know you were here."

"I can lie and say someone else brought it back for me." Rachel shrugged.

The vendor looked back and forth between Rachel and Christopher, not understanding their exchange in English. Rachel smiled at him and switched to Pashto. "He says I don't need a new scarf."

Christopher spoke Pashto almost as well as she did, but this was a carefully practiced game they played to test how willing the vendors were to interact with a woman. "He says I have twenty scarves already. I don't. I only have nineteen!" she lied easily.

The vendor broke into a hearty laugh and looked at Christopher, then back at Rachel. "Women are all the same! Anything fine and shiny, and their eyes get pulled in. My wife, I swear she gets amnesia every time she sees a crystal vase or a scarf or shoes, and she forgets that she already owns all of those things! Our home is filled with all the things she's purchased. She forgets she already has something similar."

"I guess that's why you don't let women wander around by themselves here." Rachel winked then quickly translated for Christopher to keep up the pretense.

"One of many reasons," the vendor said humorously.

"I was going to buy a scarf as a gift for my mother," Rachel explained to the vendor. She made sure to meet his eyes so she could see how he responded.

"Ah, yes, fill up her home!" He winked. "What does your mother like?"

"Jesus," Rachel laughed.

Christopher was standing beside her with his arms crossed over his chest, trying not to laugh. He was good at pretending to not understand conversations, but she knew he would think this one was a little too amusing.

"What else?" the vendor chuckled.

"I honestly don't know. We aren't very close."

The vendor nodded. "It's a shame. My daughter is fifteen. She despises her mother right now."

"Yeah, I think most girls go through that." Rachel winced. "Hopefully it gets better."

The vendor nodded again and dug through a stack of silk. "I presume in America, being Christian, she won't be covering her hair with my silk?"

"Likely not."

"She has your coloring, perhaps? Blonde with green eyes?"

"Yes," Rachel agreed. Her hand immediately reached for her headscarf, tugging it down and tucking it around her face a bit tighter.

The vendor winked and pointed to his eyebrows, letting Rachel know that that had instead been the clue. He pulled out a deep emerald green scarf from the bottom of the pile. "Try this." He handed the scarf to Christopher, who then draped it around Rachel's neck and shoulders. Christopher's breath caught in his throat as he looked at her.

"Not the most modest by our current standards here, but in America, I think you tend to accentuate your beauty in public, yes?" the vendor asked.

Rachel smiled. "Yes, we sort of take the opposite approach from the women here. How much is this?" Rachel asked, pointing to the green scarf.

"It's 3,400 afghani," the vendor told her.

"How much is 3,400 afghani? $45?" Rachel asked Christopher in English.

"Yeah, about, give or take some change," Christopher confirmed.

"How about 2,250?" Rachel tried to negotiate with the vendor.

"For something so beautiful? No, no. 3,000."

Rachel raised an eyebrow. "2,500."

"Ah, you are tough, aren't you?" the vendor teased.

"Should we meet in the middle and say 2,750?" Rachel suggested.

"Will it help to make peace between you and your mother?" he asked.

"Maybe?"

"Alright, as an offering of peace, I will go down to 2,800, but do not tell anyone." The vendor held his index finger to his lips, indicating it was a secret. "You must give it back so I can wrap it for you. It is a gift." Rachel handed over a wad of cash then reluctantly took off the scarf and held it out to him. He took it from her, careful not to touch her hand. Then he folded it neatly into a box, wrapped it with a red ribbon, and handed it to Christopher. They finished grocery shopping and rushed back to the house, knowing everyone would be hungry.

Chapter 15:
NOVEMBER 2018

SUNDAY MORNING CAME QUICKLY, and Rachel was up before the sun. She was lying in bed next to Christopher and kicked him in the shin to wake him up.

"What do you want?" he mumbled.

"I need a ride."

"No, you don't. Go back to sleep." He pulled her pillow out from under her head and put it gently over her face in an effort to make her stop talking.

"I do though." She wiggled out from under the pillow and rolled on top of him so that she was straddling Christopher.

"Where are you trying to go?" Christopher asked seriously, staring up at her.

"To Pari's house."

"Why?"

"Her husband is coming home."

"For fuck's sake," Christopher wined and covered his face with both hands.

"Come on, you know I'll get arrested if I go by myself."

She had a point. Women weren't supposed to walk alone outside and they sure as hell weren't supposed to be driving. "Rache, you're sure you want to do this?"

"You know very well I'd sacrifice my life, my heart, and my soul to save one innocent person."

Her words were sincere. They always were. He knew exactly what she was about to do and why she did it. Fighting for innocent lives, fighting for the greater good, no matter the risk or the toll it took on her. "Fine. Get up."

Rachel was up in a second, already getting dressed. She handed him a change of clothes, and Christopher got dressed too before following her reluctantly out to the truck. "What's the plan?" he asked once they were on the road.

"Do you really want to know, or do you want to wait in the truck?"

Christopher weighed his options for a minute, certain that Rachel intended on killing Pari's husband. Of course, in this scenario, he would be a defenseless civilian. Even if the man deserved to die, Christopher was fairly certain that the Geneva Convention wouldn't consider Rachel's judgment of the situation a fair trial. He was used to this of course. She did things like this all the time. They both knew women couldn't get a fair trial in cases of rape. They needed four male eye witnesses who were willing to testify that it was in fact rape. A highly unlikely scenario, especially given that Pari was now married to her rapist. "How are you going to kill him? If you're just going to shoot him or something, then you don't really need me."

"Not sure that would be making my point." Rachel tried to suppress the satisfied smile that was taking over her face. As good of a person as she tried to be, Christopher knew she enjoyed killing people when she thought they deserved it. And Pari's husband definitely had it coming. The guilt of killing weighed on her though, just like it did every soldier.

"Alright, I'll come in with you." Christopher agreed. "You know I always have your back."

Twenty minutes later, Rachel and Christopher parked outside of Pari's house. Rachel unlocked the house with the keys Pari had given her the other day and led Christopher inside to wait for Pari's husband. An hour later, a man came through the front door. Christopher and Rachel both moved so they were between him and the door, blocking his escape.

"Are you Pari's husband?" Rachel asked.

"Yes, who are you?" the man asked her.

"Not important." She drew her handgun and aimed it at his forehead. "Find a paper and pen," she ordered. She forced down the guilt that was weighing on her conscience, knowing this was technically murder and probably a war crime. But it was the right thing to do. With Pari gone, he'd find another woman to rape and abuse. This was for the greater good. This was helping women. His actions were justified under the reigning patriarchy, and she needed to end it, or at least put a dent in it. Pari and her daughters deserved justice and, unfortunately, Rachel's personal brand of retribution was all they would get, even if Rachel wished she could offer them more.

Rachel followed him to another room and watched him rifle through a desk, finally procuring a paper and pen with shaking hands.

"Good." Rachel smirked. "Now write the following: *Due to my negligence and disrespect for my wife, both she and my daughters are dead. I have failed as a husband in the eyes of Allah.*" Rachel read over his shoulder as he wrote. "Now pick up the kitchen knife." She nodded toward the kitchen counter. He looked at her, then at Christopher. Christopher drew his gun too.

"Better do what she says," Christopher warned.

"Why? I die either way, right?"

"Wouldn't you rather die with honor, confessing your sins and taking responsibility for your mistakes?" Rachel asked. Her stomach turned and a metallic taste filled her mouth. Her body may not like what she was about to do, but she was fine with being judge, jury, and executioner if it would help keep other women safe.

Pari's husband stared at her, not sure what to say.

"Pick up the kitchen knife and get on your knees," Rachel ordered again. She tucked her gun into her waistband then pulled a pair of latex gloves out of her pocket and put them on. She picked up the knife off of the counter and handed it to him, then forced him to his knees. "Be a man. Take responsibility for your mistake and let Allah save you and take you to paradise, or be a coward and force me to do it for you. As I understand, Allah doesn't reward cowards." This would be his one last chance at redemption, or salvation, or whatever he wanted to call it. She wasn't going to tell him again.

Pari's husband put the knife to his own throat and tears started streaming down his face. He didn't move.

"Coward, then." Rachel scowled. The man could rape young women, abuse his wife and children, but he couldn't take responsibility for his actions. His tears told her he knew what he'd done was wrong, but it didn't make her feel anything for him. No empathy, no concern for his life. He'd had such little concern for the lives of Pari and his daughters. He had left them home alone for days on end with no food, and then when he was home, he beat them. She took a deep breath to steady herself. *Fight sin with sin,* she thought to herself. *You're going to hell anyway. May as well make it count. Pari deserves justice, revenge, vengeance. He needs to die.*

She stood behind Pari's husband, put her hand over his, pressed the blade into his throat, and pulled the knife across his neck. She took a step back, releasing her hand and letting the knife drop to the floor. His body followed, blood gushing everywhere.

"Alright then," Christopher said, pressing his lips into a thin line. "Now what?"

"Now I have the leverage I need to demand Zarah give me answers," Rachel muttered.

Chapter 16:
DECEMBER 2018

A WEEK HAD PASSED and Rachel had finally secured an invitation to Zarah's home. She had been invited over for tea. Zarah lived in one of the modern high-rises that had been sprouting up ever since the civil war in the '90s had destroyed much of the city. Christopher walked with her, of course. He took the elevator up with her to the fourth floor, but decided to wait outside of the apartment so that Rachel and Zarah could speak privately. Rachel entered the apartment and greeted Zarah in Pashto before removing her shoes.

"Your home is beautiful," Rachel said as she followed Zarah down a narrow hallway to a sitting area. Zarah motioned for Rachel to take a seat on a cushion on the floor. Rachel looked around the sitting room and admired an elaborate tapestry that hung on the wall, the vases of fresh flowers, and the gold-framed photos propped around the room. It was posh but somehow still modest. It almost reminded Rachel of her childhood home. The thought threatened to unnerve her, but she had to focus. Before she took her seat, she couldn't help but notice a familiar face in a photo on the windowsill. *Target acquired.*

Rachel took her seat on the floor, crossing her legs and sitting straight. Zarah sat across from her and pushed back her headscarf. Rachel did the same.

"No men here," Zarah noted, giving Rachel a small smile. "Tell me how you came to speak such impeccable Pashto?"

"I studied international relations and religion at university, focusing on the Middle East," Rachel explained. "Now I'm the translator for a group of researchers who are visiting the university here."

Zarah nodded. "You're a skilled liar, Rachel. Your knowledge of Muslim customs is remarkable for an American, especially someone so young. I assume you were not raised Muslim?"

"No," Rachel confirmed. "I was raised Christian."

Zarah nodded again. "Raised Christian, but you are no longer a true believer of your faith?"

Rachel looked down before responding. "Not particularly faithful, no."

"But you will come to pray in a mosque?" she asked Rachel, pointedly.

"How else am I going to meet any women or make any friends while I'm here?" Rachel's honesty and quick wit caused them both to erupt in laughter.

"You have been spending time with Yashfa?"

"Yes. We go to her sister's house once a week," Rachel confirmed. "Thank you for introducing us."

"Of course." Zarah paused for a moment, sadness creeping across her face. "It was not always like this, you know," she said. "Before, when I was young like you, and certainly long before me, things were better. For women, I mean."

Rachel nodded, understanding.

"I would like to help you and your military friends," Zarah said, leaning in as if she were about to share a secret. "Yashfa and Veeda have told me things." She let out a chuckle and shook her head. "Researchers. Sure. So many stories from all of you Americans. It's the land of great storytelling, is it not? All those films you make." She paused for a moment. "But you are young, and I am old, and I've heard all of these stories before. And so, I ask you, my dear, what is it that you are really doing here?"

"We're looking for some people we'd like to speak with," Rachel confessed. There was no point in lying to her. Rachel was sure Zarah could guess precisely what Rachel and her team were doing in Khost and was sure she had already heard plenty from Yashfa. Rachel stood up, walked to the windowsill, and picked up the photo she'd noticed when she came in. She looked at it for a moment, at the group of five men huddled together, before handing it to Zarah. "I need to find the man in this photo." Rachel pointed at the man in the middle of the group—Saad Ayad.

"Hmm," Zarah mused. "Yes, these men have done some not so good things, and hurt many people, I'm afraid."

"How do you know them?" Rachel asked kindly.

"This one," Zarah pointed at the man standing next to Saad Ayad, "this one is my husband's brother. Or he was. He died."

"I'm sorry to hear that."

"That he died or that he was friends with the man you are looking for?"

"Both," Rachel answered honestly.

Zarah took a sip of her tea. "Why are you looking for Saad?"

"The U.S. government would like to ask him some questions."

"I see." Zarah nodded. "Then what?"

Rachel raised an eyebrow, sure that Zarah already knew the answer to that question. There was no way Rachel was going to confirm her suspicions.

"I will try to help you. I may know where he is," Zarah said with a bit of hesitation.

"Thank you," Rachel said genuinely. "Do you also know his sister, Amina Barech?" Rachel asked, trying her luck.

"Veeda's cousin." Zarah winked. "I guess you didn't do enough research."

"Clearly not!" Rachel gasped.

"She and Veeda do not speak." Zarah gave a wave of her hand as though she wanted to brush aside the topic of Amina entirely.

"Why not?"

"Because she's terrible to Veeda. Hits her, is jealous of her. Veeda is a very beautiful girl. Her father will use her, marry her to someone for some horrific purpose at some point. She will likely make a better match than even Amina did, and it makes Amina very angry, especially since her husband is always looking at Veeda now that . . ." Zara trailed off.

"I've seen a photograph of Amina. She's beautiful," Rachel stated.

"She was."

"Was?"

"There may have been a bomb." Zarah pressed her lips together. "Amina's husband started looking at other women after that. I'm sure he'll take a second wife soon."

"I see." Rachel winced. "Why do you want to help me?"

Zarah shrugged. "Women should help women."

"Sure, but turning on your family is bold. If Saad Ayad was friends with your brother-in-law . . ."

"My son died because of these men. Two of my daughters died at their hands as well, or their guards' hands. This hatred and desire for control, it needs to end. We need to go back to how it was before, when women were seen as equals." Zarah looked at Rachel with genuine concern in her eyes. "You must be careful, Rachel. These men are not kind to women." She pointed at the photo and stared directly into Rachel's eyes. "They can be cruel. They have lost sight of the true meaning behind the prophet's teachings and have been corrupted by promises of wealth and power."

"Why do you keep this photo if these men killed your family?" Rachel was curious.

"Two reasons." Zarah held up two fingers. Rachel saw both sadness and determination in her eyes. "It is the only photo we have of my brother-in-law. And, it reminds me of what I've lost, why I've lost so much. It reminds me to keep fighting back."

"I understand," Rachel said. "I'll be careful. Are they all affiliated with the Taliban or just Al-Qaeda?"

Zarah shrugged. "Is there much of a difference at this point?"

"Technically, yes, in terms of their doctrine, rules of engagement, and strategies. But you may not want a political science lecture."

"Evil men who degrade women are all the same to me," Zarah stated.

Rachel grinned. She couldn't have said it better herself. "How can I repay your kindness?" she asked, genuinely grateful for the help.

"You can keep going," Zarah answered. Rachel looked at her, confused. "You can keep fighting. Fighting in the way that men cannot. Just as you are doing now by being mindful, kind, and demonstrating grace and gratitude.

The women of Afghanistan need a champion! May Allah let it be you."

Rachel smiled a soft smile. "I'll do my best," she replied.

"We'll see how you do. Give me your telephone." Zarah reached out her hand. She called herself from Rachel's phone and saved Rachel's contact information.

Rachel chuckled and took Zarah's phone from her, updating her contact information in Zarah's phone so it was listed under *Skylark* rather than *Rachel*, then showed the screen to Zarah.

"Not a spy at all." Zarah covered her moth with her hand and shook her head.

Rachel covered her hair and put her shoes on. Christopher wasn't in the hallway when she went out, and she figured he'd gone outside to get some air. She headed for the stairs, wanting to stretch her legs after sitting for so long. She went down one flight of stairs, then two. Just as she was about to round the third flight of stairs, a door opened off to the side and someone's hands grabbed her, pulling her into a dark room. She instinctively bent her elbow at a ninety-degree angle and rotated her arm, thrusting her fist up behind her and listening intently for the crack of a broken nose. The sound was a welcome one, as was the blood dripping down her hand, but it hadn't been enough. She flew through the air before landing with a thud on the floor.

Rachel's head collided with the floor, sending a wave of pounding nausea through her. Suddenly someone was standing over top of her, holding her down. She kicked up her legs, wrapping both of them around one of her assailant's necks and twisting her body, trying to get the advantage over one of them at least. It was no use. She glanced around the room, taking in everything she could. Four men with limited weapons, or objects she could turn into weapons. Bile rose up in her throat. Four against one was a game she wouldn't win. She hoped there were only four of them. She could only see four of them.

Someone put a wet cloth over her face. She knew what was coming next.

Amateurs. She was a fucking Navy SEAL for Christ's sake. She could hold her breath just fine. But if they wanted to waste their time waterboarding her, that was up to them. Nothing she hadn't been through before. She held her breath and closed her eyes as the water rushed over her face. She sang to herself in her head, trying to distract herself, knowing exactly how long each song was so she could better keep track of time. After a few rounds, the cloth was removed.

"Who are you?" said a man's voice in Pashto.

Rachel coughed the water out of her lungs. "You know, it works better with cold water," Rachel said, sticking to Pashto as well. She knew better than to give any hint that she was American. "Ice water is best." A boot collided with her ribs, causing her to cough again. "Lazy piece of shit. Be a man and kick me like you mean it!" She laughed, hoping to provoke her assailants so they'd make a mistake.

"Who are you?" the voice asked again.

"I'm your worst fucking nightmare," Rachel said menacingly. She listened carefully to the voice, trying to see if she recognized it, trying to get any clues at all about who these men could be. The cloth was put over her face again. It was time for round two. Rachel tried not to laugh as the tepid water spilled over her face. She focused on counting seconds and minutes.

"Tell us your name!" the voice demanded as the cloth was removed from her face yet again.

Rachel caught a hint of a different accent in the voice. Pashto wasn't their native language, though she suspected Arabic was. She spit the water in her mouth directly into the face of the man closest to her. "You don't deserve to know my name," she told them in Pashto. She didn't want them to know she spoke Arabic in case it came in handy later. Her eyes had adjusted to the darkness enough to see the fist coming for her face. She grabbed her assailant's arm, pulled it toward her, and bit his wrist, hard. He screamed with pain and another man reached to pull her hands off of the first. *Big mistake.* With one arm and one leg free now, she could more than fight back. She kicked her leg up, striking one of the men in the face, then whirled her body around to spin on her back.

She managed to get her hands around one man's neck and pulled him to the floor beside her, then rolled on top of him. She quickly slid herself up his body and pressed her knee into his throat, shifting all of her bodyweight into that knee so that she could feel the air leave his trachea. A second man fisted her hair and pulled her head backwards. Rachel shifted her attention to the second assailant, directing her elbow right into his balls. It was a direct hit, and he fell to the ground. She allowed herself a moment to revel in his cries of pain before standing up to kick him in the face.

Fucking piece of shit. She wanted to say it out loud but knew she had to hide that she was American. She put her boot on his throat. It only took seconds. That was two unconscious, at least. She didn't have time to check if they were dead. The other two men were coming at her fast from the kitchen. They each took one of her wrists in their hands and forced her to her knees, twisting her arms behind her head. Then she felt the rope.

Christopher was getting nervous. His phone wasn't getting reception in the apartment building hallway, so he'd gone to wait for Rachel outside. That had been an hour and a half ago. In total, Rachel had been inside with Zarah for four hours and thirty-six minutes. He knew Rachel could get chatty, but he'd never met anyone other than his sister who could talk for this long. His lips were tight as he realized he would be leaning against the apartment building for an undetermined, ridiculously long time. It was fine, though. If Rachel was forming a relationship with Zarah, if she was getting information, then it was good. But if she wasn't . . . He had no way of knowing what was going on inside that apartment. Rachel could more than handle herself. They all knew that. It didn't mean she didn't need backup occasionally. His stomach turned in knots. He didn't know why. Hunger, dehydration, or his instinct telling him to worry—that something was wrong. He pulled out his phone to text Matt.

Hawk to Nightingale: *How fucking long can tea take? Not even my sister talks this much and she talks incessantly!*

Nightingale to Hawk: *It's been hours. You're sure she's still in there?*

Hawk to Nightingale: *There's no signal in those concrete buildings. I'm on the street, but there's no other way out as far as I can tell.*

Nightingale to Hawk: *Security cameras?*

Hawk to Nightingale: *I saw a few.*

Nightingale to Hawk: *On it!*

Christopher knew that Matt would get Daniel to hack into the building's security network so they could review the footage from the security cameras. He'd only seen a few cameras in the stairwell, and one in the elevator, and he hoped that was enough to calm his nerves.

An hour went by. People came and went in and out of the building. No one Christopher recognized. Another hour passed before his phone rang.

"Hawk, we're in," Matt told him from the other end of the line. "Reviewing the footage now from when she entered the apartment. We're clicking through until we get to the point where you left the hallway, then we'll slow it down."

"Can you get a list of residents in the building?" Christopher asked, trying to mask his concern.

"Yeah, Raven's on it. So far, no names we recognize. No one suspicious. We're running background checks on everyone though, and Raven is passing the names along to our contact at the agency," Matt assured him. "Do you have any indication that something went wrong, or are you just bored?"

"Feeling nauseous."

"Sick? Dehydrated?" Matt asked.

"Don't think so," Christopher said coolly.

"Fuck," Matt muttered. "Just feels off?"

"Yup."

"I'm at the point where Hawk goes down the stairs now," Christopher heard Daniel say in the background. "Slowing down the feed now so we don't miss anything."

"Please tell me you aren't watching that in real time?" Christopher asked.

"No, we're watching it at three times actual speed so we don't miss anything, but so it doesn't take fucking forever either," Matt said.

Time was passing slowly. More slowly than Christopher had ever experienced. He glanced at his watch. It had been thirty minutes since Matt had called. "What is happening on that footage?" Christopher asked, annoyed that Matt hadn't updated him, despite staying on the line.

"A whole lot of nothing. No movement," Matt told him. "You want me to send backup?"

"It would be a bit suspicious for all of us to stand here."

"What else is around there?"

"All residential," Christopher told him. "There's a café a few blocks away."

"I'll send Aiden and Michael to set up there," Matt said.

Rachel was bound on her knees. One man was behind her, kneeling on her legs and holding her arms. The other man stood in front of her. She could tell by his body language what was coming next. She swallowed, resigning herself to what was about to happen. Contemplating the best way to handle the situation. To cooperate or not cooperate? That was always the dilemma. She ran scenarios in her head. This was far from the first time she'd been in this position. With two men, the scenarios got more complex. She had a choice to make and seconds to make it. Flirt and flatter the men, or fight back. She had no idea who they were, but she knew Christopher was outside, somewhere, assuming he hadn't been ambushed too. She couldn't think about him now. She had to think about herself.

"Open your eyes!" the man in front of her yelled. He slapped her across the face with the back of his hand.

"You really want your friend to watch?" Rachel asked, looking up at him. "What's more enjoyable for you? Having a willing participant or using force?"

The man blinked at her then looked at his friend.

"What the fuck?" the first man asked his friend, switching to Arabic. Rachel kept her face neutral, happy that they confirmed her suspicions about Pashto not being their first language.

"Fucking American whores," the second man complained. "Always willing."

Shit, Rachel thought to herself.

The first man's face hardened. "We'll see." He stuck to Arabic, clearly thinking Rachel wouldn't understand. He grabbed her by the hair and drug her to an adjoining bedroom. Rachel fought back just enough to make him think she was resisting. He closed the door behind them, picked Rachel up, and threw her onto a mattress on the floor so she was on her back, unwittingly giving her the exact advantage she'd been hoping for.

He pulled at her clothes.

She tugged at the ropes. *Fisherman's knot, clove hitch.*

The man pulled up her shirt to expose her breasts.

Rachel slid her thumbs along the row of knots, trying to confirm the order before untying them as swiftly as possible. *Two square knots . . . overhand knot.*

Her pants glided down until they were around her ankles.

She focused on her hands, blocking out what the man was doing to her. She knew that thinking of anything else would only distract her and slow her down. This was not the time for emotions, certainly not fear. This was the time for perseverance.

One last knot . . .

The knots slid free in the same moment he flipped her onto her stomach. Just as he climbed on top of her, she reached up, looping the rope around his neck and pulling as hard as she could before flipping him onto his side. She rolled to face him, not letting up on the rope for a second, and watched as the life went out of his eyes.

There was one more man in the kitchen, but that would be easy now that she could reach her knife. She pulled up her pants and straightened her blouse, then sauntered out of the room. "I think it's your turn!" she said as enthusiastically as she could manage, still sticking with Pashto. The man sat in a chair at the kitchen table. "Oh, just the way I like it!" Rachel exclaimed happily as she straddled his lap. Men were always careless once their dicks got involved. She circled one arm around his neck and smiled brightly at him. He smiled back and cupped her ass with his hand.

"You're making this too easy," he teased.

Her eyes never left his as she reached her right hand down to where her knife was strapped inside her boot. She pressed the cool metal of the blade to his neck and pulled it, swiping the edge across his carotid artery.

Rachel went to check that the two assailants she'd rendered unconscious earlier were dead as well. She checked each of them for a pulse, felt none, but plunged her knife into the side of their necks for good measure. She knew she didn't have time for any sort of emotional processing. She needed to clean up. She was soaked in blood and was sure she looked like shit. She pulled out her phone and dialed a number. She relayed her location, the address, the apartment number, and what she'd been wearing when she was dragged inside. The receptionist on the other end told her she'd need to wait approximately ninety minutes for the cleanup crew to arrive. One of many perks of also working for the CIA.

When she was sure there was nothing else she could do, she lowered herself to the floor in the corner of the room and tucked her knees into her chest. She tried to suppress the panic and fear, but she started hyperventilating and tears streamed down her cheeks. But she was alive. She wasn't hurt, not really. This was far from the first time a man had tried to force himself on her.

She was thinking about Christopher though. What would she tell him? What would he think? More importantly, what would he do? He was the calmest person she'd ever met—until one of his friends was in danger. Then he was ruthless.

Christopher was still on the phone with Matt when a sophisticated couple with large rolling suitcases entered the building. He held the door open for them and watched as they got in the elevator. He kept watching from the doorway until the elevator stopped on the second floor. There was nothing suspicious about them per say, but they just didn't fit. His stomach turned in knots as he tried to suppress the feeling that something was very wrong. Christopher waited anxiously on the line with Matt and the rest of the team as they watched the security footage. He caught sight of Aiden and Michael moments later as they made a lap around the building then fanned out to check the nearby streets. They spent a half an hour searching before Aiden walked past him, shaking his head *no*. There was no sign of Rachel anywhere. She must still be inside the apartment building.

Exactly ninety minutes after Rachel had made her phone call, the doorbell rang. A man and a woman with large suitcases came in and issued Rachel clean clothes that perfectly matched what she was already wearing. She showered with a rubber liner in the tub, which would catch any hair, blood, or flakes of skin, making cleanup easier and ensuring no DNA was left behind. As soon as Rachel turned off the water, the woman came in to clean her cuts and apply makeup to her bruises and other injuries. Once she finished her inspection of Rachel, she helped Rachel get dressed.

"Walk." The woman pointed to the other side of the room.

Rachel took several long strides.

"No." The woman shook her head. "Your gait is off. You look injured. Do better, or I'll have to drug you."

Rachel wrinkled her nose. The pain in her ribs was sharp. She didn't mind it, but she wouldn't be able to hide it either. Certainly not from Christopher. He knew her mannerisms and body language like the back of his hand. She didn't want him to worry. Didn't want anyone to worry. She was fine.

"They've got a signal jammer," the man who had come to help clean up said. "I also found this." He handed Rachel a burner phone. She scrolled through the texts. *Take the blonde*, she read. She'd been set up. But by who? She pressed the number to dial it.

"Are you finished?" a woman answered in Arabic.

Rachel recognized her voice instantly. "Yes, I am, Zarah. I hope I passed your test."

Zara chuckled on the other end of the line. "We'll know in a minute." The line went dead.

Rachel smiled to herself, happy to know it had been a test to earn Zarah's trust, and she'd passed. She decided the guys definitely didn't need to know about this little incident of female bonding.

"Drug me," she told the woman. She pulled down her pants to get an injection of whatever delightful, likely experimental, cocktail was on today's menu, courtesy of the CIA. The woman gave her the injection and a second syringe for later. There was a knock on the door. Rachel opened it. Zarah looked her up and down, a concerned expression on her face.

"You look fine," Zarah noted.

"Of course I'm fine," Rachel told her as she opened the door wider to let Zarah in.

"There's nothing to clean up!" Zarah remarked, glancing around the apartment in shock.

"Have I earned your trust yet?" Rachel asked.

Zarah marveled at the spotless apartment. "You understand why I did this?"

"As some sort of ridiculous test, I assume." Rachel coughed. She still had water in her lungs and a bruised, if not broken, rib. It hurt despite whatever drugs she'd been given.

"If they catch you . . ." Zara looked forlorn as she considered what to say. "If you are intent on speaking with Saad, capturing him, spying on him . . . Rachel, if they catch you, this is what they will do. I had to be sure you were prepared for that."

"It's my job to be prepared for this sort of thing. I'll get him, Zarah. I promise you, I will."

Zarah nodded. "Saad Ayad attends evening prayers at the White Mosque. He will be there tomorrow night." She gave Rachel a sly grin. "Welcome to the resistance."

Hours ticked by. They guys were working too slow. Daniel was being overly detail-oriented, as always, and watching the security camera footage at a not-fast-enough speed. Christopher couldn't shake the feeling that something was very wrong. He was about to tell Matt to yell at Daniel to hurry up when he heard several voices yell on the other end of the line "Fuck!"

"Apartment 212. Second floor. Right across from the elevator," Matt stated urgently.

Christopher was through the front door before Matt even finished, sprinting up the stairs. He didn't need to know what they'd seen on the security footage. If they gave him an apartment number, it meant there was a problem. His heart was pounding and his mind was racing, trying to prepare him for whatever horrible scenario he was about to walk into.

"What the fuck, Christopher?" a familiar voice brought him back to the present moment. He'd nearly collided with Rachel on the stairs. She had her palm on his chest, a step above him, and was looking into his eyes.

He felt his beating heart calm under her touch, and he swallowed the saliva that had filled his mouth, which he only now realized had been dry for hours. "You okay?" he asked her, shocked to see her standing on the steps, alive and well.

"Yeah, all good," she said casually.

Christopher eyed her suspiciously, then looked down at his phone. He'd never hung up the call with Matt and could hear Matt's voice yelling. He put the phone to his ear. "She's right here. What the fuck did you see on the footage?"

"She got pulled into another apartment. Is she okay?" Matt asked.

Christopher looked Rachel up and down. She looked fine. "Yeah, all good. My phone works inside again . . ."

"That's weird," Matt said.

Christopher hung up with Matt and put an arm around Rachel's shoulders as they walked out of the apartment building and into the street. He didn't want to admit it, but he'd been worried the entire time she'd been inside and panicked as soon as he'd heard Matt's voice calling out an apartment number over the phone. Navy protocol and fucking Taliban bullshit laws be damned. He wasn't letting go of her.

Chapter 17:
DECEMBER 2018

THE NEXT NIGHT, THEY all headed out in pairs an hour before evening prayers, taking their places around the mosque. They had thin bulletproof vests under their clothes, knives and handguns stashed wherever they could, and backpacks with extra ammo. Michael had his sniper rifle disassembled and stashed in his backpack. Aiden had the communications equipment in his. Everyone was ready in case they got eyes on their targets and had the opportunity to detain them.

Rachel put on her headscarf and headed out with Ryan, locking the door behind her as always. They walked to the front of the mosque and sat down on a bench where they would have a clear view of the entrance. The White Mosque much resembled Khost Central Mosque, but was smaller and bright white instead of sand colored. Rachel watched as people chatted casually and made their way inside.

She felt anxious. Everyone wanted to go home, and she hoped they weren't distracted by thinking about Christmas too much. Distraction led to sloppiness. Sloppiness caused mistakes. There was no room for error on this mission. Their lives and her career depended on it. They needed to capture their targets and maintain their cover long enough to get out of the country. She pushed back thoughts of her own family and the dread of going home for Christmas, instead watching as Christopher and Matt made their way inside.

"Hawk and Nightingale are inside the building," Rachel said. She touched her hand to her right ear, activating the communication device securely in place. She heard several tapping noises in response and a few echoes of *copy that.*

Ryan pulled out his cell phone and brought up a website with tourist information for the region. He read the webpage out loud, reciting information about the province and the city. Rachel already knew everything he was telling her, but she pretended to be interested while discreetly looking around at their surroundings. She knew he needed something to entertain himself with so he didn't fidget too much, and they needed to blend in.

"What took so long with Zarah yesterday?" Ryan asked as he scrolled through photos on his phone.

"What do you mean?" Rachel asked as innocently as she could.

"All day tea?" Ryan furrowed his brow. "You're usually quicker at getting information from people."

"I was making a friend, not interrogating her," Rachel whispered.

"Hawk was worried. We all were."

"Well, I'm fine and so are all of you."

"So, the CIA cleanup crew being there was just a coincidence?" Ryan smirked.

"I have no idea what you're talking about."

"Uh-huh. Unlike everyone else, I watched the video all the way through. Up until you came back down the stairs and were safely outside with Chris." Ryan leaned into her, being sure to jab his elbow into her ribs. She winced. "Who'd you kill, Sky?"

"Keep your fucking mouth shut, Raven," Rachel muttered.

"You know I won't say anything. I was just curious."

"Ryan, shut up and check your ten." She nodded her head towards the ten o'clock position, bringing Ryan's attention to the man she saw approaching the mosque.

Ryan turned his head slightly to the left. "I see him."

Rachel touched her ear again. "Target one is approaching the building".

"Sky, I've got eyes on target two around the back of the mosque," Michael reported back to her.

"Copy that, Eagle. Follow him. Report back anything actionable"

"Understood, Skylark."

Two of their three targets in the same area, at the same time? Zarah's intel was already paying off.

An hour passed without much action. Just people out for evening strolls, making their way between the market and home, or work and home. Rachel snapped to attention as people started making their way out of the mosque. Prayers were over.

"Eyes on targets one and three coming out of the mosque," Rachel announced, overjoyed to see that Ibrahim Ayad had been inside all along. "Looks like they're headed toward the main road," Rachel informed the team.

"I still have eyes on target two," Michael announced. "He's been shopping and running errands."

"Do you need someone to relieve you?"

"No, we're good. It's crowded everywhere we've been."

"I've been tracking him with the drone," Nate added. "No worries, Skylark. We know what we're doing."

"You could have given the rest of us an update," Rachel complained.

"We said we'd report back if something was actionable. You wanted to know that he bought a pomegranate?" Michael asked.

"Not really," Rachel conceded, happy to hear that they had eyes on all three targets. "Hawk, Nightingale, do you copy?" She assumed they had their earpieces switched on again now that she could see them coming out of the front door of the mosque.

"Yes, we found targets one and three inside the mosque. Following now, as you can probably see if you're still on the same bench. Go ahead with your update Skylark. We copy," Christopher whispered back.

"We've got eyes on all three targets. You have one and three. Stay on them. Raven and I will back you up. Eagle has eyes on number two, and Crane is tracking him with the drone."

"Copy," Matt answered back.

Ryan and Rachel got up off their bench and strolled toward the main road, staying a half block back from Christopher and Matt, who were about a hundred feet behind their targets.

"Blackbird to Skylark. Do you copy?" Aiden asked. He was with Michael, following target two.

"Loud and clear, Blackbird," Rachel responded.

"Target two has entered a house ten blocks east of the Mosque, just past the grocery store, then one block north of the main road."

"Can you and Eagle keep eyes on the entrance?" Rachel asked.

"Yeah, we're good here. Hanging at a bus stop," Aiden confirmed.

"Anyone else see anything?" Rachel asked

"Negative," the men reported back.

"Alright everyone, move in. Take the streets parallel to the main road. Head east. Raven and I will stay on Hawk and Nightingale. Who can get the truck fastest?"

"On it!" Aaron said.

After walking six blocks, Rachel saw Christopher and Matt turn down an alley up ahead.

"Sky, you and Raven take over," Christopher said.

Rachel and Ryan sped up their pace. Christopher and Matt had been following their targets too closely for too long. It was smart of them to turn down the alley and have Rachel and Ryan take over.

"Hawk, take that alley down one block over and walk with us," Rachel ordered.

"Copy that," Christopher said.

Rachel and Ryan walked at a quick pace along the main road. As they passed the alley, she turned her head and saw Christopher one block down, walking in the same direction. She turned her head to the right at each intersection, locking eyes with Christopher through the crowd of people on the sidewalk every chance she got.

"Eagle to Skylark, I've got eyes on you. You're headed our way."

Rachel couldn't believe what she was hearing! Were all three targets going to the same location? She and Ryan walked one more block before they saw that the men they were following entered a building. Michael and Aiden were standing across the street at a bus stop, talking.

"Targets are inside," Rachel announced. She was exceedingly happy for Zarah's help. Mild torture incident aside, it had all been worth it.

"Stopping here," Christopher announced from the backside of the building.

"Someone relieve Eagle and Blackbird. They've been there too long," Rachel ordered, still walking straight ahead with Ryan.

"Condor and I have Eagle and Blackbird in our sights. Covering now," David said. He and Daniel sat down on a bench at the bus stop as Michael and Aiden walked away.

"We've got Hawk and Nightingale," Jason said right after.

"Great! This is our chance to move. All three in the same location will not happen again. Remember, the objective is capture, not kill. Eagle, did you notice any good sniping positions?" Rachel asked.

"Yes ma'am. Shouldn't be a problem," Michael answered.

"Good. Take Blackbird with you so you have the radio," Rachel ordered. "Alright, let's be careful. We have no idea who or what else is in that building."

"I'm going with Eagle and Blackbird so I have cover and can monitor everything with the drone," Nate announced just as Aaron parked the truck and got out.

"Good." Rachel signaled for Aaron to go around back to rendezvous with Jason and Brendon on the backside of the building. The three of them would set up a solid perimeter in case someone tried to escape out the back. Then she watched as Michael, Aiden, and Nate disappeared around a corner on the opposite side of the street. David and Daniel left their spot at the bus stop and made their way toward the front door, behind Rachel and Christopher, guns in hand. Ryan and Matt were right behind them.

The sun had set, leaving the city in darkness except for the street lamps.

Most people would be inside their homes by now, eating dinner or even putting their kids to bed. "Surveillance teams, stay in place," Rachel ordered over comms. "Eagle are you in place?"

"I could put a bullet right between your eyes if I wanted to, Sky," Michael laughed. "I don't see any movement through any of the windows though."

"Okay, hang tight. Let's try to stay quiet." Rachel glanced over her shoulder and checked that everyone had silencers attached to their handguns.

They moved in, walking silently up the front steps. Rachel led the way, and Christopher was right behind her, as always.

Christopher leaned up against the front of the house as Rachel picked the lock on the front door. In she went, gun poised and ready. She moved stealthily from room to room, the men falling in line behind her and splitting off into pairs to clear one room after another. Two men were in the kitchen, leaning against the counter, talking, and sipping tea. Rachel recognized them immediately from the photo in Zarah's home.

"Hostiles," she said, aiming her gun at one of them. She pulled the trigger as the other man dropped to the floor. "Thanks, Hawk."

"No problem," Christopher answered.

"I have kids," Ryan announced over comms.

"Gender and ages," Rachel requested.

"Young. Seven, eight? Girls."

"Keep them calm," Rachel ordered. She kept moving.

"First floor living room and bathroom all clear," David announced.

"Kitchen too," Rachel told them.

"Haven't found any computers or phones yet," Daniel told them. As always, he was focused on finding the stolen malware code and anything else tech related that may come in handy.

"First floor is clear, other than these kids," Ryan confirmed.

"Advancing to the second floor," Rachel told everyone. She headed up the stairs, knowing they would all be right behind her, except for Ryan and Matt. Rachel immediately heard the muffled screams of a few women. They were likely hiding and trying to stay quiet. Rachel knew they were getting close. There was a large family room at the top of the stairs where five women were sitting, clutching six children. Christopher, David, and Daniel were behind her, unmoving, and pointed their guns at the women.

"Calm, calm. We won't hurt you," Rachel whispered to the women and children in Pashto. She signaled for them to move downstairs so they would be safely out of harm's way. She saw a flash of metal in the corner of her eye and turned toward the woman who was holding a knife. Rachel froze and raised her handgun over her head. "I don't want to hurt you," she repeated in Pashto. She got no response, so she repeated it in Arabic. The woman looked terrified. "What is your name?" Rachel asked, deciding Arabic was the correct language.

"Who are you people?" the woman responded in Arabic.

"We're here to help," Rachel insisted. "Tell me how I can help."

"We don't need help." The woman pointed her knife at Rachel but did not approach.

"If you keep pointing that knife at me, one of my men will shoot you. I don't want you to get hurt. I don't want anyone to get hurt. We are here for the men. The men, who I would guess, have taken your right to choose, your right to make decisions for yourselves, your right to go outside without them."

There were tears in the woman's eyes, and Rachel couldn't tell if she was afraid or grateful. Maybe both?

"I am looking for Saad Ayad," Rachel tried again. Rachel watched as the woman's eyes involuntarily darted to the long hallway at the mention of his name. Rachel continued on. "Two of my men are downstairs with the children."

"If they harm those children, I will kill you all," the woman shrieked.

"I assure you, we would never harm a child," Rachel said calmly. "The men downstairs have medical supplies and some food and water. You are welcome to any of it. Or if you go downstairs to the other children, I will speak with the men who are hiding up here like cowards, letting the women and children defend them, and then we will leave. We will not hurt any of you or your children as long as you do not act aggressively toward us or indicate in any way that you mean us harm."

"If you harm my husband or take him, I will be left with nothing. My children will be left with nothing," the woman protested.

"What is your name?" Rachel scanned through a thousand photos in her mind, trying to deduce who this woman could be. "Is your name Noor? Noor Ayad? Your father is Imdad Barech and your husband is Saad Ayad's nephew, Ibrahim Ayad."

The woman's jaw dropped with disbelief, and it was all the confirmation she needed.

"Is Amina Barech here too?" Rachel asked. She watched as one of the children's eyes darted to a woman sitting on a sofa with her back to the stairs. "Okay, I want to help all of you. I do not want to hurt anyone. Please go downstairs. None of these men who are with me will hurt you."

Three of the women got up and rushed toward the stairs, ushering the children along with them. David followed them, his gun lowered but still ready in case they tried to leave the house.

"Amina and Noor, my name is Sky. I want to help you. I want to help your children," Rachel repeated, speaking Arabic again.

"Help us? I'm certain you're here to kill our husbands. How is that helping us? It just leaves us alone. Then we cannot go out. We cannot do anything," Noor told her. "All these wars, all the killing, is just leaving women alone and widowed with children, unable to provide for them. We cannot go out without a male family member, and they're all dying. I won't let you kill my husband."

"Okay, that makes sense. I know that's a big problem. I don't have an immediate solution to that. I'm trying to get rid of the Taliban, of all these groups who want to tell you what to do and take your freedom and agency away, but it's going slower than I'd hoped."

Noor scoffed.

Rachel tried again. "Would you like to go to the U.S.? You would be safe there." It would be harder to convince Director Cruse this time, but she would do it all over again. She had plenty of people she could call in favors from, if she had to.

"We would rather die," Amina seethed. She still sat on the sofa, her back to Rachel.

Christopher glanced over at Rachel and shrugged. Rachel breathed in sharply realizing Christopher was more than happy to kill Amina so that she wouldn't have to. Rachel wasn't giving up that easily though.

"Why, Amina? Help me understand, please."

"Because your country is evil."

"I sort of think the Taliban and Al-Qaeda are evil. America has its problems, sure, but women are allowed to study, to work, to make decisions for themselves."

"No, you have weak men who cannot provide for women, so women must do everything on their own. Work, support the family, care for the children, and care for their husband. It's no good," Amina argued.

Finally, she turned her face toward the stairs. Rachel was instantly taken aback by the raised scars interwoven like a spider web on Amina's damaged face. It was a stark contrast to the young, vibrant beauty she'd seen in photos. Suddenly her jealousy of Veeda's gorgeous face made sense. Rachel's mind flickered back to the first time she'd gone home after being deployed. Her mother had been shocked and horrified by the scars left from nine months of combat. But her own scars were nothing compared to this. Amina's face was unrecognizable.

"Tell me about the bombing, Amina. Tell me what happened to you. I've seen photos of you. I know you were beautiful. You still are, just maybe not in the same way."

"Was it one of your husband's car bombs?" Christopher asked. "Because if so, then we have that in common."

Amina sneered. "No. You people did this to me, and now my husband cannot look at me because of what your country has done." Hatred and disgust dripped from her tongue.

"Sounds like he's pretty weak," Rachel stated. "You're sure you don't want to come to America and trade up for a better man?"

"No, America is full of pathetic men with no courage. They are busy bombing schools. Bombing things when you cannot see what they really are, who is there, what is happening. Your country did this." She pointed at her face.

"When was that? Tell me about it," Rachel requested.

"Ten years ago. Your country set off a bomb in the northern part of the city. At my children's school. My–" Her words broke off. "Your country killed three of my children. So, no, I don't want to go to America. I despise America."

Rachel nodded. "I understand." Her mind flashed back again. She knew a factory had been the target of the drone strike, not the school. She knew because she had been on the ground collecting the intel and confirming where the factory was. Had she transmitted the wrong GPS coordinates? Had she let herself get bested by a fucking map again? Or had someone higher up made a mistake? She would never know, and she couldn't admit it out loud, but she may very well have been responsible for that school getting bombed. It would just have to be another thing to lock away, to decide later if she wanted to know the truth or the extent of her impact on that situation. She couldn't think about that now. Focusing on the present moment, the task at hand, was the only way forward.

"Have you lost a child?" Amina asked her.

"No," Rachel answered honestly.

"Then you cannot understand. My dead children are here in Khost. They will always be here and I will never leave them."

"Amina." Christopher lowered his gun. "My brother died fighting in this ridiculous war." Josh had died in the Persian Gulf, not Afghanistan, but it was close enough to the truth. "I saw what that did to my mother. She was devastated. She wandered the house, begging Jesus to take her so she could be with her son. Obviously, that didn't happen. She couldn't function she was so depressed and grief stricken. I know how hard it was for me, losing him. But losing a brother is not the same as losing a child, let alone three children. I can only imagine the pain you're in."

Tears welled in Amina's eyes, and Christopher took a step closer. "We understand your pain and devastation, Amina. I promise you that we do. We've all lost people. A lot of people. If we can do anything to help you, we will. We just need to speak with your brother."

For a moment, Rachel thought they had finally gotten through to Amina. Broken down her barrier. Rachel almost missed the silent signal pass between Amina and Noor—the subtle nod of Amina's head—but then Noor charged Rachel with the knife, and all hell broke loose. The metal glinted off of a lamp and the air caught in Rachel's throat. She sidestepped and spun, hitting Noor in the face with her handgun. Noor cried out at the pain. Rachel hated hitting her, but the knife had been mere inches from her arm.

"Do not try that again," Rachel ordered as she forced Noor to her knees. She kept her hands around Noor's throat as Daniel got busy securing Noor's wrists and ankles with zip ties. "I told you we would not harm you as long as you did not act aggressively toward us."

"Amina, that was unnecessary," Christopher said. "I understand we're technically enemies, but we don't want to hurt you. We never want women or children to have to pay the price for what men are doing. We . . ."

Rachel looked over at Christopher just in time. A switch flipped in her brain, a primal instinct unleashing fury, rage, and a violent possessive need to protect. Rachel rushed him, her gun raised, pushing Christopher out of the way just as Amina pointed a shotgun at his heart. Without thinking, Rachel pulled the trigger on her own gun, and Amina collapsed to the floor.

Rachel and Christopher moved in, their guns still trained on Amina, while Daniel kept his gun aimed at Noor.

Christopher reached down to check Amina's pulse. "Good shot." Rachel's bullet had hit Amina right between the eyes.

She was dead.

"Terrible shot," Rachel muttered. She clutched her side, pain suddenly shooting through her ribs. She was certain she'd broken a rib during the previous evening's events in Zarah's apartment building. She must have strained it when she moved to knock Christopher out of the way.

Killing Amina had not been part of the plan, but Christopher dying would have been so much worse. She wanted to save Amina, liberate her from a controlling and likely abusive home situation. But she'd do anything to keep Christopher alive. She'd do anything to keep any of her men alive. They came first. *Her* mission came second, then the Navy, and then the goddamned CIA was last. Her own life meant nothing. She was simply a carefully trained weapon of war.

"Looks like I got here just in time," David joked. In all the chaos of the past few minutes, Rachel hadn't even realized David had come back upstairs.

"Sparrow, help us look for more weapons or explosives or fucking anything, would you?" Rachel's tone was more aggressive than she meant it to be, but the pain from her broken rib was getting the better of her.

"Yes, ma'am." David's lip curled at Rachel's frustrated impatience. He moved the cushions and pillows off the sofa, quickly finding a revolver.

Rachel walked back over to Noor and looked her in the eye. "What else am I going to find up here?"

"Nothing." Noor spat on Rachel's boot.

"Thanks. Those were getting dirty." Rachel smiled down at her. "Do you have any other weapons up here?"

Noor just stared at her.

"Here's the deal, Noor. You can keep me happy and I can keep treating you with respect, or you can piss me off and instead of *me* searching you for weapons, I'll let one of the men do it." Rachel was in no mood for fucking around. Noor had already almost stabbed her once, and Amina had nearly killed Christopher. She was out of patience, but knew she'd never actually let any of the men touch Noor unless it was absolutely necessary to keep someone alive. Noor didn't need to know that though.

Noor's eyes grew wide with fear. "My husband keeps explosives in the kitchen."

"Thank you." Rachel signaled to David, and he ran downstairs immediately.

"Do you know anything about stolen documents or hard drives or USB sticks from the United States?"

"What?" Noor asked.

Rachel took a deep breath and tried to calm down now that Noor was cooperating. "Someone stole something from the U.S. government, and we would like it back. Have you heard the men mention anything like that?" she asked kindly.

"No." Noor shook her head and looked at the floor.

"Do they tend to say things around you?"

"No."

"Are you lying to me?" Rachel's hand was on Noor's head, ready to uncover her hair. She'd never actually do it with men in the room, but Noor didn't need to know that either.

"I'm not lying," Noor insisted, tears building in her eyes.

"Where are the men?" Rachel removed her hand from Noor's head and crouched down in front of her, meeting her eyes. The poor girl had had enough.

Noor looked toward the hallway.

"What are they doing?" Rachel asked.

"Talking."

"Are they armed?"

"I don't know." Noor seemed sincere.

Rachel pointed at the floor. "Stay here."

She looked at Daniel and then again at Noor. "Hawk, you're with me." Rachel moved immediately, making her way down the hallway, opening doors and closets, until she came to the end and found a door that was locked. *Bingo.* She pointed her gun at the lock and blasted it to pieces. She kicked the door open, gun poised and ready. There was a table in the center of the room with documents and maps spread out. Clearly, someone was planning something. The room was empty though, so she stood in the doorway, waiting for Christopher to finish clearing the rooms on the other side of the hallway.

"Empty?" Christopher's breath was warm on her ear.

"We'll see." She took three paces across the room and looked out the window. No sign of her targets. Just Jason, Aaron, and Brendon casually sitting on a park bench across the street, chatting. Rachel nodded toward the closet. She stood in front of it, gun poised and ready while Christopher inspected the closet door. No wires, no explosives, but it was locked. They didn't want to risk shooting any of their targets, so he raised his leg, propelling his foot down on the doorknob with enough force to break it off.

"Down on the ground!" Rachel yelled in Arabic as the closet door fell open, exposing three men. The youngest of the three men, Munir Omarkhil, reached down. Rachel saw a flash of metal and took the shot. Her bullet hit him right in the shoulder. He cried out in pain as blood stained his shirt.

"Targets acquired," Christopher announced over comms.

Once they were back at the safe house, Rachel headed straight for the shower. Christopher followed her. "May I help you with something?" Rachel raised an eyebrow at him.

"You okay?"

Rachel looked down at her bloodstained clothes then met his gaze again. She was obviously not okay.

Christopher closed the bathroom door so they could have some privacy. "Talk."

"I wish those women could understand that I was trying to help them," Rachel said. She'd been over it in her head a thousand times since that moment. She understood the cultural and ideological differences. It wasn't personal, but she was still convinced she was right. She wanted to empower them, to give them the agency to fight back and be free to do whatever they wanted.

Christopher placed his hand over hers, making her jolt. His hand was warm and calloused over her own. "Sky, not everyone thinks like you do. What you see as oppression, these women see as safety and security. It's all they've ever known. Just like all you've ever known is punching every man that looks at you wrong in the balls."

Rachel couldn't help but laugh. She leaned into him, letting him pull her into a hug. She hadn't wanted anyone to get hurt, let alone killed. She'd wanted to help those women. She understood Amina's grief and their fear of a new culture, of leaving their lives in Afghanistan behind, but she also knew their lives would be better, eventually, in America. It shouldn't have been shocking that Noor and Amina believed wholeheartedly in the ideals they'd been taught. Rachel's arrogance, her confidence that her way was the best way, was starting to crumble. She was used to being right about things—smarter than everyone else—but she needed to remember not everyone thought like she did. Not everyone wanted what she wanted. Christopher was right. What she saw as oppression, Noor and Amina saw as safety and security.

"Thanks for saving my life by the way," Christopher said, his voice barely above a whisper.

"You would have done the same."

"Yeah."

Rachel tipped her face up to his and saw the sadness and fear in his eyes. All the feelings they weren't supposed to feel. They were supposed to be tougher than that, but near misses made you think and feel everything you weren't supposed to. She put her palm on his cheek and he met her gaze. She rose up to her tiptoes and pressed her forehead to his. "I didn't want to kill Amina," she said softly.

"I know."

"But I'd kill her a hundred times over to save you." Rachel's voice was sincere and warm and caring. Full of love and respect, with a hint of longing. "I'd kill anyone for you," she murmured.

Christopher stared into her eyes, his heart racing as he put one hand on her waist and pulled her closer to him. The index finger of his other hand was under her chin, tipping her face up to his. He brushed his thumb over her lips. "I . . ." He was interrupted by pounding on the bathroom door.

"I don't hear any water running, so get the fuck out of there so other people can shower!" Aiden yelled through the door.

"Give me your jacket and pants. I'll start the laundry," Christopher said, releasing his grasp on Rachel. She quickly stripped and wadded her clothes into a ball, handing them to Christopher before she turned on the shower and got in, careful to hide the bruise that had formed over her ribs.

Chapter 18:
DECEMBER 2018

RACHEL AND RYAN SNUCK out of the apartment once everyone was asleep. They needed to question the three men they had brought in. The team hadn't found anything particularly useful at Saad's residence. There was nothing to indicate that he had or even knew about the stolen USB stick. Rachel was exhausted and annoyed. Normally she and Ryan loved doing interrogations, but they hadn't slept in days and needed to be on a flight in a few hours.

"Don't you have someone permanently based here who can do this?" Rachel complained to Director Cruse.

"No one as skilled as the two of you. See what you can accomplish between now and when you need to go to the airport," Cruse told her.

"Can you get us a dog?" Ryan asked.

"I'll look into it, but probably not."

"Fucking hell," Ryan said once Cruse left the room. "What's the plan, Sky?"

"Seeing as how I'm already pissed off, I vote we skip diplomacy and get straight to the point." Rachel took off her leather bomber jacket and looked around the room. "What do we have to play with?"

Ryan's eyes narrowed. "What do you want, and I'll go find it."

"Surprise me." Rachel grinned. She went into the interrogation room Saad Ayad had been moved to and closed the door behind her. He looked down at the table, unwilling to look at her.

"Look me in the eye you sorry piece of shit." Rachel got right in his face. "Your sister is dead because you're a fucking coward. What kind of a man hides in a closet, letting his sister and kids pay the price for his sins? You think that's going to get you into paradise? That's your fucking *jihad*?" She spat in his face. "Look at me." He refused. She grabbed his beard and forced his face up to hers.

"You're a fucking whore," Saad yelled, looking her up and down.

"Yes, I most certainly am. A whore for the U.S. government. But you didn't play your cards right, so you won't be having any of that sort of fun." Rachel's eyes flashed with hatred. She'd been called worse, and really, she couldn't disagree with the man. Not in this instance anyway. Interrogator, assassin, paramilitary operative, SEAL—whatever they wanted to call her, which ever agency was paying her—the job was the same. Kill or be killed, manipulate others to get information, turn off the human side of yourself, push yourself physically and mentally to the breaking point to accomplish whatever mission she was assigned, always putting duty and honor above all. Always acting for the greater good, no matter what toll it took on her. "Where's the USB stick?"

"What USB stick?" Saad asked in return.

"How did you get the code?" Rachel asked.

"What code?"

"Oh, it's this computer code some jackass stole from us that can control nuclear reactors and shut down Iran's power plants. Apparently, it's saved on a green USB stick," Rachel explained with a casual flick of the wrist.

"I don't know anything about computers," Saad admitted.

"I didn't think you did. In fact, I was fairly certain that you were too busy planning to blow something up to bother with cyber warfare. Based on the explosives we found in your home, I'd say I was right. But my boss thinks he's smarter than me." Rachel shrugged. "Anyway, while I believe that you didn't take the USB stick and that it's likely not in your possession currently, that doesn't mean you don't know who does have it. So tell me. Who in Al-Qaeda would want to spy on Iran?"

"Fuck Iran. We don't care about them."

"Sure, you do," Rachel insisted.

"No." Saad shook his head.

Rachel took his hand in hers and snapped his pinky finger, effortlessly breaking the bone. He cried out in pain, screaming and cursing her in Arabic. "Who in Al-Qaeda is interested in spying on Iran?" she repeated, doing her best to ignore his cries of pain. She couldn't see him as human, not if she was going to get the answers she needed.

"If you're so smart, then you would know Al-Qaeda is not a centralized hierarchical organization. We are comprised of many smaller–"

Rachel slapped him across the face with the back of her hand. "I don't need a political science lecture. I know who you work for and I know who you work with. Who in your group would be interested in Iran?"

"No one."

Rachel held his gaze as the door opened and shut.

"Thought this might be fun." Ryan grinned, holding up a hammer.

"Sure makes things easier." Rachel pressed her lips together to suppress her smile. Violence wasn't the answer, except when it was necessary. She shut down her emotions—guilt, shame, fear, and empathy—and leaned into her training. She needed information and Saad had it. How she got that information from him was something no one needed to know about, except for her and Ryan and whoever read the CIA interrogation report she would have to write, which would be full of half-truths to cover their asses anyway. It was all something to discuss with whichever deity decided her fate in the end. Heaven, hell, purgatory, or getting reincarnated as something or someone awful? That was a problem for another day. "Apparently, Al-Qaeda isn't interested in Iran and is just some lowly disorganized mishmash of idiots," Rachel summarized for Ryan.

"That is not what I said!" Saad protested.

Rachel pressed his hand into the table and struck it with the hammer, listening for the crack of bones.

"Bored already?" Ryan raised an eyebrow at Rachel. Usually, she was more patient.

Rachel got in Saad's face again. "Who would be interested in controlling Iran's power plants?"

Nothing but silence. The asshole didn't even blink.

Ryan picked up the hammer and struck Saad in the ribs, then burst out laughing when the man cried out in pain. "Shut the fuck up. I didn't even hit you that hard!"

"I mean, Raven, the man hid in a closet and let a group of women and children defend him," Rachel teased.

"You're going to kill me regardless, so why should I speak?" Saad said.

"Because I can kill you kindly, or I can kill you slowly," Rachel told him, cocking her head to the side. She and Ryan both excelled at killing people slowly. "You hold all the power here. You decide when this is over."

Saad stared at her, seeming to consider her words. He took too long. Rachel picked up the hammer and broke another finger. Saad winced and yelped with pain.

"Speak, Saad," Rachel commanded.

"Go fuck yourself," Saad said in perfect English.

"Tell me about Iran. What does Al-Qaeda have planned regarding Iran?" Rachel tried again.

"Al-Qaeda has much more important things to do than worry about Iran," Saad assured her.

"Sure, but this code isn't country specific. It would give you access to the nuclear reactors of whatever country you wanted, so wouldn't you want this code for yourself to use on whatever targets you want? The U.S. for example," Ryan told him.

"You go fuck yourself too. Better yet, fuck her into submission so she can learn to behave like a proper woman." Saad nodded toward Rachel.

"No, thanks." Ryan looked at Rachel, completely disgusted. "That would be like fucking my sister."

They kept going back and forth for hours. Saad didn't have the USB stick and kept insisting over and over that Al-Qaeda was not interested in cyber warfare. Rachel sat in a folding chair across from Saad, her head in her hands and her fingers tangled in her hair, elbows on the table. She was irritated and exhausted, and they needed to get to the airport. "Fine, Saad. You keep insisting that no one in Al-Qaeda has our USB stick or code, so who does have it? Come on. I know you've got a lot of friends. Surely you've heard something." Rachel was practically pleading with him for information.

"I don't know," Saad repeated. Ryan broke his last finger. That was ten broken fingers and two broken ribs. "ISIS. ISIS would want something like that!" Saad screamed through his pain. And there it was, her suspicions confirmed. Saad never had the USB stick. So why had Leftwich sent her on this wild goose chase?

"And how would you know that? Why should I believe you?" Rachel demanded.

"Our families may have made a little exchange recently," Saad said hesitantly.

"What trade?"

"My cousin . . . She's being traded."

"Thank you!" Rachel pressed her palms together like she was praying and looked up. "Now I just need to know exactly which of your cousins is marrying which ISIS shithead specifically."

Saad stared at her defiantly. Ryan threw a quick jab to his face shattering Saad's cheekbone.

"Tell me now, or I'm going to leave this room and come back with a dog and let the dog bite your balls off," Rachel threatened, knowing full well Cruse couldn't get them a dog.

"Well . . . it's not entirely official yet." Saad looked down and to the side. His face was flushed, his breathing heavy. "Only one man works with energy and cyber warfare."

"Name," Ryan demanded.

"Samir Al-Abadi. He made a deal with someone in exchange for . . . something! Some computer thing. I really don't know more," Saad shouted frantically.

Rachel froze in place as the hairs on her neck stood up. She felt a throbbing pain in her thigh. She knew that name. It was a name that had followed her since 2007. "What did you say?" She thought she might be hallucinating from lack of sleep.

"Samir Al-Abadi is doing something with energy and nuclear something in Iraq. I make car bombs. I am not an engineer. I don't know what exactly he is doing, but I've heard this mentioned. I swear to Allah this is the truth."

"Oh, fuck," Ryan said, noting Rachel's hardened expression. Her face turned to stone. "Sky? Are we done?"

"We are far from done." Rachel clenched her jaw so tight she could barely get out the words.

Rachel stared at Saad for a minute as thoughts and feelings and memories—horrific memories—flooded her mind. She heard Ryan's voice as he tried to get her attention, and she refocused on the task at hand—killing Saad Ayad. She considered calling Christopher and letting him come and put the bullet in the back of Saad's head himself, knowing Christopher wanted revenge for the car bomb that had almost killed him. But he couldn't find out she and Ryan spent their free time interrogating terrorists on behalf of the CIA. That was a secret no one could learn. She held out her hand, palm facing up, and waited for Ryan to detach his pistol from the holster before handing it to her. She aimed at the center of Saad's forehead and pulled the trigger.

She did it for Christopher, but also for Ryan. Killing a defenseless civilian, which Saad technically was, was a war crime. She would never let anyone but herself take on that burden, trained interrogator or not. Ryan checked Saad's pulse, nodding to confirm he was dead.

Part II:
VALOR

Chapter 19:
DECEMBER 2018

RACHEL ARRIVED IN SAN Diego on the evening of Monday, December 24th after spending a few days in San Francisco with Christopher and their friend Luke from Team Onyx. She was wearing her usual jeans and white tank top, paired with the combat boots she always kept her tactical knife discreetly tucked away in. Her hair was in a high ponytail, which she pushed out of the way as she threw her beige duffel bag over her left shoulder, ever grateful for Stephanie in the logistics department for getting Indigo on chartered flights and not routing them through bases on their way home. How Stephanie managed it, especially with the assault rifles still in their bags, Rachel didn't dare ask. The team had once shown up to deal with an eminent threat and had found themselves undersupplied, so they had implemented loopholes to the protocol so that Indigo would never be without their rifles.

Rachel's father, Admiral Thomas Ryker, was waiting for her at the train station when she arrived, his silver hair cropped short, perfectly in keeping with Navy uniform standards. "Hey baby girl!" he said, happily pulling her into a tight hug. He eyed her bag. "You know you're allowed to use normal luggage when you're on leave?"

"Hi Daddy," Rachel responded. His blue eyes lined up with hers perfectly as she ignored his comment about her bag. She couldn't tell him she'd just gotten back from deployment and had elected to go on a road trip through California instead of going home to pack properly to see her family. Instead, she slid her aviator sunglasses down from where they were perched on top of her head and flashed him a sweet smile.

"Ready to go? It's about a thirteen mile drive to the house in La Jolla, so not too far, but there will be traffic," Tom said.

"I'm good," Rachel answered. She smiled at how he specified how many miles the trip would be, making her think of Christopher. It always drove her crazy when he talked in terms of miles since she knew speed and traffic were more pertinent factors that the specific distance.

"What were you doing in San Francisco?" Tom asked once they were in the car.

"Visiting a friend," Rachel answered coolly.

"I see . . ." her father replied. This was going to be a long few days indeed. "Well, your brother's already at the house. He's on leave until January 15th. You're more than welcome to stay that long too, if you'd like."

"I have plans for New Year's," Rachel said before he could continue.

"Plans where?" Tom prompted.

"At home," Rachel replied hesitantly.

"And where exactly is home these days, Rachel?"

"Florida."

"Florida's a big state."

"Tampa, Florida," Rachel clarified. It was close enough to the truth and only a forty-minute drive from her apartment in Clearwater Beach. There was no reason for her father to have too much specific information about her.

"So, you're at the Naval Operational Support center then?" Tom asked.

"Yeah," Rachel lied.

Tom nodded, and they kept driving in silence for a few minutes. "Still in logistics?" he asked.

"Yup. You know me, Daddy. I just love figuring out how to get supplies to people." Rachel tried to sound genuine, but it came off more sarcastic than she intended.

He gave her a side eye, clearly skeptical. "You know Jamie is stationed at the air base in Key West."

"Uh-huh," Rachel said, looking out the window. She had no idea where her brother was stationed, nor did she care. As far as she was concerned, her brother was a lazy idiot who wasn't living up to his potential. She had more important things to keep track of than what Jamie was doing.

"Rachel," her father prompted. "At some point, I'd appreciate a response consisting of more than five words."

Rachel groaned and inched down in her seat, staring out the window.

Once they arrived at the house, Tom parked the car in the garage and they headed inside.

"Rachel! Sweetheart!" her mother cried enthusiastically.

"Hey, Mamma," Rachel replied, giving her mother a cold, very brief hug.

Anna-Beth Ryker was a tall blonde like her daughter and southern to the core. Her face was rounder than Rachel's but with the same high cheekbones, green eyes, and straight nose. Anna-Beth believed wholeheartedly in Southern hospitality, good manners, and God. Her hair was curled and teased and she was dressed elegantly in a blue dress and low heels.

"Why don't y'all live on base?" Rachel asked as she glanced around the entryway.

Anna-Beth cringed.

"That's why." Tom chuckled, noting his wife's facial expression. "You know your mother hates being on base."

"There wasn't any base housing that was suitable when we moved here," Anna-Beth offered.

Rachel could imagine just fine what her mother considered *suitable*. Having spent most of her life on military bases, Rachel knew no base would have a house half as nice as the one they were currently standing in.

Anna-Beth gave Rachel a quick once over then said, "Come with me sweetheart, I've got a room all ready for you."

Rachel blinked twice, not buying the warm, caring tone for a second. She followed Anna-Beth through the house, which was much too large for a family of four, let alone the two people actually living there, and took the stairs up to the second floor.

"Here we are! Figured you'd want an ocean view," Anna-Beth said happily. "Jamie's just down the hall."

As if on cue, Lieutenant Commander Jameson Ryker walked into the room. He leaned up against the doorjamb and crossed his arms over his chest, his long, lean muscles flexing underneath his perfectly tanned skin.

"Your hair looks just like dad's." Rachel grimaced at the similarity between her brother and her father.

"Umm, yeah, so when you join the Navy, they sort of give you this book with a bunch of rules for how you can dress and have your hair," Jamie teased, running a hand over his cropped blond hair that was a hint darker than Rachel's.

Rachel wrinkled her nose. Most of the SEALs ignored the uniform guides as often as possible, which for her team, was more often than not since they typically needed to blend in wherever they went. "Yeah, I threw that out."

Rachel sat at the dining room table between her father and Jamie and across from her mother. She was excited that her mother had made a pot roast with potatoes and carrots and decided it was in everyone's best interest if she focused her attention on her plate.

"Rachel, how long are you staying?" Anna-Beth asked.

"I dunno. Why?" Rachel hadn't really given the trip much thought.

"I need to know so I can plan and get things set up."

"What things?" Every muscle in Rachel's body tensed.

"I have several people for you to meet," Anna-Beth told her.

"What people?" Rachel stared, horrified, at her mother, already knowing what was coming.

"Clearly you and Jamie can't figure out how to meet anyone on your own. I understand Jamie. He's deployed so much. But you, Rachel, clearly need help with this." Anna-Beth pointed at Rachel with her fork as she spoke in between bites. "I have several girls for Jamie to meet too."

"Fine with me, Mom!" Jamie exclaimed excitedly.

"God, it's like some weird upper-class version of prostitution." Rachel sighed.

"How is it prostitution?" Tom asked. "Your mother is simply introducing you to some people. I'm sure you can manage to be polite and pleasant for one meal, Rachel."

"Yeah, it's what's expected after the meal that's the issue," Rachel muttered. She had too much experience with this forced practice. Drinks or dinner with someone her mother deemed a worthy potential husband, always someone tedious and entitled. Someone with no sense of reality, no understanding that money didn't make them as important as they believed. It was always followed by the expectation that she'd do whatever the guy wanted and keep her mouth shut about it.

"Well, church starts at nine tomorrow," Anna-Beth announced.

"Yeah, okay. I'm fine here by myself," Rachel said as she picked at her food, her appetite quickly disappearing.

Anna-Beth looked at Rachel, confused. "What do you mean 'here by yourself?'" she asked, dismayed. "Everyone is going to church."

"I will not now, nor ever, be going to church or participating in any sort of organization that promotes the subjugation of women." *Unless it's absolutely necessary to collect intel for a mission.* She could tell from the look on her mother's face that she would have to explain. "1 Timothy 2:11-15 states 'A woman should learn in quietness and full submission. I do not permit a woman to teach or to assume authority over a man; she must be quiet. For Adam was formed first, then Eve. And Adam was not the one deceived; it was the woman who was deceived and became a sinner. But women will be saved through childbearing—if they continue in faith, love and holiness with propriety.'"

"What's your problem with that excerpt?" Anna-Beth asked.

"You *don't* have a problem with it?" Rachel was shocked. "Basically, it's saying you're never allowed to disagree with Dad."

"I rarely disagree with your father."

"Why is that?" Rachel asked calmly before taking a bite of her food. If it weren't for the considerable amount of family money her mother had inherited, she'd really have no agency and nothing to do, at least as far as Rachel could tell.

"Because we are very compatible. If you choose the correct spouse, someone who has the same values as you and respects you and you respect them, then you won't need to argue. I realize that's difficult for you to understand, seeing as no one will put up with your nonsense for longer than, what, a day?" Anna-Beth stated, haughtily.

Rachel chose to ignore the last part of her mother's statement and attempted to preserve peace with her father for the moment. She had always suspected that he didn't disagree with her mother because of her mother's sizable trust fund. "But you'll still have to submit, according to Timothy. How do you interpret the word *submit*?"

"Well, you shouldn't undermine your partner in public." Anna-Beth explained.

"What about at home?"

"I don't think it's appropriate to argue in front of one's children either."

"Just argue *with* your children?"

"Rachel, every argument we have ever had was because of you and your outrageous, and oftentimes dangerous, behavior," Anna-Beth stated sternly.

"What about the part where it says 'women will be saved through childbearing?'" Rachel asked.

"Women should have children. It's what differentiates them from men. It's necessary to the continuation of humanity."

"So, if a woman can't have a child, she won't be saved?"

"I never said that."

"No, 1 Timothy 2:11–15 says that."

"I'm not sure that's what it means," Anna-Beth insisted.

"It's word for word what it says, Mamma. How else should I interpret that?"

Anna-Beth's eyebrows knitted together with concern. "You aren't getting any younger, Rachel. You really do need to settle down and find a good husband. I have several recommendations, and as soon as you tell me how long you're staying for . . ."

"I do not want your recommendations. Based on past experiences with your recommendations, I'm thinking it's in my best interest to say no."

"What?" Anna-Beth asked.

"Well, let's see. There was the guy who told me he was gonna put in the prenup that he was allowed to have sex with other women, but that he'd buy me jewelry every time there was a new woman. That was somewhat fucked up. Then there was the guy with the foot fetish. That was interesting, I guess. But my favorite might've been the guy who said he was going to put a lock on my closet, and he was going to choose my outfits for me every day and install cameras so he could watch me wandering around the house all day . . . I don't remember if that was the same guy who had a whole plastic surgery plan as I aged. That might have been a different guy. But sure, Mamma, they were all lovely people who went to church and had trust funds." Rachel smiled brightly at her mother, hoping she'd made her point. She had the good sense not to add *and wanted to control every second of my life.*

"Rachel, how many times do I have to tell you not to make up lies about people?" Anna-Beth scolded her.

"I promise, my imagination is nowhere near screwed up enough to come up with any of that on my own. I also promise that's not the worst things," Rachel insisted. "Besides, Jamie knows the foot guy." She jabbed her thumb in Jamie's direction just as a quiet chuckle escaped his lips, confirming he knew exactly who she was talking about.

"In any case, you're thirty-four. You need to take this seriously and find a husband and have children," Anna-Beth continued.

"What the hell would I do with a child? I work all the time." Rachel looked horrified. "Besides, I do not want a child." She was sure to emphasize every word.

Anna-Beth sighed. "Maybe it's for the best. You'd probably just get drunk and give it a gun to play with or something."

"Anna-Beth, don't be ridiculous. Rachel knows all about gun safety," Tom chimed in as though it were at all helpful.

"Tom, she learned this risk taking and destructive behavior from you! I'm sure she'd copy your parenting style too."

"How could I have learned much of anything from him? He was never home," Rachel pointed out.

"What behavior?" Tom ignored Rachel's comment and scowled at Anna-Beth.

"Teaching a child to box when they are three years old?" Anna-Beth gave Tom a harsh look of disapproval. "Teaching a girl to box at all, regardless of her age—"

"That's just a life skill," Rachel interrupted as she shoveled a fork full of food into her mouth. Even if she was fairly certain that was how she learned to cope with her emotions using physical pain. She'd surely learned the drinking from her father too.

Rachel looked at Anna-Beth with contempt. "There are numerous Bible verses telling women to stay silent, defer to men, and remain in submission without question. It implies that women are property and that their only value is their ability to produce offspring. It's absurd and highly offensive!" She couldn't help but think of Pari and hope that she and her daughters had made it somewhere safely. That led to thoughts of Veeda, still single and doing her best to enjoy the little bit of freedom she still had. It was distracting her and causing her to losing her composure, which would only cause her to lose the argument. After a deep breath, she pushed her friends in Afghanistan out of her mind and tried again. "I do not need to be judged for choosing not to have children. And I'm not going to church to listen to some man who has never met me ramble on about my supposed sins and all the things I'm doing wrong, none of which I consider to be wrong. When the Christian church starts judging men the way they do women, then I'll reconsider my position."

The stern look of disapproval on Anna-Beth's face was proof she wasn't making her point. She sighed and tried again. "I've read the entire Bible, and the Torah, and the Quran—in Arabic, might I add." Rachel spoke calmly now. "I've been to the Library of Alexandria, traveled all over the world to look at original versions of some of these holy books. The original intent of most of what any of the prophets taught was egalitarianism, peace, and love, but the scriptures have been corrupted, manipulated, and reinterpreted by men in the pursuit of power, control, and dominance."

Anna-Beth gestured towards Rachel and looked at Tom. "Can you make her stop, please?"

"Rachel, I think you're done," Tom said.

Rachel shook her head. She was far from done. "Show me the Bible verse telling men to keep their dicks in their pants and treat women with respect. Show me! I'm pretty sure there's a few about taking care of your wife and treating her with respect, whatever they mean by that. But until they put a ring on it, apparently they get to treat women and girls however they want."

"Tom?" Anna-Beth said sternly, not taking her eyes off of Rachel for a second.

"What do you want me to do, Anna-Beth? She's an adult, she has an opinion and fairly sound arguments, I'd say," Tom said.

Rachel sighed. At least it was an attempt at defending her, but she may as well be in Afghanistan. The similarities were getting to difficult to ignore.

"She's getting hysterical," Anna-Beth argued.

"Seriously?" Rachel couldn't believe her ears. "Mom, that is an incredibly offensive word."

"Okay, so now you're going to give us a linguistics lecture as well?" Anna-Beth raised an eyebrow.

"Happily." Rachel challenged. She could lecture her mother on any number of topics related to religion, linguistics, or philosophy.

"Tom, make her stop," Anna-Beth demanded.

Rachel looked back and forth between her parents, then saw Jamie looking down to hide his smirk. "You want Dad to hit me?" She scoffed. "So, nothing changes around here, just like I thought." She got up from the table and marched out of the kitchen. "Where's your fucking Bible so I can look up child abuse in there?"

Rachel found a drink cart with a bottle of whiskey and clean glasses in her father's study. She was pissed. She knew she shouldn't be, but she was. This was how her mother always acted. This was why she hadn't been home in ten years and why she rarely called anyone she was related to. She poured herself a large drink and sat down in one of the oversized armchairs. Visiting her parents was like living under the fucking Taliban. Being told who to marry, how to dress, how to act. Not being allowed out without her father, mother, or Jamie with her. Being threatened with violence if she disobeyed. The parallels between her life and the lives of her friends in Khost was becoming glaringly apparent. She was lost in thought and didn't notice that her father had come in and closed the door behind him.

Tom poured himself a drink and sat in the chair across from Rachel. "When were you in Egypt?"

"A few years ago," she said, not wanting to offer any more information. The truth was that she had gone with Christopher on their way home from one of their deployments. Not something she could talk about with her father.

"Your mother means well," Tom continued, changing the subject. Rachel winced. "She just has different ideas about things than you do."

"She's an idiot for buying into a belief system that constantly tells her that she's a bad, terrible, evil person. What the fuck has the average human done that could be so bad they should burn in hell? The entire concept is baffling."

Tom looked at his feet. "The things war teaches us," he said, taking a long sip of his whiskey. "You were only over there for two years, but I'm sure working in intelligence, you saw some heavy shit."

Rachel shrugged.

"I know war changed me, and I was a fighter pilot," Tom continued, seemingly trying to find some common ground. "You don't see as much as a pilot. It's less bloody. There's more distance between you and your kills. Plus, you get to go back to base and sleep every night. I know that couldn't have been the case for you."

"I'm fine, Dad," Rachel assured him.

"Fine isn't the same as good, baby girl."

Rachel was irritated and decided to treat her half glass of whiskey like a shot of tequila. Getting up to refill her glass, she sighed. "I appreciate you checking on me, Daddy. And yes, I saw some shit. I did some shit. I don't need Mamma's pastor telling me I'm going to hell for wearing a short skirt. If I'm going to hell, trust me, I already know why."

Tom couldn't help but laugh at Rachel's candor. She had a way of being shamelessly blunt with her words. "How many kills?" Tom asked her.

"Too many to count." Rachel answered matter-of-factly.

Tom nodded. "You can talk to me about it if you want," he offered. "There's also a support group at the vets center tomorrow, if you want to go?"

"I have people," she assured him kindly. "People who were with me, you know, and people who weren't with me, but did similar things . . ."

"Just an offer. No pressure. I'm happy to know you have people," he said sincerely before taking a sip of his drink. "Rachel," he paused until she met his gaze. "Honey, you do keep a lot of things secret. You don't have to. Not from me, anyway. I get with your mother. She's always wanted to change you, mold you into someone you aren't. Make you into what she thinks would be a better version of herself. But with me? I don't know when it started to be like this. I used to come home and you'd come running to me and tell me everything. Every single little thing you did, right down to how many cookies you snuck when your mamma wasn't looking."

Rachel's laughter was nearly silent and escaped her lips in a small puff of air. "I don't mean to be hurtful and keep you out. It just has to be this way. For now at least." She glanced over at her father. "Do you need to hit me to appease Mom? I don't care if you do."

"No, Rachel. Ignore her and please do not look up child abuse in the Bible. I really don't want to listen to that argument."

"Spare the rod, spoil the child." Rachel smirked. Tom winced in response.

Chapter 20:
December 2018

EVERYONE WAS UP BY 0600 on Christmas day, so they decided to have a quick breakfast and open presents since church wasn't until 0900. Rachel froze in the hallway as she made her way toward the living room. "Shit." she muttered to herself.

"What?" Jamie asked.

"I didn't get anything for Dad."

"Did you get something for Mom?" Jamie asked, a concerned look on his face.

"Yeah." Rachel moved her head up and down slowly.

"Good, cause I didn't." Jamie looked guilty for what Rachel figured may be the first time in his life. "Let's just say both presents are from both of us."

Her gut wrenched, hating the idea immediately. She knew better than to trust Jamie, but she didn't have another option. "I didn't get anything for you either," Rachel admitted.

Jamie smirked at that. "I didn't believe you were coming, so same."

"Fucking hell," she muttered as she followed Jamie into the living room, already knowing something bad was about to happen.

Rachel sat on the floor near the Christmas tree, picking up pine needles off the floor. She knew it was a useless endeavor, but she needed something to do while her mother handed out presents to everyone. Once all the presents had been distributed, they took turns opening them one at a time. Just like they'd done when she was a kid. Her father gave her mother a pearl necklace, as though she didn't already have several, but Anna-Beth insisted this one was somehow different. She gave Tom a new watch. More materialistic consumerism buying people items they already had. Rachel eyed the necklace and the watch. She knew they were both obscenely expensive and that she could have come up with a hundred better ways to spend that money. Jamie also received a new watch from Anna-Beth.

It was Rachel's turn next. She unwrapped her gift and opened the small box. It was a gold cross, accented with diamonds and strung along a thin gold chain. "Thanks," she said, doing her best to be polite. She guessed the price could probably feed a family of four for a month.

Anna-Beth picked up the box containing the scarf Rachel had bought for her in the Khost market. "Who is this from? There's no card," she asked.

"It's from me and Rachel," Jamie said quickly before Rachel had the chance to even open her mouth.

Anna-Beth untied the red ribbon from around the box. She removed the lid and set it aside, then slowly pulled the scarf out of the box. "Jameson, I love it! And it was nice of you to include Rachel."

"I bought it," Rachel said. "It's from Khost, Afghanistan."

"This was so thoughtful, Jamie," Anna-Beth reiterated, ignoring Rachel completely.

"You're welcome, Mom!" Jamie was beaming with pride.

"Right," Rachel muttered under her breath. She looked at the floor, choosing to believe her mother was being careless with her words and that the slight hadn't been intentional. She silently cursed herself for ever agreeing to Jamie's plan, if she even actually had.

Jamie opened his gift from Tom. It was a very expensive bottle of whiskey. Rachel went next and found a matching bottle. "You know us well, Dad," she joked.

"Appreciate it and don't drink it all at once," Tom told them. He opened his gift next and found a whiskey tasting set of twenty-four whiskeys from around the world.

"That's what you got him?" Rachel gave Jamie a sideways glance, not at all impressed.

"Alright, let's get ready for church then. We need to leave in an hour," Anna-Beth announced. "I'll have to change what I was planning to wear so I can wear this beautiful scarf! Jamie, how did you get a scarf from Afghanistan? Weren't you on a ship in the Persian Gulf?"

Rachel winced at that. The last time she'd been on a ship in the Persian Gulf had not been a good day. It had been a terrible day in fact. The day that cemented her hatred of ships and aircraft carriers. It was a day she never wanted to have to think about.

"You know, Mom, I just make things happen," Jamie lied with a bright smile on his face.

"I got it through someone I work with," Rachel countered.

"Oh," Anna-Beth said. "Well, Rachel, it was nice of you to help your brother with that."

Rachel plastered on a fake smile. "Yeah, no problem. I'm glad you like it." There was no use in correcting her. Anna-Beth would never believe her anyway. "Where do you keep your cleaning supplies?"

"Why?" Anna-Beth asked.

"Because I need something to do while you're at church, and your house is filthy." The house was immaculate, actually, but it was the quickest way to insult her mother and get under her skin.

Anna-Beth glared at her, clearly offended. Rachel got up and walked over to a picture that was hanging in a large gold frame on the wall. She ran her finger over the top of it, collecting trace amounts of dust, then shoved her finger in her mother's face. "Don't even get me started on the hard water buildup on the showers and faucets."

"There is no hard water buildup anywhere in this house," Anna-Beth said through gritted teeth.

"Maybe you need glasses." Rachel shrugged. "I'll fix it for you, Mamma." She flashed a bright smile.

Jamie broke into a quiet chuckle. "Rachel, you know it's a house, not a ship, right?" He pulled her hand toward his face, inspecting her finger. "Seriously, I need a microscope to see this dust you're claiming is there."

"The cleaner comes once per week. I let her take off for Christmas," Anna-Beth stated defensively.

"Right, so . . . where are your cleaning supplies?" Rachel cocked her head to the side, deciding to take the win.

"Cleaning supplies are in the hall closet." Anna-Beth said begrudgingly.

Rachel got to work deep cleaning her mother's kitchen. She scrubbed the counters and cleaned the microwave and oven, pulling out all the appliances so she could clean behind them as well. She needed to do something to take the edge off her emotions.

"Something is seriously wrong with you," Jamie said as he walked by and saw what she was doing.

"A lot of things are wrong with *you*," Rachel retorted.

"What'd I do?"

"You're a fucking liar, Jamie. You always have been. Have you ever even been to Afghanistan?"

"No. Not technically. It's sort of landlocked, and I'm stationed on an aircraft carrier."

"So, how could you have gotten a scarf from there?"

Jamie shrugged.

"Is it really so hard to say 'I'm glad you like the scarf, Mom. Rachel got it for you.'"

"We decided it would be from both of us," Jamie reminded her.

"Yeah, you're right, it's my fault for expecting you to not be a total asshole. I cannot believe you actually took credit for the idea to get it *and* the actual procurement."

Jamie shrugged again. "Why does it matter?"

"*Why?*" Rachel yelled. "Are you fucking kidding me? I swear, you are the dumbest, most selfish person I have ever met! I should have known better than to trust you or think that you'd matured at all."

"I'm not dumb or selfish. You're just overly sensitive about everything," Jamie said.

"Seriously?" Rachel threw the sponge she'd been using into the sink and turned, staring at him with disbelief. "I got that for Mamma. I went out of my way to do something nice for her in an effort to make peace and make her hate me just a tiny bit less. I won't even say I was hoping to get my mother to actually like me, just hate me slightly less. That's all. And you took that opportunity away by taking credit for getting her the scarf. Do you really not understand that?"

"It's not that big of a deal, Rachel." Jamie rolled his eyes.

"Fine. It's not a big deal," Rachel said coolly as she picked up the bucket of cleaning supplies and headed for the downstairs bathroom. She slammed the door behind her.

She sprayed the shower down with a bleach-based cleanser, scrubbed the walls, rinsed them off, then slid down the wall so she was sitting on the floor. The scent of bleach was overpowering, and she was sure better ventilation would have been a good idea. She was also sure she'd been exposed to worse things though. She was mad. There was no reason to be mad. Everyone was behaving exactly how they always did: Jamie was doing whatever he wanted and lying his way out of trouble or conflict; Anna-Beth was believing every word he said and blaming everything on Rachel; and Tom was doing his best to stay out of it. Things had always been like this, ever since she could remember. She bit her bottom lip hard enough to draw blood, trying to force her emotions to stay in check.

The trauma and chaos of war were easy enough to lock away in her mind, but the trauma of her childhood was another monster entirely. One not easily manipulated or controlled, and therefore best avoided. She knew once this monster was awake, it would be a while before it went back into hibernation. Her vision was blurry from her tears and her head was pounding as blood pumped through her body, causing her heart to race.

Only a couple more months until we deploy again.

War was the best way to drown out these memories. The adrenaline and stress of combat, of any mission, made her hyperfocus on the present moment, causing her mind and body to forget that the past existed. That it had ever happened at all. She would happily fill her mind with the horrors of war if it would replace the memories of her childhood. Then the Persian Gulf flashed through her mind, and she squished her eyes closed as tightly as she could manage.

Deploying in February. Finding Samir Al-Abadi. Finally finding Samir.

The thought came as a comfort, a welcome distraction, and her mind shifted from her family of birth, to her chosen family—her team—and their next mission. Finding Samir, wherever he was.

Chapter 21:
DECEMBER 2018

ANNA-BETH ARRIVED HOME FROM church in a flurry of excited energy. She was on Rachel in a heartbeat. "Upstairs. Get changed," she ordered.

"What? Why?" Rachel looked up from where she was polishing a silver candlestick. She saw her father's cautionary gaze and Jamie's smirk and knew she wasn't going to like whatever was coming.

"Archer Davenport and his mother will be here in an hour. Seriously, have you not looked at your phone?" Anna-Beth scolded.

"No, I was cleaning your house." Rachel furrowed her brow.

"Well, Cinderella, time to get ready for the ball!" Jamie snickered.

"Fuck you. What is happening?" Rachel pointed at Jamie.

"Don't worry, I'm going on a date with Penelope St. James, so I won't be here." Jamie grinned.

Rachel grimaced. Of course Jamie was going to take advantage of whatever disgusting social connections their mother had. "Can you even get a girl without Mamma's help?"

"Rachel, we don't have time for your petulance. Get upstairs and I will find you something to wear," Anna-Beth said.

"All I have are jeans and t-shirts, Mamma. Or Navy uniforms. Always have those," Rachel warned her.

Anna-Beth grimaced. "We'll have to make do with something out of my closet then."

"Dad, you promised!" Rachel pleaded desperately.

"It's out of my hands," Tom told her. "If I were you, I'd go help her pick out what you're wearing before she gets too set on anything."

An hour later, Rachel was sitting on the sofa in her parent's living room, clothed in a red long-sleeve dress that was tailored just above her knees. The Queen Anne neckline exposed more cleavage on Rachel than Anna-Beth would have preferred, but she eventually conceded it may be for the best. Anna-Beth had pulled Rachel's hair taunt in an elegant updo, not having had time to wash, dry, and curl it properly.

Rachel tried to ensure her sighs weren't audible as Archer Davenport rambled on about whatever business venture he was working on. Rachel didn't care. He was a mildly attractive man in his early forties, with blonde hair and blue eyes. There was nothing remarkable or interesting about him. The fact that he had to bring his mother along on chaperoned dates didn't make her feel any better about him. She covered her mouth to stifle a yawn.

Tom's eyes bore into her from across the room.

"My company just got a contract with the DOD to develop . . ." Archer said. It caught Rachel's interest momentarily, until she realized she probably wouldn't have anything nice to say to anyone who worked for a defense contractor. She did her best to tune him out, until her mother's voice, silky and sweet, interrupted her thoughts.

"Isn't that interesting, Rachel? Perhaps you'll be ordering some of these things to distribute to the Navy soon. Rachel works in Navy logistics, you know." Anna-Beth sounded proud.

Rachel knew her mother's pride was fake. Rachel raised an eyebrow. She'd barely been listening, but she'd heard something about safety equipment. "I would absolutely love it if our sailors and soldiers could get better protective equipment. The ballistic armor and helmets we have now aren't doing their jobs. The vests are too heavy, and the helmets are practically worthless."

"Right, well, we have these helmets we're developing with built-in communications capabilities . . ." Archer rambled on.

Rachel dropped her face into her hand and pinched the bridge of her nose. "No one cares if the comms equipment is built-in. No one has any problem shoving an earpiece into their ear. What we need are helmets that are lightweight and actually protect against both concussions and AK-47s. Do your helmets do either of those things, or are they more like fancy hats with some tech thing in them?"

"Umm." Archer looked at her confused, then looked at Tom.

"Don't look at him!" Rachel laughed, gesturing to her father. "He hasn't worn a helmet in decades. Probably hasn't even seen one in a while. I, on the other hand, deal with these things every day, and I've been reporting for years that our men are slipping and falling and getting concussions. Bullets are hitting them right in the fucking forehead because the helmets don't go low enough. They need to cover enough that even when some cocky jackass shoves the helmet back on their head trying to look cool, it still covers their full forehead without limiting visibility or affecting the attachment of NVGs or other equipment. Do you know why that's important?"

Archer just stared at her for a second.

"If the helmets don't cover enough." Rachel folded her fingers, mimicking a gun, and pointed to her temple then to the center of her forehead, just above the bridge of her nose. "A very good friend of mine died because of poorly designed helmets. Concussions are a regular occurrence. Just from joking around and falling, or from vehicle crashes, or explosions. You know the U.S. ships a bunch of arrogant eighteen and nineteen-year-old boys off to war, right? Do you think they're using their protective gear correctly, or are they messing around trying to look cool? Then we've got covert, top tier squads, SEALs, Delta, helmets make them conspicuous and get in the way of doing their jobs. They actually do need fancy hats, but skip the tech, make them out of Kevlar or something useful. Kevlar baseball hats," Rachel mused, considering what materials were available that might be at all functional. She, of course, was one of the arrogant jackasses who typically skipped putting on her helmet, not wanting it to affect her speed, agility, or visibility.

"Wow," Archer stared at her, dumbfounded, with his lips parted and eyes wide. "You don't want to leave the Navy and come work for my company, do you?"

"No. Not a chance in hell." Rachel shook her head vigorously.

"Why not?" Archer furrowed his brow.

"Because I find the notion of defense contractors to be abhorrent," Rachel stated. "You overcharge the military for products that are poorly designed and don't live up to the promises made. We've got stealth planes that aren't stealth, helmets that can't pass ballistics tests, lightweight vests that fall apart and are poor quality, ceramic plate inserts for the vests which, yes, do stop bullets, but that's assuming you don't drop the ceramic plate or it doesn't get damaged in transport. Those things break all the time and no one wants to haul extra ceramic plates around with them just in case some of them break. Defense contractors are greedy, grabbing money that could be better allocated to the VA and veterans benefits to treat the injuries sustained from shoddy equipment."

"She's not wrong," Tom said, sipping his iced tea.

"You are absolutely fascinating," Archer gushed. "I'd love to take you out to dinner."

"I don't live here," Rachel stated.

"Tonight?" Archer tried.

"No, tonight's no good for me." Rachel was trying to come up with a way to get out of this date without pissing off her mother too much.

"Drinks instead of dinner?" Archer tried.

"No, thank you." Rachel stood up and left the room, but Archer was hot on her tail. He cornered her in the kitchen as she reached for a glass to get some water.

"Rachel, one drink, one car ride. Come one." His hand was on her waist in an instant.

Rachel stopped in her tracks, cursing herself for not strapping her knife on for dinner. "Anyone ever tell you it's a bad idea to touch a combat veteran without their permission?" Rachel warned, her voice cold as ice. Archer slid his hand down, grazing her hip until his hand was on her thigh, pressing her hips into him. "If you don't take your hand off me in the next two seconds, I will break your nose."

"You're gonna break my nose?" Archer scoffed.

"Would you prefer a knee to the balls?" Rachel asked seriously as she turned to face him. He wasn't getting the point. "Seriously, what's your play here? You're gonna sexually assault me in my parent's kitchen?" Rachel raised an eyebrow, daring him to make another move.

"You're smart and beautiful, Rachel. What can I say?" Archer tried to excuse his behavior.

"Last warning."

"I heard you might be uncooperative." With one hand, Archer pressed her hips into him even harder, just as his other hand went for the back of her neck. Rachel was just about to raise her knee when he suddenly let go of her, taking a step to the side as Anna-Beth and his mother walked into the kitchen.

"So, you two are going out for drinks?" Anna-Beth asked.

"Nope," Rachel stated firmly.

"Why not?" Anna-Beth asked.

"I have my period," Rachel lied, hoping that might cause Archer to lose interest.

"That should in no way affect your ability to go out with Archer for a drink, or dinner," Anna-Beth told her.

"Well, I'm still gonna have to say no." Rachel fled the kitchen as quickly as she could, searching for her father.

She rounded the corner to Tom's study when she heard her father's voice, talking to someone. "Christmas has been good. My daughter is here visiting."

"Nice to have the whole family there for once," a man replied. Rachel paused, recognizing the voice, though she couldn't place it. "What's the situation with this project you're working on though? Have they determined how bad the fallout will be?"

"Well, the server was hacked apparently," Tom said.

"How does that happen?"

"You're asking me?" Tom tugged on his ear. "Trust me, they've explained it about a thousand times and I'm none the wiser, Richard."

Richard? Was her father on a call with Admiral Richard Leftwich? She pressed her back against the wall and kept listening.

"Anyway," Tom continued. "The server was hacked, but from what I understand, the whole thing is useless without the hard drive or USB encrypted password, something or another."

"They need a second USB to activate it?" Leftwich checked.

"Seems that way."

Second USB? Neither of them had mentioned a first USB, just a server being hacked. She wasn't that bad a tech to miss that detail. She'd missed the beginning of the conversation though and assumed that's why it didn't make sense.

She wanted to keep listening, but she heard footsteps in the hallway coming toward her. A man's footsteps. She knew Archer and her father were the only men in the house, and since her father was in the study, it could only be one person. She nudged the door open to her father's study and slid through, closing the it quietly behind her.

"Give me a minute, Richard. My daughter just walked in," Tom said.

Rachel jerked her chin, gesturing toward the laptop. "Is that on mute?"

Tom's head dipped in confirmation. "What is it?"

"Do not make me go out with him, Dad. Do not let Mamma make me go."

"Who, Archer? Why the hell not? He seemed nice enough and more than happy to listen to you ramble on about protective gear."

"Yeah, well, he just felt me up in the kitchen and made some insinuations."

"What sort of insinuations?"

"You want me to knock that asshole out and piss off Mamma by defending myself from unwanted advances, or do you want to tell Mamma I'm not going anywhere with him now or ever?" She got right to the point.

Tom held up a hand, indicating she should stop. "Do not knock him out. That would make things worse," he told her. "What did you tell your mother?"

"Menstrual cramps."

"Fine. Go upstairs," Tom conceded.

"What's that?" Rachel asked, eyeing a shiny purple USB stick on Tom's desk. She leaned over, close enough that she could read the jumble of letters and numbers written on the back: *RMR092184*. Her initials and her date of birth.

Tom glanced down to see what she was looking at, then answered nonchalantly, "Photos of you. Weren't you going to hide from your mother?"

"Yes. Thank you." Rachel fled the room and sprinted upstairs.

Chapter 22:
DECEMBER 2018

RACHEL SPENT THE NIGHT of December 25th tossing and turning. She couldn't stop thinking about the day. All the memories that had come flooding back, and Archer. He'd just gotten more turned on the more she'd said no. She wanted to kill him, certain he'd assaulted plenty of girls in the past and that he'd go on to assault plenty of girls in the future. She knew she could get away with it if she planned carefully enough.

Her father having a meeting with Admiral Leftwich was strange too. She didn't know what her father was working on these days, but she was quite sure it wouldn't involve the SEAL Middle East Special Projects squadron. Maybe they weren't working on anything. Maybe they were just friends? She knew her father was friends with Admiral Eastwood, or they had been when she was a kid, so it was perfectly plausible that it was a social call. Her thoughts were interrupted by a noise coming from downstairs. The creek of a door, then footsteps . . . boots. It wasn't her father or Jamie. She'd been listening to them walk around her whole life. She pulled out her phone and texted her father a few doors down the hall, knowing he was a light sleeper.

Rachel to Dad: *Heard a noise. Stay with Mamma. I'll check it out and get Jamie if I need backup.*

Tom responded with a thumbs up.

Rachel carefully and quietly made her way out into the hallway and down the stairs. She stopped when she reached the bottom, listening intently. She distinctly heard the footsteps of two people. One in the living room, and one in the kitchen. Carefully peeking around the corner of the wall, she saw a man in full tactical gear with his back to her. Rachel laughed to herself silently. This is what she trained for, after all. This was her area of expertise and one of the things she loved doing most.

She quietly snuck up behind the man in the living room, careful to stay undetected. She reached her arm around his neck, squeezing tightly in just the right place, at just the right angle, until he lost consciousness. She carefully and efficiently laid him down on the floor, mindful that any noise would alert the other intruder to her position. Then she moved toward the kitchen. The open floor plan of the house made it difficult to remain undetected for long. The second intruder saw her, then lunged with substantial force, but she slid out of his way with ease. Turning quickly, Rachel delivered a swift elbow to his stomach, then rotated her bent arm upwards so her fist could make contact with his nose. There was a loud crack as blood began to stream down his face.

The man grabbed her from behind and she used the full force of her body to bend forward, throwing him over her shoulder and onto the floor. He grabbed her ankle, knocking her off balance. Rachel fell beside him with a thud. The man got on top of her, punching and hitting her twice in the abdomen before she flipped him over, using a move she'd long since perfected. She was on top of him now. They struggled for several minutes before he pushed her off of him and got up. She rolled away and stood up too, ready to go again as adrenaline coursed through her veins, masking the pain she should be feeling.

As the man advanced toward her, Rachel bent over backwards. She'd always known cheerleading would come in handy. She placed her hands on the floor in a backbend and swiftly kicked her legs up one at a time, hitting the intruder under the chin twice before knocking him backwards. Now she moved in on the offensive with a quick jab and cross combo to his face, followed by a roundhouse kick to the side of the head. He recovered quickly, shoving her into a wall. As he came at her again, she lifted her knee, timing it perfectly to hit him in the stomach. He let out a quiet grunt, recovered, and grabbed her again, trying to throw her across the room. She held on tight, attempting to subdue him. The collision of their opposing forces resulted in a loud crash as they both flew through the nearby sliding glass door.

As she rolled over to ascertain where her attacker was, she saw Jamie running toward her, gripping his pistol tightly in both hands. He stood over the man, gun pointed at his head.

"What the fuck Rachel? Are you okay?" Jamie asked.

"Yeah, I'm good," she said. She sat up to pull shards of glass out of her skin, wincing slightly as she pulled out a large piece from the side of her thigh. "Watch him. There's another one in the living room. I'll get something to detain them with."

Jamie's face furrowed in confusion, probably astonished by how calm Rachel was. She was badly injured, with cuts and scrapes and several deep wounds from flying through the glass. But other than a wince and a slight limp, she wouldn't allow it to affect her. She could feel Jamie's eyes on her as she made her way through the kitchen and into the garage, where she returned with a pack of zip ties. As she made her way back through the living room, she bent down to grab the other unconscious man by his hair, then dragged him behind her. She schooled her face into cool disinterest as she set to work securing the men's hands behind their backs and binding their ankles together.

Jamie asked again, "Seriously, what the fuck? I know you can fight, but you just took out two men in tactical gear on your own. Why didn't you come get me?"

"Didn't need you," Rachel responded frankly.

"Clearly."

Once both men's arms and legs were secured, Rachel turned them so they were lying face down on the ground outside.

"Go check on Mamma and Dad, and call this in," she ordered.

Jamie ran upstairs and she turned her attention back to the intruders. This was clearly more than your average home robbery. Regular criminals breaking and entering didn't tend to have bulletproof vests or night vision goggles. Given her father's rank as Admiral and her highly classified work as a SEAL, it was unclear who the intruders' target was—her or her father—but she intended to find out.

The first intruder was still unconscious, but the second . . .

Rachel knelt on his back and yanked his head backward by his hair. "Who sent you?" she tried in English.

No response.

She tried again in Arabic. He struggled under her weight. "Tell me who the fuck sent you, and who your target is." Rachel had both hands around the man's throat, loose enough that he could still breathe and speak, but tight enough that he knew she had the upper hand. He didn't respond, so she tightened her grip, choking him just enough for it to be unpleasant. "Why are you here?" she tried again, loosening her grip.

"USB . . . code . . .," the man choked out in Arabic.

"Who sent you?"

"Al . . . Abadi."

Rachel tensed at the name. These men had come for her. Somehow, Samir knew she was after him, and somehow, he had followed her.

Chapter 23:
DECEMBER 2018

THE NAVY SENT A team of federal agents to the house within twenty minutes of Jamie's phone call, along with ambulances and paramedics. Rachel, Jamie, and their father all showed them their military credentials.

"Commander Ryker, we're going to need to take you to the hospital, ma'am," an agent told her.

"Unnecessary," Rachel countered. "I've got a medic kit in my room." Blood was running down her thigh where she'd pulled out the large shard of glass, among other places.

"It's not up for discussion, I'm afraid," the lead investigator, Special Agent Hope, informed her.

"I'll go with you," Jamie volunteered.

"Don't you need to take my statement?" Rachel asked, ignoring him.

"Yes, but first you need medical attention." Hope pointed toward the ambulance in a way that suggested she wasn't taking no for an answer.

Resigning, Rachel and Jamie climbed into the ambulance. Rachel was still picking shards of glass out of her arms and legs, even though the paramedics were there.

"Commander Ryker? We're going to need you to stop doing that until we get to the hospital and the doctors can do a full workup," one of the paramedics chastised her.

Rachel rolled her eyes and pulled out her phone. She took a photo of her legs, then her left arm, and texted them to Christopher.

> Hawk to Skylark: *WTF did you do?*
> Skylark to Hawk: *Break in at Mom and Dad's. Minor incident with a sliding glass door, but all good.*
> Hawk to Skylark: *Sounds fun! Sorry I missed it. Still at home?*
> Skylark to Hawk: *Stupid feds insisted I go to the hospital. On route now to UCSD health emergency.*
> Hawk to Skylark: *On my way!*

Rachel leaned her head back against the headrest, eager for this to all be over.

Jamie met her gaze, his eyes full of suspicion and interest. "Where'd you learn to fight like that, Rache? That guy was destroyed! And you took the first one out without leaving a mark on him."

"The Navy," she stated, annoyed with his stupid question. She was tired, and it took all of her concentration to remember which lie to tell. Lying to her family about her job, lying to Christopher about her relationship with the CIA . . . It was getting more and more complicated and exhausting. Jamie was still staring at her, waiting for her to continue explaining. "And Dad. He taught you too. Or at least he tried," she said, doing her best to insult him. She stared up at the ceiling of the ambulance, willing them to drive faster. Since she was stable, they were driving without lights or sirens, so they hit traffic. There was always traffic in San Diego, and she was happy she didn't live there.

After waiting for what seemed like an eternity, a doctor and nurse finally came into her room. She had continued picking the glass out of her skin and had made a little pile on the cart beside her bed.

"Well, I see you've gotten a head start," the doctor said, his jaw hanging open in awe.

"I've dug a bullet out of my own leg, doc. I think I can handle a little glass," Rachel answered. Seeing the doctor's confusion, she continued. "Navy combat vet. Iraq and Afghanistan."

"I see." The doctor's brow furrowed. "Well, I can get you some painkillers if you want."

"Don't need them," Rachel said, continuing to remove the glass from her arm. It hurt like hell, but she loved it. It calmed her down and reminded her she was alive. Painkillers would only make it harder to think. She had to be able to think so she didn't divulge any of her secrets to her family, and so she could help the federal agents, whom she was already sure would screw everything up.

It took a couple of hours for the doctor to finish pulling all the glass out of Rachel's skin and to run all the tests he insisted on doing before finally informing her that he wanted to keep her overnight to watch for signs of internal bleeding. After the doctor left, Rachel glared at Jamie. "Are you just going to sit there and stare at me, Lieutenant Commander?" she asked, using his military rank and her brash commanding officer voice for full effect.

Jamie's irritation was evident in his eyes. "No. I guess we're going to be here for a while. I'll go grab some coffee. You want anything?"

"Whiskey'd be nice," Rachel replied coolly.

"Yeah, I'm guessing they don't have that here," Jamie said, pulling the curtain closed as he walked away.

As Jamie walked toward the vending machine area, his mind wandered. He knew Rachel had been with an intelligence unit for about two years before deciding to get out of combat and work in logistics. Something their parents were thrilled about. He could never see Rachel working in logistics though. It was too structured and boring for her. His little sister thrived in chaos and craved adventure. It didn't make sense.

He slid some change into a vending machine to get a chocolate bar and then made his way to the coffee station. He poured himself a cup of coffee, electing not to get anything for Rachel. Whatever he got her would be wrong anyway, and he'd rather not hear about it. Content with his choice of snacks, he made his way past the nurses' station, toward Rachel's curtained off cubicle.

"I'm looking for Commander Rachel Ryker's room, please," Jamie heard a man say.

Jamie looked over just as the nurse asked the man, "Are you family?"

"She's my commanding officer, and she knows I'm coming to get her so . . ." The man trailed off.

Jamie walked up to him. "Hey, Lieutenant Commander Jameson Ryker," he said, reaching out his hand. "I'm Rachel's brother. She knows you're coming?"

"Lieutenant Commander Christopher Williams," the man said. "I'm her second." Christopher flashed his military ID before stretching out his hand to shake Jamie's.

"Good enough for me," Jamie replied. He was a little surprised anyone would volunteer to spend time with Rachel, but he'd take help managing her from anyone who offered. "She's over this way." Jamie led Christopher back to Rachel's cubicle and pulled the curtain open. "You've got a visitor," he said as he walked in with Christopher right behind him. Jamie plopped himself back down in the chair beside her bed, eager to expose his sister's lies.

Christopher stood by the foot of Rachel's bed with his arms crossed over his chest, staring at her with an amused smile. He couldn't help but laugh when he saw her. She had tiny cuts all over her body and a disgruntled expression on her face. "Causing trouble again, Commander Ryker?" he joked.

"Haha, very funny," she said sarcastically. "Can you please convince someone to let me out of here? I tried explaining it wasn't necessary, but . . ." She let her eyes dart over to Jamie.

Christopher instantly knew what she meant. She couldn't adequately explain to the doctors how minor this actually was without Jamie, and by extension her parents, finding out she was a SEAL. Christopher understood the importance of maintaining her cover since her father, the Admiral, had the power and influence to pull her from their missions if he knew. Admiral Eastwood had actually created a fake personnel record for Rachel and restricted her father's access to her real one.

"I'll see what I can do," Christopher agreed. He left her, careful to close the curtain behind him, while he went in search of her doctor.

"Hmm," Jamie pondered out loud.

"What?" Rachel asked shortly.

"Nothing. Just a lot of things that don't add up."

"Maybe you're just bad at math."

"Nope. Definitely pretty good at math. Tell me, Rachel, if he's your second in command, and the two of you work in logistics, why are both of you in such good shape? You don't need to be in that good of shape to sit at a desk. Plus, he's definitely sporting a non-regulation haircut. At least two inches too long. Major uniform violation."

"Why do you care about his hair? Besides, we're both on leave. He can do whatever he wants with his hair," Rachel deflected, trying not to smile. She loved Christopher's hair just the way it was.

"Nope. Not buying it." Jamie watched Rachel's face for clues. "If I didn't know any better, I'd guess he's a SEAL, and the two of you are dating and that he's your *friend* you were visiting in L.A. last week, or at Coronado, where I'd assume he's stationed. But I know your love and dedication to the Navy would prevent you from ever even thinking of breaking the fraternization rules, so it can't be that."

Rachel rolled her eyes, not liking where this was going.

"Don't worry, sis, I'll figure it out." Jamie winked before putting his feet up on her bed. He leaned back in the chair, arms crossed over his chest, with a suspicious smirk on his face. "I find you downstairs after you've subdued two intruders, more or less silently, might I add. The sliding glass door breaking is what woke me up. That's a bit more advanced than what Dad taught us, and the Navy doesn't teach that to just anyone. Not even intelligence officers going behind enemy lines, and certainly not logistics officers. If I didn't know any better, I'd say you're both SEALs, but I thought they don't let girls do that." Jamie paused for a moment before looking at his sister. "There's a first time for everything, I guess," he said with a glint of merriment in his voice.

Christopher came back in moments later, closely followed by Special Agent Hope.

"We can go," Christopher said matter-of-factly.

"We're moving your family to a safe house, Commander," Special Agent Hope said. "We don't know which of you was the target, so you'll have to stay there until our investigation is over."

Jamie's head jerked around, He stared at Rachel curiously.

Rachel met his gaze for a mere second before turning her attention back to Christopher. "You're coming with us?"

"Of course." Christopher nodded.

"And . . . you're staying?" As much as she wanted him to stay, being in the house with her parents and Jamie was likely to be awkward. Or he could do what he did best and mediate between her and her family.

"You know I've got your six. Besides, if someone breaks in again, you're hardly in any shape to do anything about it." Christopher winked.

Rachel burst out laughing. They both knew a few cuts and scrapes and shards of glass would barely slow her down.

Chapter 24:
DECEMBER 2018

THE SUN WAS STARTING to come up when they arrived at the safe house. Rachel's parents were already there. Her mother was pacing franticly and her father was speaking with one of the agents in the kitchen.

"Rachel, are you okay?" Anna-Beth asked fearfully upon seeing her daughter's injuries.

"I'm fine, Mamma," Rachel insisted.

Anna-Beth looked Christopher up and down, trying to deduce if he was one of the investigators.

"Lieutenant Commander Christopher Williams, ma'am. I work with Rachel. I was on leave in Los Angeles, so when she told me what happened, I figured I should make the drive down to make sure she was alright. It's a pleasure to meet you, Mrs. Ryker." Christopher stretched out his hand to shake hers.

"Well Lieutenant Commander, how kind of you! And please, call me Anna-Beth, I insist." Anna-Beth's Southern drawl was even thicker than Rachel's was when she was trying to be charming.

"Special Agent Hope, what's the current status?" Rachel asked, her voice booming with power and confidence.

"We're currently investigating some leads to figure out the reason for the home invasion. We've identified one of the men, so we're well on our way."

"What about the house?" Rachel asked.

"My team is investigating the house and collecting evidence–"

"No, this house. The one we're standing in," Rachel interrupted her. "Tell me about the status of this house. How many times have you used it as a safe house? How secure is it, really?"

Tom came into the entryway, a confused expression on his face. "What'd you do, Rachel, read the procedural manual for how to set up a safe house on the drive from the hospital?"

"Admiral Ryker, sir." Christopher stood at attention.

"At ease," Tom ordered. "Rachel, sweetheart," he continued, "I'm sure the agents know what they're doing. They do this all the time. All you need to do is settle in and relax."

Rachel forced a sweet smile onto her face to mask her irritation at her father's insistence she relax. Which of his children did he think he was talking to? Of course she wasn't going to relax. She never did. "Of course, Daddy. I'm just checking," Rachel answered sweetly, emphasizing her Southern drawl to be as thick as maple syrup.

Special Agent Hope locked eyes with Rachel. "We've got agents at each entrance of the house and have used this house several times before without incident. We also have a one-mile perimeter setup being monitored by SDPD under the pretense of DUI checkpoints."

Rachel nodded and pursed her lips as she made her way around the house, Christopher following close behind her. She insisted that Hope introduce her to the other agents and double-check that the all the doors and bulletproof glass windows were secure. Then she went outside to observe the house's surroundings. The house backed up to an open field of sand grass. They were still on the coast but farther south from La Jolla. They had been in traffic, so she wasn't sure exactly how far they had driven, but she was sure Christopher knew.

She continued her exploration of the house, opening cupboards and closets as she went, trying to get a sense of her surroundings. Christopher followed close behind her. He had been assigned a bedroom down the hall from Rachel's once it was made clear he wasn't leaving.

"Hope, how are you keeping the perimeter secured?" Rachel asked as she pointed out the window at the view of the Pacific Ocean. "Are you and your team prepared if someone were to approach from the water?"

"Not an issue," Hope assured her.

"Not an issue because you have cameras or someone on watch down there?" Rachel raised an eyebrow.

"Not an issue because no one is approaching from the water."

"I'd approach from the water," Christopher commented.

"Well, of course *you two* would," Hope whispered. "Normal people would not."

"Get a camera down there, please," Rachel requested. "And when are you going to take my statement?"

"We have time. Settle in."

"How are you going to investigate if you don't know what you're investigating?" Rachel asked her.

"Okay, what is your statement?" Hope asked, defensively crossing her arms over her chest.

Rachel raised an eyebrow at Hope's apparent lack of interest. "The two men who broke in were sent by Samir Al-Abadi."

"Fucking hell," Christopher muttered. "They told you that?"

"Yeah." Rachel looked at him and nodded then turned her attention back to Hope. "If I leave, my family would be safer. Al-Abadi wants me. I've been hunting him, and he's been hunting me for the better part of a decade."

"No one is leaving," Hope stated.

"Alright, but he's gonna keep sending people. I promise if he found me at my parent's house, he will find me here and keep sending people to kill me until he has proof I'm dead."

"Very true," Christopher agreed.

"Commander Ryker, I assure you, my team is on top of things."

"Work faster," Rachel requested. "And I'll get you backup."

"Not necessary!" Hope protested.

"It's entirely necessary," Rachel argued.

"We can't bring more people, unvetted, into the safe house," Hope explained.

"My team is vetted, I can assure you." Rachel tried not to laugh at the absurdity of Hope's statement and went to see what weapons the agents had with them.

Rachel walked through the kitchen several hours later, just after Anna-Beth had pulled something out of the oven. Anna-Beth turned around and grabbed Rachel by the arm. "Did you have a plastic surgeon stitch up these cuts, or was it an ER intern?" Anna-Beth asked, inspecting every inch of Rachel's skin carefully.

"Umm . . ." Rachel stared at her for a moment, then looked down at her arm. "I did this arm." She pointed at three stitches on her left arm. "Some sort of doctor did my leg. I didn't ask to see their credentials."

Anna-Beth's eyes were frantic. "What do you mean, you did that arm?"

"Well, the doctor was going really slow so . . ."

"So, what? You picked up a needle and helped?" Anna-Beth was horrified.

"It's nothing I haven't done before, Mamma."

Anna-Beth sucked in air, trying to steady herself. "They're doing great things with laser technology now. We'll need to look into that."

"Huh?" Rachel wrinkled her nose, having no idea what her mother was getting at.

"You think men want to marry a woman with scars all over her body?" Anna-Beth asked. "Really, Rachel, you're difficult enough as it is given your personality flaws and strong opinions on everything. Your looks were really all you had going for you, and now this? How do I explain this?" She gestured with her hand at Rachel's body, scanning her critically from head to toe.

"That I defended my family? I defended my country?" Rachel suggested. "You might be dead right now if I hadn't done what I did. Do you realize that?"

Anna-Beth pointed to a large scar on Rachel's arm, seeming to ignore everything Rachel said. "This might be the worst one. It's next to impossible to cover up.

"I got a Purple Heart and some other medal for that one," Rachel told her, shrugging her off. She did *not* want to think about the day she'd been shot three times as she and Christopher dragged their friend's lifeless body to the back of their team's truck.

"I will look into the laser treatments for you." Anna-Beth clasped her hands together in front of her chest.

"It's fine, Mamma. These ones probably won't even scar." Rachel pointed at the several small cuts on her arms. "Besides, I'm not getting married, and certainly not to anyone who can't accept me for who I am. You have to stop trying to change me and stop trying to make me some watered down version of myself!"

"How'd you get this one?" Anna-Beth asked, pointing to a burn on Rachel's right wrist.

"I'm not talking to you about war, Mamma," Rachel stated plainly as she pulled her wrist away.

"This is exactly why women should not be in combat. Can you even have children? Have you looked into that? You are running out of time and options," Anna-Beth insisted.

"Dad?" Rachel yelled as loudly as she could. She needed to be rescued, quickly, before she lost her temper.

Tom, Jamie, and Christopher were in the kitchen seconds later. "What? Why are you screaming?" Tom asked, clearly annoyed that Rachel had interrupted whatever he'd been doing.

"Can you please explain to Mom that I don't need some sort of weird laser procedure to remove my scars?"

"What?" Tom asked again, this time confused.

"She's telling me I need to have all my scars removed so that men will like me and want to marry me because . . . I don't know why."

"Who the hell are you trying to marry?" Christopher chuckled.

"No one!" Rachel was exasperated.

"I promise, Rachel has no problems getting men to like her," Christopher said as seriously as he could manage.

"She seems to have a problem with keeping their interest, though," Anna-Beth told him.

Christopher glanced at Rachel, trying to get a sense of how he should answer, if he should answer. She looked defeated.

"Is dinner ready?" Tom interjected, hoping that would put an end to the discussion.

"Yes!" Anna-Beth ushered everyone around the dinner table. As everyone took their seat, she said, "Rachel, it's your turn to say grace."

"No, I don't think that it is," Rachel stated.

Anna-Beth's eyes darted to Christopher then back to Rachel.

"I need to say grace to impress Williams, somehow?" Rachel furrowed her brow, gesturing toward Christopher. "I promise he knows I don't go to church." Anna-Beth stared her down, making her feel tiny and insignificant. Powerless. She refused to feel any of that and took a deep breath, determined to fight back as best she could. "Fine, I'll say grace," Rachel agreed with a twinkle in her eye. She'd had just about enough of her mother's opinions and that cold, unfeeling part of her, the part that made her such a good soldier, such a good interrogator took over. She quickly switched to Arabic, knowing it would irritate her mother even more than if she said it in English. "Dear God, please do your fucking job and bring peace to the world and alleviate human suffering, specifically war, famine, and plague, which I know are the favorites of the god of the Old Testament. Amen."

Anna-Beth stared at Rachel with rage. "What the hell was that?"

"It was me praying," Rachel stated.

"I don't think it counts if no one understands you," Anna-Beth argued.

"God understood me. Isn't that the important part?"

"Fine, would you care to translate?" Anna-Beth made it sound more like a demand.

"I asked God to alleviate human suffering, specifically war, famine, and plague."

Christopher bit the inside of his cheek, trying not to laugh.

Tom looked at him skeptically. "Is that what she actually said?" he asked Christopher.

"Yes sir, that's exactly what she said," Christopher lied.

"Rachel, typically grace is for thanking God for the food we are about to eat," Anna-Beth reminded her.

"Wait? When was God here delivering groceries? I can't believe I missed that! Sure would've loved to meet him!" Rachel exclaimed wholeheartedly.

"If you'd like to act like a child, then I guess we'll have to treat you like one." Anna-Beth scolded Rachel like she was six years old, hatred and fury filling her eyes as she took Rachel's plate and dumped the food in the trash.

Rachel looked at Christopher, schooling her face to remain neutral, almost bored. "See, God's already not listening. Maybe he's sleeping. Or maybe he's dead," she said, raising her eyebrows satirically.

Jamie was laughing right along with Christopher. She knew he understood her joke perfectly well.

"What is so funny, Jameson Ryker?" Anna-Beth glared at him, both hands on her hips.

"Mom, really? She just prayed for God to alleviate the world from famine, and then you threw her food away. You don't see the irony in that? It was kind of fucked up, actually."

Tom was laughing now too and got up to get a clean plate. He scraped half of his food on it to give to Rachel.

"No, Daddy, I don't need that. If she wants me to pray, I'll pray. Fasting will only help me get closer to God, and maybe then he'll listen," Rachel insisted. "Your god is male right?" She leaned forward toward Anna-Beth. "I wanna make sure I'm praying to the right one."

Jamie was laughing again and Christopher had his eyes fixed to the table, jaw clenched, clearly trying to behave.

"Rachel, don't be ridiculous. You have to eat," Tom said.

"It's fine. I really don't. I was informed I'm supposed to be concerned with my looks, so I probably shouldn't eat. Besides, If I can jump out of a plane and survive behind enemy lines for two weeks with only three days' worth of food, I think I can survive skipping dinner," Rachel said as though this was a perfectly normal life experience.

"When did you do that?" Christopher asked.

"On my second deployment. You know, hanging with some intelligence assets before switching to logistics." She tried to play it off as though it were no big deal.

"Oh, that makes sense," Christopher nodded, playing along.

"If you were there for two weeks, why did you only pack three days' worth of food?" Jamie asked.

Rachel winced slightly. "Because I was only supposed to be there for two days." Rachel tried to ignore the emotional pain that was creeping up on her as more images from that fateful day in the Persian Gulf flashed before her eyes. "Fortunately, I had the good sense to pack extra food when I realized the mission was going to be an utter shit show, but I didn't have any more room in my pack, so that was all I had." Rachel blinked twice as another image popped into her head. An image she never wanted to see.

"Well, I thank God every day that you decided to stop with that nonsense, and you're home safe and sound," Anna-Beth said. "Two years of that was more than enough, I'd say."

"I am much happier with what I'm doing now," Rachel said truthfully. "Not sure God had much to do with it, though."

Christopher kicked her under the table. She tugged twice on her earlobe in response, mimicking the double tap they would do on their earpieces to respond *yes* when they couldn't speak. She hoped he understood she was going to need help staying grounded. If not, it was going to be a long night.

Everyone finished their dinner while Rachel sipped her water in silence, trying to stay calm and focus on her breathing. Trying to force the memories away and halt the flashbacks before they took over.

As soon as everyone finished eating, Rachel collected the dishes and started cleaning up. Christopher quickly jumped in to help her.

"You okay?" Christopher asked once they were alone.

"We'll see."

"Flashbacks?"

"I haven't been sleeping and the stress . . . Being with these people . . . I can't. If that comes up again . . . that deployment." She shook her head. "I'm not feeling particularly stable."

Christopher nodded, and she knew he understood what she meant. They both had plenty of experience with flashbacks and trauma triggers.

"You know there's a dishwasher?" Tom interrupted as he walked into the kitchen and saw them both elbow-deep in sudsy water.

"It's fine. This is easier," Rachel insisted.

He gave them a critical look. "You two want a drink?"

"Sure," Christopher answered tentatively.

"You two can drink. I'm fasting, remember? But I'll come hang out," Rachel said, following her father into the living room. She didn't think alcohol would be helpful given the storm that seemed to be brewing in her head.

"Cut the shit Rachel. You aren't fasting. Have a drink," Tom said as she sat down in one of the armchairs.

Jamie came in and joined them too. "Mom's pissed," he stated, falling into a chair as Tom handed him a drink.

"Well, what did she expect?" Rachel asked.

"Did you really survive two weeks on three days' rations?" Jamie asked Rachel.

Rachel took a sharp inhale. "Yes, I did. To be fair, I was a little busy killing people and trying not to get killed myself to realize I was hungry so . . ."

A surge of pain exploded down her thigh, forcing her to take a deep breath. Her head was throbbing too. She blinked twice, trying to get the image in her head to go away.

"Well, good to hear you're happier doing what you're doing now. Whatever that is," Jamie said, taking a sip of his whiskey and eying her suspiciously.

"Yes, well, I think my experiences being undersupplied on so many occasions while in combat really inspire me to ensure that everyone has adequate supplies when they deploy. It's actually a–" she paused, gritting her teeth down on another surge of pain "–very valuable experience that has made me very good at my job now." She tried to keep the mood light, but every question about that deployment was pulling memories out of her mind. Memories she'd rather didn't exist and very much preferred to ignore.

Christopher nearly choked on his whiskey. "You are obsessive about supply orders." It was true. Tom and Jamie just didn't need to know they were her own team's supply orders.

Rachel sat with them, trying to remain engaged in the conversation, but she kept snapping back in time, pictures and sounds from that deployment flashing through her mind like a dusty old film reel. She could hear the assault rifles, the grenades. Could feel the bullet digging its way deeper into her leg, knowing she had several miles to go before she would reach her extraction point. She remembered the feel of her knife digging into flesh, body after body, until she finally dug it into her own, trying desperately to extract the bullet. The smell of the alcohol wipe from her medic kit that she had used, trying to clean and sterilize the blade. She could nearly feel the pain again as she remembered digging her knife into her thigh, hoping, praying that the bullet would magically dislodge itself somehow. It was dark and dusty. She'd been convinced that if she didn't die from blood loss, she'd get shot again on the way to her extraction point, and if by some miracle she survived that, she was confident she'd die of an infection from what she was doing to her leg.

She remembered sifting desperately through her backpack, looking for a suture kit and cursing herself when she remembered she'd used it on someone else the day before. After a few deep breaths, she had gone to option B and held a lighter to her tactical knife, heating the blade as much as she could before holding it to her flesh, forcing herself to remain silent through the entire procedure so she didn't alert the enemy to her position. She had bit down on her left hand while her right hand pressed the hot blade to her thigh. She had forced her left elbow on top of the blade to add pressure, hoping and praying that the knife was hot enough to seal the wound and that she didn't vomit from the stench of her own burning flesh.

No, Christopher didn't know this story. She'd never told anyone the full story. She'd only briefly mentioned in her report that she'd been shot by the enemy in the thigh. She'd been awarded another Purple Heart for it, along with a Silver Star for her heroism in battle. Both of which she'd tried to refuse.

She suddenly wished she wasn't fasting and could drink, but she wanted to make her point to her mother even more. She felt something warm pass her leg, and her eyes focused in time to see Christopher's forearm graze her thigh as he reached for the whiskey bottle, nudging her hand off of her leg as he did.

"Rachel!"

The sound of her mother's voice and the warmth of Christopher's touch snapped her back to the present moment. She whipped her head around in a panic to look at her mother. "What Mamma?" she asked, serious and wide-eyed.

"What the hell were you doing?" Anna-Beth asked. Everyone was staring at her.

Rachel had no awareness of what she'd been physically doing and hoped she'd been sitting in the chair quietly. "I was praying," she lied. Or it was a sort of lie. She had actually been praying to God in her memories, so she supposed it counted.

"What the hell did you do to your leg?" Anna-Beth asked. "I swear, Rachel . . ."

Rachel looked down at her leg and pulled her shorts down, trying to cover the burn on her thigh and the fresh fingernail marks around it. "That's from the sliding glass door." She was too distracted to come up with a believable lie.

"No, those claw marks are from your fingernails," Anna-Beth corrected her. "We have talked about this, Rachel."

"Talked about what?" Rachel furrowed her brow, not alert enough to understand what her mother was scolding her for this time.

"Something is seriously wrong with you, Rachel," Anna-Beth told her.

"Of course there is," Tom raised his voice. "She's a fucking combat veteran, Anna-Beth. Leave her the fuck alone."

"Get it together, Rachel," Anna-Beth stated firmly.

Rachel took a steadying breath. She was really losing patience. Her mother was bad enough. Flashbacks were terrible. Both at the same time, however, were unbearable. "Dad, what's the code to the gun safe here, or do I need to ask Special Agent Hope?" Rachel asked as innocently as she could, her eyes boring into her mother. It came out firm and unfeeling instead. She knew she had a gun in her duffel bag, multiple guns actually, but she was at least cognizant enough to know better than to mention it.

"Why? Who are you planning to shoot? Yourself or your mother?" Tom asked with a hint of amusement in his voice.

"Which answer gets me the code?" Her voice was cold as ice.

"Tom?" Anna-Beth said harshly.

"Right." Tom shook his head and chuckled. "Rachel, you have company. Your mother would appreciate it if you would mind your manners."

"I've seen her behave much worse than this, I can assure you," Christopher said as he took a sip of his whiskey.

"I expect you to sort this out," Anna-Beth said, her eyes boring into Tom.

"We're all good," Tom assured her. He waited for Anna-Beth to leave the room then refocused on Rachel. "When's the last time you slept?"

Rachel shrugged.

"And when did you last eat?"

Another shrug.

Tom sighed. "I should have dragged you kicking and screaming to that support group," he said under his breath.

"Fuck off," Rachel muttered as she got up and left.

CHAPTER 25:
DECEMBER 2018

CHRISTOPHER FOUND RACHEL ALONE in the kitchen the next morning, drinking coffee. "Did you sleep?" he asked her, knowing she barely slept on a good night.

"Yes, eventually."

"And you ate?"

"My father sat on my bed and stared at me until I ate a protein bar and a yogurt." She rolled her eyes.

Christopher glanced around quickly to make sure they really were alone. "What was the flashback about last night?"

"The thing Jamie was asking about." Rachel averted her eyes.

Christopher nodded. "Do you need or want to talk?"

"Nope. Well . . . hell, you've seen the scar on my leg. I was thinking about that."

"Bullet?" Christopher asked, realizing that in all the years they had known each other, it was a story he'd never heard.

"Yeah."

Christopher laughed and shook his head, knowing he could probably guess what had happened. "What did you use to get it out?"

"My tactical knife. I didn't have a suture kit so . . ."

"Fuck, that hurts," he said. "You had a lighter but no suture kit?"

"I *had* a suture kit, but I used it on someone else the day before, thinking I'd be able to get out, and because they would have died . . . I was close to the evac, supposed to be getting on a helicopter, but then some shit happened."

Christopher grimaced. "Well, you sure weren't exaggerating about your family."

"Nope," Rachel said.

"I mean, your dad's just trying to keep the peace, but your mom . . . wow."

"Yup. I could literally walk up to her with my hair on fire and tell her I was on fire, and she'd tell me to stop being dramatic and accuse me of lying."

"Umm, I know you don't normally exaggerate, but that sounds like an exaggeration."

"I promise you, it's not."

"She must have some redeeming quality?"

"She provided me with three meals a day and a bedroom?"

"And?" Christopher prompted.

"She was an excellent mother to Jamie, other than spoiling him and making him somewhat entitled."

"Well, Jamie aside, it seems like your problems with your mom are affecting your relationship with your dad," Christopher pointed out.

"I suppose." Rachel raised an eyebrow.

"You like your dad."

"Sure." She shrugged.

"Maybe try making amends with your mom? Be the bigger person. You'll feel better if you do it. If you at least try. Then it's on her if she wants to try too."

Rachel wrinkled her nose and looked at the floor. "Do you *have* to solve everything all the time?" she grumbled.

"Yes." Christopher nodded.

"Ugh! I really hate you sometimes," Rachel complained.

"Shut up. You know you love me." Christopher smirked.

Anna-Beth was standing in front of her bedroom window, a canvas and an easel set up in front of her and sheafs of old newspaper spread out on the floor. She was painting a picture of an old stone church centered in a rose garden.

"Do you need something, Rachel?" Anna-Beth asked, her eyes fixed to the easel.

Rachel winced. It didn't matter that she was the child and her mother was supposed to be the parent. That had never been the case, not really. *Be the bigger person. Forgive and forget.* Sure, she'd gone out of her way to provoke her mother on several occasions, but she'd been neglected and dismissed and alone her entire life. She knew she hadn't done anything to deserve that. No child could. She didn't know what she was going to say, but she had to start somewhere.

"That's a pretty church," Rachel said from the doorway.

"Thank you. Why are you up here?"

Excellent question. Rachel thought for a minute. She was up there because Christopher was right. If she wanted peace, she would have to make peace. But she didn't want peace. She wanted to haul ass to the Middle East with her team and hunt down Samir Al-Abadi. That didn't seem to be happening anytime soon, though, seeing as she'd yet to receive any intel about where he actually was, so she would have to stay here and try. Try to forgive things she considered unforgivable.

"I came to apologize. I'm feeling restless and anxious, and I don't want to be here. I'm taking my feelings out on you," Rachel said slowly, her eyes fixed to the floor.

"What is your problem, Rachel? Why can't you be normal?" Anna-Beth put her paint brush down and turned to look at her daughter.

"How do you define normal?" Rachel tensed, suddenly feeling attacked. She'd never been normal, didn't want to be normal. She wanted to be better than normal. But when her mother said it, it sounded like she was defective somehow. Broken.

"Calm, rational, responsible, caring to other people, caring about what happens after you die, attending church, wanting to spend time with your family."

"I am calm, rational, responsible, and caring," Rachel insisted. Her mother was right about the last three, though.

Anna-Beth shook her head and refocused on her painting.

"I'd maybe want to spend time with my family if they were nicer to me. You want me to be more caring? When have you actually shown you care about me, even a little?" Rachel asked. So much for focusing on apologizing rather than arguing.

"All the time, Rachel. Constantly. All I have ever done is try to save you from yourself."

"You just try to change me," Rachel said sadly, shoving her hands into the back pockets of her jeans and looking at her feet.

"You need to change."

"Of course." Rachel's head bowed involuntarily towards the floor. Anna-Beth was constantly trying to change her. Even after Rachel had given in and done or become what her mother had wanted, it was never good enough. She had always treated Rachel like her watercolors—something she could pour water over and dilute if she didn't like the version she'd created. "Fine, Mamma. What do I need to change? How can I get you to like me even a little?"

"You could start by going to church and showing that you're putting in some effort to better yourself, taking responsibility for your own wellbeing for a change."

"How is church going to do that?" Rachel furrowed her brow, trying to ignore the fact that her mother had more or less admitted she didn't like her. It was fine. She could just lock away all the pain and anger and save it up to use as fuel on the next battlefield.

"Regular prayer will help keep you grounded and self-aware."

"I meditate every day. It's basically the same thing," Rachel told her.

"It's not the same thing," Anna-Beth insisted, shaking her head.

"Agree to disagree then." Rachel sighed and looked out the window.

"Church is where you will find a husband," Anna-Beth added.

"I don't want a husband." Rachel wrinkled her nose.

"You need someone to keep you balanced, make decisions for you, someone to give your life meaning. Someone you can take care of, and they'll take care of you. I do realize you can probably barely take care of yourself—"

"Mamma, I take care of myself just fine. I have a pretty important job with a lot of responsibility. I manage to keep myself and other people alive. I absolutely do not need a husband bossing me around, telling me what I can wear and where I can go and what I'm allowed to buy and when! I have a job, I have my own money, I can manage my own life."

"Not from what I've seen."

"You haven't seen me in ten years."

"Whose fault is that?" Anna-Beth raised an eyebrow.

"I would happily permanently move to a combat zone to avoid arguing with you about husbands and babies and church." It was a cheap response. She'd rather be in combat than do most things.

"You are so dramatic, Rachel!" Anna-Beth scolded. "Really, you're just proving my point. You need someone to make decisions for you so you aren't so stressed, and you can relax and be calm."

"Like you? You're so calm all the time? Mamma, I've never seen you calm." Rachel couldn't help but laugh at the hypocrisy.

"I'm not calm when I'm around you because I have to worry about you too much. If you were married with a family . . . I know you had several offers."

"Who should I have married?" Rachel asked.

"Your brother's friend Richard would have been a good match," Anna-Beth suggested.

"You mean the guy who tried to sexually assault me and I kicked his ass?" Rachel raised an eyebrow.

"What did I tell you about making up stories?"

"Ask Jamie. He was there. I can give you a list of people who were there and watched the whole thing."

"I have seen you around men, Rachel. If you wear that short of shorts and skirts and flirt shamelessly with men, then what do you think is going to happen?" Anna-Beth asked. "Seriously, this is why I am so insistent you attend church so you can learn to behave properly."

"You really just made me want to go to church even less." Rachel winced.

"Why are you so against church?" Anna-Beth's voice was harsh. She put down her paintbrush again and turned to face Rachel, both hands on her hips.

"For all the reasons I've already told you. Because women aren't seen or treated as being equal to men. I'm not saying men and women are the same. They're obviously not. But demanding women be silent, putting restrictions on their behavior and limiting their choices, is wrong."

"Such as?"

"Forcing women to carry their rapist's child to term or, in the case of high-risk pregnancies or medical complications, forcing a husband to watch their unborn child kill their wife when it was preventable."

"Abortion is murder, Rachel."

"But murder in war is okay?" Rachel raised an eyebrow, knowing her mother was as pro-military and pro-war as they came.

"Two very different things, Rachel." Anna-Beth dismissed the idea with a casual flick of the wrist. "Soldiers killing soldiers is not the same as murdering babies."

"Children die in war every day, Mamma. Schools get bombed, houses get bombed, kids get scared and run to their parents in the middle of an ongoing firefight." Her mind flashed back to her encounter with Amina and her story of how her children were killed in a bombing. Rachel took a deep breath to steady herself. "When it is soldiers against soldiers, that just means those children are losing their fathers or mothers, and women are losing their husbands, men are losing their wives."

"No one is blowing up schools, Rachel." Anna-Beth gave a dismissive wave of the hand. "Besides, that has nothing to do with you going to church. You need some mental health care. I've been telling you that for decades, even since before you joined the Navy. Church would be a good start though."

"I can't make peace with a god who's more concerned about what I'm wearing than the suffering of people all over the world," Rachel stated sincerely, knowing that arguing about the husband issue wouldn't be helpful.

"Where did you get the idea that God cares about what you wear?"

"1 Timothy 2:9-10, 'I also want the women to dress modestly, with decency and propriety, adorning themselves, not with elaborate hairstyles or gold or pearls or expensive clothes, but with good deeds, appropriate for women who profess to worship God," Rachel recited. "The Bible is telling women how to dress, but setting no expectations for men. Tell me, Mother, how is that Bible verse preaching anything different from the Taliban?"

"Obviously the Christian Church is not the Taliban, Rachel." Anna-Beth shook her head. "Really, you care about this too much."

"Of course I do!" Rachel tried not to yell. "It's my life. How I'm treated by people, by society? Of course I care about it. Making the world safe for women and girls is the only thing I care about. I didn't go over to the Middle East to fight against the Islamic extremists, to stand up to them and their hateful views toward women, to fight for freedom and equality, only to come back here and be treated like shit just because I happen to be female. Things need to change here too!"

"I really don't think it's the same thing at all, Rachel. No one is stopping you from having a job or getting an education. No one is forcing you to cover your hair or face."

"No, but they're trying to deny rape victims access to safe abortions, trying to force young women to have children they don't want which actually very much limits their ability to educate themselves and have a good job. If you don't want abortion, then make condoms and birth control free and easily available. Teenagers and young adults aren't going to stay abstinent. Let's be honest about that. It's unrealistic."

"People need to accept the consequences of their actions," Anna-Beth stated firmly.

"What about when women are victims but they can't prove it was rape or abuse?" Rachel challenged.

"If it were, then there would be proof."

"I think the baby and the woman swearing under oath that she did not consent is proof. But no one ever believes women or girls. Not even other women. You never believed me about anything. You still don't!"

"What are you talking about?" Anna-Beth crossed her arms over her chest and stared at Rachel.

"Well, other than the incident with Richard Wheeler." Rachel couldn't help but roll her eyes. "Your father's maid. What was her name? Mirabelle? I told you your father was hurting her. I'm very sure he was sexually assaulting her."

"How could you possibly know it wasn't consensual?"

"He was her employer. The power dynamic makes it sexual harassment at best, if not sexual assault or rape."

"You were a child, Rachel. I'm sure you misunderstood what you saw."

"Right." Rachel winced. Her mother's words were like a slap in the face. "I came up here to try to make peace with you, Mamma. I'm trying. I guess I'm also failing." Rachel turned on her heel and stormed out of the room, running down the stairs back to the study.

"How'd it go?" Christopher barely got the question out before he saw the tears rolling down Rachel's cheeks. He pulled her into a tight hug without thinking, tangling his fingers in her hair and resting his forehead on the top of her head. Her entire body was shaking with silent sobs. He'd seen her cry before, but not like this. Frustrated tears and grief weren't the same as this level of emotional vulnerability. He couldn't help but think she was beautiful. It was like he could see her soul, and it was stunning.

He pulled her close and buried his face in her hair, wishing he could take away all her pain. "What the fuck shampoo have you been using?" he asked as he caught the scent of lavender coming off her hair.

"Stop smelling my hair, Williams. It's fucking weird," Rachel complained, even though she buried her face in his chest and wrapped her arms tighter around him, letting her tears saturate his t-shirt.

"It smells like flowers," Christopher said, taking a deep inhale as he pulled her closer. He combed his fingers through her hair, noting her messy bun was even messier than usual and falling out. He slowly untangled her hair from her hair tie, letting it fall over her shoulders, before twisting it in his fingers and twirling it into a bun. He'd dealt with enough drunk girls over the years to know how to fix their hair, his little sisters included. He'd been forced to correct his bun-twisting technique on several occasions when Rachel had been too injured to use her arm, helping her so that she wouldn't be in violation of uniform code. He paused a moment longer than he should have, his fingers still tangled in her hair, before looping the hair tie around her bun, securing it back in place. He kept one hand on the back of her head, pulling her into him, as his other hand grazed up and down along her spine. Some sort of weird instinct was trying to take over, some sort of need to comfort her and reassure her that she was safe. He was fighting the urge to kiss the top of her head. His lips needed something to do. "Really good shampoo," he murmured instead.

"Stop being weird and find me some terrorists to kill," Rachel muttered as she dug her fingernails into his back, pulling him closer to her.

Chapter 26:
DECEMBER 2018

RACHEL SPENT THE NEXT morning harassing Special Agent Hope for information about the investigation. Hope was surprisingly uncooperative.

"Do you still have the two intruders in custody?" Rachel asked, both hands curled into fists and resting on her hips. She was trying to be patient.

"Yes, we do," Hope assured her.

"Take me to talk to them," Rachel demanded.

"Commander Ryker," Hope looked around, "I've seen your record. Enough of it at least. Advanced interrogation . . . I can't let you anywhere near the suspects. You aren't authorized to work on U.S. soil."

"I will get authorization then."

"Stand down, Commander," Hope ordered.

"May I at least leave and check myself into the barracks at Coronado?" Rachel tried.

"Request denied."

"I'll just go above your head."

"Where do you think I'm getting these orders from?" Hope asked. "Your C.O. told me to keep you here."

"Eastwood?" Rachel furrowed her brow.

"Higher than that." Hope pursed her lips.

"Leftwich?" Rachel tried. The look on Hope's face told her she was correct. "That fucking asshole. You know, he was on the phone with my dad the other day. I don't know why."

"You don't need to know why."

Rachel narrowed her eyes. "Your insistence on not including me is making me more suspicious. I don't know how many times I need to explain to you, I am the target. Let me go and my family will be safe. Let me bring the rest of my team here, and we'll set up a trap to get Samir Al-Abadi and whoever he has working for him."

"I assure you, my team has everything under control," Hope insisted.

"I'm sure you do not, but I'll get some backup and then it will be." Rachel turned on her heel and went to find Christopher.

"We need a strategy session," Rachel told Christopher. He was sitting on the bed in his room, and she promptly went in and closed the door behind her.

"Easy enough," Christopher agreed. He quickly sent a text to Matt and Ryan, setting up an emergency video call. The four of them could strategize and assess, then call in the rest of the team if needed. Rachel explained the situation—about the break-in and the intruder mentioning a USB stick and Samir Al-Abadi. She knew she was missing something, some key piece of how Samir had tracked her here, but she had no idea how Samir could have possibly found her at her parent's house in San Diego.

"Hang on," Ryan said. "Al-Abadi has the code we were looking for *and* he somehow got someone to follow you to California?"

"Wait what?" Matt asked. "How the fuck did we get from Saad Ayad to Samir Al-Abadi?"

"We were informed of that information," Rachel said evasively.

"Informed by who?" Matt asked.

"That's what Saad told the CIA," Rachel stated.

"Okay, thanks for sharing, I guess," Matt complained. "If we ignore the obvious question of why Saad Ayad, a member of Al-Qaeda, knows what Samir Al-Abadi, a member of ISIS, is doing and assume the intel is credible, how did Samir find out your name, or your parent's address?" Matt asked. The fear was evident in his voice.

"I don't know!" Rachel yelled. "Look guys, I'm too focused on not killing my mother or my brother, so my brain isn't working as well as it usually does. That being said, two guys in full tactical gear broke into my parent's house and told me Samir Al-Abadi sent them. The federal agents are being less than forthcoming with information, but I did learn Leftwich ordered them to keep me here. I don't know why."

"Why is he even involved? Eastwood should be the one to make that call. Leftwich surely has better things to do than worry about where you're sleeping," Christopher pointed out.

"That's my point!" Rachel yelled.

"Okay, calm down," Matt said. "What are next steps?"

"The agents here refuse to secure the perimeter. The entire back of the house is vulnerable," Rachel said,.

"What?" Ryan asked, clearly confused.

"The house backs up to the beach and the feds keep telling us normal people wouldn't approach from the water," Christopher clarified.

Rachel nodded and continued. "And, I think we all have enough experience with Samir Al-Abadi to know that he never shows his full hand the first time. He always attacks, but not with his full force. If he had two men infiltrate my parent's house, I promise he has more men ready to go. This is how he operates. He tries to get the job done with as few people as possible, and if they fail, he hits again with a larger force, usually quite quickly. If I hadn't been there, two men probably would have been plenty."

"For fuck's sake," Matt muttered. "Ryan and I will fly there later today. We'll be there in the evening, and we can come up with a plan."

"Good, I'm still missing something though," Rachel said, trying to scrape her brain for the missing piece.

"Have you spoken to Veeda?" Ryan asked.

Rachel's eyes flashed with realization.

"What?" Christopher asked.

"Saad Ayad said his cousin was getting married- traded. She might know something," Ryan reminded her. Rachel's phone was out of her pocket before he could finish, switching her keyboard over to the Pashto alphabet so she could communicate with her friend.

>Skylark to Veeda: *Haven't spoken to you in a while. How are you?*
>Veeda to Skylark: *I got married.*
>Skylark to Veeda: *I can't tell if you're happy about that or not.*
>Veeda to Skylark: *Me neither.*
>Skylark to Veeda:. *Who did you marry?*
>Veeda to Skylark: *His name is Ammar Al-Abadi*
>Skylark to Veeda: *Is he related to Samir Al-Abadi?*

Rachel stared at her phone, wondering if Veeda knew she married into a family of terrorists. She knew Veeda's father was responsible for financing several Al-Qaeda terror cells, but it seemed she had in fact been traded to ISIS for some reason. She waited and waited for Veeda to text her back.

>Veeda to Skylark: *Sorry I was cleaning up from dinner. Now I'm in the kitchen hiding and making tea. Yes, he is Samir's nephew.*
>Skylark to Veeda: *I assume you've met Samir.*
>Veeda to Skylark: *Yes, he's here all the time.*
>Skylark to Veeda: *Where are you?*
>Veeda to Skylark: *Iraq, where I live now.*
>Skylark to Veeda: *If you tell me specifically where in Iraq you live, I'll come for a visit.*
>Veeda to Skylark: *Really? So fun!!!*
>Skylark to Veeda: *So much fun! Also, I need to know where Samir is and what he is doing at all times.*
>Veeda to Skylark: *Are you taking over leadership of the resistance from Zarah? ;)*

Skylark to Veeda: *We're all in this together. Keep me updated on where he is and where you are.*

After tilting her phone so Christopher could read the messages, she relayed everything to Matt and Ryan.

"When are we going to Iraq?" Ryan asked.

"As soon as possible," Rachel said through clenched teeth.

"Lovely." Christopher sighed.

"There is absolutely nothing lovely about Iraq other than the possibility of getting to put a bullet through Samir Al-Abadi's face." Rachel's body tensed, ready to strike. She'd been to Iraq plenty of times before and had very few positive memories of it.

"Save it for when we find him, Rache," Christopher said, placing his palm on her lower back.

She took a deep breath and immediately calmed down at the warmth of his touch.

Chapter 27:
DECEMBER 2018

CHRISTOPHER FOUND RACHEL AT the window, using binoculars to look out at the Pacific. She'd been on edge since their video call with Matt and Ryan. "The guys just got their rental car. They're on their way," Christopher told her.

"Look over here," Rachel said, pointing out the south-facing window. "Two o'clock."

Christopher took the binoculars and looked where she pointed. "Definitely got some movement. Can't tell what it is," he said.

"Yeah. Come look over here." Rachel guided Christopher down the hallway to a bedroom with a window facing west. "Now look out here," she instructed.

"I count eight," Christopher said, referring to the eight men clearly in view on this side of the house. "Looks like they're gearing up."

"Looks like they swam here, just like we kept telling Hope they would," Rachel said, annoyed.

"Can't do much about it now," Christopher said.

"I'm gonna do a whole hell of a lot about it." Rachel shoved the binoculars into Christopher's hands and ordered him to stand watch, keeping eyes on the targets. Then she sprinted downstairs to where Special Agent Hope was brewing a cup of coffee in the kitchen. Rachel marched up to her and told her all she'd observed, making a point to emphasize that she had been right all along.

"Commander, I assure you, my team has it under control. The perimeter is secure," Hope said dismissively.

"It's definitely not. Come look," Rachel said, her voice as commanding as it would be any other time she was about to lead her team into a fight.

"Fine," Hope conceded, following Rachel back up the stairs.

Christopher pointed out of the west-facing window and handed Hope the binoculars so she could watch for herself as the eight men crouched down in the sea grass adjusted their earpieces and loaded their rifles.

Next, Rachel took Special Agent Hope to the south-facing window. "Look out here. It's a little harder to see, but something's up." There were dive bags on the ground, fins, and boxes of what looked like ammunition next to the men.

"Definitely movement. I count four," Special Agent Hope said. "Are they setting up a perimeter?"

"That's what it looks like," Christopher agreed.

Rachel jumped into action, taking charge of the situation and running downstairs to where Tom was sitting in the kitchen. "Dad, you need to get Mamma and Jamie and hide in the upstairs hall closet where there aren't any windows. Stay there until Williams or I come to get you, and be quiet. No noise."

"Rachel, this isn't your job," Tom argued.

"Like hell it isn't."

"Rachel!"

"We really don't have time for this discussion. Now get out of my way and do what you're told." Rachel pushed past him and made a beeline for her bedroom.

"Hope, where are your extra vests?" Rachel yelled to Special Agent Hope, who was standing in the upstairs hallway. Without giving her a chance to respond, Rachel brushed past her and into her room, grabbing her duffel bag and throwing it up on the bed. She unpacked quickly, happy that she still had her rifle and pistol with her from their last mission, even though they had left their helmets and bulletproof vests at the safe house in Khost since they didn't want to carry them around.

Christopher was in the room down the hall from Rachel, unpacking his guns and loading them with ammunition. "What are you thinking?" he called down the hall to her.

"Everything you've got Williams. I hope you didn't pack light."

"I've got an M4 and a Sig P," Christopher responded, using shorthand to refer to his standard SEAL issue M4A1 assault rifle and 9mm Sig Sauer P266 pistol.

"Same!" Rachel called back to him. "Ammo?" she asked him urgently.

"Hopefully enough. I guess we'll see."

"What are the boys bringing?" Rachel yelled to him.

"Don't know. They flew commercial. They aren't on official travel orders," Christopher reminded her, knowing that meant they definitely wouldn't have assault rifles with them.

"Alright, we'll do our best," Rachel said, bouncing into the room. Without thinking, she changed into her Navy-issued desert camo utility pants, a dead giveaway as to what her job really was. She filled her pockets with extra rounds of ammunition and slung her rifle over her shoulder, then tucked her pistol securely into the back of her waistband for easy access and secured her tactical knife in her right boot, as always.

Christopher finished loading his guns before going to check that Tom, Jamie, and Anna-Beth were safely hidden in the closet. "Secure," he called out to Rachel just as they heard a loud pop, followed by a thump against the back door of the house. It was a sound Rachel and Christopher had grown used to—the impact of a bullet from a long-range sniper whizzing through a body. They had Michael to thank for that.

"Fuck!" Rachel said. "Hope, where are your extra vests?" she asked again.

Hope pointed toward the living room where bulletproof vests, as well as extra guns and ammunition, were being unloaded out of a gun safe. The other agents were stocking up on ammunition as well.

"Nice!" Rachel said as she put on a vest and grabbed a few extra clips of ammunition for her pistol.

Christopher and Rachel headed to the back door of the house where the agent had been shot. He was bleeding, but fine enough for now. The bullet had gone straight through his shoulder. Three other agents moved in and were headed toward the assailants. Rachel and Christopher ran out, side by side, no instructions or planning necessary.

"Lay down some cover fire," Rachel ordered the agents as she and Christopher caught up to them. The agents did as she requested, firing their service weapons toward the four assailants so that Rachel and Christopher could move in. Rachel heard Christopher fire. The sharp pops and cracks of his assault rifle told her all she needed to know. She turned her body forty-five degrees to the right, just in time to see one assailant stop to reload. She hastily fired off a few shots, not having enough time to aim. She heard a loud shrieking pop to the right of her and saw that Christopher got the kill shot, blood streaming down the man's face from where the bullet landed right between his eyes.

"One down, three to go," she said to herself. She waited a moment for the smoke from her gun to dissipate. Combined with the bright sunshine, it was obscuring her view.

"Left, Sky," Christopher called to her.

Rachel turned to her left and dropped to one knee, taking aim with her rifle and squeezing the trigger to fire off multiple rounds. "That's two!" she called over to him. Her heart was racing. Adrenaline was surging through her body, keeping her mind sharp and her muscles fueled.

She and Christopher kept advancing, squinting against the setting sun, until they heard several shots fired behind them. They turned around and saw the agents were in a firefight with the remaining two assailants. As they ran to their aid, they heard the echo of shots fired in the distance.

"Take the right, Hawk," Rachel called out as they came up behind the remaining two assailants. Their assault rifles screamed out, executing the two men seconds after one of the agents was hit in the arm.

Rachel and Christopher ran side by side, always in sync with each other. As they passed the injured agent, Christopher asked, "You good?"

"Yeah! Go!" the agent responded, grabbing his arm to try and stop the bleeding.

Rachel and Christopher took off as fast as they could toward the east side of the house, where the remaining agents were up against eight men. The agents were outnumbered and outgunned. Rachel signaled to Christopher to slow down as they approached. Still moving swiftly, they exercised caution as they moved in toward the eight assailants.

"You wanna cover or run?" Rachel asked Christopher.

"Run," he answered quickly.

Rachel laid down in the sand grass and propped herself up slightly, her rifle poised and ready to provide cover fire. She hoped to draw the assailants to their position and away from the agents. Christopher sprinted ahead, trying to flank the group of eight before they could spread out too much. She heard the blast of his rifle, saw the flash and smoke, then jumped up to move in with him. Running at top speed, she saw movement in the grass to her left. She grabbed the pistol from the back of her waistband and fired off three shots, two to the assailant's chest and one to his head, never stopping or slowing down.

"How many you get?" she asked as soon as she caught up to Christopher.

"Two," he answered.

"I got one, so five left?"

"Think so."

Just then, they heard the piercing bang of shots fired from the front of the house. Pistols.

"Sounds like our backup's here," Rachel said.

"Nightingale, where are you?" Christopher asked, pressing his finger to his ear to activate the microphone on his earpiece. He was hoping Matt or Ryan had planned ahead and had connected their Bluetooth earpieces to the two-way radio he'd left in the house.

"Just got out of the car," Matt said.

"We're at the front entrance, headed around the east side of the house," Ryan added.

Christopher echoed their position to Rachel, since she wasn't on comms.

"Good thinking," Rachel said, tapping her ear as he looked at her. She hadn't thought of comms equipment, but of course Christopher had. Maps and technology, those were his specialties. "Ready to move?"

Christopher nodded, and they moved northwest, back toward the house and the agents.

"Heading to you," Christopher said so that Matt and Ryan would be ready for them. Rachel and Christopher moved as quickly as they could through the sand grass, checking for any sign of the assailants and listening to the high-pitched bang of pistols firing off.

Rachel could feel the adrenaline rushing through her veins. Her mind became hyperalert and focused on the task at hand. Everything slowed down. She listened to the pops and bangs up ahead and waited for Christopher to parrot back the kills Matt and Ryan had made on their end.

"They got two. Three left," Christopher told her. She dipped her head in acknowledgement and they kept moving.

"Down!" Rachel called out. Christopher immediately dropped to the ground. She fired off several rounds in rapid succession and took out two of the assailants. "One left if we're counting right," she said. Just then, she heard a whizzing sound go past her. "Fucking hell!" she screamed, grasping her left arm. There was one final crack and flash from Christopher's assault rifle as blood started trickling down her arm.

"Check for clear," he said over comms to Matt and Ryan before turning to Rachel. "How bad?" he asked, already understanding she'd been hit.

"Flesh wound," she answered, wiping the blood off her arm as best she could, even if she knew it would keep bleeding. She and Christopher ran over to the agents to set up a plan to ensure the area really was clear and that they had taken out all the assailants. Matt and Ryan met them on the east side of the house.

"Nightingale, get to work on the wounded," Rachel ordered, happy to see he had a medic kit slung over his back.

"You are the wounded," Matt said, eyeing her arm.

"Fuck you, I'm fine. Help everyone else first. Raven? Hawk? Let's check for an all clear. Let me know if you find anyone not all the way dead."

Rachel, Ryan, and Christopher divided up the property, walking, pacing, and wandering in a grid pattern, making sure the assailants were all dead and looking for any helpful clues to confirm who had sent them or where they had come from. As Rachel wandered, she regretted her perfect aim. There was no one left alive to question.

"We've gotta do something about that arm, Skylark," Matt said once they had regrouped. He'd already stitched up the two agents who had been shot.

"It's fine," she answered. "Just a flesh wound. Looks worse than it is."

"I'm sure, but let me have a look anyway, just for fun," he teased as he watched the blood run down her arm. Matt escorted Rachel into the house and had her sit on the kitchen table so she was at the right height for him to see her arm better. He cleaned and inspected the wound while Ryan flirted with Special Agent Hope and Christopher ran upstairs to get her family.

Tom, Anna-Beth, and Jamie followed Christopher downstairs, where they saw Matt putting a few stitches in Rachel's arm.

"Lord Jesus!" Anna-Beth exclaimed. "What in God's name happened?"

"It's fine, Mamma," Rachel responded, sliding off the table.

"Everything good?" Tom asked, looking at Special Agent Hope.

"I've got two agents with gunshot wounds, plus Commander Ryker," she said, pointing at Rachel. "Nothing too critical. Twelve assailants accounted for, all dead thanks to these four." She pointed at Rachel, Christopher, Matt, and Ryan.

Rachel headed for the bottle of whiskey on the kitchen counter. She took a long swig from the bottle, then said, "Told you that you'd need our help."

Christopher stifled a laugh.

The agents got to work moving the dead bodies and filing the necessary paperwork while the SEALs caught up. Rachel was in the middle of hearing how Matt proposed to Charlene when her father yelled from the other side of the house.

"Rachel Marie Ryker, get your ass in here!" Tom shouted from the study.

"Whoopsies," Rachel said lightheartedly as she sauntered off to see what her father wanted to yell at her for. She entered the study, making eye contact with her father and smiling. He was standing in the middle of the room, and Jamie was sitting in a chair next to the window. "You summoned me?" Rachel asked mockingly.

Tom motioned for her to close the door. "Would you mind telling me what in the hell is going on?" Rachel looked at him dismayed, acting as though she didn't understand the question. "Rachel Marie Ryker!" Tom continued. "Do you mind explaining to me why there are three U.S. Navy SEALs in this house, acting as though you are their commanding officer?"

"Who's a SEAL?" Rachel asked innocently.

"Cut the crap, Rachel. We're not stupid," Jamie interjected.

Rachel looked back and forth between Jamie and her father, then shrugged as though she had no idea what they were talking about.

"Either you're dating one of them, and they're all covering for you, or you are also a SEAL. Those are the only two viable explanations. You have assault rifles with you, for God knows what reason, and given the pants you're wearing, I know you're part of a Naval Special Warfare Unit!" There was fury in Tom's voice.

Rachel smiled at him sweetly, determined to charm her way out of this. "Daddy, I simply do not know what you are referring to." She laid on her Southern drawl as thick as she could, ignoring his comment about her camouflage pants, which were in fact restricted to be used only by SEALs and other sailors assigned to Special Warfare Units. Wearing them in front of him had definitely been a huge oversight on her part, but they were much easier to run in than skinny jeans.

"Last chance," Tom said.

"Oh, last chance for what exactly?" Rachel challenged him. "What are you gonna do?"

"I'm sure I could come up with something to take each of you up on in court-martial if I tried hard enough."

"Rachel, just tell us!" Jamie said.

Rachel looked up at the ceiling and let out an audible groan. "Fine. Yes, the four of us are SEALs. Are you happy now?"

"Since when?" Tom demanded.

"Well, Williams and I did BUD/S, what? About eight or nine years ago. When was 2009?" She put her index finger to her lips as though she was confused. "Anyway, Johnson joined our team two years after that, and Rhodes about two years after him so . . ." Rachel shrugged again, as though none of this was interesting to her.

"The Navy didn't admit women to SEAL training in 2009," Tom insisted, knowing full well that the Navy didn't officially admit women to the program until 2015.

"Well, they sure tried to tell me I couldn't be there, but it was a little difficult for them since I outperformed all the men on the entrance tests for BUD/S, and in most of my courses. I mean really, Daddy, you didn't actually think I got promoted so fast as a logistics officer," she said, a hint of derision in her voice.

"Which team are you on?" Tom asked.

"I'm afraid that's classified."

"Did you forget again that I'm an admiral?"

"No, sir, but the answer's still the same. Are we done?" Rachel asked.

Tom was not letting her off that easily. "Where are you based?" he tried.

"Classified," Rachel responded shortly, knowing that would only help him narrow down his search.

"Rachel Marie!" Tom shouted at her.

"Daddy, I'm sorry. Admiral or not, this happens to be above your security clearance."

"It shouldn't be above my security clearance," Tom retorted. He looked over at Jamie and motioned for him to leave the room. Once Jamie had gone, Tom continued. "Rachel, the only reason something you are doing would be above my security clearance would be–"

"It's above your clearance, Daddy," Rachel insisted coolly, raising her voice.

Tom leaned his palms on his desk and looked down. "Special Projects, then."

"Daddy, why did you think you got transferred here and didn't get that job in D.C. that you wanted eight years ago? I mean, they couldn't really appoint you to the National Security Council, or Joint Chiefs, or whatever it was, now could they?"

"What do you mean?"

"I mean that my career as a SEAL was a higher priority for the Navy than your career was, and no one wanted you in D.C. where you would have a high enough clearance and enough involvement to interfere in what I was doing."

"And why is that, Rachel?"

Rachel shrugged and then, stone-faced, turned on her heel and fled the room. There was no way she was answering that question. "Williams, let's move," Rachel called out to Christopher as she ran up the stairs. Her father had gotten enough information that, if he really wanted to, he could pull up her team's mission reports and figure the rest out for himself.

They both quickly packed their belongings and their gear, having already returned the bulletproof vests to Special Agent Hope. As they ran back down the stairs, each with their duffel bag in hand, Rachel called out "Let's go boys" and advanced rapidly out to Matt's rental car, with all three men following closely behind her.

Once they were in the car, she let out a sigh. "Get me the fuck out of here, please."

Matt laughed as he pulled the car away, thoroughly amused by the fact that her father had just yelled at her like she was a teenager.

Ryan, seated in the passenger seat, turned around and handed Rachel the bottle of whiskey he'd taken from the house. "Fun family Christmas," he joked, winking at her.

Rachel huffed out her frustration. "Yup. This is precisely why I don't come home," she said, taking a sip from the whiskey bottle before passing it to Christopher. "Cover's blown, by the way."

"Yeah, we kinda figured," Matt replied. "Where do you wanna go?"

"Don't care," Rachel said. "We've got nine more days before we need to be back on base, getting ready to deploy again, so anywhere but here or there."

CHAPTER 28:

JANUARY 2019

ON THE AFTERNOON OF January 10th, Rachel was at the Virginia Beach oceanfront, perusing the small boutiques. She hated shopping, but knew she needed some civilian clothing to take with her on their upcoming deployment. Time had gotten away from her. She'd never actually made it home to Florida. They had all flown from San Diego to Dallas, Texas, where Rachel, Matt, and Ryan each switched planes, and Christopher had convinced his sister to come pick him up and drive him back to his family's ranch, which was a ninety-minute drive from the airport. Rachel had elected to go straight to Dam Neck to follow up on the intel from Veeda and start putting together a plan to go to Iraq and find Samir. Figuring out how he'd tracked her to San Diego would have to wait, but the barrage of media stories circulating about federal agents stopping a drug cartel in San Diego—the perfect cover story for the shoot-out—had been amusing. She'd been on base for over a week before she remembered she needed to go shopping. She knew Iraq in the spring was hotter and more humid than Khost had been in the fall. She also knew they had a training—planned by Christopher—at 1600, so she needed to shop quickly.

Rachel was about to go into the dressing room to try on a few blouses and pairs of lightweight pants when she received an emergency text from Christopher to the team's group chat at 1445.

> Hawk to Indigo: *Fuck up with the schedule, get to base ASAP for training.*

Rachel rolled her eyes and texted him back.

> Skylark to Indigo: *WTF Hawk? What do we need to bring?*
> Hawk to Indigo: *Nothing, all supplies are here.*

Each team member texted back their current location and estimated arrival time.

Rachel, happy she'd borrowed a truck from base, drove as fast as traffic would allow and arrived at the base at 1510. She ran to their meeting spot, irritated. "What the hell?" she yelled at Christopher.

"What? It clearly says 1500 in the team calendar. Not my fault none of you knows how a calendar works," Christopher said.

Rachel pulled up her email showing him he clearly wrote 1600 in the information he sent out to the team.

Christopher shrugged. "You know, always be prepared and what not." He winked at her.

The rest of the team arrived by 1530, and Christopher got to work explaining what they would be doing. Pointing at the map of the area, he said, "Our mission is to swim from Fort Boykin to Huntington Park Beach, where there will be beer waiting. This is a race, so if you're late, the beer might be all gone. We leave in five minutes, so you all had better haul ass. Camo is over there for those of you not in uniform." He pointed to a pile of extra utility pants and jackets.

Rachel raised her hand to ask a question. "Hawk, you are aware that we're about to deploy to the desert?"

"So?" Christopher said. "We're SEALs. We do water."

"Just in case Samir decides to take up swimming?" Ryan joked.

"Yes," Christopher said seriously. When his response elicited laughter from the team, he pulled up a map of Iraq on his phone. "For those of you who don't recall, there are two rather large rivers in Iraq—the Tigris and the Euphrates."

"Here we go," Rachel said under her breath as she braced herself for the geography/social studies/political science lecture that she was sure would be long-winded.

"What I hear you saying," Aiden said, cutting Christopher off before he could get too engrossed in whatever he was rambling on about, "is that due to a rather miniscule chance that we'll need to swim across a river while in Iraq in pursuit of Samir, we need to freeze our asses off now?"

"Correct," Christopher pointed to the pile of uniforms again.

"I fucking hate you." The corner of Rachel's lip tugged up as she walked past Christopher to change with everyone else. Christopher smirked knowing the only thing Rachel hated more than being cold was being wet *and* cold.

Everyone changed as quickly as they could and loaded into a Navy-appointed van, with Christopher getting behind the wheel to drive. It took ninety minutes to get to Fort Boykin, a wooded picturesque park on the west bank of the James River. They arrived just before 1700. Christopher led the team at a fast sprint to the water. Some men headed straight in while others paused on shore to take off their shoes or clothes.

Rachel took off her jacket and boots, tying her jacket around her waist and her boots around her shoulder, before entering the water. It was cold, and the current was strong. Normally, she loved swimming, but she was in no mood for this. Christopher's schedule fiasco had clearly been on purpose.

Despite being one of the last to leave the shore, Rachel was in the lead. She was a strong swimmer, but the current was stronger, pulling her under the water more than she wanted it to. She started treading water while she unbuttoned her pants, sliding them off with some effort. Then she cinched the waistband closed as tight as she could with her belt so that as little air as possible would escape, making a flotation device to deal with the roaring tide that kept pulling her down. Next, she took the hair tie out of her hair and tied a knot around one of her pant legs. Then she took a deep breath and blew into the still open pant leg, continuing to do so until the pants were properly inflated. She secured both pant legs with her hair tie, looking down as she did.

"For fuck's sake!" Rachel muttered to herself as she noticed her now very see through white tank top. Her red lacy bra was showing and her matching red thong was definitely not up to Navy uniform standards. This was definitely not a good day.

Christopher passed by her, having made a flotation device of his own. "Did I not mention this is a race?"

"Fuck you!" Rachel yelled back at him.

Rachel slowly made her way to shore. She was embarrassed, but that wasn't going to help things.

Get your fucking head straight, Ryker, she lectured herself silently. *There has to be a graceful way to handle this.* She was only half-way across the river so she had time to come up with a plan.

She swam slowly, playing out potential scenarios in her head as each member of her team passed her by. She was mad at Christopher for pulling this prank with the schedule, but she was mostly just mad at herself. *Always be prepared.* Fuck, she'd fucked up. She'd known she was cutting it close by going shopping, but it was the only free time on her schedule for the foreseeable future, at least while the shops were open.

She hated that this was even an issue. She knew her team respected her. She knew they didn't think of her in that way, but she needed to maintain her confidence, her dominance, and to keep their respect. She had clawed her way to the top, even in the hardest moments, to prove to herself—to prove to all of the damned Navy, really—that a woman could be just as strong, just as worthy as any man out on that battlefield. She had worked ten times harder to get to where she was, never quitting. Even when she had to dig a god damn bullet out of her leg, she'd stood right back up and kept going. She remembered her grandmother, Rochelle Amelie Ryker, and how she fought with the French Resistance during World War II. Rachel had never met her, but she'd grown up listening to stories of the beautiful Rochelle, seducing Nazi officers and stabbing them with her knife. She had always wanted to be like her grandmother. It was a big legacy to live up to though.

Rachel had too much to fight for. There were too many women to save and too many evil men to kill. She wasn't about to give up because of a little bit of lace.

Ryan called out to her as he passed. "What, you don't like beer anymore?"

"No, I only swim for whiskey," Rachel responded.

She was used to changing in front of them, rarely having any privacy when they were deployed, but then they were changing too. And she sure as hell wasn't wearing red lacy lingerie under a see through tank top on deployment!

Ugh. Okay, now fix your face.

She saw several beach chairs lined up, but everyone had their back to her, crowded around the coolers of beer. She forced her face into a bright, flirtatious smile and swished her hips as she glided out of the river. Just as she was knee high in the water, she tossed her pants, jacket, and boots onto the beach and called out to the boys in a playfully seductive voice that emphasized her Southern drawl. "Well that sure was fun! Now, which of you boys is gonna get me a beer?"

They all turned to stare at her as she sauntered over to one of the beach chairs, putting a little extra swing in her hips. Christopher choked on his beer, shocked, and looking more embarrassed than she'd ever seen anyone before. His eyes were wide and his face flushed. She'd pulled it off!

"Dry clothes are in the van, Sky, if you want," Christopher said, shoving his hands in his pockets and looking at the ground. It was the first time in ten years he hadn't been able to look her in the eye.

"No thanks, I'm good!" She forced herself to smile as she chugged the beer Matt had gotten for her. "What else did you bring?" she asked, waving the empty bottle in the air. Christopher was still staring at the ground.

"You good?" Ryan whispered in her ear as he handed her another beer.

"Fuck off," Rachel muttered.

Ryan gave her a reassuring squeeze on the arm. "I'll be sure to submit your nomination for your academy award." Rachel glared at him, but he wasn't done. "I've never seen Chris this uncomfortable before. It's kind of funny. At least he knows he fucked up," Ryan chuckled. "You want me to get you a dry jacket or towel or something?"

"It is not funny, Ryan," Rachel whispered. Then she noticed the guys had all changed into dry clothes.

"I think that's the first time you didn't win a race, Sky," Aiden interrupted as he walked over to her, seemingly oblivious to what was happening.

"I let y'all win on purpose, Aiden," Rachel lied.

"Why?"

"So I could watch everyone and see what y'all were doing, who used what strategies."

"Oh," Aiden said. "It was a test then. How'd we do?"

"How do you think you did?" Rachel raised an eyebrow at him and cocked her head to the side, surprised he wasn't picking up on the palpable tension between her and Christopher. But that was Aiden, sweet and somewhat innocent, always focused on the positive.

"I think we did pretty good," Aiden said proudly. "I got a little distracted . . . Sort of tried to slow Ryan down."

"Yeah, thanks for jumping on my back." Ryan shook his head.

"Why is Chris just over there playing on his phone?" Aiden asked, looking back and forth between Rachel and Christopher. "You two get in a fight?"

Rachel stared at Aiden, wide-eyed for a moment, before sending him away to get her another beer. Before she could blink, David tossed her a dry towel.

"What's this for?" Rachel grumbled.

"Your hair. I'm guessing you're cold."

Rachel raised an eyebrow at him.

"The rest of us don't have long hair. Clara and the girls have me well trained." Rachel flashed him a small but appreciative smile then used the towel to wring the excess water out of her hair. A wife and two pre-teen daughters would make David more aware of the challenges of having long hair. "I see the point you're making, by the way. No need to be a hero. We all know you hate being cold."

"I'm just sitting here." Rachel shrugged, but she couldn't ignore the goose bumps all over her skin.

"Uh huh." David winked then turned his attention back to the men. "Drink up and let's move. We've got places to be!"

"We don't have anywhere to be," Christopher stated.

"You think you're the only person who can plan things?" David challenged.

"Yeah, come on, it's fucking freezing out here," Jason complained, giving Rachel a wink from across the beach.

"Alright, let's go." Christopher clapped his hands together then pointed to the parking lot where he'd had some of their support staff leave a van along with the dry uniforms and beer.

"Please wear these on the drive home," Ryan requested, tossing Rachel a dry pair of pants.

"What? You don't like my outfit?" Rachel feigned offense, putting her hand over her mouth and letting her Southern drawl drip thick as ever. This was her Scarlet O'Hara moment. "And here I put in all this effort getting dressed up for Hawk's birthday, and no one even appreciates it?" Her dramatics made everyone laugh, even Christopher, as she desperately tried to lighten the mood.

"Put on the damn pants!" Ryan demanded. "If you wanna get drunk and take off all your clothes at the bar later, no one's gonna complain," he added, knowing very well that as drunk as they had seen her, Rachel had always managed to keep her clothes on. She put on the dry pants and a dry jacket and helped the men pack up the van so Christopher could drive them all back to base.

"Who votes Hawk doesn't plan any more skills training until he takes a course on how to make a proper schedule?" Rachel asked once they were all loaded up and on the road. Everyone burst out laughing, agreeing that this would be the first and last time that Christopher was put in charge of planning skills training.

Back at base, everyone returned to their respective rooms, promising to meet at the main entrance in forty-five minutes. Christopher walked to his room, which was in the same hallway as Matt and Ryan's room.

"Well, that was interesting," Ryan said.

"Total fuck up, Chris," Matt echoed.

"I seriously cannot believe I just did that!" Christopher was mortified that he'd put his commanding officer, and best friend, in that position. "In the ten years I've known her, she's never not been prepared to jump into action. Seriously, what the fuck was she wearing? Did you guys know she has underwear like that?"

"I have never thought about Rachel's underwear before, nor do I want to," Matt said.

"I'm sure she's pissed." Christopher shoved his hands in his pockets.

"To be fair," Ryan said, "I think you're more embarrassed about it than she is. I mean really, she has nothing to be embarrassed about."

Matt laughed, and Christopher groaned unhappily. She'd had to play it off in front of the rest of the team to maintain their respect, but he was sure he'd hear about this from Rachel later in private. "I should go talk to her and get yelled at now before we go out with everyone."

"How are you gonna get into the women's hallway? I highly doubt your ID is programmed to open that door," Matt reminded him.

"I'll figure it out," Christopher muttered. He turned quickly and headed for the other corridor, not wanting to admit to Matt, Ryan, or even himself that he really just wanted an excuse to see her again. He couldn't stop thinking about her and how the approximately three hundred squats she did per day really paid off.

Large double doors leading to the women's corridor were blocking his way, but he knew someone would need to go in or out soon enough. While he wasn't as good as Rachel at sneaking into places, he was a close second. It took ten minutes for the door to open, and he carefully blocked it with his foot as a female petty officer made her way through the door. He waited for her to turn the corner, then slid in through the door. He'd only been in this hallway once before, when Rachel had been injured and he and Matt had helped her to her room with her bag. She didn't have a permanently assigned room on base since they were rarely there. He walked slowly, trying to decide where she might be. He got to the end of the hallway and turned his head to the right then the left, deciding which way to go. Suddenly he saw her walking down the hallway with damp hair and wrapped in a plush white towel. He took five long paces and was standing right in front of her.

"You are not supposed to be back here," Rachel stated. She took a step away from him, and he took a step forward. Her back landed against the wall, and he was right in front of her. He could feel the steam coming off her body, feel the softness of the towel wrapped around her, and could smell her shampoo.

"I know." Christopher's mouth filled with saliva as he looked at her.

"Do you need something?"

"No . . . I just wanted to . . ." His mind went blank, and he was struggling to remember why he'd come looking for her. He brushed the backs of his fingers along her arm, feeling her warm, soft, bare flesh.

"Lieutenant Commander Williams," Rachel said sternly. "I'm fairly certain you aren't supposed to be touching me."

"Hmm." Christopher nodded absently. He couldn't take his eyes off her, and he'd seemingly lost control of his hand.

"Would you like to be relieved of duty and court-martialed?"

"No." His voice was barely above a whisper.

"Then I suggest you go back to your room, because that's what's going to happen if anyone sees you back here, and I highly doubt a court would believe that you, an expert navigator, got lost on a base you've been to probably a thousand times."

"Rachel," he started quietly.

"Lieutenant Commander Williams, unless you've had gender reassignment surgery in the past fifteen minutes, you need to stop touching me and get out of this corridor immediately before someone else sees you." Her voice was commanding but quiet.

"Everyone's at dinner." Christopher's voice was low and sultry.

"Why did you come over here?" Rachel asked, trying to make her voice calmer.

"To talk to you." He stared into her eyes.

"About what?"

"You don't like what I'm doing?"

"I didn't say that." Rachel choked on the words as his skin and fingernails brushed up and down her upper arm.

"Right." Christopher smiled. "You didn't say that."

"What did you need to talk to me about?"

"Today."

"More words, Williams."

"To apologize."

"For what specifically?"

"For pulling that prank with the schedule and putting you in a position where–"

"You didn't like my outfit?" Rachel teased.

"Fucking hell, Rachel!" That got his attention, and it was his turn to be stern and serious. He ran both of his hands through his hair as he looked down at his feet. "I'm sure you're mad at me, so just get the yelling out of the way so you don't have to yell at me in front of everyone later."

"I would never yell at you in front of everyone. You know that."

"Alright, so, yell."

"I think you're feeling bad enough already. Not really sure what I can contribute."

"How are you feeling?" Christopher asked.

"I'm feeling like I want to go to my room and get dressed so we can go out and celebrate your birthday."

"Okay, but what are you thinking?" he asked.

"I'm thinking we're going to be late if you don't get out of my way and let me go back to my room," she lied.

"We're good?" Christopher asked. He put his hands in his pockets as he looked into her eyes.

"Always." Rachel smiled softly. She put her palm on his chest, pushing him gently away from her, and made her way past him to her room.

At the bar, Christopher ordered a double whiskey neat for himself and another for Rachel.

"It's your birthday!" Rachel exclaimed over the loud music. There was a live cover band playing at the front of the room. "Aren't I supposed to be the one buying you a drink?" she said it a little flirtatiously, wanting to re-spark the sexual tension from the hallway outside the women's shower.

"It's to make up for earlier. The scheduling issue and sneaking into the women's hallway," Christopher said seriously. "I know you said we were good, but . . ."

Rachel clapped him on the shoulder. "Seriously, no harm, no foul. Let it go!"

Christopher was surprised. He thought she would be mad. But like Ryan had said, Rachel had nothing to be embarrassed about. His reaction to her dressed like that . . . he should definitely be embarrassed, and probably ashamed, that he was thinking about her like that at all. He should probably feel bad about seeing her in her towel outside the shower too. He'd seen her straight out of the shower plenty of times. They all lived in such close quarters when they were deployed. But something about this time had been different.

"No, no, I don't want a drink for my birthday. Not from you anyway," Christopher said. Deciding to believe that everything was good and back to normal, and taking a cue from Rachel's earlier tactics, he lowered his voice and whispered in her ear seductively. "I want something else from you for my birthday." He grinned.

"Lieutenant Commander Williams, is it your goal to make me kick you in the balls on your birthday?" Rachel was shocked. Flirting was one thing. They did it more often than they should. But this was the third time today he'd gotten close to crossing a line that couldn't be uncrossed.

"Wait for it," Christopher said with a wink.

About forty minutes later, the band stopped playing and the lead singer said, "We have a special guest joining us tonight as a birthday present to her friend. Miss Rachel Ryker, would you care to join us on stage?"

Rachel shot Christopher a look, finally understanding that this was what he had meant earlier. She joined the band on stage and sang ". . . Ready for It?" and "Wildest Dreams" by Taylor Swift before leading the entire bar in singing "Happy Birthday" to Christopher. She held eye contact with him the whole time, directing every word of each song to him. Christopher couldn't take his eyes off of Rachel as her melodic voice rang out in perfect harmony with the band. Singing somewhere between a high alto and a low soprano, her voice had a velvety tone with a unique mix of rich dark notes and a bright upper range. Her charisma and stage presence made her light up the room. She was a total natural.

When she was done singing, she jumped down from the stage. Christopher's eyes followed her as she headed straight to the bar where several men offered to buy her drinks. He watched as she politely declined and then walked straight towards him.

"Happy birthday, Williams," she said gleefully. "I hope you liked your present."

"Yes, thank you. I thoroughly enjoyed it." He flashed her a wide grin.

"Well, I hope it makes up for your birthday last year," Rachel said.

"One hundred percent makes up for last year." The year before, they had been at a base in Iraq, preparing to head out for a mission. Things hadn't been going well. Supplies had been delayed, intel had been bad, and to make things worse, the power had kept going out on base. They ended up celebrating his birthday with a few beers they got from the understocked commissary, which they split between the entire team, and everyone crowded around a laptop to watch Christopher's favorite movie, *The Lion King*. The original animated one from 1994, of course. The team had done their best to make the day fun, which was no easy feat, given the situation they were in. This year was definitely much better.

"Well, not to take away from Chris's birthday, or our successful crossing of the James River," Matt interrupted after he gathered the whole team. "But I have something for each of you." He pulled a stack of metallic silver envelops out of his jacket pocket and handed one to each member of the team.

"What are these?" Ryan asked.

"I went over your head Skylark and checked the date with Eastwood." Matt winked at Rachel. "Even if we all need to be emergency evaced out of a firefight, we will all be in Lexington, Kentucky in May for my wedding."

"Eastwood promised you that?" Rachel was more than a little skeptical.

"No, he promised Charlene that," Matt corrected. "She will be contacting you all with details of how she expects you each to be involved. Please open the invitations and RSVP so she knows what food you want. We already know you're coming."

"Please tell me Charlene doesn't expect me to be a bridesmaid and wear some sort of hideous dress." Rachel wrinkled her nose.

"No, she does not," Matt assured her.

She leaned in closer to him so only he could hear. "I will not miss my opportunity to take out Samir for your wedding, or anyone else's."

"What about a funeral?" Matt asked.

"Only if it's mine." Rachel narrowed her eyes at him.

Chapter 29:
FEBRUARY 2019

CHRISTOPHER LED INDIGO THROUGH the desert of northeastern Iraq, walking and wandering on foot through a rather desolate part of the country. He would do anything for a beer right about now. His throat was as dry as the desert they were drudging through, and a far cry from the birthday party Rachel had thrown him four weeks ago. Their official mission was to track Samir Al-Abadi to recover the USB stick with the stolen malware code, which Samir allegedly had. Step one, though, was to find Veeda since she could lead them to Samir.

Rachel was giving him directions to the village Veeda lived in, or trying to. She kept showing him her cell phone as she exchanged text messages with Veeda, who it seemed was even worse at geography than Rachel was.

"How does she not know where she is?" Christopher complained.

"Well, she was only allowed to go through like sixth or seventh grade. You know, girls weren't allowed in schools in Afghanistan for quite a while, so she sort of missed out."

"What's your excuse then?" Christopher teased.

Rachel punched him in the arm. "There is a village close to here, somewhere, and that is where Veeda is," Rachel assured him for the hundredth time.

"You said that an hour and sixty miles ago." Rachel was fond of using words like *close* and *soon*, which irritated Christopher to no end.

"Well, I don't know what to tell you. She says it's about halfway between Hatra and Tal Afar, but to the side, but not as far as Al-Ba'aj. And there's a school. It's not on any of the main roads. It's not my fault she lives in the middle of nowhere."

"Quite literally," Christopher grumbled.

"I'm excited to see Veeda again!" Aiden grinned.

"You are going to get that girl and yourself killed, Aiden. Leave Veeda alone," Rachel chided him.

"She's my friend!" Aiden protested.

"According to Islamic Law, she is her husband's property, and I highly doubt he would approve of you being her friend."

"Well, there's nothing here, so let's get back in the truck," Christopher suggested. They kept driving while Nate operated the drone so they could look several miles off the roads—if you could call them roads—looking for villages. Rachel kept rambling on about Samir and the enslavement of the Yazidi people who used to live in the area, eventually spiraling off on several tangents to ensure Aiden was caught up on Samir Al-Abadi's full resume. It took about five minutes for Aiden to say "Oh that guy" as he realized who exactly Rachel was talking about and how many times the man had come close to killing them all, but she didn't shut up.

Christopher looked at his phone, which was connected to the truck's Bluetooth, and put on "Slow it Down for You" by The Goo Goo Dolls.

"Good song!" Rachel exclaimed.

Christopher took his eyes off the road for a second to watch her face as she listened to the song. He'd picked it on purpose. They always chose songs for each other with some sort of message or hidden meaning, some sort of inside joke.

"You'd like me to shut up about ISIS and focus on the present moment?" Rachel scrunched up her face.

"Among other things," Christopher chuckled.

Rachel looked down at her hands. "You really would, wouldn't you?"

"What?"

"Slow down the whole world for me and help me get back control of all the chaos?"

"Always." Christopher smiled.

"I wish you lived closer to me," Rachel said sadly.

"What? Are you ever even home?" Christopher was a bit taken aback.

Rachel shrugged. "You know what I mean."

"I'm not sure I do." He furrowed his brow and glanced over at her, not wanting to take his eyes off the road but also wanting to assess her mental state.

"Just move to Florida so we can hang out all the time and do cool stuff like this!"

"You don't see me enough?" He raised an eyebrow at her.

"No." Rachel shook her head vigorously, trying to make her point.

"I'm not moving to Florida, or anywhere," Christopher told her.

"Why the hell not? We'd have so much fun!"

"Why would I move and then have to pay rent? I live on my parent's property more or less for free!"

"Then move in with me!" Rachel actually sounded serious.

"Why don't you move to Texas if you want to be closer to me all the time?" He gave her a sideways glance, trying to figure out how serious she was being.

Rachel grimaced. "I don't think you live next to the ocean."

"There's a lake."

"Not the same."

"I guess we'll have to keep getting on planes to see each other and do fun, crazy shit then," Christopher teased.

Rachel pouted at his dismissal of her idea, then she saw what Aiden was doing. She snatched her phone back from him but wasn't fast enough. He'd already added Veeda's cellphone number to his contact list and had likely committed it to memory.

"By the way, Sky, if you move to Texas, you'll be closer to me, too," Aiden pointed out.

"Yeah, I'm very certain there's no ocean in Oklahoma." Rachel cringed.

Christopher decided to ignore them both and turned up the music. As the team's navigator, he was deciding where they went. But even he had to admit they were driving aimlessly, looking for a needle in a haystack. Or one young woman in a village that may or may not be anywhere near where they were driving.

They finally came to a village and jumped out of the truck to wander around. They quickly came upon ten Americans running a school and medical clinic, and Rachel was convinced they were finally in the right place. Matt promised to return with boxes of medical supplies. Rachel promised to track down paper, pens, and anything else that could be used in the school and deliver it to them on their next pass through the village.

Rachel and Christopher made the rounds, talking to the aid workers, talking to some of the girls at the school and their parents. She was happy to see that the general population wasn't necessarily embracing the idea of limiting girl's education and women's rights, even if it was being done to them anyway.

"We are so happy to have these people here," a man told them in Arabic. "I want my daughter to know how to read, to be able to add numbers. These are important skills."

The man's wife nodded. "I would give my life so that my daughter could keep this. Playing with other children in a safe environment, meeting people from another culture—that is everything. Reading and math are good too, sure, but this—what these women and men are doing, learning our culture and teaching us theirs—this is how we heal. All of us. This is how we will prevent the next war, assuming this one ever ends."

"It will end," Rachel assured her. "I will end it, or I'll die trying."

The man had a soft smile on his lips.

"Do you know who is funding the school?" Rachel asked.

"It is some organization, I'm not sure. American." He shrugged. "But mostly we must thank a man called Ammar Al-Abadi for fighting to keep it open. It was supposed to close last fall, but he gave some money," the man told her.

"Where do I find him?"

"Oh, he is not here so often. His wife is, though. She is very involved with the school. Good people, good family." He nodded.

"Maybe I could talk to his wife? Just to express my appreciation," Rachel asked, even though both she and Christopher knew Veeda was his wife and that she had to be around somewhere.

"She comes here sometimes, or is in the shops."

Rachel nodded and thanked them for the information. She took several paces away from them and pulled out her phone.

Skylark to Veeda: *Where are you? I found the school.*

Just then, Rachel saw a young woman wearing a bright red scarf over her hair come out of the medical clinic.

"Hey!" Aiden called out to her in Pashto. Rachel's eyes darted to him, and she made her way across the street to where he was standing. Veeda was walking toward him too.

Veeda greeted them both and then switched to Arabic as she introduced them to the medical staff at the clinic, as well as a few of the teachers at the school.

Rachel switched back to Pashto, realizing that her team and Veeda were likely the only ones in the village who could speak it. "How is this possible? How is your husband, a member of the Islamic State, funding a school that lets girls attend?" Rachel asked seriously.

Veeda shrugged. "Something about small changes, getting people on his side. I don't know."

"Give the people something small they want so he can get them on board with something big, and then he'll take away the small thing once they are." Rachel pursed her lips. "That's what I would do."

"I told my husband girls could be more dutiful wives if they were able to read the Quran for themselves and that knowing math will make them better cooks and that it was very important to me. As long as I appear to be a dutiful wife and daughter, the school will remain open." She puffed out her chest and stood tall, proud of her achievement.

"Then you'd better not be talking to Aiden, or any of the guys, unsupervised," Rachel reminded her. "Now about Samir . . ."

"What about Samir?" Veeda asked.

"Keep me updated on where he is, please."

"So you can make him disappear?" Veeda teased with a wry smile.

Aiden laughed, causing Veeda to light up as she made eye contact with him. "Honestly, Rachel, I never know where he is until he's standing right in front of me. They never tell me anything. Besides, they all speak Arabic all the time. Everyone in this place speaks Arabic. Which I can, but not as well, you know? It's like being a child all over again. I can understand the words but not always what people mean."

Rachel and Aiden both nodded. "How many people here speak Pashto?" Aiden asked her.

"Basically no one," Veeda pouted, confirming Rachel's earlier assumption.

"Cool, so we have our own secret code." Aiden grinned and gave her a wink.

"People can see you." Rachel reminded them. "Veeda will get in a lot of trouble if anyone tells her husband she's behaving inappropriately with other men."

"I'm not worried, Rachel," Veeda said nonchalantly.

"See, not a problem." Aiden's grin grew wider.

"This is exactly why I don't have children," Rachel muttered.

"Why?" Veeda asked.

"Because I'm too busy looking out for all of you!" Rachel chided. "You are an intelligence asset, Veeda. You are very important, essential even, to finding all of these terrible people. On top of that, you're my friend and I want you to be safe."

"Is Aiden essential?" Veeda asked playfully.

"Yes," Rachel replied shortly.

Chapter 30:

FEBRUARY 2019

AFTER A FEW DAYS on base to resupply, Indigo loaded their truck with school and medical supplies, along with their regular gear, and headed back to the village.

"We brought supplies for the school and medical clinic," Rachel told Cara, the head teacher, the second she'd jumped out of the truck.

One of the other teachers, Rae, was with her and started unpacking the boxes immediately. "This is all great, Rachel! Exactly what we needed!" Her dark eyes lit up as she cheered.

"We have a request for Band-Aids," Matt said, walking up to Rachel with a woman named Karima.

"Band-Aids?" Rachel's brow furrowed.

"Yeah, you know for like cuts and scrapes and shit."

"Oh, I don't know if we have those," Rachel told him.

"Yeah? No one falls down and gets a skinned knee ever?" Karima asked.

"If they do, they just pour some water on it and keep walking," Rachel said.

Karima laughed and shook her head. "That doesn't work with kids."

"Right." Rachel cocked her head to the side. "You're a doctor I'm guessing? I didn't meet you last time we drove through."

"Nurse," Karima corrected. "I'm technically working at the clinic, but we've found that it's more effective if I'm at the school and can see the kids in their natural environment. The medical clinic can be scary, so they get nervous, and it feels too serious and then they don't want to talk as much. At the school, it's more relaxed. Plus, I can line them all up and check for lice and ear infections and give them vaccines and all that. More efficient for me and more comfortable for the kids. Then, if I know one of the kids has an appointment at the clinic, I try to make sure I'm there for it so they have a face they're more familiar with."

"Wow, that's a fantastic approach!" Rachel commended her.

"She's teaching the kids about nutrition and hygiene too," Matt added.

"I am loving this! You're all doing such incredible work!" Rachel exclaimed. "If you need anything else, let me know and I can check if we have it on base, or if I can get it here somehow. There's a woman managing the supply warehouse, and I told her what you're all doing and she's very excited to help."

"Umm, actually." Karima's eyes flashed with a hint of embarrassment. "Feminine hygiene products would be helpful."

"Oh! Tampons, pads, menstrual cups. What do you want?" Rachel asked as Matt hurried away.

"Whatever we can get."

"Do you need condoms?"

Karima laughed. "Couldn't hurt. I guess we scared Matt away."

Rachel scrunched up her face. "No, he's not embarrassed by tampons. He probably went to get you some!" Sure enough, Matt was back a few minutes later with two boxes of tampons in hand.

"Thanks!" Karima looked at Rachel. "You don't need these?"

"No, I have an IUD. No period, all set. Those are for bloody noses," Rachel explained, pointing at the boxes.

"Yeah, you cut them in half lengthwise and stick them up a broken nose," Matt explained.

"Then you keep walking." Rachel winked.

"You're sure you don't need these?" Karima asked Matt.

"I saved a box for us. I'll bring you more on our next pass through. We've got all that stuff on base for the female staff."

"Condoms too even though no one's allowed to be sleeping together. But the nurses like to hand them out to everyone going on leave or headed home," Rachel said.

"Sort of like a congrats-you-didn't-die gift." Matt winked, and Karima burst out laughing.

Chapter 31:
APRIL 2019

RACHEL WAS UNLOADING SCHOOL and medical supplies to give to the aid workers in the village. They had been in northern Iraq for two months with no sign of Samir Al-Abadi. Everyone was getting frustrated. As soon as Rachel was out of the truck, Cara and Rae came running up to help her, with Veeda close behind them.

"He was here," Veeda said to Rachel in Pashto.

"Who?"

"Samir."

"When?"

"Yesterday, with my husband."

"He's gone now?"

"He'll be back in a few hours," Veeda explained.

"What were they doing?" Rachel asked, passing a box of paper to Cara.

"I don't know, Rachel." Veeda sighed. "Wandering around."

Rachel pulled up the photo of Samir Al-Abadi on her phone and showed it to Cara and Rae. "Did either of you two see this man yesterday?" she asked them in English.

"Yes . . ." Rae answered with a bit of hesitation.

"Just wandering around, or did you hear anything he was saying?"

"He was with Veeda's husband and a third man," Cara said. "They walked past the school around 1000 yesterday while the kids had recess. I didn't hear what they were talking about."

"Thank you!" Rachel hugged her. "If you see him again, let me know." She helped carry the remainder of the school supplies inside then went for a walk with Veeda.

Speaking Pashto so no one would understand, Rachel asked, "When will they be back today?"

"For tea this afternoon."

"At your house?"

"Yes, I will have to serve them tea," Veeda confirmed.

"Will you sit with them the entire time?"

"No. They will send me to another room so I cannot hear them."

Rachel sucked in air, her chest rising and falling with effort as she tried to think. "What if we bug your house?"

"Bugs? No, I just cleaned." Veeda looked horrified.

"No, not insects, not like that. Technology. Small listening devices so we can record what they are saying."

"You spent all fall trying to convince me you were not a spy." Veeda pouted playfully.

"Spies lie." Rachel winked and poked Veeda in the ribs, causing her to burst out laughing as they walked down the street.

"What do these things look like? How do they work?" Veeda asked.

"Not my department. Let's find Daniel and Christopher, or Aiden, because I don't think Daniel can explain it in a way we'll understand. He's very technical about things. Too smart for his own good, but we love him anyway."

Thirty minutes later, Veeda had confirmed that her home was empty. She and Rachel leaned against the front of the house, seeming to soak up the last of the afternoon sunshine while Daniel, Aiden, and Christopher were inside. Veeda had been fascinated by Daniel's gadgets. By the end of his explanation about everything, during which Christopher and Aiden took turns simplifying the more technical aspects, Veeda was begging for an earpiece and callsign of her own so she could be a spy too. Aiden debated it for a bit, finally landing on *Minivet*, a sleek black bird with red markings, like Veeda's hair and red scarf.

It took the guys forty minutes to install small listening devices throughout Veeda's home and connect them to a receiver, which was plugged into a recording device and left in a drawer under Veeda's clothes. Daniel made sure it had a memory card that could store the recordings for eighteen hours of audio, showed Veeda how to turn the device on and off, and remove the memory card. Then they all left, hoping for the best.

Veeda found Rachel at the medical clinic the next day where she and Matt were helping take inventory of their supplies.

"There were three of them," Veeda blurted out in Pashto as soon as she saw Rachel.

"Three of who?" Rachel asked, writing something down on her clipboard then passing it off to Matt.

"My husband, Samir, and another man."

Rachel glanced around casually, then reached out her hand for the memory card. "Who was the third man?"

"I do not know him," Veeda said. "Aquib something."

"Faizan?" Rachel asked.

"Why do you know who all these people are?" Veeda furrowed her brow.

"It's my job." Rachel shrugged. "Did you hear anything they were saying?"

"Not much past hellos and how's your family," Veeda admitted.

"Thank you for this." Rachel held up the memory card. "Can I give you another one?"

"I suppose."

"You can turn it on while they're there, or you can have it on all the time.

It's up to you. Then find me and I'll give you a new memory card whenever you need one."

"Okay." Veeda grinned. "I really am a spy now! Zarah would be so proud of me!"

"You're doing great, Veeda."

"What is your plan though?"

"What do you mean?" Rachel cocked her head to the side.

"You wanted to make these men disappear."

"I need to make sure they aren't planning anything first, that no one is in danger, then we'll detain them."

"And then?" Veeda raised an eyebrow.

"And then we'll talk to them."

"And kill them," Veeda whispered like a child conspiring to sneak into their parent's room, looking for their Christmas presents.

Rachel pressed her lips into a tight line. "The less you know, the safer you'll be."

"Safe from what?"

"If they find out you're helping us—"

Veeda cut her off. "I don't care, Rachel If they kill me . . . What am I doing anyway? Cooking and cleaning. I have no life here, not really any friends. The teachers and doctors, I like them, but they'll all go home eventually. Maybe new people will come, but you'll all go back home and I'll be here." She looked at the ground as a wave of sadness washed over her face. "I wish . . . I wish I'd had more time in Khost. Maybe . . . maybe I should have left with Pari when you helped her. Maybe I should have—" She stopped talking abruptly when Aiden appeared in the doorway. "If only we'd had more time."

Rachel winced and looked at the floor. "You really like him, don't you?"

"How could anyone not?" Veeda said sadly.

The next day, Daniel was reviewing everything he'd listened to with Rachel and Christopher. They didn't have much to go on, but Samir Al-Abadi and

Aquib Faizan had both been at Veeda's home for several hours. They had to agree with Veeda, though. The men spoke about everything and nothing.

"Is it some sort of code?" Daniel guessed.

"No, we just don't have the context," Rachel said.

"What do they mean by 'making improvements to help our brothers and sisters?' That could be anything." Christopher wrinkled his nose as he summarized the recorded conversation between Samir and Aquib.

"Do they mean the school and clinic?" Daniel asked.

"Doubtful." Rachel sighed.

"Samir seems very calm and rational," Daniel commented.

"He always is," Rachel nodded.

"Aquib Faizan being there, being here, worries me," Christopher said

"Because we have a school full of girls and several American women in this village and he's known for human trafficking?" Rachel cocked her head to the side.

"Precisely." Cristopher frowned.

"Hey Rachel, how do you know so much about this guy anyway?" Daniel asked.

"Seeing as tracking them is our jobs, I think the better question is why don't you know more about them?" Rachel deflected. "It's not a good situation, but Cara and Rae and Karima . . . none of them will leave the village. The school and the clinic are their passion."

"What do we do?" Christopher asked.

"We poke the hornet's nest."

Rachel charged out of the room with Christopher and Daniel trailing after her. She made her way through the streets until she found Cara and Rae at the school, locking up for the day. "Do either of you have lipstick?" Rachel asked them.

"Why?" Cara furrowed her brow.

"Don't worry about it." Rachel laughed quietly to herself.

"I think Karima has lipstick." Rae wandered off to check.

"Did you see that man I asked about again today by any chance?" Rachel asked Cara.

"Yeah, he was walking on the street that parallels the main road. I saw him when I was on my break and followed him. Let me show you." She led Rachel through the village, past rows of tiny houses, then stopped outside a small brick building.

"Do you know what this building is?" Rachel asked, staring at it. She wrinkled her nose with confusion. There weren't any signs, no markings, nothing to indicate what it was for.

"This is where the power generator is. See the solar panels on top?" Christopher pointed at the roof. "This village isn't on the national power grid. They just have this small local power plant," Christopher explained.

"Hmm . . . Not sure I want Sammy playing with the electricity."

"Sammy?" Christopher raised an eyebrow. "You gave him a nickname?"

"Don't worry about it." Rachel waved her hand casually in the air, hoping he'd drop the subject. She walked back to the school where Rae was waiting with a tube of bright red lipstick. She had Cara unlock the school so she could get a paper and pen then wrote a note.

Dearest Samir,
You know I'm looking for you, and you know I'm close. Hide and seek is over. Tag, you're it! XO Skylark.

She put the lipstick on and kissed the paper right next to her name, then pulled a small vial of jasmine oil out of her pocket and shook out a drop of the oil onto the paper.

"What the hell are you doing?" Christopher grimaced.

"Just leaving a note for my friend." Rachel winked and quickly folded the paper in half, then wrote Samir's name on it so he would know it was for him. She found some tape and marched back to the building containing the power generator and taped her note to the door.

"Provoking terrorists again, are we?" Christopher teased. This was definitely not the first time she'd done something like this.

"We need to draw him out. From the recording, it doesn't seem like they have anything planned that's an immediate threat. Nothing we need to monitor and get details on, so we need to just get *him*."

"Risky," Christopher noted.

"Worth it." Rachel grinned.

Chapter 32:
APRIL 2019

INDIGO HAD BEEN BACK on base for two days resupplying and enjoying sleeping on cots in the barracks rather than the ground camped several miles outside Veeda's village. No one was convinced the cots were better, but it was nice to have a bit of variation. Christopher was shaken awake suddenly. He blinked his eyes open to see Aiden's face, full of panic, right in his.

"What do you want?" Christopher mumbled.

"Veeda's missing," Aiden whispered.

"What?" Christopher was too tired to have any idea what Aiden was talking about.

"She's not answering her phone and she didn't meet me."

"Meet you?" Christopher practically yelled.

"Shh!" Aiden hissed and covered Christopher's mouth. "Do not wake up Sky."

Christopher turned his head to the side and saw that Rachel was in fact asleep on the cot next to him. She rarely slept, and when she did, they all did their best to avoid waking her. This, however, was not a situation Christopher wanted to be in charge of. He hit Aiden on the arm and gestured toward the door before getting up to follow Aiden outside. "What do you mean, she didn't meet you?" Christopher asked again, once they were alone.

"Umm, yeah, so I've been meeting up with her at night. The nights her husband isn't there."

"For fucks sake." Christopher looked at the ground and crossed his arms over his chest. "Promise me you aren't sleeping with her."

"No!" Aiden seemed horrified by the idea. "I'm not an idiot, Chris. Don't get me wrong, I'd love to sleep with Veeda, but I have not and I will not."

"For some reason, I don't believe you." Christopher scrubbed his hands over his face, trying to fully wake up.

"Okay, well, not really the point. The point is that she's now missing, which is why I got you. You know, since you're the tracker."

"No, you got me because you know Rachel would fucking kill you if she knew you'd been sneaking off to meet up with Veeda."

"Well . . ." Aiden's eyes were fixated on the toe of his boot.

Christopher sighed. "She didn't meet you, she's not answering her phone. Is her phone off?"

"Yes."

"Where were you supposed to meet her?"

"One kilometer outside her village."

"Have you been taking the truck in the middle of the night?" Christopher glared at him.

"Not our truck. I know how obsessive you are about the odometer, so I've been taking a different truck." Aiden pursed his lips and averted his eyes.

Christopher stared at Aiden, unblinking, with his hands on his hips. "So, you knew you were doing something you shouldn't be doing."

"She's my friend!" Aiden tried to defend himself.

"Whatever." Christopher pulled up a map of the area on his phone. "Show me exactly where you were supposed to meet her."

Aiden took the phone and zoomed in on the map. Christopher looked at it and sighed. "You drove all the way there, waited for her, then came all the way back here to get me?"

Aiden nodded.

"So, she's been missing for at least . . ."

"Ninety minutes," Aiden finished for him.

"Go wake up Daniel. I need him to run a trace on her phone and see where it was the last time it was turned on."

Aiden sprinted inside the barracks to Daniel's cot, and Christopher leaned against the wall. He knew if Veeda's husband even suspected she'd been talking to Aiden, let alone meeting up with him in the middle of the night or recording his conversations with his uncle, that she was probably already dead, and if she wasn't, she would be soon. That was the most likely scenario. Or her husband had come home, in which case she couldn't sneak out. Or her husband had taken her somewhere. They had no authority to meddle in Veeda's marriage, even if they all wanted to. He took a deep breath and went back inside.

Daniel was sitting cross-legged on his cot with his laptop balanced on his knees, typing away. It took a few minutes to trace Veeda's phone. "Last place her phone was on was a few blocks from her house," he whispered to Christopher.

"Can you turn it on remotely?" Christopher asked hopefully.

"I can try," Daniel muttered.

"We need to go to the village," Aiden pleaded.

"If you were just there, why didn't you go into the village and check on her?" Christopher asked.

"I'm gonna just show up at her house in the middle of the night? I'm not stupid or suicidal," Aiden insisted.

"I'm not so sure." Christopher gave him a sideways glance, spurring Daniel into a fit of laughter.

"Shut the fuck up before you wake up Sky!" Aiden whispered.

"Because you know she'll murder you for hanging out with Veeda?" Daniel teased.

"This is taking too long," Aiden complained.

"Alright, we'll get in the truck and head over there, just the three of us. We'll keep working on getting her phone back on while we're driving," Christopher decided. He walked over to his cot and quickly got dressed while

Daniel did the same.

"Just the three of us?" Daniel glanced back at the barracks as they walked to the team's truck.

"I'd really rather not have Rachel murder Aiden." Christopher wrinkled his nose. "For all we know, Veeda is safe in her bed with her husband. Until we know there is actually a problem, I'd rather not make this a problem." Christopher got into the driver's seat, with Aiden riding shotgun and Daniel in the backseat, working furiously on his laptop.

"God, I wish Hall was here," Christopher sighed.

"Hall?" Daniel asked.

"Lux, Team Onyx," Christopher clarified.

"What's the problem, Hawk? You don't know how to do recon?" Daniel teased.

"Not nearly as well as Lux," Christopher admitted begrudgingly. Luke Hall, aka Lux, had gone through SEAL training with him and Rachel and was hands down the best reconnaissance specialist in the entire U.S. military.

"You're sure they aren't in country?" Daniel asked.

"Yeah, Skylark and I just saw him in San Francisco when we got back from Khost. They're on leave."

They got to the location where Aiden typically met Veeda and got out of the truck, immediately clicking on flashlights to search the area.

"Tire tracks," Christopher noted.

"Yeah, that's from my truck earlier," Aiden confirmed. "Veeda usually walks up the path over there." He pointed to a narrow footpath leading back to the village.

Christopher led the way down the path, sweeping his flashlight to look for footprints, blood, or anything else that would indicate someone had been there recently. There was nothing. They worked their way down the path and through the village to Veeda's home. Christopher looked around, flashlight in hand. The door had been left slightly ajar. He pointed at it, and they all unclipped their night vision goggles from their belts and put them on before going inside.

"Holy fuck." Christopher barely got enough air into his lungs to say the words as he looked around Veeda's living room. The dark, chocolate syrup-like puddles on the floor told him plenty. Only blood looked like chocolate syrup through the gray-green of night vision goggles.

"Do we know whose blood this is?" Daniel asked curiously.

"Veeda's, I'm assuming," Christopher told him.

Aiden looked nauseous.

Daniel nodded and they got to searching, careful not to step in any of the blood. "Hawk?" he called to Christopher from a back room. Christopher walked to him, and Daniel pointed at a safe sitting on the floor.

Christopher knelt down, and got to work cracking it while Daniel searched the rest of the house and Aiden paced back and forth impatiently. Twelve minutes later, the door on the safe popped open. They knew each other so well they didn't need to ask for help. They knew who was best at what. Christopher reached in and pulled a stack of files out. He flipped through the documents, handing half to Aiden so he could do the same. "I've got maps, locations, photos of a compound," Christopher said.

"Guys." Daniel came back into the room. "Two things. First, the recording device is still in place. Or was. It's now in my pocket. Second, I've got some interesting reading material here." He held up a spiral-bound book.

"What is it?" Christopher asked, reaching out his hand to take it.

"It's like a journal or project management notebook, manifesto sort of thing. It explains all about tolerating the aid workers, getting Americans here that they could kidnap and use as leverage."

"I hate it when we're right about this shit," Christopher grumbled.

After a thorough search of Veeda's home, Christopher, Daniel, and Aiden went to the house where the aid workers had been staying. They made their way through the house quickly. There was no sign of forced entry or any sort of struggle. The house was empty, other than a white envelope on Cara's pillow that was addressed to Skylark. None of the aid workers knew their call signs, they'd only used first names. But someone knew Skylark.

"Fuck." Christopher dropped his head into his palm. "Trace their cell phones," he ordered Daniel.

"I got Cara's phone to turn on," Daniel told him fifteen minutes later, holding up a tablet that showed a map and a small red flashing dot.

"What about Veeda?" Aiden asked.

"We have a duty to rescue the Americans, not Veeda," Christopher said bluntly. As SEALs, their duty was always to help the Americans first, but Christopher hoped desperately that they would be able to save Veeda too, if she wasn't already dead. From the looks of her house, she very well might be, and was likely wishing she were.

"But–" Aiden started to protest.

Christopher cut him off. "But we'll save her too, if we can. We all care about Veeda, Aiden." He moved to look at Daniel's screen.

"I should have married her," Aiden murmured.

"Excuse me?" Christopher glared at him.

"In Khost, when I met her. I should have taken her home and married her."

"You'd known her for a day. You spoke to her once," Christopher reminded him.

"Once is all it takes, apparently," Aiden said sadly.

"For what?" Daniel glanced up from his screen to look at Aiden.

"To know you've found the girl of your dreams."

Daniel scoffed at Aiden's starry-eyed expression and turned back to his screen. Christopher pinched the bridge of his nose and looked at his feet.

"They were moving, but now it looks like they've stopped," Daniel explained, pointing to his screen.

"Then we have GPS coordinates," Christopher concluded as he studied the screen for a minute. "Time to wake up the rest of the team."

Forty minutes later, Rachel marched into the house where the aid workers had been staying, with the rest of Indigo right behind her. Nate had the drone in the air, headed for the location Cara's phone was pinging from.

"Hawk, I see the compound," Nate told Christopher, tilting the remote for the drone so he could see the screen. "It looks pretty big. There's an open courtyard and . . . Fuck! We've got action," he confirmed. "Can't see Cara or anyone, but definitely plenty of insurgents."

"You found them?" Rachel asked.

"We think so," Christopher said. "We've got an enemy compound in any case, and Cara's phone is pinging from there."

"What about Veeda?" Rachel asked.

"We don't have eyes on any of them," Christopher told her.

Rachel walked over to look at the screen with Christopher and Daniel and saw the red dot that indicated Cara's phone was on and broadcasting a signal, then turned her attention to the screen for the drone. "This compound is this dot?" Rachel asked, pointing back and forth between the screens.

"Yeah. Eyes on the compound and insurgent activity. No sign of the hostages, but that's where Cara's phone is currently, so it's an educated guess that they're there," Christopher confirmed.

"We can't just go hit a compound," Rachel pointed out.

"I know." Christopher crossed his arms over his chest. He knew Rachel was right. They were looking for Samir and would compromise their entire mission if they hit an enemy compound without provocation. They needed eyes on Samir Al-Abadi or one of the aid workers. Eyes on Veeda wouldn't even be enough. Cara's cell phone pinging from there was a good indication, but they couldn't confirm that she was there, only that her phone was.

"We need to show you something," Christopher told her. He led her upstairs to Cara's room where the crisp white envelope addressed to Skylark was waiting for her.

"Interesting." Rachel pouted her lips and walked toward the bed. She picked up the envelop from Cara's pillow and opened it. There was a USB stick inside. "Wouldn't it be nice if this was the damned malware code we've been looking for?" Rachel held it up for Christopher to see.

"You're delusional if you think someone just returned the malware code to us." Christopher furrowed his brow.

"Well, who has a computer with them so we can see what the fuck this is?" Rachel asked.

"Give it to Daniel," Christopher said.

Rachel made her way downstairs and handed Daniel the USB stick. He popped it into a laptop and opened the file. It was a video.

"Anyone who doesn't feel compelled to watch a mystery video, go in another room please. We have no idea what's on here, but I'm guessing it's not porn," Rachel ordered.

Everyone laughed and most of the men went upstairs or into the kitchen, knowing ISIS had a bad habit of filming beheadings, among other horrific things. Aiden stood in the corner where he could listen but not see.

"You good?" Daniel asked, pointing at the laptop. Rachel knew he had no desire to watch the mystery video if he didn't have to.

Daniel left the room, but Christopher and Ryan joined her, standing on either side of her. Rachel pressed play and a man about her age, with dark hair and a beard covering a sturdy jawline, came onto the screen. She immediately recognized Samir's full lips, straight nose, and oval face—and that damned purple and black checkered scarf that Rachel knew had been purchased at a market in Basrah, Iraq in February 2008. She didn't know if he always wore it because he actually liked it or if it was just to fuck with her. He likely wondered the same about her scenting her note to him with jasmine oil.

"I have ten Americans," Samir started. "I will happily trade them for one American. One specific American. She goes by Skylark. Surely the U.S. government is more than willing to trade one person for ten? If not . . ." Samir trailed off as another man sat down beside him.

"Fuck," Christopher muttered.

"It seems we have some friends in common," Samir continued speaking. "This whore, I will not trade back to you though." The camera panned to the side, to Veeda. She was on her knees and a man stood behind her, his fist tangled in her hair. Rachel pressed pause.

"Well, I'd say that's enough provocation." Rachel smirked.

Rachel and Christopher spent the entire fifty-two minutes and seventeen seconds drive strategizing. They agreed to split their team in two, with half of them going in the front door of the compound and half of them going in the back. Or at least what they assumed was the front and back, based on what Nate could see with the drone.

"You want to take David with you?" Rachel asked Christopher

"Why?"

"So you don't blow up the entire compound and kill us all," Rachel teased.

"I would not!"

"Every time we let you play with explosives, the blast ends up being twice as large as planned."

"Better," Christopher corrected.

"No, bigger is not always better." Rachel laughed.

"Good to know," Christopher winked.

"As if that's an issue." Rachel was trying not to giggle.

"What?" Christopher's eyes were wide.

"Nothing." Rachel did her best to sound innocent.

"You're looking when we're all changing?"

"Seriously? I wake up next to you most mornings. Now, stop flirting with me and focus." Rachel rolled her eyes.

"I second that," Aiden complained. "Veeda is in danger. Cara and Rae and Karima and everyone are in danger, and you two are sitting there like . . ."

Christopher was horrified by what Rachel had said and decided it was best to ignore Aiden for the time being. "I am not flirting with you. I do *not* flirt with you, and I do *not* make explosions too big," he insisted.

"You do though."

"Which?"

"Both." Rachel's eyes darted to Aiden and she saw the corner of his lips tug up slightly.

"Whatever. I'll take David if it makes you feel better, and Ryan since you guys are best at picking locks," Christopher said.

Rachel poked him in the ribs before nodding toward Aiden. Christopher winked back, understanding that she was trying to get a rise out of him to distract Aiden.

"Good. Matt's with me then. Two officers per group."

"Right, but then our two best medics are together," Christopher pointed out.

"Hence why you and I are usually together, and Matt and Ryan are usually together," Rachel reminded him.

"But you and I are best at dealing with hostages, so it's better to split us up so when we find them we can keep them calm. Fuck, you just had to leave that note and provoke Samir!" Rachel's comments may have been in jest, but Christopher's irritation at the entire situation was real.

Chapter 33:
APRIL 2019

THEY PARKED TWO KILOMETERS from the compound, where they suspected the aid workers were being held. Nate got their drone back in the air after bringing it down to replace the battery, then sketched out a quick map of the compound.

"We're good to go, Skylark," Nate told her. Daniel and Aiden nodded in agreement that all of their tech and comms equipment were working properly.

Christopher led the way toward their destination on foot, with Rachel and the rest of Indigo right behind him, moving at a quick pace but not running, knowing they needed to stay alert and conserve energy for the coming firefight. Daniel was right next to her, a recording device in hand. He was rewinding and fast-forwarding the tape, and Rachel listened to all the key parts of what had been said in Veeda's home before they got there.

"She fought back." Rachel frowned.

"She fought like hell, it sounds like. And from the look of the place . . ." Daniel let out a low whistle. "I've listened to most of it. She didn't say anything about you or us or the recordings. She had several choice words for her husband and Samir though."

"I really hope she's not already dead," Rachel murmured. Daniel put his hand on her shoulder to comfort her, even if they both knew there was no point.

Rachel led her group to the front of the compound and stopped outside a black door. For a front entrance, it was smaller than she was expecting, but whatever. She heard the crackle of static in her ear and adjusted her earpiece.

"Did someone say something?" Rachel asked. There was no response, and the five men behind her all shook their heads. "Okay. Who's got my explosives?" Rachel asked.

Brendon ran forward, handing her a small bomb just big enough to blast the door to the compound open, but not big enough that anyone could get hurt. She attached the bomb to the door before lighting the fuse and ran a hundred feet back to where everyone else was waiting. Rachel was inside the compound seconds after the lock shattered, instantly opening fire on anyone and everyone she could see. Her assault rifle sang loud above the shouts and screams. Matt, Michael, Aiden, Jason, and Brendon fell in line behind her as she skillfully made her way through the compound in search of the hostages. As they rounded a corner into an open courtyard, fifteen insurgents rushed them, firing at her group.

"Fucking hell," Rachel muttered.

"Skylark, what's happening?" Christopher asked.

"We're taking fire. In the courtyard," Rachel yelled over the pops and cracks of the assault rifles reverberating off of the surrounding walls.

"How the fuck are you already in the courtyard? You're fast, but you aren't *that* fast," Christopher shouted back.

"What?" Rachel asked. "We went through the door Crane said and the fucking courtyard was right here."

Christopher sighed. "You went through the wrong door, Sky."

"Fuck." Rachel pressed her back against the wall as bullets flew everywhere. She signaled to her men to do the same.

"Did you turn the screen upside down?" Christopher asked.

"Not sure this is the time for teasing, Hawk. Besides, I wasn't holding the damned screen."

"Fuck. Crane, did you have the video right side up from her side or from yours?"

"From mine," Nate said. "North, south, east, and west were all clearly marked."

"Well then I know what went wrong, and I know exactly where you are, Sky," Christopher told her. "We're coming up from the side of the courtyard, diagonal from you. Advancing toward you now. Hang tight."

He always turned maps and screens so it was right-side up from Rachel's viewpoint, since he knew she had a hard time flipping the map around in her mind.

"Copy that," Rachel said. She signaled to the men behind her to move back. It was no use though. The enemy was advancing quickly, and they didn't have good cover. Christopher needed to move the other half of their team quicker. She waited as seconds faded to minutes and listened as bullets ricocheted off the walls.

"Sky, we see the courtyard. Engaging now." Christopher's voice caused her to let out a sigh of relief. She peered around the corner and watched as the insurgents turned and refocused their attention on Christopher's group.

"Fuck," Rachel muttered. They had the enemy surrounded but somehow still didn't have the upper hand. If there was ever a time for a miracle or any sort of divine intervention, this would be it.

"Hawk, fall back for a minute. I'm gonna do something," Rachel said.

"What?" Christopher asked.

"We've got two grenades, and it looks like we only have hostiles in the courtyard. Can you confirm from your viewpoint?"

"Affirmative. Hostiles only."

Brendon and Jason both took the grenades out of their pockets and passed them up the line. Rachel pulled the pin of the first and threw it toward the insurgents before quickly doing the same with the second grenade. It helped, but not enough.

"Go ahead and reengage. Repeat, Hawk, you're clear to engage."

"Looks like you got a couple, Sky. Thanks!" Christopher laughed.

"Yeah, not enough. I didn't have a good angle," Rachel complained. She focused on her breathing, peering around the corner periodically. Waiting for an opening, a break in the fire so she could shoot back.

"Hold fire. Hold fire!" Nate shouted over comms as Rachel saw what he must be seeing on the drone. A group of men were leading Veeda out of a building on the other side of the courtyard, dragging her by her hair as she struggled to get away.

"We need to move, Sky," Aiden yelled to her.

"Stay put, Blackbird."

"We need to get to Veeda," Aiden argued.

"Hawk, do you see what we see?" Rachel asked.

"We see her," Christopher confirmed.

"Daniel, any way to call Cara's phone and patch me through to whomever answers?"

"Sure," Daniel said hesitantly.

She waited as the phone rang. And rang. Until finally Rachel heard the click of someone coming through on the other end.

"You have ten of my people, plus Veeda," Rachel said in Arabic, not waiting for the person to speak. Her voice had dropped in pitch and morphed into a cold, menacing tone that was devoid of her typical Southern charm—completely unrecognizable as her own. "Tell everyone to drop their weapons, and we'll make the trade. Me for them."

"Who are you?" It was a man's voice that came through on the other line.

"Skylark. Samir wants me. Where is he?"

The man laughed. "You think Samir Al-Abadi would disgrace himself by being in the presence of such filth?"

"Wouldn't be the first time. Where is he?"

"Not here."

"Where are the ten Americans?"

"They're safe . . . for now."

"Sky," Aiden interrupted, though his eyes were not on Rachel. They were trained across the courtyard, where the men were forcing Veeda to her knees.

Sensing his next move, Rachel stretched out her arm and shoved Aiden's back up against the wall. She held her grip on him, keeping her forearm braced against his chest, despite his struggling. She gritted her teeth, stuck between a blackbird and a terrorist.

"I don't typically negotiate," Rachel turned her attention back to the phone call. "But since my presence was specifically requested, I felt sort of special. Made me curious. What exactly does Samir want me for?"

"What the fuck do you think?" Rachel heard Christopher mutter through her earpiece.

"Samir's a good guy. He wouldn't hurt me," Rachel insisted.

"He will force you to your knees and teach you your place, you filthy whore," the man yelled at her.

"He won't. Now, why don't you let Veeda go. My men can take her home, and you and I can hang out and wait for Samir to get here."

"She, too, is a filthy whore. Associating with Americans. Speaking with men, lying to her husband. Refusing to lie with her husband."

"Oh, she's not that bad. Just a dumb girl. I'm sure she didn't mean it," Rachel tried to negotiate.

"She's a fucking angel," Aiden yelled, clearly not liking Rachel's characterization of Veeda as dumb.

Rachel used her entire body to shove Aiden against the wall again then glanced down the line of men behind her, wondering why none of them were helping her detain him.

"She has disgraced her family."

"Where are the Americans?" Rachel yelled, trying a different tactic.

"Crane to Sky and Hawk," Nate said through the earpiece. "I think the hostages are in a room in the building across the courtyard from Skylark and to the left of Hawk's group. According to my thermal scanner, there's a group of people in there. Whether it's the hostages or more insurgents, I can't say–"

Before he'd even finished his sentence, another man had come up behind Veeda, knife in hand. It looked more like a machete really, and Rachel knew instantly what was coming. The men forced Veeda's head forward. Rachel's eyes darted from Veeda to the other side of the courtyard where the hostages might be. She lost focus just long enough for Aiden to shove past her, his rifle raised and aimed at the man seemingly intent on killing Veeda. He pulled the trigger and everything in Rachel's view slowed down. The man standing behind Veeda crumpled to the ground. There were screams of pain. The sound of bullets leaving chambers, and then ricocheting off the walls.

She looked to Aiden, who was rushing straight toward Veeda, then across the courtyard to where Nate thought the hostages were. In that split second, she was torn between duty and what she knew was right. She wanted to help Veeda, but if she chose Veeda over the aid workers and something happened to any of the Americans, it would be an unforgivable black mark on her service record. It would be just the sort of excuse Leftwich needed to get rid of her once and for all. She took one last look at Veeda. The girl was beaten to a pulp, caked in blood, struggling to breathe. Not from fear, but from pain. Debilitating pain. They'd need a medivac to get her back to safety, and based on the injuries Rachel could see, it didn't look promising.

One life for ten, she thought to herself. Veeda's life for the ten American hostages.

Fine.

But Samir wasn't here. The men here didn't want to trade.

One life for ten.

Everything came back into focus. There wasn't any more time to think, to rationalize. Bullets were flying everywhere. Rachel took a deep breath and sprinted across the courtyard in the direction they suspected the aid workers were. Her finger was securely pressed down on the trigger, taking down insurgent after insurgent on her way, trying to get them away from Veeda and Aiden. Trying to clear a path forward for herself. She listened to the ricochet of bullets off the walls as her eyes scanned ahead of her for danger—and for Christopher. Suddenly she saw him in the hallway in front of her, on one knee, rifle raised.

"Run, Sky. I've got you covered," Christopher assured her.

She took her finger off the trigger and sprinted towards him. Within seconds, she was kneeling on one knee right beside him trying to catch her breath.

"Blackbird's hit! Man down, man down," Matt yelled over comms minutes later.

Fucking hell, Aiden. Rachel's head swiveled towards the courtyard. It was chaos. She couldn't see Aiden or Matt—or Veeda. She squeezed her eyes shut as her throat tightened, forcing her fear and concern away. She considered turning back but knew she had to push forward. She couldn't think about Aiden or Veeda now. Matt would save them if he could. She pushed away her emotions and refocused on what she could do. What she did have control over. She let the sound of assault rifles ringing out all around her drown out Matt's voice. Christopher's hand on her arm brought her back to the present moment. They locked eyes, and she saw he was as concerned as she was.

Rachel covered the microphone on her earpiece and looked Christopher dead in the eye. "We have to keep moving," she said quietly. "No time for emotions." He nodded. They opened door after door, checking and searching. The echo of gunfire from the courtyard was continuous. They kept going from room to room until they had finished the first floor. Then took a narrow staircase down into a dimly lit basement. *Pop, crack, pop.* Rachel fired, killing three men within seconds. She'd only fired three shots, but the echoes off the sandstone walls made it sound like more.

Christopher was in the doorway right behind her. The smoke from Rachel's rifle hung in the air, but he saw ten people, seven women and three men all in their late twenties to early forties, arms and legs bound, sitting and kneeling on the concrete floor. They all looked exhausted.

"We have the hostages," Christopher announced to the rest of the SEALs.

Rachel was already moving, her rifle hanging at her side as she worked to untie them. "You're safe, we've got you, you're going home," she kept assuring them, looking each of them in the eye, making sure they felt seen and heard and safe.

"Rachel, we're okay," Cara assured her.

"Are any of you hurt?" Christopher asked, very positive that none of them were okay.

"We're good," Karima assured them. "Just scared and a little shook up."

"Okay. We'll get you out of here as soon as it's safe to move you," Rachel told them, not believing them for a second. They seemed unharmed at least, other than bumps and bruises and chafing from the ropes and zip ties binding them.

Rachel got up and walked to guard the doorway, leaving Christopher sitting on the floor with everyone else. He had a unique ability to calm people down in even the most chaotic of situations, an ability which he could turn on and off at will. "Hostages are good. Let us know when we're clear to move," Rachel said over comms. There was no way she was going to move them until the firefight in the courtyard was over. It was too risky, and she didn't want them to have to see the carnage. They had practiced this routine, her guarding the door and him changing the energy—the vibe—of a room too many times to count. They knew each other's strengths and weaknesses and rarely needed to actually discuss or plan a course of action. She put her fingers up to her earpiece and sighed. "Skylark to Crane, do you copy?"

"Copy, Sky," Nate replied.

"Do you mind getting on the phone with someone to get us and evac out of here? I'm sort of busy."

Nate chuckled. "I'm on it. You focus on guarding the hostages."

"Will do," Rachel said, trying to keep her tone light since she knew the aid workers could all hear her.

Christopher was sitting on the floor across from Cara, speaking to the ten aid workers calmly and softly, explaining to them where they were, what day it was, and what was going on outside. He outlined the plan to get them out of the compound and back home to safety, urging them to take deep breaths as he passed around his and Rachel's canteens of water. Rae was panicking that no one would be in the village to run the school. Christopher assured her they could get someone from the base to take care of it and that they'd be able to go back to the village, if they really wanted to, after a quick trip back to the U.S. He knew it was a lie. There was no way any NGO was sending anyone here. Not for a long while anyway.

Ten minutes later, they heard Ryan on comms. "Fight's over. You're good to move the hostages, Skylark." He sounded dejected.

Rachel took the lead, followed by the ten aid workers, with Christopher taking up the rear. They moved slowly and deliberately back up the staircase and down the hallway. She had them line up in the hallway, their backs to the windows while she went out to check the damage. Her breath caught in her throat as she saw Veeda, dead on the ground. A knife had wounded the side of her neck. Her eyes were still wide open, staring at Aiden, who was also dead.

Fuck. Another friend dead. Another friend she couldn't save. She had chosen the Americans over Veeda. Ten people's lives for one. Ten people who weren't in immediate danger, instead of one young woman who very clearly had been. Veeda's death was on her. So was Aiden's. If she'd done more to intervene on Veeda's behalf, he wouldn't have rushed past her in an effort to save Veeda.

She walked over to Matt, who was kneeling over Aiden's lifeless body. The rest of Indigo were finishing their search of the compound to be sure they had executed all the insurgents.

"Bullet to the carotid artery," Matt told Rachel sadly as he looked up at her. "Nothing I could do. Her too, but . . . knife." He gestured toward Veeda's lifeless body.

Rachel winced, thinking about the knife piercing Veeda's delicate neck. Somehow, it was worse than Aiden getting shot. Soldiers died. Innocent young women weren't supposed to. Certainly not right in front of a team of Navy SEALs who had sworn to protect the lives of others above their own. Veeda's life had been over before they got there though. They had all known that, even if they didn't want to accept it. That's why she had stopped Aiden. She knew what was coming and she hadn't wanted Aiden to watch his friend, the girl he probably loved, get killed. Now they were both dead, and while Aiden and Veeda had both made choices that contributed to that happening, Rachel had too.

Rachel and Matt both knew a severed carotid artery wasn't fixable. Maybe in a top tier emergency room in the States if you were lucky, but not here, not while under heavy fire, not with the limited supplies they had. Rachel knelt across from Matt, Aiden lying dead between them, and put a hand on Matt's shoulder. She could tell he was trying to keep it together and maintain his composure, but what was the point? She was devastated, so why shouldn't he be? They did need to get the aid workers out though, so it wasn't time to fall apart. Not yet.

Aiden looked peaceful lying on the ground. Matt had already closed his eyes. Rachel moved the rifle hanging around Aiden's shoulder to the side and crossed his arms gently over his chest, knowing he'd be easier to carry that way, while Matt pulled a black bag out of his medic kit. The one supply in there that no one ever asked for. They never talked about that bag, never mentioned it, and always hoped they'd never have to resupply it. No luck on that one today.

"Last words?" Rachel asked, wondering if Aiden had said anything to Matt. Matt shook his head. "Quick?" Matt nodded. "Okay."

Rachel gave him a small smile, the only sign of gratitude she could manage. She bent down and lifted Aiden's upper body, one last hug staining her jacket with his blood, as Matt unzipped the bag. There was nothing to say, just things to do. Things neither of them wanted to do. She worked on autopilot beside Matt, getting Aiden's body ready for transport, as thoughts flew through her head.

It took us too long to get here, and now she's dead and so is he. Stupid guys not waking me up earlier. It should have been me. My life for theirs, Rachel scolded herself. *I should have helped Veeda first. I should have acted, then they'd both still be alive.*

"What about–" Matt glanced over at Veeda, interrupting Rachel's thoughts.

"We can't leave any DNA on her body." Rachel scrunched her eyes closed, shaking her head. "I don't know. Matt, I don't know."

"Okay, breathe." Matt held up both hands, sensing the panic in Rachel's voice. They had all come to love Veeda and see her as a friend, but Rachel had been especially close with her.

"They wouldn't have killed her without her husband and her father's permission," Rachel noted. "I . . ." She looked down. "We have to leave her. We're not even supposed to be here."

"Sky," Christopher said, walking over to her. He handed her a white envelope identical to the one they had found on Cara's pillow.

Rachel ripped it open.

> *Dearest Skylark, if you're finding this note, then you took too long to find me. I don't want any Americans other than you. I wonder who you chose to save though? Your friend or ten people you barely know? Impossible choices, especially for someone whose country was built on dreams. The hostages weren't the only thing I have that you want.*

Also in the envelope was a picture of Samir holding up a purple USB stick, a bright smile on his face. Rachel cocked her head, thinking for a minute. Something was nagging at her, as though she recognized some clue, but it wasn't making sense. They were supposed to find a green USB stick. Why would Samir be bragging about having a purple USB? Grief clouded her thinking. Grief that she had to shut down until her men and the aid workers were safely home. She put the letter and the photo back into the envelope, folded it in half, and slid it into her jacket pocket.

The SEALs called all clear, and they made their way to the extraction point where the aid workers would be airlifted home. The mood was somber as Rachel and Matt carried the black bag containing Aiden's body. No one knew what to say. Aiden had sacrificed his life in an attempt to save Veeda, and had inadvertently saved the rest of them, and they knew it.

Chapter 34:
APRIL 2019

AFTER A LONG DAY of traveling, Indigo and the ten aid workers arrived exhausted and hungry at Dam Neck Naval Base. Rachel helped get the aid workers settled in an empty warehouse where cots had been set up for them.

As she was headed back to their barracks, someone called to her. "You've got a call from HQ Commander Ryker."

Rachel nodded and followed a Petty officer to a secure room, where her boss was waiting to speak with her via video call. Clearly changing out of her blood-soaked uniform would have to wait.

"Admiral Eastwood." Rachel stood at attention.

"At ease, Ryker. You've had a long flight," Eastwood said kindly. "Just wanted to check in and see how things are going. I got your preliminary action report. You know you don't have to write those on the plane, right?".

"Didn't have much else to do, sir. Figured I may as well be productive."

"Well, as always, your team did good work," Eastwood continued.

Rachel looked at her shoes. She was tired and feeling defeated. She did not consider the mission to have gone well. Casualties happened in war, of course, but they were not something she considered to be part of a successful mission. She also knew her note to Samir had provoked him. It was her fault the hostages had been taken to begin with, and now the kids in that village—the girls—had lost their access to education and reliable health care. Her dedication to her career and the Navy had taken priority over protecting the aid workers and keeping that school and clinic open in the village. Not to mention Veeda. She'd had two competing priorities, two competing goals, and she'd made her choice. Her fear of losing her career, failing their mission, and having Admiral Leftwich rip everything away from her, everything she'd worked so hard to build, had mixed with her need to kill Samir and had blotted out her common sense.

"Also wanted to let you know you're being promoted to captain," Eastwood interrupted her thoughts. "Williams is getting promoted to commander, and Johnson to lieutenant commander. I'll let you tell them. Your new pins and insignia should be there in the base commander's office there at Dam Neck."

"I'm not sure we deserve those promotions, what with the casualty and losing an asset."

"Promotions were a long time coming," Admiral Eastwood continued. "Try not to beat yourself up, Ryker. It's war after all. Shit happens and we don't get to control everything. Your team saved ten people. Ten good, kind, and caring innocent people who were trying to help other innocent people. That's the part you focus on. That's the part you think about."

"Yes, sir," Rachel answered, still unconvinced.

"I think you'd also like to know that the Islamic State has taken credit for taking the aid workers hostage. Samir Al-Abadi personally has taken responsibility, or says his group was responsible at least. Like you thought. He also confirmed they are focusing more on cyber warfare, so that should be fun. There's a video."

"Show me the video," Rachel demanded.

Admiral Eastwood played it for her. Samir was still wearing that damned scarf, talking about the importance of a united Iraq, a united Islamic State governed by Islamic law. It was Samir's typical speech. He followed that up with a five minute soliloquy on the changing landscape of war and his pending shift to cyber warfare, warning the U.S. and the West that changes were coming. That they needed to be afraid.

Rachel listened with a stoic expression on her face, nodding along with his words. Her eyes darted around the screen, looking for any clue as to where he might be. She didn't miss the picture of a Eurasian skylark placed strategically behind Samir in the video, a detail she had no intention of pointing out to her boss. Eastwood didn't need to know the details of her history with Samir. He didn't need to know she'd provoked him on purpose, trying to draw him out, and he didn't need to know that this video had been created as a message specifically for Rachel's eyes and ears. Samir knew she was after him and was confirming that she'd been close. The video ended with Samir smiling and holding up the purple USB stick. This time, she caught a glimpse of what was written on it. Most of the text was covered by his fingers, but she saw that whatever was written on it ended with the number 84.

The call ended, and she went to the base commander's office in search of their new insignia. She didn't think they should promote her, given the fact that Aiden and Veeda had died. She didn't consider fatalities to be cause for promotions, but the Navy sure seemed to. It was like some sort of consolation prize. But it wasn't her call. The base commander had their new pins ready for her. She sent a text to Matt and Christopher, asking them to come meet her. While she waited for them, she hesitantly removed the silver oak leaf pin from her collar and replaced it with a silver spread eagle.

"Commander," Matt and Christopher said in unison as they entered the base commander's office.

"Captain," Christopher corrected, noting Rachel's new pin.

Rachel forced a proud smile onto her face. She didn't think any of them should have been promoted but knew the guys would be happy for the pay bump at least, even if she was fairly certain they weren't that proud of themselves either. Pride and fatalities didn't go together. "Commander Williams." She pinned a silver oak leaf onto Christopher's jacket. "Lieutenant Commander Johnson." A bronze oak leaf for Matt.

They thanked her and shook her hand, knowing better than to complain or make any comments in front of the base commander, before they all returned to the barracks for some much needed sleep.

Chapter 35:

APRIL 2019

RACHEL SPENT AN EXTRA day on base after sending the rest of the team home so that she could complete a stack of HR paperwork, making it official that Aiden was off the team and formally requesting he be replaced. She'd spent the rest of the day memorizing Aiden Bennet's service record. She knew it all, since they'd served together for most of his career, but she needed to have the details straight before she went to see his parents in Daisy, Oklahoma.

Crisis calls weren't officially part of her job as team leader or squadron leader, but she insisted on meeting the family of everyone killed in action under her watch. Aiden had been the first person to die on her team since she officially took over leadership. She had done this even before taking over though, as a SEAL and as an intelligence officer. And even before that, when she was a child. She had always accompanied her father when he did crisis calls, knowing that going with him would likely be her only opportunity to see him that week.

She picked up her rental car in Dallas, a blue Chevy Sedan, and drove the one hundred and seventy-four miles to Daisy, Oklahoma. It was a cute name for a town. The reason for her visit? Not so cute. Tears filled her eyes as she remembered every single crisis call she'd ever had to make. Every family she'd visited, telling them their son, daughter, spouse, father, or mother was dead. She had observed Navy chaplain after Navy chaplain try to comfort these people, trying to help them make meaning from the loss. Some were better at it than others.

Her mind flashed straight to the last crisis call she had made. Straight back to June 2014, when Commander Henry Tull, her friend and former commanding officer, had died right before her eyes. He had been team leader for Indigo and leader of their squadron when Rachel and Christopher had joined the team. She had taken over both roles from him the second the bullet went into his head and his blood spattered onto her.

Henry had been driving them through the Nangarhar Province of Afghanistan when the bullet pierced the windshield. Rachel had watched from the middle back seat as Christopher immediately took over driving, reaching across Henry's dead body to take the steering wheel, accelerator, and brake. They had all practiced driving like that before, just in case, hoping they'd never have to actually do it but knowing they probably would. Christopher had pulled the truck over, then got out. They needed to move Henry's body to the back. He thought it had been safe. But Christopher had been hit too, in the right knee. Rachel had taken multiple bullets to the right arm, and Aiden had been left in the truck, lying on the front seat, yelling into the radio at anyone who would listen, begging for help.

Rachel flexed her fingers and shook out her arm, wincing at the memory. At the time, she'd barely felt the bullets, thanks to the adrenaline. But she could feel it now. She'd been promoted that time, too, as soon as Aiden had gotten the call connected to HQ. It was by far the worst way to get promoted. Even worse than getting promoted to captain following Aiden's death.

Aiden, she thought as tears flooded her eyes. She forced herself to blink, trying to refocus on the road and the present moment—Aiden Bennet's crisis call. This wouldn't be the official crisis call, of course. A Navy chaplain had done that already before she got back to the States. But the family deserved to hear it from her, to know what really happened, or as much as she could tell them, anyway.

She stopped at a gas station a few miles from her destination to use the bathroom and check her appearance. *Fix your face, Ryker,* she said to herself calmly. After splashing some cold water on her face and taking a few deep breaths, she got back in her car and continued on.

She pulled up a dirt driveway to a single-story, light blue ranch-style house that was surrounded by a lush green field. She parked the car and checked her appearance one more time in the rearview mirror before grabbing a file off of the passenger seat and making her way to the front door. *Breath Ryker, fucking breathe. This is about them, not about you.*

She rang the doorbell, and a petite woman answered the door, dressed in a loose-fitting black blouse and gray trousers.

"Mrs. Harper Bennet?" Rachel asked

The woman's brows knit together.

"I'm Captain Rachel Ryker, U.S. Navy SEALs. I'm—I was—Aiden's commanding officer, team leader, and good friend."

Harper fingered the dog tags hanging around her neck at the mention of her son's name.

"I know the Navy chaplain has already been to see you," Rachel continued. "But I wanted to personally come and see how you and your husband are doing, and see if I can answer any questions either of you may have about what happened to Aiden." Rachel raised her hand holding the file she had taken with her from the car. "I have Aiden's service record here, partly redacted, I'm afraid. If you would like, I'd be happy to go through it with you, maybe help give some meaning and purpose to his death." Rachel's voice was steady, full of compassion and empathy.

"I was going to make him a pie." Harper's voice was barely above a whisper.

"I know you were," Rachel said kindly. "I've been hearing about the best apple pie in the world for the past eight years. I know you make him one every time he comes home."

Harper nodded, a slight smile on her face, as she slowly wiped the tears from her eyes, and motioned for Rachel to come in. She got to work fixing tea, and Rachel immediately jumped in to help, doing her best to ignore the numerous photos of Aiden scattered around the house. She needed to stay focused and composed if she was going to get through this. Despite having done this probably a hundred times, it was always harder when it was a close friend. Aiden's father, Jacob, came into the kitchen a moment later, followed by Dorothy, Aiden's grandmother.

"I am truly sorry for your loss," Rachel said after introducing herself to them. They all sat down at the kitchen table, each with a steaming hot mug of chamomile tea. Rachel noticed an urn sitting on a shelf near the table and furrowed her brow. She knew Aiden would be buried.

Jacob saw her confused look. "The family dog," he told her. "We had to put her down a few years ago."

"Dixie. I remember." Rachel nodded.

"Aiden was so mad at us." Harper looked at the table.

"No, he was mad at me and mad at who or whatever gave his dog cancer," Rachel corrected.

"Why was he mad at you?" Dorothy asked.

"It was easier to blame me that he was deployed than to really deal with it, I think."

Harper winced. "I'd guess you get that a lot."

"I do." The corners of Rachel's lips curled slightly. She was more than happy to take the blame so other people would feel better. "If you're ready." Rachel opened the cover of the file to the first page and flipped it around the table. "I'll tell you as much as I can and as much as you would like to hear. I know everyone has a different tolerance for hearing about war, so if it gets to be too much, please let me know. I have nowhere to be until Aiden's funeral so . . ." She trailed off, looking at them.

Jacob Bennet nodded at Rachel to proceed. She explained Aiden's time in BUD/S, the first round of SEAL training in Coronado, as well as his two deployments as a SEAL, before going through more training to join Special Projects. Then she got to the part she knew every single detail of. "Petty Officer Third Class Aiden Bennet was assigned to the Middle East Specialty Division, Team Indigo, as a communications specialist in July 2011, at only twenty-two years old. I was already on the team but not yet promoted to team leader," Rachel said. Then she walked them through Aiden's career, mission by mission, in as much detail as she was allowed, sharing anecdotes and memories about Aiden as she went. She told them about how she had usually ended up sitting between him and Christopher when they were driving anywhere, since Christopher was lead driver and team navigator, and Aiden had been responsible for making sure their radio and satellite phones, and all other means of communication, were up and running. She had almost eight years of stories to share with them from deployments and leave. Serious stories of Aiden acting with honor and valor in combat, and funny stories too. She told them about the day Henry had died, how instrumental Aiden had been in getting the team back to safety. She also told several parent appropriate stories about their time while on leave. She told them every story she had to tell. How he was in combat, how good he was with the radio and phone, how he could always seem to get a cell phone signal, even in the most remote locations.

"He was obsessed with his cell phone." Jacob shook his head.

"Always making noise and fiddling with some sort of gadget," Harper recalled.

Rachel smiled kindly. She paused and watched them for a minute. Both Harper and Jacob were crying. Tears of sadness, grief, and joy all coiled into twisted expressions on their faces. Dorothy was calm—not stoic, but composed.

Rachel got up from the table and went to refill the kettle and make more tea. She had already been there for five hours. Her own emotions were competing for her attention. She made a fist and pressed her nails into her palm, forcing her feelings back into the tiny box in her head where she kept all the bad memories and difficult emotions locked away. She opened cupboards until she found bread, peanut butter, and some strawberry jelly to make the one thing she knew she couldn't fuck up, then cut each sandwich diagonally. She brought the tea and two sandwiches over to the table, putting them in front of Harper, Dorothy, and Jacob. She'd done these enough times to know that grieving families rarely remembered to eat.

Harper stared at her plate, a soft smile on her face. "You cut them into triangles."

"I have been informed on several occasions that sandwiches must be cut into triangles. I've never fully understood the reasoning, but anytime Aiden had a sandwich or anyone made him one, it had to be cut into triangles for whatever reason." Rachel shook her head.

"It was easier to hold with one hand so he wouldn't have to put his phone down, I think." Jacob's lip tugged up into a half smile.

"He said it tasted better," Harper corrected.

"I heard it's because that's how his mom always did it." Rachel winked. "What questions do you have so far?" Harper, Dorothy, and Jacob were all silent. "Okay, well, that brings us to February 2019." Rachel paused again, checking to see if they were ready for more, then explained everything that had happened between February and April, including the events leading up to Aiden's death. Rachel paused and looked down at the table. Her hands were clasped together so tightly that her knuckles had turned white. "We wanted to help Veeda too, but our duty was to the ten Americans. Aiden . . . we all found that unacceptable, but Aiden ran, rushing the men who had Veeda, trying to save her. His actions distracted the insurgents so I could run to the hostages," Rachel explained. "We were all really close with Aiden. He could make friends with anyone, anywhere." Rachel paused. "I don't know if it's comforting for you to know, but he didn't suffer long, and he wasn't alone."

"Did he say anything?" Jacob asked.

Rachel shook her head. "It went too quick. I asked Matt, our medic, he said Aiden didn't say a single word, which for Aiden was strange. He was always talking. The last thing I heard him say . . . We were pinned down, stuck with our backs up against a wall. I told the guys behind me—Aiden was with me—to back up and stay put until it was safe to move. Aiden argued that it wasn't going to be safe, he needed to get to Veeda. The next thing I remember, he was off and running."

"He knew what he was doing." Jacob's smile didn't reach his eyes. "He knew he was taking a risk."

"I wish I had stopped him. I really do." Rachel looked at the table. "It happened so fast. Not that it's an excuse."

Harper clasped her hands together on the table, her knuckles white, as a tear rolled down her cheek. "I think . . . you're never ready to lose a child, but in a way, we've been waiting for this for years," she said quietly.

"Since he came home from school his sophomore year of high school, he'd met a Navy recruiter. They'd had some sort of assembly at school about building character, and some Navy guys and Army guys . . . I don't know, they were telling the kids about how to be your best self, how to lead, that sort of thing. Aiden came home and told us right then and there that he was going to be a Navy SEAL. It was the first time in his life he really buckled down, made a goal and stuck to it. Then when he got through training . . ." Jacob looked at his wife.

"The first time he handed us those life insurance forms." Harper frowned.

"It's a shock but not a surprise," Rachel summarized, knowing death was always shocking and sudden in the moment, but that military families were rarely truly surprised when someone died. They waited on edge every day their loved one was gone, hoping and praying they would come back, and always keeping a contingency plan in the back of their mind in case they didn't.

Rachel hesitated and looked at Aiden's family. Tears were streaming down their faces. No hysterics or sobbing, just red puffy eyes and quiet tears. They were all so calm and collected, the polar opposite of Aiden, who had always been loud and energetic.

"Your son's quick thinking and swift action saved the lives of ten American aid workers and eleven SEALs, myself included." Rachel paused, waiting to see if that sunk in, if they could really hear it and feel it. She put one of her hands on each of his parents', forcing them to make eye contact with her. "Aiden died a hero. And I don't mean that in the overly patriotic 'every sailor, every soldier is a hero' sort of way. He truly died with honor and valor. We would not have been able to complete our mission and rescue those people if it had not been for Aiden. He sacrificed his life to save them." A few minutes later Rachel asked, "What questions or concerns do you have for me?"

"What about the girl, the woman he ran to help?" Dorothy had been quiet so far, but she looked Rachel straight in the eye when she asked about Veeda.

Rachel took a sharp inhale. "Unfortunately, despite our best efforts, she died. The men who had her . . . They knew she'd been working with us, speaking to Aiden without her husband's permission or supervision." Rachel tried to swallow the lump in her throat. "Veeda's father was helping finance terror cells and married her off to a man very much involved in terrorist activity." She pressed her lips together and nodded to herself. "They were planning to kill her for disgracing her family, betraying them, for helping us. Honestly, as soon as they drug her out into the courtyard, I knew. They had beaten her to the point that she was struggling to breathe. Even if we had been able to get to her, save her, she likely would have died in the helicopter. I don't think Aiden could accept it. I think he might have been in love with her. Aiden shot some of the men detaining her, but they managed to stab her in the neck." Rachel pointed to the soft spot where her neck and shoulder met. "She was beautiful and sweet, and had the situation been different—very different—and if she had lived here, if she had been part of a more progressive family . . ."

"He was in love with her." Dorothy smiled.

"Can't really blame him." Rachel pulled up a photo of Veeda on her phone.

Jacob shook his head and chuckled. "I see the problem. She's absolutely beautiful."

"He told me about her, I think. He told me he met a girl in Afghanistan and showed me a photo of her. I think it's the same girl," Dorothy said.

"Yeah, it's the same girl." Rachel exhaled.

The corner of Dorothy's upper lip curled. "He told me over Christmas that he never regretted anything so much as leaving that girl behind in Afghanistan. He wanted to go back and get her and bring her here."

"I suspected as much." Rachel looked down at the table. "We all loved Veeda. She was an amazing human being, a great girl. Courageous, bubbly, beautiful, smart. A friend and an irreplaceable intelligence asset."

A small smile crept onto Harper's face. "You lost two friends then, Captain Ryker?"

"Yes, ma'am," Rachel admitted.

Dorothy nodded. "Hopefully they find each other in heaven."

"That's what we're all praying for," Rachel agreed.

"Two lives gone to save twenty-one others." Dorothy put a finger to her lips, seeming to consider her own words.

It was after 1900 before Rachel left the Bennet's home. She caught a glimpse of a blanket folded haphazardly on the couch and knew she was about to lose control of her emotions. Aiden had always been too busy talking to fold anything properly. It was why he was never assigned laundry duty. She had spent hours following Aiden around, refolding blankets and towels. It had always gotten on her nerves before, but now she found it endearing. Sweet, overly sociable Aiden who was too busy telling stories and asking people about their day to focus on folding a blanket properly.

Rachel got in her rental car and drove away, making sure she was far out of sight before allowing herself to cry. She had spent seven hours taking in Harper, Dorothy, and Jacob's feelings, helping to carry the weight of their suffering, their loss, while pushing her own emotions aside. Once her tears were so thick that she couldn't see, she pulled over and let it all out—everything she'd been feeling from the second she'd heard '*Blackbird's hit, man down*' announced over comms. From the second she ran to Aiden's lifeless body. She sat in her car on the side of the road for twenty minutes before wiping her eyes, checking her face in the mirror, and thanking God for whoever invented waterproof mascara.

After a few deep breaths, she took out her phone and texted Christopher. Within seconds, her phone rang.

"You okay? How'd it go?" Christopher asked, not bothering to say hi.

"Seven hours. I was with them for seven hours." Her voice was shaking.

"Where are you?" Christopher asked.

"In my car on the side of the road," she answered.

"I mean, where is your car?"

"Oklahoma," she said. Realizing Christopher would want a more specific answer, she clarified, "A few miles south of Daisy, Oklahoma."

"Where are you headed?"

"Don't know. I've never been here before." She meant both physically, that she'd never been to Oklahoma, and emotionally, that she'd never felt this defeated.

"Why don't you come here? It's only a two hour drive, and we're both going to the funeral next week. Hell, Matt's wedding is the week after, so we can make a road trip of it," Christopher suggested.

"That won't be weird?" Rachel asked.

"Why would it be weird? What? You can share a bed with me, with any of us in a hotel, but you can't come to my house? I stayed with your family, remember?" Christopher asked.

"Oh god. Your parents will be there." The prospect of meeting Christopher's parents was tying knots in her stomach.

"Yeah, and my sisters." He waited a moment, then sighed at her silence. "I'm texting you the address and directions," Christopher told her. "Come here. My family knows all about keeping things classified. Can you drive, or are you too upset?"

"I'm good," Rachel assured him. "See you soon."

Chapter 36:
APRIL 2019

AN HOUR AND A half later, Christopher was standing in front of his parent's house, knowing Rachel would make what should have been a two hour drive in considerably less time. He didn't have to wait long until a blue Chevy Sedan turned through the main gate and pulled up to the house. He grabbed her duffel bag from the back seat and slung it over his shoulder while she collected her phone and some papers off the front seat, then got out of the car.

"Good?" He asked her, studying her face and body language.

Rachel met his eyes. "Could be better, could be worse."

Christopher saw she was exhausted and decided she could wait until breakfast the next morning to meet his family. He led her down a narrow dirt road to his cabin and gave her the tour.

Rachel followed him around the cabin, which was a single-story, two bedroom, one bath with a wraparound porch and an open kitchen-living room. The décor was simple, though not minimalistic, and was cozier than the homes of most men. She showered and changed into exercise shorts and a t-shirt.

"Drink?" Christopher asked when she came out of the bathroom showered and dressed, her hair still wet but knotted up in a high messy bun. Rachel nodded, and he poured her a large glass of whiskey. "Wanna talk about it?" Christopher asked her.

"I think I've talked enough for one day," Rachel answered. They drank in silence until their glasses were empty. Rachel decided it was time to sleep and they both went to their respective rooms. Rachel, exhausted from her day, fell asleep immediately.

Christopher lay awake on his bed with his door closed, unable to sleep. He rarely had trouble sleeping, but his thoughts kept drifting to Rachel in the next room. He wished he could take some of the weight off her shoulders, help her bear the burden of all the responsibilities she carried, plus the extra duties she assigned herself. Going to see the Bennets had been her choice, something she felt she needed to do as the person responsible for making the calls that got their son killed. She had done the same thing nearly five years prior when Henry Tull had died. She had insisted on going to see his parents too, sitting with them all day, talking to them, listening to them, comforting them—all to her own detriment, it seemed. Christopher knew Aiden's death wasn't on Rachel. It was on the person who shot him. Taking a bullet through the carotid artery was messy business and an almost immediate death sentence. They all knew that, but Christopher was very sure Rachel was blaming herself, anyway.

His thoughts floated effortlessly from one memory to the next, over their time together, remembering the first day they met. They had both grown since then. Christopher had been impressed enough that she had already made Lieutenant Commander at such a young age and couldn't help but wonder what she had done previously to earn the rank. Over the coming weeks, he had gotten to know her. Not as a hot blonde who could kick some serious ass, but as an intelligent, quick-thinking strategist. It didn't take long for the rest of their class to fall in line behind her and let her lead the way.

The evolution of Rachel Ryker, he thought to himself with a laugh. She had gone from a brazen, somewhat arrogant, young woman who was determined to prove everyone wrong and make a name for herself, to a thoughtful, humble, empathic leader. She could still be plenty brazen, of course. He'd never seen anyone so fearless, so lacking in shame or so confident and self-assured. An image of her walking out of the James River, soaking wet in nothing but a see through white tank top and red lingerie, popped into his head. He'd been so embarrassed that he'd put her in that situation, but mostly he had been embarrassed by his own arousal at seeing her like that. It hadn't been since the first day he met her, on the bus going to SEAL training ten years ago, that he had thought about her like that. He tried to push the image out of his head, tried to think of her only as his superior, his commanding officer, and his best friend in the entire world.

CHAPTER 37:

APRIL 2019

RACHEL WOKE UP THE next morning at 0600. She laid in bed, looking at her surroundings and trying to remember where she was. *Okay, it's definitely weird,* she thought to herself as she realized she was at Christopher's house. Best friends or not, over the past ten years, she had never been to his house and he had never been to hers, other than the brief forced stay at the safe house in San Diego with her family. That really wasn't the same thing though. They were all so careful to protect each other's identities that even their families didn't know the names and faces of their team members. Secrecy and discretion were key. If anyone's identity was compromised, they wanted everyone's families to stay protected. As the only female SEAL, secrecy was even more crucial for Rachel.

She got up and dug through her clothes, unsure what she should wear. She settled on jeans and a white Navy t-shirt with blue text. Knowing Christopher typically slept longer than she did, she quietly went out to the kitchen to see if he had any coffee, not wanting to wake him up. She found the coffee pot and coffee. "No milk," she muttered as she inspected the fridge. She shouldn't be surprised. It was Christopher's house, and he didn't put milk in his coffee.

She noted that there wasn't any food either, not that she could cook.

Feeling restless, she found a spot on the living room floor and laid down on her back. She did set after set of sit-ups and push-ups as quietly as she could. What she wanted to do was run, run as far and as fast as she could away from this situation. She didn't understand why she felt so weird about being here. Like Christopher had said, they had traveled the world together, slept in the same bed, slept on the same piece of dirt sharing a blanket. This shouldn't be weird. *It's not like he's your boyfriend taking you home to meet his parents for the first time.* No one had ever taken her home to meet their parents. She had been friends with Carter—her husband, technically—since elementary school. His parents had already known her very well before they had started dating, and she had never seriously dated anyone else, opting instead for the simplicity that comes with one-night stands and random hookups.

The door to Christopher's room opened at 0700, interrupting her thoughts. "Good morning," Christopher said, noting she was mid push-up. "Did you get any sleep?"

"Are you kidding?" Rachel asked, continuing her set without looking up. "I slept so hard I forgot where I was."

Christopher laughed, knowing it was an occupational hazard. Getting on a plane and waking up somewhere else was a typical occurrence for them. "Well, I assume you remember where you are now." He watched her for a minute as she flipped onto her back to do sit-ups.

"You don't have any milk," Rachel stated.

"No, I guess I don't. But breakfast is in thirty minutes and there will be plenty of milk and coffee there."

Rachel finally stopped exercising and lifted herself up onto her elbows to look at him. "Breakfast?" was all she asked. They had gotten so used to each other, knew each other so well, that they had developed a sort of shorthand, rarely needing to say full sentences.

"Yeah, we'll go up to the main house for breakfast. My mom is kind of obsessive. Says feeding us is her way of showing she loves us, but I think it's some sort of secret plot to keep track of where we are and interrogate us about what we're up to. So, breakfast is at 0730, lunch is at 1230, and dinner is at

1800. If you're late, she will spend the entire meal making you explain why."

Rachel stared at him, dismayed. "Fuck, it's like being on a ship!"

"Except the food is much better." He gave her a wink and paused. "Oh, one more thing. She's going to insist on saying grace. Just to warn you."

Rachel rolled her eyes. Christopher stared at her, waiting for her to say something about the evils of organized religion.

"Her house, her rules, I guess," was all Rachel said.

"Well, don't tell her that! She'll make us go to church!"

Rachel knew that Christopher gave in and went to church with his family occasionally. She knew, because he usually spent the entire service texting her to complain about it.

Christopher jumped in the shower, and Rachel helped herself to a glass of water before going outside to sit on the porch. She sat on a chair, drinking a glass of water and playing on her phone as she waited for Christopher to lead the way to the food he had assured her existed.

Christopher led Rachel up to the main house and through the front door. His parents and his sister were already in the kitchen. "Good morning family," Christopher said casually as he came in. "I'd like you all to meet Captain Rachel Ryker, U.S. Navy SEAL, and my C.O."

"Hey, y'all," Rachel said with a small wave. "Thank you for letting me come to stay."

"You are more than welcome, dear!" Mary said, giving Rachel a hug. "I'm Mary, Christopher's mother, and this is Bob and Jackie." Mary pointed to each person as she said their name. "And that," she was pointed behind Rachel at a young woman with a blonde shoulder-length haircut, "is Sara. She's off studying to be a veterinarian, but apparently wanted some free laundry and food, so she came home for the weekend. She's headed back to school after we eat."

Christopher quickly introduced Rachel to Sara, and the whole family sat down for breakfast. Rachel's eyes darted up to a framed flag, folded neatly into a triangle which was sitting on a shelf behind the kitchen table.

"So, Rachel," Bob started as he sat down. "How long have you been working with Christopher?"

"We did SEAL training together, so that's what? Ten years?" Rachel responded politely.

"I thought they didn't allow women into the SEAL program until 2015?" Bob asked. As a former Navy sailor himself, Rachel knew he probably liked to keep track of these things.

"Well, that is the Navy's official story," Rachel said.

Mary reached out her hands expectantly. "Grace first!"

Rachel obliged, taking Jackie's hand and then Christopher's. Everyone bowed their heads and Mary prayed. Rachel bit the inside of her cheek to stop herself from saying anything rude. *This is definitely weird*, she thought to herself again, trying not to focus on the feel of Christopher's warm hand in hers.

"Rachel?" Jackie asked, taking a bite of her pancakes. "If you're Christopher's boss, does that mean you can kick his ass?"

Rachel laughed. "Yes, that's exactly what that means."

"I would pay good money to see that!"

"Jackie," Mary warned. "Be nice to your brother."

"I am being nice. I'm just being *nicer* to Rachel," Jackie clarified.

Christopher gave Rachel a lopsided grin. "Well, it's usually a pretty fair fight actually."

Rachel scoffed. "You're dreaming, Williams!"

"The only reason you're a better fighter than me is because of all your crazy backflips and cheerleading high kicks and shit," he stated. "That's the only reason you have the advantage."

"I'll let you keep believing that," Rachel said haughtily.

"Jackie and Sara did cheer too, all through high school," Mary offered, trying to change the subject.

"Oh, so then I guess you two should have a pretty easy time kicking Christopher's ass too, since that's apparently the only reason I can do it," Rachel said as she looked at Christopher, smiling brightly. "Or maybe there's a little more to it than that?"

Christopher pressed his lips together, conceding the point. "What do you want to do while you're here, Ryker? We've got six days until we need to be in Oklahoma, then a week until we need to be in Kentucky."

"Well, you're more than welcome to join us for church later. Service starts at 10:00 sharp. We usually leave here by 9:30."

Christopher choked on his food and quickly averted his eyes from his mother.

"That's a kind offer, Mary, but I'll be in church the next two weekends for a funeral and a wedding. I think that will just about meet my quota on churchgoing for the foreseeable future, but thank you anyway," Rachel said politely.

Mary looked at Christopher. "You're staying here with Rachel then, I guess?"

"Yup," was all Christopher managed to get out, trying not to laugh at Rachel's attempt at diplomacy. "Thought I'd take the former rodeo queen for a ride, if it's alright with Jackie. Don't want to mess with your training schedule." Jackie was a horse trainer and breeder, running both of her businesses from her own cabin on their parent's property. She was the boss when it came to anything horse related.

"I think I can squeeze you into the schedule," Jackie responded. She looked at Rachel and twirled a lock of her dark hair with her finger. "Rodeo queen, huh? For real, or is he just giving you shit?"

Rachel smiled sweetly. "Former barrel racer," she stated, meeting Jackie's bright blue eyes.

"You've seen her ride?" Jackie asked Christopher, trying to get a better assessment of Rachel's riding abilities.

"Yup, we did the Dalyan Trail in Turkey a few years back. There you've got steep trails, beaches, forests. We've also ridden in Cappadocia, also in Turkey," he clarified, realizing the rest of the family may not know where that was.

"And we did a safari on horseback in Botswana, and another in Kenya," Rachel added.

"Yeah, Botswana was the first time Henry put you in charge of team building." Christopher's eyes squinted as he suppressed a quiet laugh.

"He regretted it, didn't he?" Rachel's eyes sparkled.

"He didn't regret it enough to not let you be in charge of it the next time. Which is how we ended up in Cappadocia."

"Remember how we were riding around, looking for cheetahs, and Aiden wouldn't stop talking and scared all the animals away, then Henry threatened to use him as bait if he didn't shut up?" Rachel laughed.

"Yeah," Christopher said sadly. He looked up at the ceiling, and Rachel's face turned to stone. If she felt anything, it was entirely indiscernible. "Anyway, I think she can handle anything we've got," Christopher concluded.

Jackie looked suspiciously at them. "You two just go on vacation together all the time?"

"It's not vacation, it's team building," Rachel corrected. "The main benefit of being team leader is that I get to plan all the team building activities, so naturally I pick what I want to do and then make the team do it with me." She shrugged. "Just happens to be a lot of cool places to ride horses."

Jackie laughed. "Yeah, I'd probably do the same!"

Jackie led the way to the barn after breakfast, with Christopher and Rachel in tow. Looking at Christopher, Jackie said, "You want Blaze I assume?" Blaze, Rachel had learned, was Christopher's favorite horse. Then Jackie eyed Rachel curiously. "Let's see what Seabreeze thinks of you." Seabreeze, or Breeze for short, was an American Quarter Horse, small and quick, stocky but agile, feisty, and perfect for western-style riding, sport, and cattle-handling. She was a five-year-old mare with perlino coloring, making her as blonde as Rachel. Christopher said nothing, realizing it was a test, and knowing that Rachel would pass with flying colors. Jackie had raised Breeze from birth and trained her herself. No one rode Breeze but Jackie, due to her stormy temperament.

Rachel took her time grooming Breeze. She was patient and thorough, but efficient. Breeze was as calm with Rachel as she was with Jackie. Before Jackie could bring over a saddle and bridle for her to use, Rachel had untied Breeze and led her into the large adjacent riding arena, closing the gate behind her.

"What's she doing?" Jackie asked Christopher. He shrugged, having no idea what Rachel was doing.

Once in the arena, Rachel looped the lead rope around Breeze's neck before tying it in a knot securely under the horse's chin, making makeshift reigns. She stroked Breeze's back, applying a bit of pressure and weight as she did. After a few minutes, Rachel stood calmly next to Breeze's neck, facing her rear, and swiftly lifted herself, kicking up her leg to mount the horse. Breeze was calm under Rachel's weight, standing perfectly still until Rachel lightly tapped her heels and leaned forward, urging Breeze to walk. After a few laps around the arena, she accelerated Breeze into a lively trot, sitting easily and steadily the entire time. Rachel sped up again, this time into a swift canter. She looped around the arena a few times before cutting across diagonally and changing directions. "Alright girl, let's see what you can do," Rachel said quietly to Breeze. Responding to Rachel's slight tap of the heel, Breeze opened up into a gallop.

"Shit, even I wouldn't try that on Breeze," Jackie said, stunned.

After a few laps, Rachel brought Breeze to a sudden halt and instructed her to take a few steps backwards, then stopped again before proceeding forward. She repeated the exercise a few times before dismounting and leading Breeze back to the gate.

"I think I'm in love!" Rachel said to Jackie and Christopher as she led Breeze over to the tack area. "I assume you recommend saddles on the trails, though?"

"Probably a good idea," Christopher said in awe. He'd seen Rachel ride plenty of times, but that was something else. They quickly finished saddling their horses before Christopher led the way out of the barn and up a large hill. They rode fast and hard through the forest and over small streams until they reached the top of a ridge that overlooked a lake. "That's Lake Tawakoni," Christopher said. "It's not a real lake. It's a manmade reservoir, really."

"It's beautiful." Rachel examined the large lake that was surrounded by dense oak forest. They stayed for a while, admiring the view, before advancing their horses along the ridge and following a trail to the west. After several miles, the trail swooped around into a gradual slope, which ended in an open meadow rich with wildflowers. They raced their horses through the meadow and back to the barn, laughing and joking with each other as they did. When they got back to the barn, they quickly untacked and groomed the horses.

They ended up back at the main house. It was a two-story ranch-style house with a wide front porch that was able to accommodate several chairs and small tables. The house was built out of deep, dark timber and had large picture windows on the first floor and two charming dormers on the front. There was a guest room, kitchen, half bath, living room, and a laundry room downstairs and an attached garage full of motorcycles, ATVs, and tools. The master bedroom was up a narrow wooden staircase and to the left. To the right were four bedrooms. They each had been left as a shrine to its former occupant, with trophies, ribbons, and photographs from high school on the bookshelves.

"So that's Jackie, Sara, me, and . . ." Christopher trailed off as he pointed out which room had belonged to who, entirely unable to speak Josh's name out loud.

"Right," Rachel said, nodding. "Don't talk about that?"

"Never."

"Too hard?"

"For Mom."

"Got it," Rachel smiled mischievously and opened the door to Christopher's childhood bedroom.

Christopher followed Rachel into his old room and sat on the bed, watching Rachel scrutinize his past. He liked her being there. It felt right. She said nothing, touched nothing, just observed.

"You were really happy," Rachel stated as picked up the photograph of him next to a shiny black pick-up truck. He'd just gotten his driver's license.

"Yeah," was all Christopher said.

Rachel stared at the photo in her hand. "Less complicated."

He knew what she meant. Life before the Navy had been simpler. He had been a fairly typical high school student—good grades, or good enough to get a football scholarship for college, great friends, and way too much fun.

Rachel turned around to look at him as she leaned against the bookshelf. "Tell me."

Christopher shook his head. "I don't know. I played football, hung out with my friends. It's all right there in the photos."

Rachel nodded, thinking to herself. "Pictures lie. No one takes pictures of the bad things, and if they do, they get put in some mission report and tucked away. Not displayed for everyone to see." She pointed at the bookshelf. "No, this is the fantasy. This is what you want to remember, what you want other people to know. So, what's the other half?"

Christopher stared at her. He didn't know what to say. They had known each other for ten years and somehow certain things had never come up.

"I can see," Rachel continued, "that you never had a serious girlfriend in high school. No shocker there." She gave him a wink.

"What's that supposed to mean?" Christopher was slightly offended at her conclusion, even if she was right.

"The same girl is never featured twice in any of these photos. If you'd had a girlfriend, then at least one girl would appear in more than one photo. Besides, in case you are forgetting, I've traveled all over the world with you. I know how you are."

Christopher conceded. "No, I did not have a steady girlfriend in high school or college. Where would the fun have been in that?"

"You didn't answer the question, Williams. What's the bad part? What am I not seeing here? What are you trying to forget?" Rachel leaned patiently against the built-in bookcase, giving Christopher time to formulate an answer.

"Things were not perfect, no. Obviously nothing's perfect." Christopher paused. He knew he had to give her some sort of answer to appease her or else she would just keep asking. "I snuck out, partied too much, drove too fast, drove drunk. You know, normal stuff."

"And if I asked your mamma, what would she say?" Rachel stared him down.

"That I was reckless and impulsive and irresponsible and completely out of control."

Rachel laughed out loud.

"What's so funny?" Christopher asked.

"Oh, nothing. We're so similar now, it makes sense we would have been similar then too. Perfect on paper. You, the all-American boy, and me, the all-American girl. The ideal in so many ways, if you just focus on the photos."

Christopher was intrigued. "What's the dumbest thing you ever did in high school?"

"I borrowed my father's car when I was fourteen." She shrugged.

"Fourteen?" Even Christopher thought that was young.

"What? I needed to go somewhere!"

Christopher smirked. "You're always on your way somewhere. Can't sit still for a minute."

"What about you? What's the dumbest thing you ever did in high school?" Rachel asked.

"I got drunk and drove my motorcycle at top speed down the main road that comes up to the house. Almost hit a cow that had gotten loose."

"Any injuries?"

"Nope. Both me and the cow were thankfully fine," Christopher said with a grin.

"Hmm," Rachel looked inquisitively at Christopher. "Why? I mean, I know why I was the way I was, or am, or whatever. But you . . . I know so much about you. Everything you've told me, everything in your personnel file and service record. But there's something. Some big piece of the puzzle that's missing."

Christopher said nothing. He knew the answer to her question, but there were too many parts of the story that weren't his to tell. "You show me yours and I'll show you mine," Christopher challenged.

Rachel gave a casual wave of her hand. "Oh, you know, just the typical battle scars that come with growing up female in a patriarchal society."

"Same," Christopher said.

Rachel crossed her arms over her chest and gave him a flirtatious pout.

"No, not the same!" she insisted. "You aren't going to tell me, are you?"

"Not my story to tell."

Rachel tried to sleep that night, confining herself to Christopher's guest room, but she was restless thinking about Aiden and thinking about Christopher in the next room. He was asleep of course. He never struggled to sleep. She took Christopher's guitar from the living room and a bottle of whiskey and went outside. She walked the whole way around twice before deciding the best way to climb up onto the roof was from the backside of the porch.

She lay on her back, looking at the stars and strumming his guitar in between sips of whiskey, trying to slow down her thoughts. Sleep still eluded her, however. Part of her wanted to crawl into bed with Christopher and make him sing her to sleep. But for some reason, getting in his bed, in *his* bed in *his* house, felt very wrong. She would have to regulate her own emotions without his singing and his hugs and whatever else might happen if she went in his room. She tried to remember what had helped the last time this had happened. What had made her feel better? Suddenly she remembered.

Sex. Sex had been the answer then, but it definitely couldn't be the answer now since her only available option seemed to be Christopher . . . or Jackie, and she wasn't about to cross that line. Her best friend's sister was for sure off-limits, and her best friend, her colleague, her second in command, was even more off-limits. She'd better keep her sad, grieving, desperate ass on the roof before she did something unforgivable and unforgettable in Christopher's bed.

Grief was leading to restlessness, though, which was leading to desire—very inappropriate desires—which only led to guilt. She took off her smartwatch, careful to lay it on her stomach so it wouldn't slide off the roof, then dug the nails of her right hand into her left wrist, where she knew the marks would be covered by the band of her watch. Pain was usually the cure for guilt, and sex was typically the cure for everything else. She'd left her knife in her room though, so fingernails and whiskey would have to do.

She could hear Aiden's voice in her head, laughing and joking, whining about something not being fair, telling her some funny story about a girl he'd hooked up with. The fact that she'd never hear his voice again was jarring. Death and grief and loss weren't new experiences for her. Far from it. But that didn't make it easier. A warm tear rolled down her cheek, and she tasted salt in her mouth as it reached her lips. Memories of Aiden flickered through her mind. They'd had nearly eight years with him. Eight years was a long time, but it hadn't been long enough.

Chapter 38:

APRIL 2019

CHRISTOPHER AND RACHEL DROVE in complete silence to Daisy, Oklahoma for Aiden's funeral, wearing their blue dress uniforms. When they got to the cemetery, they parked and walked toward the burial plot. They were the first ones from their team to arrive. Matt and Ryan arrived with Charlene shortly after, followed by the rest of the team. Rachel found Aiden's parents and grandmother and introduced them to everyone.

They walked down a short pathway to a small chapel for the funeral service. There was a large photo of Aiden on the altar. He was dressed in his service khakis and had his brown hair cropped short. He had a bright smile on his face, and his eyes twinkled like brown sugar crystals. Rachel recognized it as the photo on his ID card. Next to it was a photo of him kneeling on the ground with his arm wrapped around a yellow lab. Dixie, she presumed. She'd listened to Aiden ramble on incessantly about his childhood best friend. Aiden had a lot of best friends. His dog Dixie had been just one of them.

The team spoke with Aiden's family, sharing stories back and forth about his time in the Navy and when he was a child. They sang "Amazing Grace" and listened to the chaplain recite Psalm 23 before they ended with the hymn "Morning is Broken." Aiden's best friend from high school gave the eulogy. When the service was over, they went back to the gravesite for the burial. The hearse arrived, and the casket was carried to the gravesite with a flag draped over it. The chaplain performed the rite of committal, reading Matthew 25:34: "'Come, you whom my Father has blessed, says the Lord; inherit the kingdom prepared for you since the foundation of the world.'" That was followed by "The Lord's Prayer."

Daniel, Jason, Brendon, Aaron, and Nate made up the rifle party. They gave their final salute, firing three shots into the air with M1 rifles, before fighter jets from the Air Force base outside of Dallas did an aerial flyover in missing man formation. They couldn't find a bugler, so they elected to have Rachel sing "Taps," even though she was technically part of the honor guard. She, Christopher, and Matt stood on one side of the casket while Ryan, Michael, and David stood on the other. They meticulously folded the flag thirteen times, tucking the end in to the final fold to form a triangle, the stars pointing upwards.

Rachel carried the flag with the straight edge facing Aiden's parents. When she was face-to-face with them, she saw the sun glint off of Aiden's dog tags, which were still hanging around Harper's neck. After a steadying breath, she presented the flag to Harper. "On behalf of the President of the United States, the United States Navy, and a grateful nation, please accept this flag as a symbol of our appreciation for your loved one's honorable and faithful service."

The casket was lowered. It was done. Aiden was officially gone.

The funeral reception took place at the Bennet's home, where Rachel had met them just a week before. Christopher drove. The drive would be their only twenty-minute break for the day.

"Are you doing okay?" Rachel asked Christopher.

"Nope," he said. "You?"

"God no. This is awful," Rachel admitted.

"We're halfway through the day and then we can drive out to the wilderness and disappear," Christopher said.

"I'm very much looking forward to that."

They rode the rest of the way in silence. There was nothing to say. Rachel tried desperately to think about something else. Her week at Christopher's family's ranch had been fun and she seemed to naturally fit in. Their first ride up to the ridge had been so beautiful. Christopher seemed at peace there, and it had been fun to see him in his natural environment. She thought back to his last birthday, how he had been a little flirtatious, but in a fun way. Not crossing a line, but almost. Really just a bit of teasing between friends. She was happy to have him in her life. Grateful it hadn't been him who had died.

Christopher could tell that Rachel was having a tough day. She always took on other people's feelings and never took time for her own. He didn't want to push her, certainly not now when they were on their way to the Bennet's home. They couldn't show up crying. He had seen her deal with a lot of difficult situations, but this was one of the worst. He tried to focus on driving and not think about her.

Once they got to the house, Rachel jumped into action, helping to arrange trays of food and fill glasses with lemonade and sweet tea. Christopher helped set up folding chairs in the living room and on the wrap around porch. They both needed to stay busy so that they could keep their emotions in check. This was not their day to grieve. This day was for Aiden's family.

Harper and Jacob Bennet greeted their guests as they trickled in. Rachel kept a close eye on them from the kitchen. She periodically refilled their glasses and brought them food, knowing they would forget to eat. Charlene helped Rachel in the kitchen and kept a close eye on Matt and Ryan. Christopher did the same for the rest of the men on their team. They all had their people to look out for.

"Apple pie," Ryan said, staring at the kitchen counter. The entire team gathered around, remembering all the times Aiden would brag about his mom baking the best apple pie in the entire world. Ryan cut everyone a slice and they all had to agree. It was the best damned apple pie any of them had ever had.

"Someone ask Mrs. Bennet for the recipe," Matt whispered.

"Leave Harper alone," Rachel scolded them.

"Hell no. I need more of this fucking pie." Aaron cut himself another slice and plopped it on his plate then rushed off to find Harper before Rachel could stop him. He came back ten minutes later with Dorothy in tow, signaling that he had secured the recipe.

"Did Aiden tell you all that was Harper's pie recipe?" Dorothy gave them a disapproving stare. "Who do you all think taught her?" She winked. The whole team let out a collective chuckle. "Captain Ryker, I did something for you. For all of you, I suppose." Dorothy looked each of them in the eye and motioned for them to follow her. She led them through the house to Aiden's bedroom and paused, pointing at the nightstand beside the bed. "I know I'm an old lady, and I never understood half of what Aiden was talking about with his phone and all that, but I took it to the store and they helped me print this off his cellphone."

Rachel's eyes filled with tears as she saw the framed photo of Veeda on Aiden's nightstand. And beside it was a picture of Aiden, a votive candle flickering between them. She felt like her chest was going to collapse.

"I'll give you all a minute." Dorothy gave a slight nod of her head and left the room, momentarily resting her hand on Rachel's shoulder on her way past.

All eleven of them stood perfectly silent around Aiden's bed. No one moved. They were barely breathing, collectively lost for words, until Aaron leaned down to straighten a fleece blanket on Aiden's bed.

"Don't you dare move that." Rachel's voice was hardly above a whisper.

"Can we all promise to never fold blankets properly again?" Ryan asked. There was a collective nod of agreement.

"Did you tell her we didn't get to bury Veeda?" Christopher asked after a few more moments of silence. All Rachel could do was shake her head and stare wide-eyed at the photo of her friend on the nightstand.

"We'll get him, Rachel," David said, studying her face. "We were close this time. We'll regroup and head back over. Neither of them will be forgotten."

Rachel was vaguely aware that the men were talking. Sharing memories about Veeda and Aiden she supposed, but everything was a blur as she tried to contain her rage and sorrow over the two lives that had both ended too soon.

Chapter 39:

MAY 2019

RACHEL AND CHRISTOPHER HAD one week to kill between Aiden's funeral in Daisy and Matt and Charlene's wedding in Lexington, so they decided to hike in the Ozark-St. Francis National Forest in Arkansas on the way. They hadn't planned ahead so they stopped at a store to buy supplies. They didn't need much. Rachel had her knife and they had a medic kit in the truck, so all they needed was some food, a blanket, and something to make a fire with. Rachel had wanted to wander around and explore, but Christopher insisted on stopping at the ranger's station on their way into the forest to get a paper map of the area. He led the way into the East Fork Wilderness section of the park. The area encompassed 10, 777 acres along the southern edge of the Boston Mountains. The terrain was mostly flat and scattered with hollows that were separated by steep rock walls. There were ponds, creeks, and waterfalls up to twenty feet high, perfect for swimming. They walked amongst the oak and hickory trees, quietly exploring. Christopher had chosen this area because it was more rugged than other areas of the forest and had no developed trails, just a few main roads cutting through.

Nature was the perfect medicine. Rachel's grief and guilt over Aiden's death was fading, plaguing her less and less the deeper they got into the wilderness. She hadn't let herself cry over it, hadn't really felt it other than the night she drove to meet Christopher after visiting Aiden's parents. But that had been more from exhaustion than anything else.

During the day, she could forget everything and just be present in the forest. At night, things were different though. At night, she couldn't ignore her pain and anguish anymore. Each night after Christopher fell asleep, she let herself cry silent tears for Aiden, for his mother, for his father, his grandmother, for the entire team, for Veeda, and for herself.

Christopher woke up in the middle of the night, lying on the cool ground in the forest. He was aware of Rachel lying next to him. He heard her breathing heavily and turned to look at her. It was dark, but he could see her hands over her face. She was shaking, not a lot, just enough for him to notice. He reached out for her and pulled her to him, holding her close and letting her cry against his chest until she finally fell asleep. It was obvious why she was crying; he didn't need to ask. He knew she was crying for Aiden and Veeda, and crying for herself, since she felt responsible.

The next night was the same. He could feel her sadness as she lay next to him, but she was on her side, facing away from him. He inched closer to her and wrapped his arm around her waist, burying his face in her hair. His arm was on her stomach, her arm was on top of his arm, urging him to hold her tighter. She pulled his hand up to her lips and kissed it lightly before wrapping his arm even tighter around her.

On Thursday, they packed up and headed back out of the forest to Christopher's truck. They decided to spend one night in Nashville on their way to Lexington. The drive took six hours and forty-five minutes, and they arrived in time for a late dinner. They checked into their hotel, showered, changed, and went out in search of some food. They found a good spot for Nashville hot chicken and sweet tea before heading out to a bar. It was Nashville on a Thursday night, so there was live music everywhere. They stayed out late, knowing they could sleep in the next morning since it was only a three hour drive to Lexington, and they didn't need to check out of the hotel until noon.

They were back in their hotel room by 0300. Rachel brushed her teeth and changed into sweats and a t-shirt before climbing into her bed. She lay awake for a while, listening to Christopher as he got ready for bed and waited for him to fall asleep. The guilt and pain she had been feeling came flooding back. She tried to calm herself down. Normally she would drink, or hook up with a random stranger, or jump in a car or on a motorcycle and drive off, run away either physically or mentally from the emotional pain. But she couldn't do that right now. They'd been having too much fun together, and now it was 0300. Not the optimal time for finding someone to sleep with since no one was out. Besides, they had to be in Lexington the next day for Matt and Charlene's rehearsal dinner. She could feel tears welling up in her eyes and could tell they were about to turn to loud sobs. Not wanting to wake Christopher up, she went into the bathroom, turned on the shower, and sat on the floor, hoping the sound of the water would drown out the sound of her crying.

At 0700 the next morning, Christopher found Rachel asleep on the bathroom floor with the shower still on. Her eyes were red and puffy, so he knew she'd been crying again. He sat down on the floor next to her and ran his fingers through her tangled hair. She rolled over and looked up at him.

"Have you been in here all night?" he asked, suspecting she had been.

"Yeah," she said.

"Why didn't you wake me up?"

"Why *would* I wake you up?"

He looked at her with compassion, studying her face. "So that you didn't have to be sad alone." Rachel didn't seem to understand. "You aren't the only one grieving. I miss Aiden too. You aren't alone in this."

It was never easy getting Rachel to admit her feelings, but Christopher was determined to try. She didn't open up to people easily, despite the fact that she expected everyone to open up to her. He'd found her crying twice during SEAL training. She had snuck off alone to hide, and he'd gone to look for her, knowing something had been wrong. She'd been frustrated and angry then, upset that she was being treated differently, that several of the instructors and their classmates had been going out of their way to ensure that she failed. It had been easy to comfort her then, to encourage her to keep going, to keep fighting. He'd seen her cry after difficult missions when they were alone and she was sure no one else could see or hear, when she was sure he wouldn't give her shit or say anything to anyone else. And he'd seen her cry the last time they had done this. The last time they had buried a friend—their former team leader and commanding officer, Henry Tull—nearly five years earlier. That had been the only time she'd cried in front of anyone else. It had been impossible to avoid, and only Matt, Charlene, and Aiden had seen. They had all been crying too. They had all been so close—Christopher, Rachel, Matt, Aiden, and Henry—and now of the five of them, only three of them were left. But Henry's death had brought them Ryan. If only he could get her to focus on the positive. Loosing Aiden meant someone new would come into their lives. But Aiden seemed irreplaceable. Even more than Henry had.

"You seem fine," Rachel said.

"Yeah, because when I got back, I went to go talk to a counselor about it. It was really helpful. I worked through a lot of the guilt I was feeling. Like thinking that it should have been me, stuff like that, you know? But I still miss him, and Veeda. I'm still sad when I think about it. Grief takes time." He combed his fingers through her hair, trying to keep her calm.

Rachel nodded. Christopher loved going to therapy. It was practically a hobby for him.

"I know you think you need to be strong all the time," Christopher continued. "Show that you can handle everything. But you don't. Not with me. I get with the rest of the team, but it's okay to not be okay." Rachel started crying again. Christopher laid down next to her, not touching her, just looking into her eyes and letting her get it all out. It killed him to watch her cry without intervening, but he knew it was best for her. The second he started comforting her, she would calm down and then she'd never let herself feel any of it.

After a while, she reached her hand out to hold his and he pulled her into him for a hug, holding her tight against him. She buried her face into his bare chest, and Christopher let his own tears fall with hers. He was crying for Aiden but mostly for her. Her sorrow was palpable and he sensed her pain. He knew how much she hated and blamed herself for everything and how she likely thought she should have been the one who died. If you had asked any of them five years ago who would make it out of combat alive and who would die in battle, they all would have assumed Rachel and Christopher would be the ones to die. They would've done something reckless together, something that would be called heroic after their passing, resulting in them dying side-by-side on the battlefield.

Rachel cried for three hours straight before finally calming down. She was happy to be in Christopher's arms, secretly thinking that it was the best, safest place in the world. He'd always had her back, always knew how to make her feel better. He was her best friend in the entire world and the only person she had ever fully trusted with her life, with her thoughts, with her feelings, with her body and soul. She never needed to hide anything from him, even if she did anyway. She wanted to spare him as much as possible and didn't want him to have to take on her feelings more than she really needed him to, but he was always there. He was always waiting with open arms, ready to let her cry or scream or fight him, just to get her feelings out. Just to get a little relief from the torment she was feeling. And he was always there when things were good too. Always the first to raise a glass and toast their success, to make a joke, usually a very inappropriate joke. They had known each other for nearly ten and a half years, and she could barely remember what her life had been like before they'd met.

"Christopher," Rachel whispered. "I'm okay. You can let go now." He pulled her closer instead, holding her as tightly as he could, and she knew he'd needed this as much as she had. "You're okay too. We're both okay," she whispered against his chest, realizing that he was as scared and panicked and sad as she was after all.

"Please don't die. I can't bury you too," he whispered.

"Okay. I'm not going anywhere. And if I did, hell you're always right behind me. I'm sure the bullet would get us both and we'd go together," she joked.

He held tighter and let out a laugh in the middle of his tears. "Let's hope," he said.

"Besides, I'm pretty sure we're invincible if we haven't died by now."

"You're probably right." He laughed again. "God, I love you! I can't believe I'm lucky enough to have you as my best friend."

"Matt is your best friend." She furrowed her brow, knowing he was being serious and choosing to believe he meant platonic love. That was the only kind of love they could ever have.

"Fuck Matt! He's got nothing on you!"

"Can you believe we've known each other for ten years?" Rachel asked.

"Ten years of glory and hell," Christopher joked.

"You know you're my favorite person in the entire world, Williams?" She tipped her face up toward his and stared into his eyes.

"I know you love me, Ryker." He smiled back, grazing his thumb along her chin.

Heat coursed through her entire body and her heart rate sped up. She forced herself to calm down and cursed her emotions. Clearly her brain was mixing up friendship and comfort with something else. Something she could never let herself feel, certainly not for Christopher. "I love you more than I love my actual brother," Rachel told him seriously.

"Yeah, well, I've met your brother. That's not too stiff of competition."

"Maybe not, but still. You know what I mean." Something rose up, some feeling she'd never had and couldn't name, but she forced it down. It was getting so much harder to ignore her feelings, but she had to. She'd just lost one friend, and she refused to lose another.

Christopher squeezed her hand.

"We're going to have to get up off the floor eventually, right?" she asked him.

"Yeah."

"I don't want to though," Rachel admitted.

"Okay." Christopher pulled her into him again, holding on as tight as he could.

Chapter 40:
MAY 2019

CHRISTOPHER DROVE THEM TO Lexington and let Rachel take control of the stereo, for the most part. He could only take so much Taylor Swift at once, but he knew it would distract her from being sad, so he decided to try to tolerate it. They had arrived and checked into their rooms by 1630. Given the semi-official nature of the trip, they had each gotten their own room, knowing there were too many Navy officers, including their boss, staying at the same hotel. Plus, they knew wanting to save money wouldn't be a viable reason for any of them to share rooms. It was practically like being on base.

The next day, Matt showed Rachel, Christopher, and Ryan around downtown Lexington. They had plenty of time to kill before the ceremony. They were having a beer in one of the nearby bars when Rachel said, "God, I'm so happy I get to hang out with you guys, and I don't have to be a bridesmaid. You know they're all sitting at the hotel, panicking about hair and makeup and shoes for the next eight hours. This is much easier."

"Have you ever been a bridesmaid?" Ryan asked, as though the possibility of Rachel doing anything feminine was shocking.

"Yes, I have. Many times, in fact."

"When?" Christopher asked.

"Two friends got married right out of high school and three more during or after college," Rachel explained.

"You don't have any friends," Ryan stated.

"Maybe not now! I'm never anywhere long enough to have friends. But once upon a time, I was very popular."

"Well, no one's saying you aren't popular," Christopher said. "I mean, we basically can't take you anywhere without you attracting all sorts of attention."

"Commander Williams, was that your weird way of telling me you think I'm pretty?" Rachel teased.

"Nope. That was me saying that other people seem to think you're pretty." Christopher winked.

"I dunno Sky, I think we should send you off to the bridesmaids. Maybe have you do some reconnaissance or something. Might come in handy later," Ryan suggested.

"Is Charlene aware of the fact that you've made it your mission to fuck all of her friends this weekend?" Rachel teased.

"Not all of them," Ryan clarified. "Go hang out with them and let us know what you find out."

Rachel gave Ryan a wink and left to go back to the hotel.

Charlene's hotel room was a cloud of hairspray with fake eyelashes and makeup brushes strewn everywhere. Rachel was horrified but put on a smile anyway.

"Rachel's here!" Charlene screamed.

"Oh sweetie, are you drunk already?" Rachel asked.

"No, just a little tipsy. And excited!"

"Have you eaten?" Rachel smiled. Charlene was definitely drunk.

"Yeah, we had pizza! Come sit! We'll get you all fixed up!" Charlene ordered. Rachel sat down as directed and Charlene's hair and makeup team immediately pounced on her. They twisted Rachel's hair into an elegant updo, still in keeping with Navy regulations since she'd be in uniform, and applied more makeup than Rachel had worn since college. She couldn't argue with the results though.

"Oh my god! You're stunning, Rachel!" Charlene said. "Not that you aren't always, but shit, you clean up nice!"

Rachel bowed dramatically, spurring Charlene into a fit of giggles. "Ryan is wondering which of your bridesmaids he should focus his attention on. I'm guessing Christopher is wondering too, but he had better sense than to ask."

Charlene choked on the champagne she was sipping. "Alyssa already told me she thinks Ryan is cute. As for Christopher, I don't know. He's gorgeous, he'll figure it out." She laughed with a wave of her hand.

"So, you wouldn't be mad if . . ."

"No! Everyone is an adult, so they can sleep with whoever they want. Or everyone who's single . . ."

"Okay, I'll let them know."

Christopher knocked on the door a few minutes after Charlene and the bridesmaids had finished getting dressed. "We're going to head over to the church soon. Are you coming with us or staying with Charlie?"

"Oh, I'm definitely coming with you," Rachel confirmed. Then she turned to Charlene and called out to her, "I'm going over to the church with the guys. Don't be late to your own wedding!" Charlene waved her off.

"Oh my God, the Navy should add hair spray to its chemical weapons arsenal," Rachel said to Christopher as she closed the door to Charlene's room. "I almost died in there!"

Christopher laughed, then he looked at her face and just stared.

"Why are you looking at me like that?" Rachel asked him.

"Like what?" Christopher wasn't blinking, his lips were slightly parted, and he was leaning in, his face mere inches from hers.

"Huh, I guess *now* you think I'm pretty." Rachel winked and walked down the hallway to her room. "Lobby in ten?"

"Yup, ten minutes." Christopher answered a bit absently.

When Rachel got downstairs, Ryan and Matt were already waiting.

"Ick, what happened to your face?" Ryan asked her, grimacing as he poked her nose with his index finger. "You look weird."

"Thank you, Ryan. How sweet of you to say," Rachel said sarcastically.

Matt gave her a hug and a peck on the cheek. "You look great! I'll hold Ryan down so you can kick his ass later."

"It's fine. I'll just withhold the information I received about which bridesmaid is interested in him until he apologizes and says something nice."

"Wait, what?" Ryan asked.

"Sorry I'm late," Christopher said, walking up to the group.

"Skylark, I sincerely apologize for my rude comment. I'm just not used to seeing you with makeup. As Matt said, you do look very nice."

"Is 'nice' the best you can do? I don't know if 'nice' is good enough to get the intel I have."

"You are gorgeous, stunning, and ravishing all wrapped into one! Now please tell me!" Ryan pleaded.

"Fine, although I'm doubting the sincerity of all that. According to Charlene, Alyssa is your best bet and has already expressed her interest in you. As for you," she pointed to Christopher, "I was told, and I quote, 'Chris is gorgeous he'll figure it out.' So good luck with that I guess."

"What about you?" Ryan asked.

"Oh my god, you are truly awful, aren't you? I'm not going to corrupt one of Charlene's best friends!" Rachel insisted.

CHAPTER 41:
MAY 2019

THE WEDDING CEREMONY WAS very traditional and lasted about forty minutes. Afterwards, Matt and Charlene disappeared to take photos while the rest of the guests and wedding party made their way to a nineteenth-century southern mansion where the reception would take place. Rachel was seated at the head table between Matt and Christopher and had the unfortunate pleasure of having Admiral Eastwood at the table just in front of her, watching her every move. Everyone needed to be on their best behavior. After dinner was served, the speeches started. Charlene's parents, Matt's grandparents, Charlene's sister, then Christopher. Finally, it was Rachel's turn. She highly doubted she had much to say that hadn't already been said, but she'd written a speech at Charlene's request, or insistence rather, so she'd read it.

"Hi everyone. I hope y'all have enjoyed your evening so far. For those of you who don't know me, I'm Captain Rachel Ryker, also known as Matt's boss." The whole room laughed at that. "I met Matt seven years ago when he joined my team, and we've been on quite a few adventures together since then. I can assure Charlene's parents that she's in excellent hands. Matt has always acted with integrity and honor, even in the most challenging situations, and is truly one of the kindest people I know.

"Charlene, on the other hand," Rachel continued, "likes to stir up trouble, always luring Matt off base and making him late to things. Or at least that's the story he tells me." More laughter erupted from the guests. "I sincerely have never met two people more in love or more perfectly suited for each other than these two. It has been a privilege to watch their relationship grow over the past six years, from the first time the team and I got to meet Charlene when she came to visit Matt in New Orleans, until the day he finally proposed and somehow threw together this wedding in the span of a few months.

"I already know that Matt and Charlene are destined to spend the rest of their lives together. I anticipate that no matter how much they love each other today, they will fall even deeper in love with each other every day that comes after." Rachel raised her glass, and everyone else in the room did the same. "To Matt and Charlene!"

Charlene gave Rachel a hug and took the microphone from her. "Thank you, Rachel! I would like to clarify, Captain Ryker, Admiral Eastwood, I am not responsible for Matt being late. That's all on him!" Charlene exclaimed.

"Well, it's just because you're too pretty and I can't stand to leave you!" Matt clarified, giving Charlene a peck on the cheek.

"Yeah, and if you could run faster, you'd probably be on time," Ryan jabbed.

The night continued in a whirlwind of semi-structured activities and formalities. After the couple's first dance, Rachel was leaning up against the bar talking to Charlene.

"I find it really unfair that the guys all put their uniforms on and girls come flocking, but I put mine on and nothing," Rachel complained to Charlene. "Apparently, most men are intimidated by a woman in uniform. Why do they have to be so cowardly and spineless?"

"Just go back to the hotel and change!" Charlene said.

"I can't! There are too many Navy officers here, including Admiral Eastwood. We're all supposed to be in uniform, and I don't really feel like taking shit for *not* being in uniform just for the possibility of what would likely be bad sex anyway."

Charlene laughed. "If you're okay with me telling people you're a secretary or something, I can probably help. But yeah, introducing you as the only female to ever pass SEAL training, let alone get put into leadership . . . I can see how men could find that intimidating."

"Charlene, seriously, I've been home from deployment for like a month and nothing. The most action I've gotten was Williams hugging me when I was crying about Aiden."

Charlene giggled and gave Rachel a wink.

"Matt, why aren't there any lesbians at your wedding?" Rachel asked as he walked up to her and Charlene.

"Striking out, are you?" Matt teased.

"I'm being serious! And yes, horribly. This uniform is like man repellant."

"Well, you know that you're in Kentucky, right? This is like the least liberal state in the entire country. So, even if there were a lesbian here, I don't think they'd be too open about it."

"Fuck! Why can't you be from California or something?"

Matt wrapped his arm around her shoulder and pulled her into him as he took a sip of his beer. "You know, I think this is the first time I've seen you fail to convince someone to go home with you."

"It's the fucking uniform," Rachel complained again.

"No, can't be the uniform. It's always worked for me." Matt grinned, and Charlene giggled again.

"Fine, it's the stupid patriarchal way we socialize men and boys in this country to be intimidated by strong women," Rachel corrected herself.

"See, I think that's a more accurate reason. Good luck, Sky!" Matt grabbed Charlene's hand and pulled her back to the dance floor just as Christopher was making his way over to the bar, empty beer bottle in hand.

"How's your night going?" Christopher asked after signaling the bartender to get him another beer.

"No luck," Rachel answered. "How about you?"

Christopher leaned his elbow into the bar, facing her. "I don't know. Weddings are always weird. Everyone knows everyone, it gets complicated . . . It seems your intel worked out for Ryan though." Christopher pointed across the room to where Ryan was leaving with Alyssa.

"Of course it did," Rachel said bitterly.

"Do we have to stay here?" Christopher asked.

"At the wedding or right in this exact spot?"

"Both," Christopher grimaced.

"What'd you have in mind?"

"Steal a bottle of whiskey and go somewhere less depressing?"

"How is your best friend's wedding depressing?"

"You know. Love, commitment, happily ever after? I'm never going to have that," Christopher said sadly.

"Well, that sounds more like jealousy than depression," Rachel said.

Christopher shrugged. "Whatever it is, it's unpleasant."

"Yeah," Rachel agreed. "I am happy for them, though. They're like this perfect one in a million couple that makes you think love is real and commitment works and all that."

"Well, I think it works for most people. We're just deployed so much."

Rachel choked on her laugh. "Be serious, Christopher. Combat or not, who the fuck is gonna love me like that?"

"Umm." Christopher didn't know how to answer. "You think you're unlovable?"

"Let's go." Rachel reached over the bar and grabbed a bottle of whiskey that was just barely in reach. Christopher took off his jacket and folded it over his arm just as she handed him the bottle, swiftly hiding it under his jacket.

She followed him out of the room, pressing her nails into the palms of both hands. There was no way she was having a conversation with him about just how unlovable she was. He'd seen her on her best days and her worst. There was no need to discuss the fact that no one could or should love her, or all the things that made it true. He knew the reasons already and so did she.

Christopher led Rachel to a back stairway. Rachel paused, realizing this was the 'great make-out spot' Ryan had told her about earlier. It was dimly lit and secluded. "You're taking me to Ryan's great make out spot?" She wrinkled her nose at Christopher.

"Yeah, technically." He shrugged.

"What exactly were you hoping was gonna happen?" She froze in place and stared straight ahead at the stairs.

"Drinking." He held up the bottle.

"That's it?"

"Yeah."

"Too bad," Rachel said, sitting down on the top step, just out of view from everyone else.

"How drunk are you right now?" He sat down beside her.

"Really not at all." She sighed.

"Then what's up?"

"Haven't gotten laid since we got home."

Christopher's brow furrowed with surprise. Normally that was the first thing each of them did as soon as they got off the plane.

"I've been with you so." She shrugged.

"Then let me revise my question. How desperate are you?" His upper lip curled as he squinted at her.

"I'm almost desperate enough to fuck you!" She laughed.

"What?" Christopher's eyes went wide with shock.

"Calm down, I'm joking. You don't remember when you said that to me?"

"No. When have I *ever* said that to you?" Panic and horror washed over his face.

"Last time we were in Khost, and I woke you up with a bottle of whiskey. You asked me to go get you the best thing in the world and complained you were so miserable and lonely that you were almost desperate enough to fuck me."

"Right." Christopher's face morphed into a half smirk, half cringe.

"Don't worry about it. You were half asleep."

"*Almost* desperate enough?" Christopher asked, one eyebrow raised curiously.

"If I ever get all the way desperate, I'll let you know." Rachel laughed uncomfortably before taking a sip of the whiskey straight from the bottle.

"How close to all the way are you right now?" He took the whiskey bottle out of her hand and put it to his lips as he nudged her shoulder with his.

"You want, like, a number?" Rachel wrinkled her nose.

"Yeah, give me a number." He was doing his best to suppress his smile. "Let's make one completely fine and stable and without need, and ten completely, entirely out of your mind desperate," Christopher suggested.

Rachel was happy he didn't seem to be taking her too seriously. "Seven."

"Hmm," Christopher mused as he ran his hand slowly from the base of her spine up to her neck. His thumb brushed along her skin, and he ran his fingers through the hair at the base of her skull, careful not to mess up her hair.

She could feel the warmth of his fingers. The pressure of his touch was just enough, and her heart rate increased instantly. The back of his hand slid delicately down her arm until her hand was in his, resting on her thigh. "Eight," she breathed.

He leaned into her, his breath warm in her ear. "How about now?" His voice turned low and sultry.

Rachel closed her eyes and swallowed the saliva that was filling her mouth. Tried to ignore her pounding heart and the tingling sensation in her extremities, and most importantly, all the wonderfully inappropriate ideas swirling around in her head. She opened her eyes and kept her gaze focused on the floor between her feet, knowing that if she looked into his deep blue eyes, that would be it. Maybe she was more desperate than she thought? Or maybe . . .

She shut down her thoughts instantly, knowing that nothing good could come from finishing them. "Nine." She balled her hands into fists so tight her knuckles turned white.

Christopher put his hand under her chin, turning her face toward his as he grazed her lips with his thumb, his eyes boring into hers. There was something in his gaze. Warmth, desire, longing. Rachel wasn't sure what it was. She didn't know if he was doing it on purpose just to fuck with her or if there were sincere feelings behind that look. It was intense, scorching even, almost possessive but in a good way. No one had ever looked at her like that before. The muscles in her core and pelvis tensed as the breath caught in her throat. She leaned into him, pressing her forehead to his as her lips parted. Their breath mingled and she put her palm on his cheek.

"Rachel," Christopher started. His index finger still held her chin, ready to tip her face up to his.

If she didn't stop now, she never would.

Rachel stood up as fast as she could. "Alright. Time for bed."

"Mine or yours?" he asked, actually sounding serious.

"Hilarious, Christopher," Rachel called, but there was no humor in her voice. She bolted down the stairs, cursing his blue eyes and firm but subtle touch. The exit seemed miles away as she tried to ignore the need inside her that was aching desperately like a ten, maybe a twelve. Christopher's fucked up desperation scale and his hand running up her back was the hottest thing she'd ever experienced. Or she really was entirely, hopelessly desperate. Desperate and completely fucked in the head. One of her best friends had just died, another had just gotten married, and all she could think about was sex. Sex with Christopher Williams, apparently. Maybe she was drunker than she thought. There was absolutely no excuse for thinking of him that way. He was her best friend and her subordinate. It was the definition of fraternization, let alone sexual harassment. If she acted on her thoughts even a little, she'd be out of a job and so would he. They'd both be dishonorably discharged, there was no question about it.

She had just made it to the landing, just barely out of view of the rest of the wedding guests milling around, when Christopher grabbed her wrist and spun her around to face him. They were standing so close that they were practically nose-to-nose, her face tilting up toward his once more. She swallowed, gulping for air.

"Ten," Rachel stated confidently as their eyes met. *Those goddamned blue eyes.* That look was back, full of passion and intense heat, but warm and caring and full of love. His eyes were so blue in the dim light of the stairwell that she thought she would drown. Her imagination ran wild thinking about what it would be like to kiss him. She forced her hands to behave, gripping the banister behind her and leaning against it, trying to put a few inches between them.

"Ten?" Christopher echoed. He gripped her wrist tightly with one hand and rested his other hand on her waist, pulling her into him as much as he dared.

She took a deep inhale, her chest rising slowly with each breath. Losing her restraint, she reached up to comb her fingers through his wavy, milk chocolate hair. "Eleven." She ran her tongue over her lips.

"I thought the scale stopped at ten?" Christopher asked as he pressed his forehead to hers.

"I thought we were going to bed." The words were barely audible. It was taking all her effort not to kiss him.

"Sure." His upper lip curled at her suggestion.

"Alone. Separately and alone. Definitely alone," Rachel clarified, though. her voice sounded more pleading and desperate than it ever had before.

"*Not* an eleven then."

She pulled her hand away, but it found a new spot, resting on his chest, not quite pushing him away. "Admiral Eastwood is here. Everyone is here. As entertaining as this is . . ." She glanced down the stairs, her eyes darting back and forth, ensuring they weren't being watched.

"Entertaining?"

"What do you want me to call it?"

"I want you to call it what it is."

"What is it?" Rachel furrowed her brow and met his gaze again.

"That's what I'm asking you."

"*I'm* calling it desperation. I'm pretty sure *you* could call it sexual harassment if you wanted to," she said.

"I don't want to." He pulled her closer, his hand sliding from the small of her back to her ass, pressing her hips into him.

"Alright . . . I think Corin was interested in you," Rachel tried to deflect.

"Who?" he mumbled into her hair, his lips grazing her temple.

"Charlene's sister."

"I'm not fucking Charlene's sister!" Christopher hissed, pulling his face away from hers slightly.

"Just me then?"

"Any day of the week," he said confidently, staring straight into her eyes.

"Go to bed, Christopher. This never happened." She nudged him away and rushed to the door.

Chapter 42:
MAY 2019

CHRISTOPHER HAD TAKEN RACHEL to pick up a rental car the next morning since there weren't any good flights from Lexington to Tampa. They hadn't discussed the previous night's events. It had never happened, just like Rachel had said. She was halfway home, somewhere around Atlanta, when she decided to turn and head for Montgomery, Alabama instead of Clearwater Beach, Florida. Flirting with Christopher had been a fun distraction, even if it had been highly inappropriate. She was feeling something. She didn't know what, but she knew the cure. That's what husbands were for, right? She stopped at a gas station and bought a Coke and a bottle of whiskey, then poured out some of the Coke from the bottle and added the whiskey, before she kept driving as fast as she dared. Before she thought the better of going to see Carter.

The whiskey numbed her thoughts and feelings a bit, but she kept thinking about Christopher and Aiden and Veeda. She was consumed by guilt and other things—feelings she couldn't name since she'd never had them before. Flirting with Christopher had been wrong. Sure, they flirted a little bit here and there, but last night had been something else. She really hadn't been drunk, but she wished she had been so she'd have something to blame her behavior on. He had been. But that was worse. That made it so much worse. Taking advantage of a friend, a colleague, a subordinate? Completely inappropriate, unprofessional, and unforgivable.

She was beyond drunk by the time she got to Carter's house—their house, technically. It was the middle of the night, but she didn't care. The spare key was easy enough to find, so she let herself in. She went to the bedroom where she undressed and climbed into bed with him. Wrapping herself around him, she whispered in his ear, "I need you."

"What the fuck are you doing here?" Carter mumbled, still half asleep.

"I couldn't sleep," Rachel said, slurring her words.

"God, how did you get here? You're drunk as shit, Rachel!" Carter was wide awake now. "How much have you had to drink and how did you get here?"

"Don't worry about it. You always worry," Rachel whined. "Are you going to be helpful or not?"

"Rachel, you cannot show up here in the middle of the night, drunk, and demand sex," Carter said.

"Since when?" Rachel asked as she took Carter's hand and guided it to where she wanted him to touch her. Carter pulled his hand away and got out of the bed. She followed him. He went and looked out the front window of the house and spotted her rental car.

"You drove here like this? Are you insane? You would've been safer hitchhiking!"

"You worry too much. It's no fun." Rachel was getting impatient.

"Did it ever occur to you that I have a life? You run off for months, sometimes years, with no word–"

Rachel cut him off. "What, like you're dating someone?" She scoffed. "Carter, be real, you could be dating a Victoria Secret model and would still fuck me if I asked you to. Not like that would ever happen." She fell into him and looked up, staring straight into his whiskey brown eyes that were nearly the same color as his hair.

"You can't keep doing this, Rache. Keep living like this. You're going to kill yourself!" He was standing face-to-face with her, his eyes slightly higher than hers, noses practically touching.

"I'm not trying to kill myself." Rachel pushed away from him and started searching the house for more alcohol.

"I didn't say you were trying. I said you were getting close to succeeding."

Rachel tripped over her own feet as she walked through the living room. Carter hadn't seen her this drunk in about nine years, not since after her first deployment as a SEAL. She'd never told him what had happened on that tour, and she wasn't about to start talking now.

"Give me your phone," Carter demanded.

"No."

"Yes, give me your phone. I'm going to call someone to come get you."

"Who the fuck are you going to call? Who's going to come and get me?" Rachel laughed.

Carter was standing over her, looking down at the floor. "I'm going to call Chris. Maybe he can talk some sense into you."

Rachel laughed again and used the arm of the couch to pull herself up off the floor. "No, you aren't going to call Christopher. Besides, he can't come get me. He's busy." The last person she needed to be thinking about was Christopher.

"For some reason, I don't believe you," Carter said. "Now, give me your phone!"

"Honey, if you want my phone, you're going to have to take it from me," Rachel said.

"Oh, it's that kind of night?" Carter snapped back at her. He understood what she wanted now. "You're truly fucked up, you know that, right?"

"Yes, I'm aware." She had found a bottle of whiskey and had just put it to her lips when Carter grabbed the bottle away from her and started chugging. If he was drinking, that meant he was giving in because he was going to need to be just as drunk as she was for this. She watched as he walked towards the kitchen, slamming the whiskey bottle onto the counter. Rachel winced. Not at the noise but from the realization that Carter very much resembled Christopher from behind. A shorter, less muscular version of Christopher, but she was drunk enough that it triggered the fucked-up fantasies in her head.

Carter turned around and stared at her. His brown eyes brought her back to reality and she'd never been so appreciative of brown eyes before.

"What the fuck is wrong with you?" he asked.

Rachel tripped over her feet again, falling on the floor, giggling this time. There were too many things wrong with her for her to pick just one. "First you wanted my phone. Now you want the whiskey? Make up your mind!"

"Shut the fuck up, Rachel," Carter demanded. He knelt on the floor and grabbed her by the arm, flipping her onto her stomach and pinning her arm behind her back.

Rachel squirmed under his weight. "You'll have to do it harder than that!" She easily got out of his grip and rolled onto her back again. "I'm not that drunk!" Carter used the full force of his weight to hold her down, pinning her arms over her head this time with her back flat on the floor. She wrapped her legs around his waist and pulled him in closer for a kiss. "Do your worst," she dared him.

She was desperate to feel anything other than what she was actually feeling. Desperate for physical pain to overtake all the memories that were camped out in her head like a perpetual plague of nightmares. They wouldn't go away. Watching Aiden run past her across the courtyard, hearing the call over the radio, seeing his dead body, trying to take away Matt's guilt, talking to Aiden's parents, the coffin being lowered into the ground. Aiden's death was too much for her to bear, and she was already incessantly haunted by so many memories. Then there was her guilt over Veeda. Her mind was consumed with the atrocities of war and the horrors of other things. Too many things to count. Horrible, awful things that she had seen, that she had done, that she couldn't erase any other way.

Rachel woke up badly bruised. She had fought back just enough to provoke Carter, but not enough to hurt him. She had gotten exactly what she wanted, what she needed. Physical punishment for her guilt, her shame, her hatred of herself for all the terrible things she had done. Rough sex usually did the trick. It was like medicine. The perfect drug. A seductive mixture of pleasure and pain that made all the bad feelings disappear. All of *her* bad feelings, anyway. She was lying on the living room floor alone and naked, an empty bottle of whiskey next to her, yet she was feeling better than the day before. Her head was quiet. The medicine had worked, and she finally had her relief, at least for now. She counted Carter's steps as he walked around the house and knew exactly where he was until he was on the floor next to her. She turned her head to look at him, tears falling down her face. Carter clenched his jaw, unable to meet her gaze. She could tell by the way he held himself taut, angled away from her, that he had betrayed her.

"You called Christopher, didn't you?" she asked. "That's what you were doing in the bedroom for so long." Carter said nothing. "You shouldn't have done that."

"Don't try to pick another fight, Rache. That part's done," Carter explained.

"It's an invasion of privacy," Rachel argued.

"Rachel, you have to stop taking on all the world's problems. You are not to blame for even a fraction of the things you take responsibility for." His voice was stern but full of empathy as he ran his fingers through her tangled hair.

Rachel slapped his hand away. She didn't want to be comforted. Certainly not by him. "You have no idea what I've done, what I've seen, what I've asked others to do."

"Rachel, it's war! Shit happens, and that shit is not your fault."

"Do it again, Carter!"

Carter sighed and took her hand in his. "Honey, I know we have our issues, together and separately. That sometimes we can really hate each other. I know you hate yourself a lot of the time. It's been twenty-five years that we've known each other. I know you, maybe even better than you know yourself. If you want to lie here and blame yourself for something you had no control over, that's on you. Just know that no matter what we're fighting about or how long you're away for, I love you. I love the person you are deep down. I know that girl is still inside you somewhere. War hasn't changed you as much as you pretend it has. You're still kind and compassionate. Otherwise, this loss wouldn't hurt so bad. You wouldn't blame yourself." Carter paused. Rachel was just staring at him, frozen. "Rachel, it kills me that you can't love yourself, that you won't let yourself be happy. That no matter what I say or do, you find some way to take on everyone else's shit. It's generous and kind that you want to make everyone else feel better, but it's clearly hurting you." He paused again, waiting to see if she'd say anything. He was met with silence. "Chris said that one of your guys ran into enemy fire to pull them away from the rest of you and save one of your informants. If that's what happened, then honey, there wasn't anything you could have done."

Rachel started crying again. Quiet tears streamed down her face like rain on a windowpane.

"Do you want to tell me what happened?" Carter asked, brushing his fingers through her hair.

Rachel's tears turned to sobs as she told him about Aiden, when he'd joined her team, how funny and smart he had been, everything leading up to the last mission. Then she told him about Veeda. Carter let her talk and talk. She stopped and skipped parts of the story when she needed to, either because something was classified or because it was too hard for her to say out loud. Rachel paused and her voice got quiet. "Sometimes I wish it had been me and not him, you know?"

Carter took her hand in his. "I know you can't believe this yet, but there wasn't anything you could have done."

Chapter 43:
JUNE 2019

A WEEK PASSED AND Rachel was lonely. Visiting Carter had temporarily helped ease her guilt. She had spent the next few days drunk and hooking up with strangers, trying to make herself feel better. Her drunken partying and random hookups weren't cutting it though, so she flew from Tampa to New York. From there, she took a taxi into the city and checked into a hotel in Manhattan, then called Ryan to make plans for dinner.

Rachel changed into a red halter top, dark jeans, black heels, and a black clutch. She fixed her hair—deciding to have it down and curled—put on some tinted moisturizer, mascara and red lip gloss. She tossed her ID, phone, lip gloss, wallet, and room key into her clutch. She checked the weather app on her phone and, after seeing that the temperature had dropped to the mid sixties, put on her black leather bomber jacket and went down to the lobby to meet Ryan.

"Well, don't you look nice!" Ryan said when he saw her. He was wearing dark jeans, a charcoal gray button-up, and a black jacket.

"You too!" Rachel said, giving him a hug. She winced as his arms tightened around her.

"What's wrong?" Ryan asked.

"Nothing."

Ryan looked her up and down then poked her in the ribs. She winced again and he chuckled, giving her a knowing look. "Rough sex?"

"Shut the fuck up." Rachel scowled.

"Did it assuage your guilt and grief?" Ryan asked playfully, knowing he'd been right.

"What did I just say?"

Ryan raised a quizzical eyebrow.

"No, it did not. If you'd like to kick my ass later, I'm all for it."

Ryan burst out laughing. "You know, Sky, as amused as I am by your masochistic tendencies, I really don't feel the need to participate." He linked his arm with hers so they could walk the three blocks to an Asian fusion restaurant.

They were shown to a booth in the middle of the restaurant and got cocktails before perusing the menu and ordering food.

"So, home's boring?" Ryan asked Rachel, raising his voice so she would hear him over the chatter of the other patrons.

"Yeah, well, when you run into the same people over and over, it's time for a change," Rachel said.

Ryan shook his head. "You've worked your way through an entire city?" he teased.

"Ugh, you know what I mean! And no, not an entire city, just everywhere that's walking distance. In any case, I'm finding my lifestyle less and less fulfilling," she grumbled.

"What? Drunk meaningless sex isn't meeting your emotional needs?" Ryan pretended to be surprised.

Rachel propped her elbow on the table and her hand on her fist. "Is it meeting yours?"

Ryan stared at her for a minute. "You know, I actually talk to my family and have friends here in New York that I hang out with when I'm home. I know you're more or less on your own down there. It can't be easy."

"I'm fine. Just bored," Rachel assured him. Their food came, and they started eating. "Besides, only two more months until I need to be back at base."

"What are you going to do for two months though?" Ryan asked, immediately more concerned than he'd already been. "We've been home for three weeks and you're bored out of your mind already. At some point, you're going to need to put down roots somewhere. You can't keep doing what you're doing, Sky. And before you even start, yes, I'm aware you plan to die in combat, but until that happens, while you're home, you've got to figure something out! I mean, do you even have a functioning liver anymore? And I'm guessing most of your paycheck goes to condoms at this point." He eyed the cocktail sitting next to her. Her second of the evening.

Rachel glared at him. "I came to have fun with my friend, not get a lecture!"

"I know. But your allergy to the mundane is what's going to get you killed, not combat. Promise to think about it," Ryan said. It was one thing to get drunk and fuck around for a few days here and there while they were on leave, but not every day.

"And what exactly do you do that's any different from me?" Rachel asked, knowing he wasn't much better than she was.

"I help my mom fix up her apartment and take her to shows and babysit for my sisters and then *sometimes* I go out and get drunk and get laid. Not every day. You've gotta slow down."

"Yeah. There's just so much in my head, you know?" Rachel said.

"Try therapy. Chris says it's fantastic," Ryan said, skeptically.

"You're one to talk!"

"What the hell does that mean?"

"I'll go when you go," Rachel challenged. "Besides, I keep getting cleared. Apparently, I don't have any mental health problems."

"Other than insomnia and using alcohol and sex as a distraction."

"As if the rest of you don't do that too? You and Christopher are just as bad as I am! You just don't want to admit it. Or maybe it's because I'm a woman? Maybe that's why it's a problem?" Rachel was getting annoyed now.

"No, it's not cause you're a woman. It's because you drink a bottle of whiskey by yourself most days of the week. It's a bit much. I get you're running from shit, and you know very well that I know what most of that shit is, but it's not going away any time soon, so you need to fucking deal with it."

They finished eating and meandered the streets of Manhattan, and Ryan lead Rachel past as many tourist attractions as he could. As they stood in the middle of Times Square, surrounded by people, Rachel felt alone. She was with Ryan and they were having a great time, despite his incessant lecturing, but something was missing. Her heart felt empty, if that was a thing. Getting over her guilt and grief were only part of the problem. Filling up the emptiness was the real problem—the dark void of feeling alone even when she was with other people. Her thoughts were a jumbled mess of her own trauma and Ryan's lectures on the importance of self-care. She tried to sort through it but couldn't. Every time she made progress untangling the emotional nightmare that was the inside of her mind, Christopher's face flashed before her eyes. She pressed her eyes together, but she could still feel his hand on her back, could remember what it had felt like being pressed up against him in that stairwell at Matt's wedding. She focused on that memory—his blue eyes, his warm touch, his steady voice, his bright smile. A wave of calm washed over her, and it was suddenly clear what the problem had been all week. She missed Christopher. She texted him every day, but it wasn't the same. She missed his physical presence more than she had ever missed anything.

Her face twisted into a smirk. She knew how to fix that problem. It was a pretty dumb problem to have actually, so she sent him a selfie of her and Ryan and told him to come meet them in New York.

Christopher caught the first available flight from Dallas and met up with Rachel and Ryan in Manhattan. After a day of exploring the city, they all crashed in the king-sized bed in Rachel's hotel room, with Rachel sleeping in the middle.

The next morning, Christopher woke up, surprised to find that Rachel was still asleep. She was lying on her side, facing him with her head on his shoulder, her arm around him, completely pressed up against him. Her shorts had slid up, and she had thrown the blankets off, giving him a glimpse of her perfect ass. Her t-shirt was scrunched up too, exposing her slender waist, ribs, and flat stomach. It had been tight with all three of them in the bed, but not so tight that she had to be entirely intertwined with him. Waking up like this was not a first, but she had never looked quite this . . . tranquil. Her hair was down and everywhere and smelled like lavender. Christopher wasn't used to seeing her with her hair down. It was gorgeous. Her hips and pelvis pressed against him a little more than they usually did, and her leg was wrapped securely around his, urging him closer to her. His head and his body were telling him two very different things, which normally was not the case. One thing he should do, and the other he wanted to do. He knew he had to let his head win this one, but she was so perfect lying there with him. He fought against his instincts, everything he would have done if she'd been another girl, any other girl, tangled up with him like that, looking like that. Running shorts and a t-shirt had never seemed so sexy before, or sexy at all. He glanced around and noticed Ryan wasn't there but heard that the shower was on. They were all alone—for better or worse.

"Sky," he whispered in her ear, doing his best to resist the urge to kiss her. "Time to wake up. It's morning."

She made a noise, a very cute noise, and curled in closer to him, running her hand under his t-shirt and along his chest. Not the result he was going for. He turned his head away, trying not to look at her, but he could still feel every inch of her body pressed against his, from her forehead to her perky round breasts to her perfectly toned thighs.

Ryan came out of the bathroom and saw what was happening. He took one look at Christopher's face and laughed. "Well, she sure looks cozy," he said.

Christopher gave him a desperate look, pleading with Ryan to help get her off of him.

Ryan grabbed Rachel's ankle and dragged her to the other side of the bed. "Wake up!" he yelled at her before slapping her hard on her ass.

"What the fuck, Ryan!" Rachel yelled.

"Time for breakfast, sleeping beauty," Ryan said.

★ ★ ★

That night Rachel was pounding whiskey and tequila shots, talking to people at the bar and having a great time. Christopher saw how drunk she was and stopped drinking. After what he had woken up to that morning, he wasn't sure he could control himself if he was drunk too. He thanked God that Ryan was with them, certain that nothing would happen if Ryan were in the room, or in the same bed, actually. As if she could read his thoughts, Rachel came bouncing up to him and put her arm around his waist. He put his arm around her shoulder, trying to steady her.

"I'm very drunk," Rachel stated, looking up at him. "I lost Raven, I dunno where he is." She scrunched up her face and looked around the room in search of Ryan. "Christopher?" She sounded scared and rested her hand on his bicep, leaning into him to hold herself up.

"What?" he asked.

"Don't let me leave with anyone but you, okay?"

He pulled her closer to him so he could whisper in her ear. "You okay?"

"Yeah, just don't let me leave," she said seriously.

"Promise," Christopher assured her. He stayed close to her after that, watching out for her and taking drinks away from her when she wasn't paying attention. He pulled out his phone to text Ryan.

Hawk to Raven: *Where are you?*

No answer. Christopher kept following Rachel around the bar until Ryan finally texted him back.

Raven to Hawk: *Got distracted*

Christopher rolled his eyes. He knew exactly what kind of distraction Ryan meant.

Hawk to Raven: *Sky's drunk as shit. We're by the bar. Come here.*

Ryan made his way over to the bar just in time to see Rachel trip and Christopher catch her. Rachel could handle her liquor more than well. If she was falling over, then she was very far beyond drunk, and they needed to get her home ASAP.

"For fuck's sake!" Ryan shouted.

"Youuu caaame baaack!" Rachel fell on Ryan, giving him a big hug and drawing out each word.

"You seem to be having fun," he said as he put his arm around her waist to hold her up. He gave Christopher a puzzled look. "Let's get you home, okay?"

"No, no, *we're* not going home, Ryan." Rachel placed her palm on his chest and shook her head so fast that she lost her balance again.

"Why not?" he asked. Rachel was leaning on him, barely able to stand.

"Cause I'm gonna go home with Christopher, thaaat's why," Rachel explained, as though it should have been obvious. "I already decided."

Ryan was confused. He pointed at Christopher. "That Christopher, or did you meet a different Christopher that you're planning to go home with?"

Rachel hit Ryan playfully on the chest. "Dhun't be shtupid, Ryan." She was slurring her words now but managed to stand up and walk back to the bar, to speak to someone she had met earlier.

Ryan looked at Christopher, wide-eyed. "Who is she trying to leave with?" he asked, looking over at the bar.

"She made me promise not to let her leave with anyone other than me, so I assume she means me? And I'm thinking now would be a good time to go," Christopher said as he saw Rachel reach for another shot of tequila.

Ryan was standing closest to Rachel and swiftly grabbed her around the waist, pulling her to him before she could pick up the shot glass. "Time to go, Sky. It's bedtime."

She gave him an angry look. "Buuut I'ma nah gonna go home with youuu," she explained again.

"Sky, Chris is coming too. We're all going to the same place."

Rachel giggled. "That should be in-ter-es-ting," she said, looking back and forth between the two of them.

Christopher covered his mouth with his hand as his eyes got wide. This was going to be a rough night. He put his arm around Rachel and pulled her away from Ryan. "Let's go, Skylark," he ordered her, pushing her in front of him toward the exit. "Ryan," he said seriously as Rachel stumbled ahead of him towards the door.

"What?" Ryan answered.

"Do not, under any circumstances, leave her alone with me tonight."

"I kinda think we shouldn't leave her alone with anyone, especially not you." Ryan cringed.

They walked back to the hotel with Ryan and Christopher on either side of Rachel. She had her arm tight around Christopher's waist and was refusing to let go. She started singing "Sugar" by Maroon 5 and trying to dance with him as they walked, singing the song over and over until they got back to the hotel.

As soon as she walked into their room, she took off her shirt and started taking off her jeans. Christopher immediately turned and looked at the wall. He was thinking about her in ways he should definitely not be thinking about her and knew he could not handle this. She was still singing, mostly to him, and somewhat to herself.

Ryan jumped into action and redirected her to the bathroom. He turned the shower on as cold as it went and shoved Rachel half-dressed under the water. He left her standing there and went out, closing the door behind him.

"Jesus Christ!" Ryan said. "What the fuck happened? How is she so drunk?"

"I think it's a mix of a lot of whiskey and several tequila shots. Maybe some beer," Christopher answered.

"Well, at least she's happy and not trying to murder anyone."

"No, she's just trying to do . . . other things," Christopher said as Rachel came out of the bathroom in her underwear, soaking wet.

"Are y'all just gonna leave me in there by myself?" she asked.

"Yes," Christopher and Ryan said in unison. Christopher was staring at the floor.

"Well, *that's* nah very helpful, is it?" She winked at them.

"Rachel Ryker, I will slap you in the face so hard if you do not get your shit together in the next five seconds," Ryan shouted at her.

"I dare ya," Rachel said playfully.

Christopher didn't know whether to laugh or cry. This would have been entertaining if he wasn't so turned on. Ryan walked over to the medic kit he had brought with him from home and pulled out a roll of duct tape and all the supplies necessary to set up an IV drip.

"I swear to God, Rachel," Ryan said as he walked over to her. She was still singing and dancing, using the door frame as a makeshift stripper pole. He pushed her back into the bathroom, kicking the door closed behind him. He forced her back into the shower and onto the floor. "Did you see how hot the girl was I had to walk away from because of your drunk, stupid ass?" He grabbed her arm and inserted the needle for the IV into her skin, then taped the IV bag to the wall. He shut off the water and went to get a towel to cover her up with. "Sit there, shut up, and behave!"

Ryan left Rachel in the bathroom by herself again and went back out to join Christopher, closing the door as he left. He was speechless for the first time in his life.

Christopher shook his head, his arms crossed in front of his chest. "Am I imagining things or . . ."

"Or is she coming on to you?" Ryan finished. "Yeah, what the fuck? That was weird."

Christopher didn't know if he was more surprised by Rachel's behavior or by how much he liked Rachel's behavior.

"I'm assuming you aren't feeling sexually harassed and we don't need to make a thing of this?" Ryan asked. "I mean technically . . ."

Christopher shook his head. "No, she's just drunk," he said. "This stays between us." They both knew Rachel could get in a lot of trouble with the Navy if anyone else had been there. She could get charged with any number of things and be court-martialed for this, potentially dishonorably discharged.

Christopher waited thirty minutes before checking on her, hoping that the IV had rehydrated her back to sanity. "Sky, you okay?" he asked, peeking his head in the door.

"My head hurts," she whined.

"Yeah, I'll bet it does. You drank way too much. You probably could use a second IV. I'll go get another bag."

"No, cause Ryan slammed me againssst tha wall," Rachel corrected him.

"Well, you sort of had that coming. Let me look." Rachel bent her head forward so that Christopher could check the back of her head. He went in and knelt in front of her. "It's not bleeding, but I'll go get you some ice. And some clothes," he added, looking at her half-covered with a towel.

"Christopher," Rachel said tenderly, looking up at him. "Thank you."

"For what?"

"For being you," she said sincerely.

He was kneeling so close to her, close enough to feel the damp warmth of her skin, smell her lingering perfume. He wanted to kiss her so badly, and so he leaned in, his breath catching in his throat as he tucked a strand of loose wet hair behind her ear. The green of her eyes widened, and her lips parted. Just as he thought he might do it, he cleared his throat and stood up. "Ice." He nodded and forced himself to turn away from her.

He came back to the room with a bucket of ice and rifled through her bag to find a clean shirt and pants. No more cute little shorts, he decided. She would be getting only long loose sweatpants. He took the ice and clothes into the bathroom. She was still pretty drunk, but much improved from earlier. He pulled her up off the floor and the towel fell.

"What the fuck did you do?" Christopher stared at her, at the yellowing bruise that covered her ribs.

Rachel scrunched up her face and fell into him, her palm on his chest as she tried to steady herself. He gripped her shoulders and leaned her away from him, inspecting the bruise. He slid his fingers over it gingerly, and she winced.

"Rachel, what the hell happened?"

She waved her hand as though it were nothing.

"Are you running around Clearwater getting into bar fights?"

"No, nothing like that," she said, blinking a few times before looking away.

He cocked his head to the side. Something was wrong. "Rachel, last chance to tell me, honestly, how you got that bruise." When she scoffed in response, Christopher swiftly kicked her right leg away from her left, then spun her around so that her face was pressed against the cool tiles of the shower wall. He kept one hand on her back so she wouldn't move and ran his other hand over her arms, torso, and legs, finding even more bruises, all in places that would indicate something very different from a bar fight. "Who did this to you?"

"Don't worry 'bout it," Rachel mumbled.

"Did you get carried away or was this intentional?" He poked a bruise on her hip as he crouched behind her, noting several bruises on her inner thigh.

"I dunno what you're talking about," Rachel lied.

Christopher stood up and wrapped his arms around her, pressing his face into her neck. "You're not okay, are you?"

"I'm fine."

"I know. You're always fine." He tightened his arms around her. "You did this last time too."

"What did I do what time?" Rachel murmured, either too drunk or pretending not to have any idea what he was talking about.

"After Henry died . . . We were in Kansas City on our way to his funeral, and you ran off by yourself and showed up the next morning, well, worse than this."

"Are you done judging me?" Rachel's tone was cold as ice.

"I'm not judging." Christopher sighed, pressing his lips into the back of her head. "I just want you to be safe. I guess happy is too much to hope for right now."

Rachel pulled his arms tighter around her. "This helps."

PART III:

HONOR

Chapter 44:
MAY 2020

THE MONTHS WENT BY, dragging one year into the next. Rachel had thrown herself into her work, reading every intel report, every brief, and texting every contact she had in the Middle East, desperate to hunt down Samir Al-Abadi. The team had spent two months training at Dam Neck and getting to know their new communications specialist, Sam King, call sign *Falcon*. It was still weird working without Aiden, but life went on. It had to. By May, their intel had led them to Syria.

They had spent the past month shooting their way through several compounds, losing track of how many people they'd killed, collecting intel as they went, but nearly missing Samir Al-Abadi each step of the way. While none of them minded killing terrorists, it was getting tedious and frustrating to feel like they were so close to Samir, though they never actually saw him. They collected documents, cell phones, and computers at each compound, finding evidence that Samir had been there recently. They knew they were on the right track, but somehow, he kept slipping away.

Rachel was standing next to the team's truck, laughing her ass off and pointing at it as it burned. Fortunately, no one had been injured . . . except for the truck. The truck was fucked. They'd been using it as cover while exchanging fire with several members of an ISIS terror cell until they saw someone pull out a rocket-propelled grenade launcher. Then they'd run. They'd all run.

Michael had been pissed. None of them wanted to hike through the desert, least of all him, so he'd loaded his sniper rifle and went to town, throwing caution to the wind. He'd run at top speed toward the enemy, skillfully taking them out one at a time. Rachel and Christopher had been right next to him laying down cover fire until there was no one left to shoot back. The truck had been the only casualty. All twelve members of Indigo were happy, healthy, and whole as they listened to Christopher explain that they would need to trek twenty miles per day through the desert to stay on schedule and reach what they hoped would be the final compound, according to the emails Daniel had read on the cell phone they'd just recovered.

Happy may have been an overstatement. It was unseasonably warm, with temperatures reaching a sweltering 101 degrees Fahrenheit during the day and staying at about 80 degrees at night. Rachel didn't know where exactly they were and she had stopped caring. Somewhere in Syria, in the desert west of Damascus but north of Az Zalaf, was all she knew. Christopher knew where they were and where they were going, and that was good enough. He could lead the entire team through the desert to find the next ISIS compound just fine without her input, but with the scorching heat and all their gear, morale was taking a dive.

"I always figured if I died in the Middle East, it would be from a bullet," Rachel complained as streams of sweat trickled down her face and neck. She was too tired to set a good example for the rest of the team.

"Seriously, we've been walking forever! When are we going to get there?" Ryan whined. More exceptional leadership.

"That depends on how fast we walk," Christopher answered. "We're behind schedule. We need to walk twenty miles before we can sleep. We've only gone ten."

"That's because it's so fucking hot!" Rachel exclaimed. "My mother keeps telling me I'm going to burn in hell for all my sins. I guess she was right. I just figured I'd be dead first!" There was a chorus of chuckles and swearing from the rest of the team.

"I still don't understand why we can't get another truck and why we have to walk," Michael complained.

"Where are we gonna get another truck from?" Christopher asked. "We're nowhere near a base. You think we're all gonna get airlifted back to base, get another truck, and start from the beginning? This isn't a video game. There's no whoopsies you failed, now go back and start again at the last place you saved."

"Obviously I know it's not a video game," Michael pointed out.

Christopher stopped short and stared at him before pressing his thumb and finger to the bridge of his nose "What's worse, walking a little bit or wasting a bunch of time going back to base and starting over? These assholes are moving the entire time. Right now, we're hot on their tail. There is no way in hell we're going to any base to get a truck when we can walk twenty miles today and thirty miles tomorrow and get to where we're going. Or do you have a better option?"

"Umm." Michael looked up at the sky. Nothing he said would be a good answer.

"Start walking and stop complaining," Christopher ordered.

They finally got to the tiny dot on Christopher's map that indicated their stopping point for the day and got to work setting up camp. Fortunately, they had been able to save some supplies from the truck before the engine exploded and the flames spread. Rachel glanced at her watch then looked around at everyone. "It's almost 2100. Let's try to sleep for eight hours. That gets us back up and moving by 0500. Should be cooler then. It's too dangerous to stop and sleep during the day so, it'll have to do. We'll set up watch in two hour shifts with two people per shift. That way everyone gets six hours to sleep and eat and do whatever else they wanna do."

Christopher was on first watch with David, followed by Ryan and Michael, Rachel and Daniel, then Matt and Sam. After chugging a protein shake, Rachel got ready for bed. Ryan was faster than her, as usual, and had already claimed a blanket. She went over and laid down next to him, shoving him over to one side as she did. "You have to share!" she ordered playfully. As Rachel lay down, she looked across their camp at Christopher and said, "Song, please!"

"I can't sing it until you're in bed with your eyes closed." Christopher walked over to her and looked down at her with a smile.

Rachel squeezed her eyes closed as tightly as she could for dramatic effect. He smiled and started singing. He was as musically gifted as Rachel was. A talented singer and an even better guitar player. He knew what song she wanted to hear: "American Pie" by Don McLean. Years ago, they had been stuck in the desert, hearing the sounds of machine guns several miles off in every direction. They had been more or less safe where they were, but Rachel hadn't been able to sleep, so Christopher had sung in an attempt to drown out the noise from the nearby battles. It worked. She had fallen asleep next to him, listening to the sound of his voice within minutes. The song had been renamed by the next morning and was commonly referred to by the team as "Skylark's Lullaby."

Rachel shifted in her sleep, sensing that Christopher was beside her. She turned toward him, and put her arm on his, her forehead pressed up against him.

"Hey," she mumbled in her sleep.

"Two more hours till your turn," Christopher whispered to her. He turned onto his side to face her and wrapped his arm around her, pulling her in close to him. She buried her face in his chest and fell back asleep.

Rachel woke up at 0045 for her turn to be on watch. She untangled herself from Christopher and got up. She was feeling nervous and wanted to talk to Ryan privately. A quick nod in the direction of the bedrolls had Michael darting off to bed.

Ryan flashed her a grin. "Couldn't sleep?"

Rachel shook her head. "Bad feeling."

"Well," Ryan started, "at least we won't have to do any interrogations on this trip and the CIA is staying out of things."

Rachel smirked. "When we catch my buddy Sammy, I will be having a chat with him, but that's really not the same thing."

"Your buddy Sammy?" Ryan furrowed his brow and his lip curled slightly.

"Yup. I've been wanting to have a chat with him for a while."

"You just want to know how his mind works." Ryan shook his head. "What are you gonna ask him?" He leaned against a pile of backpacks and looked up at the stars.

"I'm gonna ask him why." Rachel picked up a stick and started drawing circles in the dirt. "Why so many things. He's done a lot of things and so have I. He and I aren't so different. We just don't believe the same thing. If we did . . ."

"Yeah, that would be terrifying." Ryan gave a bitter laugh. "So we find him, you have a chat, then you kill him?"

"That's the plan," Rachel confirmed.

"You're sure the CIA doesn't want him?"

"They can't have him."

"Why not? Just hand him over after your chat. I'm sure they'll still let you be the one to shoot him once they're done with him. Hell, I'm sure they'll let you be lead interrogator."

"No. I'll chat with him, and if I learn anything pertinent, then I'll fill The Agency in on what they need to know. They can't get their way all the time."

"They do tend to kill the people who don't do what they say," Ryan pointed out.

"It's fine. They won't kill me. They need me too much. You too, by the way. Don't ever let them boss you around. You and I are way too good at our jobs, and we know way too much about too many people."

"You have so many plans, don't you?" Ryan chuckled.

"I have plans. I have information. And one day, someone will piss me off enough and enough horrible things will happen that I'll have no choice but to let everyone know all the horrific things I know," Rachel said somberly. She stared at the dirt silently for several minutes before speaking again, a hint of worry in her voice. "The gun safe in my apartment . . . There's a false bottom. There's a lot of stuff in there . . . files . . . if something happens, when I die, go get it."

"Okay. What do you want me to do with it?" Ryan asked hesitantly.

"I presume you'd read it all regardless of what I told you to do with it." She gave him a sideways glance. Ryan always followed orders, but that didn't mean he didn't reinterpret some of those orders, and if she were dead, he'd be too curious to leave anything that had been in her possession unread.

"What's the code to your gun safe?" Ryan asked.

"It's your birthday since you're the one who would need to go get everything. That way you can't forget. Six digits. Month, day, year."

"10 20 90. Alright. I'll take care of it." Ryan gripped her thigh and looked her in the eye before getting up to wake Daniel for his turn on watch.

Rachel sat up for the next two hours with Daniel, interrogating him about all things technology and trying to get a sense of what tech hadn't gotten too damaged when the truck blew up.

Realizing she wouldn't be able to go back to sleep, she elected to stay on watch with Sam, letting Matt sleep. They packed up what gear they could and organized the morning's rations so that food would be ready when people woke up. She couldn't cook, but she could mix protein powder and water while she talked to Sam.

"How are you feeling? How's it going?" Rachel asked him as she scooped protein powder into twelve shakers.

"You know . . . intense," Sam answered as he filled each shaker with water.

"Is it everything you'd hoped it would be?" Rachel joked.

"Yeah. I did two deployments with regular SEAL teams before getting into Special Projects. I guess everyone did?"

Rachel nodded. Sam didn't need to know a few of them had been exempt from that rule. "You're feeling okay though? We had quite a bit of action."

"No, it's great! I mean, people keep harassing me to use the satphone more than they should." He gestured to the only working satellite phone the team had, clipped onto the outer strap of his daypack.

"Yeah." Rachel laughed. "I assure you they will continue to do so whether you let them use it or not."

"Well, what's the general rule? How often should I be letting people use it to call home?"

Rachel shrugged. "We've never had a rule. I think the guiding principle before was if you could tell Aiden a convincing enough story as to why you needed to use it and filled him in on all the gossip, then he'd hand it over."

"That sounds expensive."

"Well, I get the bill, and I can see exactly who's calling who and when and for how long, so don't worry about it too much. Let people use the phone enough to bond and build friendships, but don't let them take advantage." Rachel gave him an encouraging smile. She didn't know the phone rules, even if she was team leader, since she never used the phone except to call a regional command center or SEAL HQ. Everyone she wanted to talk to was right here.

Her eyes moved over to Christopher. Since New York, something had shifted between them. She'd been thinking about New York a lot, trying to remember what had happened after leaving the bar. She hadn't blacked out in at least a decade, but mixing whiskey and tequila was a combination that never turned out well for her. Somehow though, that potent mixture had caused several dots to connect in her brain. She'd been putting barricades up, blocking those dots from connecting for years. It was clear now though. She was physically attracted to Christopher. Obviously, everyone was. On top of that, she was emotionally connected to him in a way she'd never been with anyone else. Their souls seemed to operate on the same frequency, the same vibration, and they were always in sync. It could only mean one thing. One horrible life changing, perspective changing, world shifting thing.

She was head over heels in love with Christopher Williams.

She couldn't be though, shouldn't be. She knew she had to shut down her feelings and make sure he never felt the same way about her as she did about him.

Chapter 45:
MAY 2020

THE REST OF THE team woke up, ate, and packed. Matt didn't seem to notice that Rachel had never woken him up, or maybe he was just used to it. They all knew she didn't sleep much. Christopher, as always, was the last to wake up. Rachel went over to him and knelt down before whispering in his ear. "Good morning, sleepy head. Time to rise and shine!"

He shifted and opened his eyes, smiling when he saw her face. "Good morning," he said groggily. "Did you get any sleep?"

"Yes, four solid hours. Now get up. We've gotta get moving, and no one but you knows where we're going!"

They headed out as quickly as they could and followed Christopher southeast, walking for six hours before stopping to eat around noon. They ate quickly and then headed off again, knowing they needed to make up as much time as possible. After walking thirty miles, Christopher finally announced they were stopping.

"Skylark, come look at the map with me," he called. She walked over to him to look. "We're about five miles from the compound where Samir's group is allegedly staying–"

"Hang on," Daniel interrupted before rushing over to them. "The phone I grabbed at the last compound is still on, still receiving emails. It looks like they moved again."

"What?" Rachel clenched her jaw and ripped the phone out of his hand to read the email for herself.

Heading back to Damascus. Left the code though in case you need the original file while we're all away.
-Samir

"Are you fucking kidding me?" Rachel muttered.

"Our original mission was to retrieve the USB stick and code. I guess we can do that easily enough if no one's home." Daniel shrugged. Christopher nodded in agreement.

"Keep this phone charged," Rachel told Daniel. "We'll recover the USB stick and then see if we've received any more texts or emails and go from there."

"Go from there?" Daniel frowned. "If we get the USB stick, we're done."

"We're done when I say we're done," Rachel corrected. "We will recover the USB then continue to track Samir Al-Abadi until I'm done killing him."

"Yes ma'am." Daniel pursed his lips as he took a sharp inhale.

"Okay, well, to refocus," Christopher cut in. "I know this compound is supposed to be empty, but probably smart to take a break here and go after dark, just to be safe."

"We should do a flyover with the drone and infrared scanner to be sure it's empty," Rachel added.

"Drone's dead," Daniel told her. "The drone itself still works, but the battery is dead, and all the spare batteries and charger were in the truck."

Rachel stared at him then blinked twice, trying to process what he'd just said. "I swear we had a conversation about this last night while we were on watch. You gave me a list of tech that got destroyed when the truck blew up. You failed to mention anything about the drone."

"The drone isn't tech," Daniel noted.

Rachel failed to see the distinction. The drone had batteries, which in her opinion made it technology. The fact that Nate operated the drone rather than Daniel hardly excused his failure to mention the drone was broken. "Okay then." She pursed her lips and glanced around, looking for Nate. He was sitting on the ground, pouting, and she took that to mean that there was no hope of reviving the drone. She checked her watch. It was 1600. "Since that email says Damascus is next, and we need a truck to get there, I guess we'll hit this compound, get the USB, and then get airlifted to a base and resupply while we figure out our next move. I'll call command and see what time someone wants to come get us tonight. It should take us, what, about an hour and forty-five to walk to the compound? Maybe a couple of hours to search and collect intel?"

Christopher nodded in agreement.

"What's the best extraction point for a helicopter and how far is it?"

"The extraction point is a mile and a half away from the compound. Helicopter would land here." Christopher pointed at a red *x* in the top right corner of the map.

Rachel got the satellite phone from Sam and got connected to Command Headquarters. She gave them the team's coordinates and confirmed the pickup location and time.

CHAPTER 46:
MAY 2020

CHRISTOPHER LED THE WAY to the compound with Rachel bouncing along right beside him. She was energetic and pumped up for the mission. Four hours of sleep really was all she ever needed to recharge. Matt was in the middle so he could get to everyone quickly in case of a medical emergency, and Ryan was in the back.

Rachel paused when they got to the compound, allowing herself a moment to stare at the Ablaq stonework, the alternating rows of dark and light stone making their way up the two-story house. It was a remarkably nice house to have out in such a remote location. She took a deep breath and tried the door. It was unlocked. She shoved the door open, her assault rifle—flashlight attached—poised and ready. Moving into the entryway, she swung around, shining the flashlight briefly in all directions. The men fanned out behind her, going in pairs to silently check the rooms downstairs. The compound was larger than they had anticipated, and it took them a long time to search the first floor, but their intel seemed to be correct. The place was deserted. Eventually, they found a room with computers and filing cabinets.

"Raven, big room toward the back of the building. Get here and get to work," Rachel whispered just loud enough that the team could hear her on their comms. Christopher and Daniel packed up a stash of hard drives, laptops, and cellphones that were lying around while Ryan got to work cracking an electronic keypad lock on a safe that they hoped contained the USB stick with the malware code.

Rachel headed up the stairs, with Matt following half a flight of stairs behind her. She climbed to the first landing before shining her flashlight and peaking around the corner to check it was safe to proceed. She advanced slowly and calmly.

Once at the top of the stairs, she made her way over to a desk. There were some papers—nothing that looked too important—and a USB stick. She reached out a hand and picked up the USB stick off the desk, turning it over between her fingers. *RMR092184* was written on the side. Her eyes were struggling to focus, her brain struggling to comprehend. She'd seen this USB before. *What the fuck?* Where had she seen this before?

She barely finished the thought when she felt two hands grasp each of her arms. She dropped the USB stick and turned, instantly putting her hands on the neck of the man standing behind her. She backed him toward the stairs and saw two other men in her periphery. The man holding her released one of his hands from her arm. She felt the cold sharp prick of the tip of a knife against her abdomen, just below her bulletproof vest. Searing pain took over. Her vision went black.

It took all her strength and focus to constrict her hands around the man's neck and twist, pressing down hard. She couldn't see but trusted her instincts and was happy for the rush of adrenaline that helped mask her pain. She heard the distinct sound of cracking bones and pushed the man in the direction of the stairs. A series of thuds followed. Then two shots fired. She felt her rifle hanging at her side, the strap slug over her shoulder and the barrel of the gun swinging into her leg as she struggled to balance. She wasn't shooting. But someone was. She was in so much pain she couldn't tell if she'd been hit with a bullet too or just stabbed with a knife. It didn't matter. It was all the same as darkness and pain and confusion took over. Then hands, more hands, grabbed her, held her as her body collapsed and her mind went blank.

Christopher heard the first shot fired and ran, rifle in hand, to the stairs. He left Ryan and Daniel to finish collecting the intel while everyone else continued searching the compound. He took the steps two at a time and got to the top just in time to see Rachel collapse into Matt's arms, covered in blood. The whole world stopped in that second. Christopher's heart was pounding out of his chest and his gut wrenched with pain and nausea. It took all of his effort not to reach for her, not to grab her away from Matt. He knew Matt was more than capable of carrying her. But Christopher couldn't help but think Rachel would be safer with him. Just when he thought the world was going to end, instinct and adrenaline kicked in.

"Skylark is down. I repeat, Skylark is down!" Christopher said over comms. "Raven has command. Finish the mission. Nightingale and I will extract Sky. Meet at the extraction point when you're done." He ran at top speed toward the extraction site with Matt right behind him, carrying a now unconscious Rachel.

As they ran outside, three more armed insurgents came running toward them from the side of the building, seeming to come out of nowhere. Christopher turned toward them, his finger pressed against the trigger of his assault rifle. He killed them one by one as he ran, firing off more bullets than necessary. All he knew was that he had to get Matt to the extraction point. He didn't know what had happened to Rachel, hadn't seen what happened, but she was bleeding badly.

They made it just as the helicopter was landing. Matt had Rachel on the ground and he was applying pressure to her abdomen, trying to stop the bleeding. That's when Christopher saw the knife. He took a deep breath, trying not to panic. Matt was the best medic the SEAL teams had. He had to have faith in his friend. His eyes darted between Matt and Rachel, who was on the ground, and then around their surroundings. Watching for danger. Watching the helicopter land. He tried to focus on what he could control—his own breathing and his rifle. That was all he could do.

He glanced down at Matt and felt a wave of nausea. Even in the dark—even with night vision goggles on—he could see Matt's typical calm resolute focus was cracking. He was trying to keep up the façade, likely for Christopher's sake. It was clear nothing was working. Rachel was losing too much blood. Christopher and Matt loaded her into the helicopter and climbed in after. Christopher took over holding pressure on Rachel's abdomen while Matt dug through the medical supplies that the crew had onboard. Christopher couldn't take his eyes off her face, desperately praying for the bleeding to stop and wishing he could trade places with her.

"Where the fuck are your blood bags?" Matt screamed at the pilot, knowing that Rachel would need a blood transfusion quickly if she was going to live.

"Didn't have any supplies to restock," the pilot explained.

Matt was furious. The entire region had been undersupplied it seemed, hence why he didn't have what he needed himself. He looked around, searching through all the supplies while Christopher kept holding pressure to the wound. Matt pulled out two kits containing sterile needles and tubing, then slid one needle into a vein in Rachel's arm before cutting a slit in the side of the tube.

"I need your arm, Hawk," Matt said, knowing that Christopher's blood type was O negative, the universal donor. Christopher winced as Matt jammed the second needle quickly into Christopher's arm, not being careful with his technique and not caring if it hurt. Then Matt slid the tube attached to Christopher's needle into the tube attached to Rachel. This was the messiest, most improvised blood transfusion ever. Matt ripped off a piece of duct tape to wrap around the two tubes, hoping it would hold them together and prevent the blood from leaking out.

"Holy fuck!" Ryan yelled as he climbed into the helicopter and saw what Matt was doing.

The rest of the team was right behind him, and they loaded in as quickly as they could before the pilot took off. Ryan relieved Christopher from holding pressure on Rachel's abdomen, and Matt went to speak with the pilot.

"We need to get to Rmeilan Air Base ASAP!" Matt ordered the pilot.

"I'm supposed to take you to al-Tanf," the pilot argued.

"It's too unstable around there. They don't have surgeons, and you just told me they're out of medical supplies! We have to go to the hospital at Rmeilan. Now! I'll call command. You fly."

Christopher lay on the floor of the helicopter next to Rachel, feeling nauseous. He wasn't sure if it was his own blood loss or hers. The past eleven years flashed through his mind: every smile, every look, every touch. He stayed next to her, holding her hand while Ryan held pressure on her abdomen and Matt repeatedly checked her vitals. They had trained for moments like this, but the training was nothing like the real thing. He stared at Rachel's pale lifeless body, willing her to stay alive by whispering in her ear, telling her to hang on, telling her everything would be okay. Matt kept assuring them all that she still had a pulse, even if it was weak. She was still breathing, just shallowly, and that was about all they could hope for.

Matt turned around, focusing his attention on Christopher. "How you doing, Hawk?"

"Fine. Focus on Sky," Christopher answered.

"She's as fine as she's gonna be until we get her to a surgeon. The only thing we can do is hold pressure and give her blood. But you can't give her too much, or you'll pass out and then both of you are fucked."

"I'm good. Not lightheaded or anything," Christopher lied.

"She's probably gotten as much as is safe for you to give. It's been over thirty minutes. That's gotta be about two pints, even with the makeshift setup," Matt said, ripping the needle out of Christopher's arm. "If you give her much more, you'll go into shock and die right next to her."

It was the first time any of them had said out loud what they were all thinking. It became real to him then, that Rachel dying was not only a real possibility, but was likely.

All Christopher could think about was what his life would be like without her. Empty was all he could come up with. Without her bright smile and twinkling eyes, her sharp wit and flirtatious banter, his life would be empty. She was his best friend, had been since the day they'd met, but maybe she was more than that too, and maybe he'd known that all along. He did his best to hide his panic, knowing Matt didn't need to be worrying about him too. Matt needed to focus on Rachel. Rachel was all that mattered. His fear was his problem, no one else's. He stayed next to her, taking deep breaths, hoping it would relieve his nausea. It didn't help. Neither did the protein bar and water Aaron was trying to force-feed him.

An hour later, they landed at Rmeilan Air Base. The surgical team was ready and waiting on the landing pad. They lifted Rachel onto a gurney and Matt jumped on top of her, doing his best to apply pressure without moving the knife. He hadn't seen the knife before it went in and he didn't know how big the blade actually was or what organs, if any, had been damaged. He talked as they ran to the operating room, explaining to the surgeon everything that had happened, how she had sustained the injury, and what field medicine he had already done, then provided her blood type and medical history. Within minutes, they had her under general anesthesia and were opening her up to see what damage had been done. Matt stood off to the side, watching as the surgeons used sponge after sponge to soak up all the blood so they could see where the wound was.

"It's her uterus," the surgeon said, looking at Matt. "The knife went straight through. If it hadn't been twisted, this would've been an easy repair."

"Can you fix it?" Matt asked.

"I can try, but she'd likely bleed out in the process. If we want to be sure she's gonna live, we need to take it out. I can keep her stable for the next fifteen minutes, but someone's going to have to make that call."

Matt sprinted out of the room soaked in Rachel's blood, but he didn't care. He found Christopher and the rest of the team sitting on the floor in a nearby hallway.

"Christopher," Matt said with an urgent and serious tone in his voice. He motioned for Christopher to follow him so they could speak away from the rest of the team.

Christopher knew it was terrible the second he heard Matt call him by his first name. Not his rank, not his last name, not his call sign, not even Chris. His full first name. His heart was racing in his chest and it was getting harder to breathe. "How bad?" he asked.

"The surgeon can keep her stable for about fifteen minutes . . . twelve probably. It took a while to run over here."

"What, Matt?" Christopher's voice was sharp.

"They want to remove her uterus. Knife went straight through before it was twisted. I know she's not really the settling down and popping out babies kind of girl but—"

"Tell them to save her life by any means necessary," Christopher cut him off.

"Chris," Matt started again.

"She can live without a uterus. She can fight without a uterus. And if she decides she wants a kid, which I'm fairly certain she does not, she can adopt one or something," Christopher yelled. "Go save her!"

"You need to call Carter. He's her husband. Technicality or not, it's his decision," Matt reminded him.

Christopher scoffed. "Like hell it is."

"I would have called myself, but I don't have his phone number. You do, and getting his number from you is faster than going through HR."

"What are you gonna do? Call him at work and tell him this? We aren't wasting time with that. He'll tell you the same thing I'm telling you!"

"Christopher . . ." Matt tried to reason with him one more time.

"If she dies because you're out here fucking around and wasting time making phone calls—"

"You cannot legally make medical decisions for her!" Matt yelled back at him, trying to get Christopher to comprehend what was happening.

"You bet your ass I can. Now run faster than you've ever run in your fucking life back to that operating room." Christopher's voice was booming as he pointed down the hallway, back in the direction Matt had come from.

"You're sure? This is illegal and could cause some issues for you. HR and the legal department aren't gonna be happy." Matt looked at him seriously, trying to drive the point home.

"You think the Navy wants to risk her dying? They need her as much as . . . Fuck." His eyes darted toward the ceiling. "Matt, just go fucking save her life! Run!" Christopher shouted.

His heart was racing and he let his back slide down the wall as he watched Matt sprint back to the operating room. He felt like he was dying right along with her. Like his soul was crumbling to ash. He needed her to live. He needed her more than he needed oxygen. His mind flashed back to all the times he'd held her, all the times he could have kissed her. He should have kissed her. He started praying, negotiating with God, begging for him to save her. Offering to trade his life for hers but knowing that could never work. They needed to be together. Everything was better when they were together, and every time they split up, something terrible happened. He should have been behind her on the stairs and not Matt. They'd split up when Aiden died too. There'd been an incident with a car bomb when they'd been in separate trucks too, and when Henry died. Sure they'd been in the same truck. But if she'd been sitting next to him instead of behind him, maybe things would have gone differently then too. Everything went better when they were together. It was like magic. Some sort of divine combination of karmic energy that kept them safe.

He sat on the floor of the hallway alone. Trying to breathe, trying to slow down his heart rate. Trying to pray or remember anything from any religion that would be at all helpful. The only thing he could think of was Psalms 23:4: "As I walk through the valley of the shadow of death, I will fear no evil, for you are with me; your rod and your staff, they comfort me."

He wasn't thinking about Jesus though, or God. He was thinking about Rachel. She was his comfort, strength, and courage. She made him a better man. She was his everything.

Chapter 47:
MAY 2020

BUZZING FLUORESCENT LIGHTS AND beeping machines. That was all Rachel noticed as her eyes fluttered open and closed. It was hard to breathe, hard to focus. She was trying to open her eyes, trying to be a part of the real world, but she couldn't. Waking up wasn't working. A problem she'd never had before. Sleep was usually the issue. She didn't know where she was or what was happening. Her mind was clouded and she couldn't think. She tried to move her fingers and felt a familiar pinch. Rolling her head to the side and forcing her eyes open was an excruciating task. She had an IV in her hand.

What the fuck?

She swallowed. A strange mix of mucus, saliva, and stress hormones suddenly surged into her mouth. Her throat was sore. These clues all helped her understand she was in a hospital, but she had no idea why. She turned her head the other way, knowing that someone from her team would be with her, and saw Christopher.

"What?" Her voice was hoarse, and it hurt to talk. It hurt pretty much everywhere.

"Don't talk, just rest," Christopher said. He looked at her panic-stricken eyes, begging him to tell her something, anything. "That compound was not empty. There were at least six men there. I don't know what happened after we got you out. Matt and Ryan are working on the report now."

"But . . . what?" Rachel was looking around the room, confused and terrified.

Christopher cut her off. "You went up to the second floor and there were three men. One of them stabbed you, but don't worry, you broke his neck and threw him down the stairs before you collapsed. Matt was right behind you and took out the other two, caught you, and then he and I took you out to the evac."

Rachel opened her mouth to speak.

"Stop trying to talk!" Christopher instructed. "You had general anesthesia. That means you had a breathing tube. Your throat is going to hurt for a while."

Rachel switched to sign language, understanding that talking wasn't an option. She signed as best as she could, given the needle in her hand and her fatigue. "Why am I in a hospital and why can't I think?"

Christopher chuckled and explained, "You can't think because you are high as fuck on painkillers. And you're high as fuck on painkillers because you had to have surgery."

"What surgery?" Rachel asked, still using sign language.

Christopher took a deep breath to steady himself.

"What surgery?" Rachel signed again, not missing the fear that had briefly washed over his face.

Christopher took her hand and looked into her eyes as he sat on the edge of her bed. "You're okay." He paused. "You're alive and well, and in six to eight weeks, you'll be good as new. Probably on medical leave for a while, but good as new."

"What surgery?" Rachel signed again, pulling her hand away. She wanted to hit him. "Just tell me."

Christopher looked up at the ceiling. "A ten-inch blade went straight into your abdomen and pierced your uterus before it was twisted. They had to remove it."

"Of course, they removed it. I can't walk around with a knife inside of me," Rachel signed.

"Sky, listen, not the knife." Christopher paused. He didn't want to say it, he didn't want to be the one to tell her, but he didn't want her to hear it from someone else either. "They had to remove your uterus in order to save your life."

Rachel stared at him, blinking. She wasn't understanding at all. He was making it seem like she was dying or something. She could live without a uterus. What the fuck was she planning to do with that anyway? "What else?" she signed.

"What do you mean?" Christopher asked.

"You're acting like I'm dying or something horribly tragic has happened, so what else?" Rachel was trying hard to remember basic anatomy, but her thoughts were muddled from the morphine.

"Nothing else. Just you no longer have a uterus, which is sort of a big deal . . . in case you ever decided you wanted kids. That's all the damage you sustained other than a ton of blood loss. Matt had to do a direct transfusion in the helicopter."

Rachel pointed at him, knowing he was O negative.

"Yeah, me," Christopher said.

"Are you okay?" Rachel signed.

"I'm okay," Christopher assured her. Not at all surprised that she was more concerned about him than herself. "You're the only one who sustained any injuries."

Rachel nodded. She let her head sink into her pillow and closed her eyes. She could feel the tears coming but didn't know why she was crying. Probably just a stress response.

"Hey, scoot over a bit," Christopher told her. He helped her move over to the side of her bed, took off his boots, and climbed in next to her. He slid his arm under her neck, letting her face rest comfortably on his arm, and held her as tightly as he could without hurting her until they both fell asleep.

The team had been set up with cots in a room close to the hospital. They were taking turns sitting with Rachel, or trying to, but Christopher refused to leave her room. After getting a few hours of sleep, Matt went to check on her and tried to convince Christopher to take a break. He walked down the hallway to her room and opened her door to see Rachel and Christopher curled up together, both asleep in her hospital bed. He turned around, quickly closing the door behind him, and made a silent promise to guard the door. Sharing blankets in the desert or a bed in a hotel room when it was just their team was one thing. They all knew there was nothing going on between Rachel and Christopher and that Rachel would happily sleep next to whomever. But hospital beds were not meant to be shared. Teammates were not supposed to hold each other, arms and legs intertwined, hands tangled in each other's hair, and heads and bodies pressed together. Sure, waking up like that was one thing. People moved in their sleep. Sometimes shit happened. Matt had woken up with his arm around Christopher or Ryan plenty of times. But in a hospital on a military base where anyone could see them and would have to report it? There was no excusing their behavior, no rationalizing it away. Christopher had no valid reason to be in her bed. It would be assumed that she pressured him, making it sexual harassment, or if he insisted he'd gotten into bed with her willingly, it would have to be labeled fraternization.

Rachel woke up a few hours later, still lying in Christopher's arms, and still high on morphine. She tilted her head up and saw that Christopher was awake too. She ran her hand along his chest. "I'm done crying now," she said, still hoarse.

"I see that," Christopher responded, tucking a loose strand of hair behind her ear.

Rachel stared at him. "Are you supposed to be in my bed?" Her throat still hurt and her voice wasn't as strong as it usually was.

"Do you want me to get up?" Christopher asked.

"No." Rachel wasn't sure what she wanted. She couldn't think straight.

All she knew was that she felt better when Christopher was holding her rather than when he wasn't.

"Rachel–" Christopher started.

"What's wrong?" she interrupted. He rarely called her by her first name.

"You almost died," Christopher said.

"Okay?" She didn't know where he was going with this. "But I didn't, so . . ."

"The second I saw you collapse into Matt's arms, I realized that I can't spend a single day without you, that every time I'm away from you, I'm miserable." Christopher paused and looked deep into her eyes.

"What are you saying? You're being super weird," Rachel said.

"Rachel Ryker, I'm trying to tell you that I'm in love with you! That I have been in love with you probably the entire time I've known you!" Christopher blurted out.

"Don't be stupid!" Rachel laughed. "You absolutely are not in love with me. You might have feelings *of* love *for* me. We are best friends, but you aren't *in* love with me. You just got scared I was going to die, and now you've lost your mind."

"Can't all those things be true?" Christopher asked.

"No, they can't," Rachel said emphatically. "You most definitely cannot be in love with me." She felt fear rising up, knowing that what she really meant was that he wasn't allowed to be in love with her. Before she could formulate a logical response, there was a knock on the door. Christopher jumped out of Rachel's bed seconds before Matt opened it to peek inside.

"Oh, good. You're up!" Matt said enthusiastically to them both. "And I see that your common sense has returned, Commander Williams," he teased after closing the door behind him. Christopher looked at him, clearly panicked. "Don't worry, I'm the only one who saw. I've been standing outside guarding the door for two hours."

"Two hours?" Christopher sounded concerned, and Rachel's eyes snapped to his.

"How long were we asleep?" Rachel asked.

"Longer than two hours." He winced.

Matt sighed and looked at the ground.

"Did you come in earlier?" Rachel asked Matt. "I thought I heard the door."

"Yeah, I did, then I decided to stand outside so no one else went in your room and saw you two in bed together."

"It must have been you then," Rachel concluded.

"I hope so." Matt frowned. "Chris, did you tell her?"

"Oh, he's said a lot!" Rachel giggled. "Matt, you should hear the dumb shit he's trying to tell me!"

Matt looked back and forth between Christopher and Rachel. "No, I think it's best I know as little about this as possible."

"You wouldn't believe me even if I told you!" Rachel giggled.

"Well, I guess the morphine's working," Matt said, slightly irritated. "The surgeon is coming to talk to you, Sky." He turned to Christopher. "Is telling her the full story of what happened one of the dumb things you told her?"

"Yes, I told her what happened," Christopher confirmed.

Rachel laughed again. "Yeah, that part was pretty stupid too."

"I'm choosing to blame your laughter on the morphine," Christopher said coolly. He wasn't nearly as amused as she was.

"Good idea!" Rachel giggled again.

"She's always a pain in the ass when I have to give her morphine," Matt said.

"What happened to taking people's feelings seriously and being respectful?" Christopher asked, trying to remain calm.

"Christopher, this is not a Share and Care session, and you have clearly lost your mind."

"I have not! I'm telling you how I feel and you're being completely dismissive." He was practically yelling.

"I think given the nature of the feelings you're sharing, me dismissing them is in everyone's best interest."

"Rachel, I swear to God." His voice raised, full of frustration.

There was another knock on the door and the surgeon came into the room. Christopher immediately stood straighter and forced a serious expression onto his face. Arguing with Rachel about their feelings for each other would have to wait.

"Captain Ryker" the surgeon greeted her, "it's nice to officially meet you, ma'am. I'm the one who operated on you."

Rachel waved her hand dismissively at him. "No need for formalities, Doc. You've already been inside me, after all!" Rachel joked.

"We may need to adjust her morphine drip," Matt said, scratching his head and looking awkwardly at his feet. "Might be a little too much."

"Are you in any pain?" the surgeon asked Rachel.

"Nope!" Rachel exclaimed, giggling again.

The surgeon turned to Matt. "I see what you mean." He walked over to Rachel's IV and adjusted her morphine dose. "If you're in too much pain, let us know." Rachel gave him a thumbs up. "Has anyone told you what happened?"

Rachel looked at Christopher and pointed to him, smiling.

"I told her everything that happened," Christopher said. "From how she got injured to the surgery."

The surgeon nodded. "Captain Ryker, your injuries were severe and caused significant damage to your uterus, which I had to remove in order to save your life."

"So I've been told," Rachel laughed again.

"You understand you won't be able to have children?"

"Yeah, yeah, I know anatomy. Never planned on the kids thing," she assured him.

The surgeon looked back and forth between Matt and Christopher, trying to get some help.

"Sky, I know you're on a lot of morphine, and I know kids have never been that important to you, but we need to make sure you understand what's happening," Matt said slowly and calmly.

"Matt, it's a uterus. I see this only as a positive. No more period, no more unwanted pregnancy, whatever. What's the problem? Stitch me up and give me my rifle back."

"Well, it's gonna be awhile before you're well enough to fight again," Matt told her.

"Why?"

"Because you just had major surgery, you fucking lunatic!" Matt dropped his forehead into his palm.

Rachel brushed off his comments with a wave of the hand.

The surgeon gave Matt a sideways glance, clearly uncomfortable with his insubordination, and tried to reason with Rachel again. "Captain Ryker, you are on a considerable amount of morphine, and we're monitoring you for postoperative infections. Your body needs time to heal."

"You're all overreacting. I'm fine," Rachel insisted, waving her hand in the air as though that would solve everything.

"Try to get up," Christopher challenged.

Rachel gave him a haughty look, certain she could get herself out of the dumb hospital bed without a problem. She tried to sit up all the way and winced. She lifted her right leg, trying to inch it closer to the edge of the bed. Her face froze in a terrified, confused expression as pain spread like wildfire through her whole body. She was dizzy, so dizzy from the drugs and the pain. This wasn't the nice kind of pain that usually made her feel more alive. This was the debilitating kind that made her wish she was dead.

"Not as easy as you thought, is it?" Christopher asked, putting his palm on her shoulder and nudging her back against her pillow.

"Do you have any questions for me?" the surgeon asked once she'd relaxed back against her bed.

Rachel blinked twice, trying to erase the emotions and the pain she was feeling. She was determined not to show any sign of weakness, not even in front of Christopher and Matt. "I would very much like to know how long I have to be here, when I can go home, and how the rest of my team's mission went, although you probably can't answer that last one."

"No, your team will have to answer the last one, but as for the first two, you will be here for one or two more days, then we will transfer you back stateside to Walter Reed for recovery. You'll probably be there for a few days to a week, depending on how everything goes. After that, you'll go home. Do you have someone who can help you at home?"

Rachel rolled her eyes.

"She does," Christopher answered for her.

"How long do I have to be home for?"

"Well, a full recovery from this type of surgery is typically six to eight weeks. How long you're home for is up to the Navy."

Rachel scrunched up her face, looking confused. "What do you mean?"

"Well, depending on how they classify your injury . . ."

The look on Rachel's face went from confusion to realization to anger in a matter of seconds. The possibility hadn't crossed her mind until that very second. "They can't pull me from combat for this, can they?" The look on the surgeon's face told her everything she needed to know.

Christopher and Matt exchanged horrified looks with each other as they also comprehended what was happening. The fact that this could be a career ending injury must have been news to them as well.

"Someone get me a fucking phone!" Rachel demanded. No one moved. She looked straight at Matt and Christopher. "One of you, get me a phone so I can call Command HQ right now. That is a direct order from your commanding officer!" Matt clenched his jaw and left with the surgeon to find her a phone.

"You should have let me die, Hawk. They're going to put me on a fucking desk," Rachel said, unable to look at Christopher. Her face had turned to stone, somber and stoic, and her tone had gone from playful to tense and defeated in a matter of seconds.

"Rache, you don't know that. They took out your uterus. You don't need a uterus. If it were your liver or a kidney or something, then maybe, but—"

"No. This is just the excuse they need." *Just the excuse* he *needs.* She knew Leftwich would use this against her.

Matt came back in with a satellite phone in hand. The surgeon had moved on to other patients. "I have Admiral Eastwood for you, Sky," he said.

Rachel took the phone from Matt and held it up to her ear. She skipped all pleasantries and started yelling immediately. Christopher could only hear her side of the call, but it didn't sound good. Ten minutes later, she screamed and threw the phone against the wall, wincing with pain as she did. It crashed to the floor with a loud thud. Matt and Christopher stood completely frozen, staring at her. No one said anything for fifteen minutes.

"Apparently, I've sustained vital organ damage and am no longer fit for combat," Rachel said calmly, still staring straight ahead.

"That's the dumbest thing I've ever heard," Matt said.

Rachel looked stoically at Christopher. "It's even more ridiculous than what you said earlier."

Christopher rolled his eyes at her. "Nothing that I said earlier was ridiculous, or dumb, or untrue."

"It was a stupid thing to say."

Christopher shrugged. "Doesn't make it untrue." He had meant every word.

"I think that's my cue to go," Matt said, leaving the room in a hurry.

"Are they really pulling you from combat?" Christopher asked once Matt was gone. He shoved his hands in his pockets and looked at the floor. They both knew it wasn't the time to argue about who felt what for whom. They'd have to sort that out later.

Rachel was silent for a few minutes. "They're going to try–" She sat up in bed, wincing slightly as she did, and Christopher moved to stand beside her. He wrapped his arms around her, hugging her tightly. "Who made the call?" she asked sharply.

"What call?" Christopher asked, more focused on the feel of her in his arms than her words.

"To remove an allegedly vital organ from my body. Did you call Carter or did the surgeon decide?"

"I made the call." Christopher admitted.

"Why?"

"You were dying. It was, according to the surgeon and Matt, the only sure way to save your life. We had minutes to decide and I wasn't about to waste those minutes trying to get a hold of Carter or anybody else, so I made the call."

Rachel wrinkled her nose. "And now Admiral Leftwich is using it as an excuse to end my career."

"End your career? You'll be on a desk at HQ. You still have your career, Rache."

"It's not the same and you know it." Her voice turned colder than ever.

"I had no idea they could pull you from combat for this. If I had thought or suspected that at all, you know I wouldn't have let them. I would have told the surgeon to leave it in and get the bleeding under control so he could repair it."

"I'm fairly certain that technically they *can't* remove me from combat for this, but it seems to be happening anyway." Rachel clenched her jaw.

Christopher was dumbfounded. It was the most absurd thing he'd ever heard. He tried to push down his guilt. There was no way any of them could have known that a uterus was necessary for serving in combat. No one else had a fucking uterus, and they seemed to serve in combat just fine.

"What did Eastwood say when you talked to him?"

"Not his call, above his pay grade, he tried to stop it, blah, blah, blah. If I accept the job at HQ, they'll promote me to rear admiral." Rachel rolled her eyes.

"You're mad."

"No," Rachel lied.

"Which thing or things specifically are you mad about?"

"I'm sorry you had to decide," Rachel said sadly, looking down at the bed.

"Me too," he said sadly. "I wasn't about to let anyone else do it though." He grazed his thumb over her cheek.

"Sort of why we have signed documents designating a legal next of kin. Also why you aren't mine."

"Is that why?" Christopher let out a quiet laugh and shook his head. "I'm fairly certain I'm not listed as your legal next of kin because I'm not your legal next of kin."

"You should have made Carter decide. He would have done exactly what you did."

"Then why does it matter?"

"Then I could be mad at him."

"Instead of being mad at me?" He raised an eyebrow at her.

"I could never be mad at you." Rachel blinked back her tears.

"Are you sure?"

"Never have been before. Why start now?" She looked down at the blanket covering her legs and twisted it between her clenched fists.

"But you're not in love with me?" Christopher asked, knowing it was the only chance he would get to sneak that question in.

The quietest of laughs escaped Rachel's lips in a small puff of air. "No, Christopher. No one in this room can be in love with anyone else in this room."

"No one can be, or no one is?"

She dropped her face into her hands. "Christopher, you need to stop and you know it."

He sighed. "No, I don't know that, Rachel." He looked down at her, pushed her hands away from her face, and tipped her chin up until she was staring into his eyes. "What I do know is that it's going to be okay. Everything will be okay no matter what happens. I promise you it will be okay."

Loud, violent sobs escaped her still sore throat. Christopher sat on the edge of her bed, holding her and trying to reassure her until she finally cried herself to sleep. He wasn't sure if she was crying about losing her uterus, never being able to have kids, being pulled from combat or him telling her he was in love with her. Probably all of it. It didn't matter. He was staying with her through all of it.

Ryan came in an hour later. Rachel was still sleeping and Christopher was sitting in the chair next to her bed, reading something on his phone. "My turn!" Ryan proclaimed. Christopher shot him a look. "Dude, I don't know what's going on, but you've been in here with her for two days. Besides, Matt needs to talk to you about something, not sure what, but it sounded urgent."

Christopher reluctantly got up and left the room.

Once Christopher found Matt, he shouted down the hall, "Hey. Raven said you needed me for something?"

Matt immediately pulled him into a nearby supply closet, where they wouldn't be overheard. "What the fuck were you thinking? It's one thing when we're in the middle of the desert and everyone is scared shitless, and she lays down next to one of us and snuggles up, or when we're on leave and don't want to pay for more rooms, but have you actually lost your mind?"

"She was crying. What was I supposed to do?" Christopher tried to defend himself.

"Well, I don't know! *Not* jump into bed with her? If anyone else had seen you, you'd probably be court-martialed! Hell, you both probably would be!"

Christopher looked at the floor. He knew Matt was right, but he also knew that he didn't care. "What was I supposed to do?" Christopher asked again, looking at Matt with tears in his eyes.

"Fuck," Matt said. "She's not dying."

"She thinks she is! God, can you imagine her on a desk? It's going to be torture for her."

"Not up to us," Matt said. "Not up to her, either. Now, you need to get your head on straight because while she's recovering and we're waiting for an official decision regarding her status, you're team leader, you're C.O. Fuck, you're probably taking over as squadron leader too. So, get your head in the fucking game and stop with all this other shit. I know you care about her, probably more than you should. Hell, we all do! But . . ."

Christopher put both hands over his face and took a deep breath. "I'm fucking in love with her, Matt." He paused and made eye contact with his friend before continuing. "I am so insanely, crazy in love with her, I don't know what to do. From the second I saw you catch her, I saw all that blood, that was it. My whole world stopped spinning. There was no Syria, no mission, no Navy protocol. There was only her."

Matt crossed his arms over his chest and looked at the floor. "Chris, think about what you're saying. This isn't something you can take back. Your career will be over, possibly hers too." He stopped, raising his head to look at Christopher, to study his face and body language. "Fuck, you already told her, didn't you? That's what she was saying earlier. That you said something stupid, even if it was true?" Christopher was silent. Matt glared at him. "Does she feel the same way?" Christopher shrugged and Matt chuckled. "Yeah, I suppose even if she did, she wouldn't be dumb enough to admit it."

"I can't go back without her, fight without her, die without her," Christopher said quietly.

"You're going to have to. You haven't done your twenty years. You aren't eligible for pension yet."

"Fuck pension!" Christopher yelled.

"Fine, what are you gonna do?" Matt was trying to be a supportive friend, but he agreed with Rachel. This was probably the dumbest thing Christopher had ever said or done.

"Whatever it takes to be with her, to make her happy, to take care of her. Whatever it takes. That's what I'm going to do," Christopher promised.

Rachel woke up with Ryan in the chair beside her. She was calmer now, and the lowered morphine dose had helped clear her head. "Where's Hawk?" she asked.

"Dunno. Nightingale needed him for something," Ryan answered.

Rachel nodded. "He's lost his fucking mind, you know."

"Who, Chris?" Ryan asked. Rachel nodded again. "What'd he do?"

Rachel laughed. "Professed his undying love for me! I tried to explain to him he just got scared, but he wouldn't listen to me. You and Matt need to straighten him out before he does something stupid, like crawl into bed with me again."

Ryan blinked at her. "Sky, what if he really *were* in love with you? Like really, really *in* love with you?"

"He's not. He's just being dramatic and stupid."

"No, I don't think he is . . ." Ryan trailed off, waiting to see Rachel's reaction. Her expression was blank. "I mean, can you honestly tell me you don't feel the same way about him?"

"Of course I don't!" Rachel said, sounding offended. "I'm his commanding officer. I couldn't be in love with him."

Ryan exhaled sharply. "See Skylark, here's your greatest fault. I know we all give you shit about your cooking and inability to use technology or a sniper rifle, and God, the maps! But your greatest fault is also your greatest asset." Rachel stared at him, clearly confused. "Your love and dedication to the Navy," Ryan clarified. He waited a minute to see if she would say anything before continuing. "If you take work out of it, put the whole fraternization thing aside, if there was no Navy and the two of you had normal jobs and lived in the real world–"

"But we don't, Ryan, and that's the point," Rachel interjected.

"But you could, if you wanted to. You could medically retire. They can't deny you your pension after this. You could retire and be with him if you wanted to." He paused, letting that information set in. "Sky, you may be able to lie to yourself, to push your feelings down and put your duty to your country first, but you can't lie to me."

Chapter 48:
MAY 2020

THE WHOLE TEAM FLEW into D.C. the next day, where Rachel was admitted to Walter Reed National Military Medical Center. Christopher stayed by her side as much as he was allowed. He had spent the rest of their time at Rmeilan trying to convince Rachel to at least consider the possibility that maybe he really was in love with her. He knew he was, and he was pretty sure she felt the same way, but so far, she wouldn't admit it.

Rachel had been assigned to a private room that had a view overlooking a courtyard filled with lush green trees and park benches. Her doctors encouraged her to go outside for short walks as much as she could, and Christopher had taken it upon himself to act as her physical therapist, despite the fact that she had an actual physical therapist assigned to help her. They were sitting on a park bench in the courtyard when Christopher took her hand in his.

"What the hell are you doing? Someone will see!" Rachel chastised him, quickly pulling her hand away from his.

"So? No one knows who we are. We're not in uniform."

"Christopher, this is not okay. We cannot do this and you know it."

"Well, I'm retiring regardless, whether you like it or not. I'm not going back over there without you. Can you honestly say that you'd go back without me?" Christopher asked.

"I'd prefer to go back *with* you. I'd prefer to go back to when we planned that fucking mission, I'd prefer to go back to the day before we went into that compound and demand that someone do another fly over with a drone! We have a drone! I cannot believe I didn't think to do that. I'd prefer the fucking CIA and Navy Intelligence do their god damned jobs correctly!"

"No, our drone got damaged when the truck got blown up," he reminded her. She glared at him and he couldn't help but smile at her irritation. "I don't think anyone's close to figuring out time travel yet, so what would your second choice be?"

Rachel shoved her fists into the pockets of the sweatshirt she was wearing and clenched her jaw.

"Look, I know you're frustrated," he continued. "I know you're pissed off and angry and probably want to go kick someone's ass right now just for the hell of it, and I promise to volunteer to be that person as soon as the doctors clear you for that level of physical activity."

Rachel couldn't help but laugh. "Every fucking time, Williams," she said. "Every fucking time in the past eleven years that I've gotten stuck in my own head, that I've let my anger take over, you've pulled me back. You're the only one who can do that."

"Ryan does it."

"No, he hands me a bottle of whiskey and makes inappropriate comments to distract me. It's not the same thing."

"Rachel, I'm being serious," Christopher said. "I'm not going back. I'm done. If the Navy lets you go back, which doesn't seem likely at this point, then go if you want. I'll be here, or in Texas, or wherever you want me to be, waiting for you to come home."

"That's ridiculous," Rachel said.

"Why?"

"You're going to just sit around waiting for me? No. You're going to be jealous that I'm over there and you're not, then I'll come home and you'll want to hear all about it, and I won't be able to tell you because you won't have security clearance anymore and then you'll resent me and hate me and regret you ever retired."

Christopher shook his head. "Nope, not gonna happen. You'll come home all hyped up on adrenaline and endorphins from your mission and we'll settle in and live in our own little world, doing whatever we want to do until you get sent back again. It'll be like war and the Navy don't exist when you're home. It'll just be you and me."

"How do you know I even want that?"

Christopher ran his hand up her spine.

"Lust is hardly the same thing."

"Pretend all you want. I know you. I know your soul. I know every thought in your head whether you like it or not."

"How?" Rachel glared at him.

"Aren't you always saying that my special talent is knowing what people are thinking?" He raised an eyebrow. Rachel glared at him as he continued. "You can pretend and push me away all you want. I'm not going anywhere, Rachel. I'm right here, forever and always, and I'll do my best to be patient while you get over yourself and decide to admit that I'm right."

Rachel was exasperated. He was living in some sort of dream world. "Have you even spoken with anyone in human resources about this? Found out what your options actually are? You can't just sit here and dream and speculate and wish."

"Yes, I'm working on that," he assured her.

"Besides, you won't actually be happy with me. Not for long anyway." She crossed her arms over her chest and leaned back against the bench.

"Is that so? Please, Ms. Ryker, enlighten me," he teased.

"Christopher, be serious. I know you want kids. You've been rambling on for the past decade about what happens when you get out of the Navy, and every single time, a wife, house, and kids were part of the picture. Were the main part of the picture, actually." She looked sad. "I can't give you that."

"First of all, you are all I need to be happy. I don't need the house and kids, only you. And second, I know you know there are lots of ways to have kids, to have a family, if that was something you decided you wanted."

"No, I don't mean physically. I froze my eggs right after graduating from SEAL training. I mean mentally, emotionally, I can't do it. Certainly not if I'm still in combat."

"Explain," Christopher said.

"I spent my entire childhood waiting for my father to come home, watching my mother worry, watching the other kids, the other wives on base after base, going on crisis calls with my dad when he was home. I could never put someone through that."

Christopher turned towards her and tucked a loose strand of hair behind her ear. "And if they do pull you out of combat permanently? What then?"

"I honestly don't know. Do you really think I could prioritize a kid over work? Especially if I'm working at SEAL Command. They may as well assign me a permanent bed there. I wouldn't do that to a kid, and I wouldn't do that to you. When my dad was home, he was mostly a good father, but that was maybe a couple of hours per week at the most. He was always gone or on the phone yelling at someone or distracted by whatever problem he needed to solve. You have to know by now that I'm the same way. You know I don't sleep, I don't stop working, and I won't stop."

"I know. But why?"

"Why?"

"Yeah, why work? Why sacrifice your own happiness for a job?"

"Christopher, seriously? You know how hard I've worked."

"We both have."

"Sure, but you know it was different for me. Becoming a Navy SEAL? I never wanted anything more in my life. Since I was about ten years old, that's what I wanted. I grew up hearing stories from my grandpa about him as a paratrooper, about my grandmother working as part of the French Resistance in World War II. Being in combat was the only thing I ever saw myself doing. Then I turned eighteen and I was told no. Women couldn't serve in combat. So I went to college. I used every political connection my parents or anyone else I knew had, trying to get that rule changed. I physically fought people—generals, admirals, whomever—trying to make my point. I fought them with my words and my fists. I wanted to make a difference. I wanted to live up to my family legacy, probably win my father's approval somehow too, as fucked up and Freudian as that is, and the only reason why I couldn't was because I had the wrong fucking chromosomes and body parts. I was always good enough, but somehow never enough.

"Now, I've made it. I've achieved my dream. If I give that up, what does that say? Especially if I gave it up for you, or any guy? No." She shook her head. "I'm not done. Not until I make admiral and maybe not even then. I'm paving the way for generations of girls and women behind me. I'm making a difference in the lives of women in the Middle East and on every fucking base I go to."

Rachel paused, finally daring to meet his eyes. "You know me. You've seen me stateside. I can't do normal social interaction. I just want to punch people most of the time. I'm gonna end up in fucking prison for hitting some misogynistic asshole."

"Probably," Christopher chuckled. "I'll be right there to bail you out though."

"I know you will be," she grumbled. "My point is, I have a certain set of skills and those skills aren't exactly transferable to other jobs. What the fuck do I put on a resume? Excels at killing terrorists with a knife? Expert at breaking necks? I'm thirty-five years old, almost thirty-six. I can't retire. I'd lose my mind and commit suicide within a month if I had nothing to do. Being on a desk at HQ? Yeah, at least I'm still in the Navy, still on active duty, but it's not the same. I'm just gonna be watching everyone else over there having fun without me, knowing I could probably get things done faster if I were over there. Knowing I could keep everyone motivated and engaged and safer if I were fighting right next to them. Instead, I'll be in D.C., feeling like my soul is dying from jealousy and lack of adrenaline."

Christopher nodded, considering what she'd said. "You know I understand the job. I understand and admire your dedication. If I could be at HQ with you, backing you up, you know I would be. But rules are rules so I can't be. Even if we weren't together, I highly doubt they'd let both of us transfer to HQ. So I'll be here, waiting for you to get home from saving the world, and I'll be ready with open arms whether you've had a good day or a shit day. I'd never get between you and your dream, you know that. I'm right here, ready to help. Tell me how and we'll crush the fucking patriarchy together, okay?"

Rachel sighed, hating that everything he was saying made sense, making him even more perfect. She sat next to him in silence, contemplating what he had said until it was time to go back inside for lunch.

Chapter 49:
MAY 2020

LATER THAT DAY, RACHEL was sitting in her hospital bed playing on her cell phone when a tall, thin woman entered her room dressed in service khakis with her brown hair twisted into a knot at the nape of her neck. She tucked her hat under her arm and pushed her shoulders back, at attention, as she waited to address Rachel.

"Out," Rachel said to Christopher, who was sitting in the chair next to her bed reading a magazine. She already knew who the woman was.

"Captain Ryker," the woman said, "I'm Lieutenant Commander Kristen Campbell. I heard you were looking to speak with a lawyer."

Christopher shot Rachel a confused look as he left the room.

"At ease Lieutenant Commander," Rachel instructed. "Yes, it's come to my attention that I'm being pulled from combat based on how the Navy has classified my recent injury. Tell me, how would you legally define a vital organ?"

"A vital organ is an internal organ necessary for life, like the heart, lungs, or brain," Kristen answered.

Rachel raised an eyebrow. "From a legal perspective, could a uterus be classified as a vital organ?"

"No ma'am, I wouldn't think so." Kristen's eyebrows knitted together at the absurdity of the idea.

"Hmmm, that's what I thought. Well, the Navy is trying to tell me it is, and they are pulling me from combat and putting me on a desk because of it. If a man had gotten stabbed where I did, I think they'd be allowed to go back."

"Captain Ryker, are you accusing the Navy of gender discrimination?"

"Maybe? I'm not a lawyer. You tell me."

Kristen paused for a minute, contemplating. "Gender discrimination, the legal definition anyway, is 'treating an applicant or employee unfavorably, disadvantageously, or unequally because of that person's sex.' It's technically a civil rights violation."

"So, what do you think? Do I have a case?" Rachel asked hopefully.

"I could make a case for that, sure. But you can't sue the whole Navy. You have to bring someone up on specific charges. So, we would need to identify who decided to categorize your injury that way and file charges with Command to have a preliminary investigation conducted. We'd need to file under Article 134, which gives the military the ability to punish conduct that is not explicitly listed in the UCMJ as a crime, as long as it is not a capital offense, which this is not. Article 134 pertains to 'all disorders and neglects to the prejudice of good order and discipline in the armed forces, all conduct of a nature to bring discredit upon the armed forces, and crimes and offenses not capital, of which persons subject may be guilty.' I would bring the charges up in a general court-martial. But like I said, we need to know who made that call so we have someone to press charges against."

"What do you need from me in order to proceed?" Rachel asked.

Kristen had Rachel sign a power of attorney granting her access to Rachel's medical records and service record. Then she sat in the chair Christopher had vacated earlier and got to work scouring Rachel's records. It was easy to identify who had classified Rachel's injury as *critical*, thus disqualifying her from combat. "Do you know an Admiral Leftwich?" Kristen asked Rachel.

"Yes, he's my C.O.'s C.O. and a misogynistic ass," Rachel explained. "He's been trying to put me on a desk for years and is decidedly unhappy that I was allowed to do SEAL training or be in combat at all."

"Do you have any documentation of that?" Kristen asked her.

Rachel handed over her phone. "Do emails count?" Rachel had saved every single piece of communication with the man, knowing that someday she would get her chance to use it against him. "There's a folder in my inbox labeled *Vengeance*. Start there," Rachel instructed.

Kristen couldn't help but laugh. She opened the folder and saw over five hundred emails that Rachel had saved over the years. She scrolled through, opening them one by one at random. "This shows a fairly straightforward pattern of hatred toward women, at least, and definitely documents that he doesn't think you should be in combat," she explained to Rachel.

"When you check my service record, test scores from training, and fitness test results, you'll see that I outperform most of the men on just about everything," Rachel said. "Regardless of that, Leftwich has been lobbying to have me removed from my position in the field, removed from leadership, and hell, probably removed from the Navy all together."

"As the person preferring the charges, you need to put them in writing and sign them under oath before a commissioned officer. The statement has to indicate that you, the signer, has personal knowledge of, or has investigated, the matters set forth in the charges and that the matters set forth in the charges and specifications are true to the best of your knowledge. I can go through all of this evidence and draft something for you and bring it by tomorrow for you to sign, if you want," Kristen offered.

"That would be very much appreciated!"

The next day, Kristen came by with a statement for Rachel to approve and sign so that she could file charges against Admiral Leftwich. It was pretty straightforward, detailing how he had tried to bar her from SEAL training and combat despite her exemplary performance and how he had argued against her promotions when they had been clearly earned. The main focus of the charges was, of course, the classification of her injury and the decision that it disqualified her from being in combat. Kristen promised to file the charges the same day, which would trigger a preliminary investigation into Admiral Leftwich's conduct. After Kristen left, Christopher came in to see Rachel.

"I filed my papers this morning," he said, eying Kristen as she walked down the hallway and away from Rachel's room. "She's been here to see you two days in a row. Why?" He pointed toward the door, watching as Kristen walked away down the long hallway.

"She's my lawyer. What papers?"

"Request for early retirement. I got that she's a lawyer, but why do you need a lawyer?"

"It's hard to convene a court-martial without one," Rachel said, as if Christopher should already know what she was talking about.

"I think I missed something," he said.

"I'm bringing Admiral Leftwich up on charges of gender discrimination under Article 134. He's the one who categorized my injury as critical, not that he's a doctor. He made the call to permanently pull me from combat without giving me the opportunity to recover and retake the fitness test. He deemed my uterus to be a vital organ."

"Okay," Christopher said, hesitantly. "You have proof of this I presume?"

"Of course. And a kick ass lawyer!" Rachel exclaimed. "Now what's this about filing for early retirement?"

"I haven't done twenty years, so I don't qualify for pension," Christopher explained.

Rachel ran her fingers through her hair. *One more thing to do.* "Send me a copy of your paperwork. I'll take care of it," she said, knowing she was much better at paperwork than he was. He definitely qualified for medical retirement, if only he would just set aside his pride and was honest about all of his injuries for once.

"Since when can someone not live without a uterus? All the rest of us serve in combat just fine without a uterus."

"Precisely the point I plan to make in court," Rachel replied.

Kristen was back the next afternoon. "You're being charged," she said tossing a file onto Rachel's lap.

"What do you mean? I'm the one filling charges." Kristen pointed at the file, so she opened it and skimmed the first page. "Fraternization charges? Fascinating. Tell me, how long did it take from the time you filed the charges against Admiral Leftwich until you received this?"

"Four hours," Kristen answered.

"And let's see who is charging me . . . Captain Simms. Fascinating indeed! I highly doubt it's a coincidence that I file charges against Leftwich and then four hours later, his chief of staff files charges against me. Do you have a pen?" Kristen handed her a pen and watched as Rachel read through the charges, making notes and crossing things out on the document. "Kissed Commander Williams at a bar in Lexington? Nope, I have never kissed anyone in the Navy. This is completely made up." She glanced over at Christopher. "Did I forget that we slept together at some point?"

"No, I think we would both remember that!" Christopher shook his head, unable to hide his amusement.

"Oh, this is highly creative but, unfortunately no, there was no tying up involved in the sex that Christopher and I didn't have." She laughed. The list of accusations went on and on. When she was done reading, she handed the document back to Kristen. "Yeah, that's all one hundred percent bullshit. None of those things happened, ever. Some of them sound fun though."

"Which ones?" Christopher's upper lip curled, clearly thinking about how fun some of those things would be.

"Shut the fuck up." Rachel glared at him.

Kristen pursed her lips, trying not to laugh. "There will be a preliminary investigation. Then you can elect to have a judge review the case and make a ruling without a full trial. If they can't find any evidence, the charges will be dropped."

"Sounds good."

As she was leaving, Kristen turned and said, "Maybe some distance until this is over. Just my legal recommendation." She pointed back and forth between Rachel and Christopher.

"She's right, you probably shouldn't be here," Rachel said. Christopher rolled his eyes and stayed right where he was sitting.

Chapter 50:
MAY 2020

RACHEL WOKE UP THAT evening by herself. She hadn't been alone since her injury, but she heard voices outside her room. She carefully got out of bed to see what was going on. She was a bit out of it, still woozy from the painkillers the doctors insisted on giving her. As she got closer to the door, she recognized her father's voice.

"Commander Williams, you will not be retiring early from the Navy, no matter what. You are a valuable asset, and you will take over as team leader no matter how my daughter feels about it."

Rachel was taken aback and decided to keep listening through the door before going out into the hallway.

"Sir, I understand that, but I'm not going back into combat without her," Christopher said. "I'm not spending a single day without her. I don't care if the Navy won't give me a pension. She's worth it."

"I can assure you, I do not know what kind of crazy ideas that girl has put in your head. She's not thinking straight and neither are you. What I do know is that Rachel has a history of going to great lengths to get what she wants, and I wouldn't put it past her to manipulate you so you'd threaten to retire if they didn't put her back in the field. I guarantee you, this thing between the two of you—and suing the Navy, which she's apparently doing—are all just a ploy to force them to do what she wants. She doesn't love you any more than you love her. She's got you convinced you do. She'll lose her court case, and you'll quit the Navy and be left with nothing. This little scheme of hers is going to get both of you dishonorably discharged!"

Rachel opened the door to the hallway. "What the hell are you doing here?" she asked her father, irate. "How did you even know I was here?"

"Are you supposed to be out of bed?" Tom asked her.

"What the fuck are you doing here?" Rachel asked again, gritting her teeth as she tried to mask her pain and frustration.

"You think I didn't start checking your mission reports after I found out you were a SEAL? And good thing I did since no one called me!"

"Why the hell would anyone call you?" Rachel asked, confused.

"Because you were injured and clearly won't be able to go home on your own."

"And what do you suppose that has to do with you?"

Tom looked at Rachel then at Christopher.

"You shouldn't be here," Rachel said passively. She was exhausted. "From what I just overheard you saying to Christopher before I came out here, and how you're talking to me, you are most definitely not wanted or needed." She had all of her weight against the doorjamb now, trying desperately to hide that she was in pain.

"Rachel, I will not stand by while you manipulate Commander Williams into destroying his career."

"I'm not manipulating him. We . . ." Rachel looked at Christopher more affectionately than she meant to. The morphine was messing with her brain.

"Unless this was going on before you were injured, in which case you've ruined both of your careers," Tom said, seeing the way Rachel had looked at Christopher.

"Do you really think so little of me, Daddy? You think I would do that to someone?"

Tom's eyes were like daggers. She winced.

"I woke up in the hospital and Christopher had decided all of this on his own. I tried to convince him to stay on active duty, to take over the team. He doesn't want to, and that's his choice. As for what's going on between the two of us, that remains to be seen, but I can assure you, it's none of *your* business. Now, are you going to leave, or am I going to call security?" Rachel stared her father down, her eyes boring into him, daring him to stay and keep yelling. He didn't budge.

"If the two of you aren't together, then what the hell's he doing here?" Tom asked, still full of furry.

"It's a SEAL thing. You wouldn't get it," Rachel said coolly.

"Never leave a man behind and all that," Christopher said. "We just take it a bit more seriously. The whole team is here, not just me."

"We stick together until everyone gets to go home. That's the rule," Rachel added.

As if on cue, Ryan and Matt came around the corner, walking toward them. "See sir," Christopher pointed toward Matt and Ryan, "there's my watch relief."

Matt and Ryan came over and stood at attention. "Admiral Ryker, sir," they shouted in unison.

"Nice of you to come for a visit," Ryan said.

Tom wasn't giving up. "Lieutenant Rhodes," he started. "What do you know about these two and their history of fraternization?" He pointed back and forth between Rachel and Christopher.

"No history that I know of, sir," Ryan assured him. "Sure, I've seen her hug him. She's hugged me too, and Matt, and everyone. But I haven't ever seen her do anything with Williams she hasn't done with the rest of us. Hell, I've even seen her hug Admiral Eastwood and even kiss him on the cheek once she finally got him to approve her supply order one time. Does any of that count as fraternization?"

"Captain Ryker is the epitome of integrity," Matt chimed in. "She loves the Navy more than she loves herself. She'd never violate any policies, certainly not commit fraternization. It would end her career. And we all know she's not planning to retire until she outranks you, sir."

"Should be any day now," Rachel joked. "I'm thinking two years as rear admiral at command HQ, then they'll promote me to vice admiral for a couple years, then admiral probably by the time I'm forty."

"Skylark." Matt looked at her with concern. "Shouldn't you be in bed?"

"Why thank you for asking! Yes, I should be in bed. I was, however, quite rudely woken up by my father yelling at Commander Williams out here in the hallway, trying to convince him I'm a manipulative whore. So, if you can come up with a way to make them leave so I can go back to sleep, I sure would appreciate it." It killed her to send Christopher away, but it was the only way she could think of to get rid of her father.

"Alright, you all heard the woman," Ryan said assertively as he nudged Tom and Christopher away from Rachel's door. "I'll text the team and let them know Matt's on watch."

Matt and Rachel stood in the hallway until Tom, Christopher, and Ryan had gone. "What the fuck," Matt said. He turned to Rachel and continued. "You really should be in bed." Rachel responded with an irritated grunt, and, with a bit of help, complied with his instructions. "Seriously, Sky, what the fuck was that?" he asked once she was back in bed.

"That was the start of the Spanish Inquisition, I'm afraid. Y'all need to be ready," Rachel continued. "They're doing an investigation."

"What do you mean?" Matt asked, confused.

"No one believes Christopher and I weren't together before or that we're not together now. The Navy is putting together a list of everyone we've ever worked with, and I mean everybody. You are all going to be questioned under oath. I don't know when, but it will be soon. They are very unhappy that Christopher wants to retire, and they are possibly more unhappy that I'm filing charges against them for pulling me from combat. This could just be an attempt to get both of us, or even just one of us, to back down. I really don't know. Just tell everyone to be ready."

"It's not like you have anything to worry about. Shit, I always figured if anyone from our team would get brought up on fraternization charges, it would be you and Ryan," Matt said.

"Oh my god, that is the most disgusting thing I've ever heard! He's like my little brother!"

"Obviously I know nothing's ever happened! Just with how much you two are always whispering and sneaking off together to gossip, it would be an easier case for the Navy to make against you," Matt clarified.

"First of all, Ryan and I do not sneak off to gossip. We politely leave the area while y'all are sleeping so we don't wake you up." There was no way she could tell Matt that she and Ryan snuck off in the middle of the night to interrogate terrorists for the CIA.

"See, it doesn't sound so great when you say it like that," Matt pointed out.

Rachel cringed. "I thought I was supposed to be resting, not having disturbing ideas put in my head."

"Well, unfortunately," Matt handed Rachel the file he was holding, "this is why Ryan and I actually came to talk to you. I'm sure your brain isn't fully functional because of the drugs, but I figured you'd want to see the final mission report before we send it in. Ryan filed the preliminary report since he actually was at the compound finishing everything while we were in the helicopter. Then it took a few days for Daniel to go through everything we collected. But there's some interesting stuff in there."

Rachel skimmed the report, reading all about how they had entered the compound, and started searching for intel. She already knew all that and decided to skip ahead to the part she didn't know and read all about how they had finished collecting the intel and blown up the compound before running to the helicopter. Then she got to the interesting part.

"Six hostels, later identified via fingerprints and facial recognition as Iranian nationals, were found and executed at the compound. It is believed that they were attempting to recover the same intel as the SEAL team. Technical expert 'Condor,' together with the rest of the team, analyzed the recovered hard drives and documents, all of which were part of a dossier of over 100,000 documents previously stolen from Iran by Mossad in 2018. These documents and files detail Iran's AMAD project, which aimed to develop nuclear weapons. Also recovered were files detailing updates made to the program, several of which were based on stolen U.S. technology, specifically malware which previously targeted Iran's nuclear

program. The recovered intel provides details of new U.S. technology in the form of an updated, more advanced malware code. The original code was uncovered in 2010 and is believed to have been developed jointly by the U.S. and Israel as part of 'Operation Olympic Games.' It previously destroyed approximately one-fifth of Iran's nuclear centrifuges by targeting the control systems.

"Can you explain this in English please?" Rachel requested.

Matt chuckled. "It's malware that is targeting industrial facilities. The U.S. developed the original code with Israel. It caused a global epidemic of computer shutdowns. Since then, the U.S. and Iran and God knows who else have been trying to get and update the code to make it more efficient and precise. The original code targeted PLC, Programable Logic Controllers, which control things like power plants or power grids. Critical infrastructure. The CIA and NSA military cyber command, together with Israeli intelligence, were trying to slow down Iran's nuclear program. It didn't really have the effect they were hoping for, hence why they're updating the code now." Matt paused, giving Rachel a minute to process everything. "So, we didn't recover the USB stick with the malware. We did recover proof that ISIS, Samir Al-Abadi specifically, has this malware code. And some other things . . ."

"What proof and other things?" Rachel asked, furrowing her brow.

"Turn the page." Matt suggested.

Rachel flipped to the next page. It was a note.

Dear Skylark,
Please be aware that your country is the enemy of the world. Not me. America is harming average citizens by playing with the power grid. You tried to harm Iran once, it didn't work, so now you're trying again. You are not the world's saviors as you think you are. I will admit, the updated code is much better. I won't tell you how I got it, but now I have it. Know that your country is not as secure or safe as you pretend.
-Samir

"Okay, not entirely sure I can disagree with his premise on this one. Why are we turning off people's electricity?" Rachel asked.

"That wasn't the intended purpose. It's just what ended up happening," Matt said. "Ask Daniel. He can explain it better."

Rachel grimaced at the thought. "That sounds like a long lecture that's going to confuse me and frustrate him."

Matt nodded in agreement. "You ready for the next part?"

"Next part?" Rachel asked, turning the page again.

The next document in the file was a large image of her father, followed by photos of her mother and her brother, with a caption reading *Admiral Thomas Ryker, lead supervisor of Operation Winter Games, together with his family.*

"What the fuck? What does this shit have to do with my family?" Rachel asked. "Matt, I don't get it. Maybe it's the morphine."

"San Diego. That's what your dad was working on when you were in San Diego a couple of years ago, and his house was broken into and you had to go to the safe house. After we got back from Khost."

"Somehow they followed me from Khost," Rachel stated.

"No. Your father was the target. They wanted the updated code."

Rachel scrunched up her face, thinking for several minutes as bits and pieces came together in her mind. "What do you mean you didn't get the USB sick?"

"We didn't find a USB stick at the compound. Just all these documents and one hard drive that Daniel's still going through."

"Did I dream it?" Rachel asked out loud but mostly to herself.

"Dream what?"

"I had it in my hand. I was confused because it had my birthday on it . . . He said it was photos of me . . ."

"Maybe try some complete sentences?" Matt's brow creased with confusion. He'd seen her on morphine plenty of times, he'd dosed her with morphine himself enough times to know it always made her loopy and slightly incoherent.

"My dad had a purple USB stick on his desk when I was in San Diego with my initials and birthday written on it. I asked him what it was and he said it was pictures of me. It was lying on his desk out in the open, so I didn't think twice about it."

"Okay." Matt was staring at her, unsure if she was done talking and not knowing what to say.

"Then," Rachel kept going, "after Aiden died, Samir left me a note and a photo. He was holding a purple USB stick." Rachel looked frantically around her room. "Where's my phone?"

"I dunno," Matt said.

"Well, find it, Matthew!" Rachel said harshly.

"Alright, no need for full names." Matt shook his head, knowing she'd start yelling if he didn't find her phone fast.

Rachel scrunched her eyes closed, completely frustrated with the situation. "Matthew Mason Johnson, find me my fucking phone!"

"I'm looking for it!" Matt yelled back as he opened cupboards and drawers and searched under miscellaneous sweatshirts that were strewn about her room. He finally found her phone plugged in on the other side of the room. He disconnected the charger and handed it to her.

Rachel scrolled through her photos immediately. Something was clicking in her brain, but the morphine was making her not trust herself. She scrolled and scrolled then paused abruptly. Rachel showed Matt the photo of Samir's note from after Aiden died. Next, she showed him the photo of Samir holding a purple USB stick. She zoomed in on the letters on the side of it, barely visible since he was holding it. "The last number is a four," Rachel pointed out.

Matt took her phone and examined the photo, then scanned the photo of the note more closely before nodding in agreement.

"You didn't find it at the compound?" Rachel asked again.

"No," Matt confirmed.

"I was holding it, then . . ." Her hand reached for her abdomen. "I was confused because it said RMR092184 on the side, and I remember thinking it was odd and also thinking I recognized it. Now I know why."

"It was in your hand when you got stabbed?" Matt asked.

Rachel bobbed her head slowly. "Pretty sure." She looked down at her hands, gripping the blanket covering her legs so hard her knuckles were white. "I dropped it. Maybe it got kicked under the desk in the struggle?"

"Maybe." Matt nodded again. "If it did, it should have gotten destroyed in the explosion when David blew up the compound."

"I don't understand though. If Samir already had the code when we were in Khost, why did he send someone to attack my father in San Diego?"

"Maybe they wanted access to the programmer and any updates they had done?" Matt shrugged.

Rachel flipped through the documents in the file. "Did you show this to my dad? He needs to see this. Fuck, you have to convince the fucking doctors to stop drugging me so I can fucking understand what I'm reading!"

"Is it the morphine though, or is it all the technical jargon?" Matt teased.

"Fuck you. I know what malware is." Rachel rolled her eyes. "Why don't they have a picture of me? Shit, maybe it's good I didn't go home for ten years."

"Yeah, maybe."

"Are you getting my dad?"

"Yes, I'm working on it," Matt assured her as he texted Ryan.

Ryan, Christopher, and Tom were back in Rachel's room a few minutes later, and Rachel handed her father the last two pages of the report that detailed the intel they had recovered. "Read that please," Rachel requested.

Tom's eyes got wide as he read, and wider when he flipped to the page with the family photos.

"San Diego," Rachel stated. "Did they ever solve that case? I suspect they didn't."

"They identified the men who attacked the house and safe house and followed the money being used to pay them," Tom told her.

"Who was paying them?" Rachel asked.

"A shell company," Tom said. "The men were mercenaries, guns for hire."

Rachel had suspected as much. "We recovered hard drives and documents at an ISIS compound, proving that ISIS has your code. Has had your code since before they attacked your home, is what we've been told. They were trying to get access to the updated code and your programmer, I guess."

"Shit!" Tom exclaimed as he perused the file.

"Iran likely has your new code now too since the guys we found in Syria were Iranian. I'm sure they were photographing and uploading images and stuff as they searched the house. So you may want to scrap that project and start over. I had your fucking USB stick in my hand. I swear I did."

"What color was the USB stick you found in Syria?" Tom asked.

Rachel gave him a blank stare. "How the fuck would I know? I was wearing night vision goggles. It was some greyish-brownish-green color from what I could tell. But I have a photo of Samir Al-Abadi holding a purple USB stick, so I assume that's the one." Rachel raised her eyebrows as she relayed the message to her father, hoping her voice was as patronizing as she was trying to make it.

"The red USB has the malware code. The purple one has the passwords and codes to install and activate it," Tom explained.

"Fucking fantastic," Rachel muttered. She showed her father the photos on her phone of Samir with the purple USB stick.

Tom's eyes were wide as he stared at the photo. "Rachel? How many intruders were there in San Diego?"

"Umm, two?" Rachel said, trying to remember.

"We had just switched to purple USB sticks the week before you came," Tom noted.

"What are you saying, Daddy?" Rachel was trying to catch up.

"If there were two intruders, and you detained two intruders . . . I remember very clearly you detained two intruders. How did they get this USB stick?" Tom asked, pointing to the photo.

"I don't know. My brain isn't working properly. I'm on too many drugs." Rachel glared at Matt.

Christopher stared at Tom. "Sir, are you thinking there was a third intruder who got away?"

Tom nodded. "There must have been."

"No, I promise I don't ever fuck up like that." Rachel chuckled at the absurdity of the accusation. "We're missing something."

"Well–" Tom started.

Rachel held up a finger, indicating that he needed to be quiet. She buried her face in her hands, humming to herself as she meditated herself back to December 2018 and the break-in in San Diego. "Who else knew about this project around the time of the break-in?" Rachel asked.

"Only the people on the project," Tom assured her.

"No, because we were sent on a wild goose chase in Khost to find a *green* USB stick with your stupid code right before that," Rachel told him. "Leftwich . . . Leftwich knew you were missing your code and he sent us after Saad Ayad which, of course, we all knew was a bullshit mission." She thought to herself for a minute. "You were on the phone with him when I was at your house. On Christmas. You had a meeting with him and you talked about something with a code."

"Isn't Khost in Afghanistan?" Tom asked.

Rachel raised both eyebrows and stared at him like he was an idiot. "Yes, it is, why?"

"Leftwich knew our server had been hacked from Iraq. The tech and intelligence departments, the NSA, everyone was certain ISIS had stolen the malware code. That was determined in July 2018. We included Leftwich in August 2018 and asked him to send a SEAL team to Iraq to investigate."

"And he sent us to Afghanistan in October 2018." Ryan grimaced.

"How good of friends are you with Dick Leftwich?" Rachel asked Tom.

"*Richard* and I know each other very well," Tom replied.

"Has he ever been to your home?"

"Yes."

"Around the time you started using purple USB sticks?" Rachel raised an eyebrow.

"Rachel Marie Ryker, are you accusing an admiral of stealing the USB stick and giving it to a terrorist?" Tom asked lividly.

"Answer the question."

"He was at my home in January 2019. We had dinner," Tom admitted.

"Rache, he's a misogynistic jackass, but I'm sure he's not working with Samir," Christopher said.

"How else would you explain it?" Rachel asked. Their conversation was interrupted by a knock on the door. Matt was closest and opened it to let in

Kristen Campbell.

"Hearings are starting," Kristen announced. "They want to talk to Rhodes." She looked at Ryan.

"Right now?" Ryan asked.

Kristen nodded.

"No time to prep?" Ryan raised an eyebrow.

"I tried to delay . . ." Kristen gave him a weak smile.

"Fuck." Ryan looked at the floor. "Do I need to be in uniform?"

"Yup," Kristen told him. "Service khakis would be preferable." She winked, noting his jeans and black t-shirt.

"I thought the whole point of being a SEAL was that you didn't have to be in uniform and do all this dumb shit," Ryan grumbled as he followed Kristen out of the room.

"Stop complaining Rhodes and go get me out of trouble," Rachel joked. She leaned back against the pillow, her mind a jumbled up mess of thoughts. Things weren't making sense, not really. She wasn't sure if it was the drugs or if she really was missing something. She racked her brain, trying to untangle the details.

Stupid Leftwich. Why was everything suddenly connecting back to him?

"Campbell?" Rachel paused as Kristen turned to look at her. "Subpoena Admiral Leftwich's emails and texts and whatever else you can get pertaining to Samir Al-Abadi, malware, or Iran."

"Why?" Kristen asked.

"Curiosity, or I'm crazy." Rachel shrugged. "Just a hunch."

Chapter 51:
JUNE 2020

CHRISTOPHER PULLED UP THE ranch's long gravel driveway and made a left-hand turn at the main house before continuing down the road toward his cabin. It had only been four weeks since Rachel had been injured in Syria, and he didn't want her to walk any further than necessary. They had flown from D.C. to Dallas where Christopher had left his truck in the long-term parking lot. He stopped the truck in front of his cabin and got out, rushing around to Rachel's side to open her door.

"I can open my own door!" she yelled.

"I'm sure you can, but you aren't supposed to. It's too heavy. You can rip open your incision still."

"It's a door," Rachel insisted. She was not being a very cooperative patient.

Christopher took her hand, helping her to step down from the truck and walk up the three steps to the front door of his cabin. He opened the front door and got her settled on the couch, then got to work fixing up her room with clean linens and bringing in her bag.

"Do you want to sleep?" he asked her when he was done.

"No." Rachel scowled.

"Are you hungry?"

"No." Rachel rolled her eyes.

He looked at his watch. It was only one hour until dinner. "I'm going to go park the truck up at the house and come back with an ATV. Are you okay sitting where you are?"

"I'm fine," Rachel assured him.

Christopher went back out to the truck and drove down to the barn where he could turn around and go back to the main house. Jackie saw him and waved him down.

"How is she?" Jackie asked, concerned. He had told his family that Rachel had been injured but he had told only Jackie the exact nature of Rachel's injuries.

"Physically fine. She has some restrictions for a while. Mentally," he shook his head, "not good."

"Yeah, she doesn't really strike me as the kind of person who can sit still and take it easy. How can I help?" Jackie asked.

"Can you take one of the ATVs up to my place while I park the truck and say hi to Mom? Rachel shouldn't be walking that much yet. I mean, she can walk, and she will walk if you let her, but it's better if she doesn't walk too much for at least a week or so."

Jackie grinned and pretended to salute him. She did it incorrectly, of course, but it made Christopher smile anyway. "I'm on it! I think Dad and Sara are up at the house too. If you want, I can hang with Rachel and bring her up to the house for dinner later?"

Christopher nodded, knowing he needed a break from arguing with Rachel. She seemed to be struggling to understand that just because she could do something physically, didn't mean it was a good idea.

Christopher went up to the main house to find his parents and Sara on the front porch.

"Honey, you're here!" Mary exclaimed as she jumped up to hug him. "Where's Rachel?"

"I sent Jackie to mind the very uncooperative patient for a while. Wanted to fill you all in on what's happening before she comes up for dinner,"

Christopher answered.

"Are you going to tell us what happened?" Sara asked inquisitively. She had finished veterinary school a few weeks prior and moved back home. Christopher hadn't wanted to burden her with the details while she was finishing her exams.

"Rachel was stabbed in the abdomen right below the bottom of her vest." He paused, hearing his mother gasp in shock. "Physically, she's more or less fine. She sustained some organ damage." He could see the wheels turning in Sara's head as she ran through human anatomy in her head. She touched her own stomach, estimating how far down a bulletproof vest would go. With two fingers pressed against her abdomen, she looked at Christopher, knowing immediately which organ he must be referring to.

"Right about here?" Sara asked.

Christopher nodded. Mary reached for her own stomach, to the scar she'd earned after having a cesarean section when Jackie was born. Bob was the only one who wasn't catching on.

"Could they repair it?" Sara asked anxiously.

"No, the knife had been twisted, so it was a decision between taking it out or risk her dying. She'd already lost too much blood. We were too far from the hospital and didn't have the right supplies." He looked at Sara, knowing she would understand. "Our medic did a direct transfusion in the helicopter." Sara's eyes went wide at hearing that, and she and Mary both had their hands over their mouths, tears in their eyes.

Sara looked at her father. "Her uterus, Dad." Bob's face went white with shock.

"Lord Jesus," Mary said.

"She's fine, Mom," Christopher assured her. "She's not upset about that part." Mary looked confused. "The Navy is pulling her from combat, reassigning her to a desk. That's the part that's killing her." Christopher paused, letting the information sink in.

"That makes you team leader then, right?" Bob asked. "I guess we'll be seeing less of you from now on. You'll need to be in Virginia a lot more, I suppose."

Christopher looked down at his shoes. This was the hard part. "Technically, I'm interim team leader until everything is officially decided, but . . ." He didn't know how to explain that he was retiring, that he was in love with Rachel, that he'd given up his career for a girl. It sounded crazy even to him, but that's exactly what he was doing.

"What is it, honey?" Mary asked kindly, sensing her son's hesitation.

Christopher looked up at her. "I've decided to retire from the Navy."

Sara shot him a knowing look.

Just then, they heard the ATV pull up. Christopher's head swiveled and he watched Rachel get off the ATV less carefully than she should have before she rushed up the porch steps to the house.

"Hey y'all," Rachel said. "Thanks for letting me come to stay with you. The doctors wouldn't discharge me to go home by myself so . . ."

"Rachel, sweetheart, you are more than welcome here any time," Mary said, giving Rachel a hug. Rachel made eye contact with Christopher over Mary's shoulder and he gave her a slight nod of the head.

"I guess Christopher filled y'all in on what happened," she started.

"He did," Mary confirmed. "How long is your recovery time?"

"They said six to eight weeks. It's been four, so I guess I'm halfway there. But then I have to train for the physical fitness test, and I'm guessing eight weeks of doing nothing will take a bit of a toll."

"You don't have to do the fitness test," Christopher said.

"Yes, I do," Rachel insisted.

"If they're pulling you from combat–" Christopher started.

"Nothing has been decided yet," she interrupted quickly to cut him off.

Christopher inhaled sharply and raised his eyebrows and pursed his lips, showing his irritation. He wasn't going to have this argument with her again, certainly not in front of his whole family. Rachel wasn't going back to the Middle East, not to fight anyway.

"Rachel," Bob asked carefully. "If you are reassigned, where do you think you'll be?"

"SEAL Command Headquarters in D.C., planning and coordinating missions for the teams," Rachel answered.

"Something she's already excellent at," Christopher contributed, trying to put a positive spin on the situation.

"It's boring," Rachel stated bluntly.

Jackie laughed. "Not exactly an adrenaline rush!"

"No, it's whatever the exact opposite of an adrenaline rush is," Rachel said. "Can you imagine sitting in an office for eight or more hours a day with all these dumb old men, having to convince them you're smarter than they are?"

"Well, now you get to show them how to plan a mission properly," Christopher said.

Rachel, clearly tired of his positivity, said in Arabic so no one else could understand, "Stop trying to make it better."

Sara pulled Rachel aside after dinner. "Hey, if you want to talk about any of it, I know Christopher is a good listener, but you know, he's a man. Anyway, Jackie, Mom, and I, we're here if you want."

"Thank you, Sara," Rachel said, giving her a hug. "And I guess I should congratulate you, *Doctor* Williams! What are you going to do now that you're done with school?"

"Oh, I'm going to live here, down at my cabin, and help with the cattle and assist one of the local veterinarians who is planning to retire soon. He's going to cut back his hours successively so I can take over."

"Sounds like an excellent plan, Doctor," Rachel said.

Sara beamed. "You know, I think I'm going to make Christopher call me that. What's higher, commander or doctor?"

"The doctors at Walter Reed seemed to be of the opinion that doctor outranked captain, so if that's the case." They both burst out laughing. Rachel wrapped an arm around her stomach, trying not to wince from the pain.

"Stop laughing, you're going to hurt yourself," Christopher chastised Rachel from across the room.

"Is your incision still healing?" Sara asked, concerned. Rachel shrugged. "Can I look? That way I know if Chris is overreacting or not."

She and Rachel went into the bathroom, where Rachel undid her jeans and pulled them down. Sara gently pulled back the bandage. "Wow, Christopher mentioned the knife got twisted, but shit! Looks like it was a pretty big knife too," Sara said as she looked at the thick red scar across Rachel's bikini line. It was several inches long horizontally, with a thin red vertical line intersecting it in the middle. She could tell Rachel's skin had been delicately tucked and pulled and woven back together by the surgeon.

"That's what I've been told. I don't really remember."

"Well, the incision is healing well." Sara traced her finger along Rachel's skin close to the scar. "It's not fully healed though, so unfortunately, you do need to be careful a bit longer."

Rachel gave Sara a wink. "I'll try to behave."

Christopher went outside and started the ATV. Rachel walked right past him, headed for the cabin. "Rachel! You aren't supposed to be walking that far!" he yelled to her. Rachel gave him the finger and kept walking. Sara, having witnessed the exchange, ran and caught up with Rachel, opting to walk with her in case something happened. Christopher followed on the ATV.

"He's just being careful because he cares," Sara reminded Rachel.

"I know. It doesn't make it less annoying though," Rachel replied.

"He's retiring to be with you, isn't he?" Sara asked.

"That's what he says. Nothing is official yet. He's technically filed for early retirement. We're supposed to serve for twenty years to qualify for pension. He's only done fourteen years, so what he's doing isn't particularly smart. I mean, he'd still have the other veteran's benefits, home loans and VA health care. All those things. But it's not a very well thought out plan. If he doesn't want to go back into combat, then he can transfer to a desk for six years and then retire."

Sara nodded. "But you two, I mean, one of you has to retire, right? If you're going to . . ."

"Yeah, well, that's still being decided too," Rachel said wistfully. She climbed the steps to Christopher's cabin, went straight into her bedroom, and closed the door.

Rachel lay on her bed, waiting to hear Christopher go into his own room. They hadn't said a single word to each other since dinner. She was irritated with the situation and irritated by Christopher's need to put a positive spin on everything to cheer her up. She didn't want to be cheered up. She wanted to be angry. After listening for a minute and deciding Christopher wasn't in the living room, she wandered outside to the wraparound porch, trying to find a way to safely climb up onto the roof. It was hopeless. She was stuck on the porch or inside the house. She wandered back to her bed and tried to sleep. After two unsuccessful hours, she got up and went to Christopher's room and climbed into his bed. He reached out his arm instinctually and pulled her in close. She curled into him, her head on his chest and arm wrapped around him, falling asleep instantly.

Christopher woke up at 0600. He had been exhausted from arguing with Rachel for the past month, but was happy to have her crawl into his bed. He understood how difficult this must be for her, having to give up the thing she loved doing most, but she needed to accept reality. Rachel was singing "Treacherous" softly in the living room, strumming his guitar as she sang. He stayed in bed for a minute, listening. He knew the song well. Jackie and Rachel were both obsessed with Taylor Swift. He also knew that Rachel chose her songs with care and that something in the lyrics was what she was thinking. Something she wanted to say but didn't know how to put into words. He listened to the lyrics carefully, trying to get inside her head before he went out to her. The situation they were in *was* potentially perilous as they stood on the edge of a life changing decision. The song choice made sense. She was admitting she was scared. He walked into the living room and smiled at her before going to the kitchen to make coffee. He brought over two mugs—one black, one with milk—before sitting down next to her and sliding the coffee with milk over to her. She finished the song and took a sip of the coffee.

Her next song choice was "I'm Only Me When I'm With You." She sang it slowly, her own arrangement of the song, sweet and somewhat sad and not at all like the radio version, which was upbeat and much happier sounding. He was starting to understand. She sang with her eyes closed, not looking at him but leaning toward him. She was completely engrossed in what she was doing, channeling all of her emotions into the song. He listened carefully to the lyrics. She was trying to tell him so many things. The song was like confession—he knew her best, he made her feel safe and whole, and she was struggling to admit it. At the same time, she was finally acknowledging her own feelings for him in the only way she knew how.

Her fingers brushed against his as she handed him the guitar.

Christopher knew he needed to make a point, force her to understand what he was thinking and feeling, so he switched to the one language he knew she'd fully understand—more Taylor Swift songs—and chose "Dancing with Our Hands Tied." He sang, looking deep into her eyes and hoping she'd get the hint.

Rachel watched Christopher play. It was the perfect song. Repressed feelings and secret love since they were twenty-five? Rumors and accusations? Loving each other the best way they knew how, even when they knew they couldn't actually act on their feelings? That damned fraternization rule had acted like handcuffs that neither of them had been able to escape.

"You really do love me, don't you?" Rachel asked when he was done. The question was genuine, like she had been uncertain about his sincerity all along.

"That's what I've been trying to tell you!" Christopher said as he put the guitar down on the floor. "I guess I should've known you'd need it in a song." He chuckled, shaking his head before looking at her with a serious expression on his face. Her upper lip curled as she leaned toward him. His body unconsciously mirrored hers until their foreheads were pressed together. "You know you only sleep when you're with me," Christopher stated firmly. He was staring straight into her eyes as he grazed her cheek with his thumb.

"That is not true!" Rachel pulled away and hit him on the side of the head with a nearby throw pillow. "I sleep just fine, thank you!"

"Then what was last night about?" he teased.

"Couldn't sleep," she admitted hesitantly.

"Yeah, like I said." Christopher took a sip of his coffee and leaned back on the couch, smiling at her, happy he'd won that one at least.

Rachel laid her head on his shoulder and sighed. "What the hell are we gonna do?" she asked, disheartened.

"We'll figure it out," Christopher assured her as he put his arm around her. "You'll see. Everything is going to be great. We just need to give it some time."

The next day, Rachel had a doctor's appointment to check her incision. It was healing well, but she would still need to take it easy for the next few weeks. No heavy lifting. No intensive exercise. No sex. Her body was basically a prison cell. She was getting frustrated and frantic. She had a physical fitness test planned for the middle of July to prove to the Navy, and whoever else doubted her, that she still had what it takes to be a SEAL and serve in direct ground combat.

Christopher was driving them back from Dallas. He could tell that Rachel was restless. "What?" he asked her.

"What?" Rachel responded, annoyed.

"You're clearly upset," Christopher said.

Rachel was silent.

"You're halfway there. Just a few more weeks and you can get back to normal," Christopher said.

Quiet tears trickled down her cheeks. Everything was so mixed up in her head. She didn't know who she was or who they were together. Her thoughts and feelings were a chaotic mess that she couldn't sort through. Christopher saw she was crying and put his hand on her thigh. It sent a shockwave of warmth through her like lightning. He'd never done that before. She felt a hunger and longing like never before, a lustful desire demanding to be quenched.

Every other thought, feeling, and fear that she'd ever had dissipated in that lightning flash. She remembered what he'd said that morning, that she could only sleep when she was with him. It was true. The only place she felt whole was in his arms, like the warmth of him replaced the missing pieces of her heart and soul that had been lost over so many years of trauma, horror, and heartbreak. She knew she couldn't act on it. Not until everything was officially decided and all the paperwork for his retirement was complete. Her loyalty to the Navy still outweighed her love for him.

"I'm taking a shower," Rachel announced as soon as they were back at Christopher's cabin. She then proceeded to take the coldest shower of her life, hoping it would calm her down and make her stop thinking about him that way. She had to stay in control of her body and her mind and knew she was going to need to find something to distract herself with. The doctor had said she could start with light exercise. *Thank God!* She finished showering and put on yoga pants, a sports bra, and a t-shirt before heading outside.

Christopher had left, but that was probably for the best. She walked to a patch of grass behind his cabin and laid down, deciding to test what her body could do. She knew she would need to swim five hundred yards in under twelve and a half minutes, then do at least fifty push-ups in two minutes, fifty sit-ups in two minutes, ten pull-ups in two minutes, and run one and a half miles in under ten and a half minutes just to meet the basic qualifications for entry into SEAL training, let alone to qualify to go back into the field with her team. The swimming and running were easy. She could complete those without a problem in less than half the allotted time before she was injured. The strength training would be hard though. She had lost muscle mass while in the hospital and her core strength had been severely affected by the surgeon cutting and sewing her abdominal muscles. She knew those were the minimum requirements to pass, to be considered eligible, but she would need to do much more than simply get a passing score in order to make her point.

Rachel tried a sit up. Everything hurt. She rolled over into a plank position to try a push-up, but there was more pain. Every muscle in her core was screaming at her to stop. Her body was failing her as much as her mind was. She wished for a second that she had died. She was feeling restless and frustrated. Physical punishment was usually her go-to solution, but her body was already punishing her enough. Within minutes, Christopher was kneeling by her side, his palm on her back, as violent, panic-stricken tears drenched her face.

"What?" Christopher asked. His voice was full of concern and love and sincerity.

"I can't do anything," Rachel said between sobs. "I tried, and everything hurts. I'm broken. Everything is broken."

"I know," Christopher said. She was sure he wanted to encourage her, to tell her it would get better soon, but also probably knew none of that would be a comfort to her like it would have been to anyone else. Instead, he laid on his stomach in the grass right next to her. "Explain," he said.

Rachel cried a few minutes longer, trying to catch her breath and put her thoughts into words. The physical pain, the physical problems, those were straightforward enough. It was all the other stuff that was confusing. "I tried to do a sit-up. Couldn't. Tried a push-up. Can't even plank for five seconds." She took a breath and Christopher waited for her to continue. "It's like I'm not me anymore and you're not you, and it's this weird mess, and it's confusing and terrible and wonderful and terrifying all at the same time." She was crying again, tears streaming down her face. "When I think about work, being stuck at Command on a desk, I feel like my soul is dying. But when I think about you . . . I really don't sleep when I'm not with you." That was all she could say. She couldn't tell him the rest of how she felt. Not without making things too real and too serious.

"How can I help?" Christopher asked. His heart was aching for her. He wanted to take away her pain and confusion and make her feel safe.

"I don't know. I'm not allowed to do any of the things I would normally do."

"Then we need to try something else," Christopher suggested. He'd spent years watching her process her feelings with alcohol, exercise, and sex, and as the doctor had just told them, none of those things were an option. Not that he processed things much differently most of the time, other than going to therapy, which he knew she'd say no to.

"Try what?" Rachel asked.

"Walking, music. I don't know, maybe this strange thing called talking?" he teased.

Rachel turned her head to look at him. "What was I just doing?"

Christopher had to laugh at that. Rachel was an expert at talking to other people about how they were feeling, but when it came to her own deep emotional vulnerability, she had put up so many walls she had no idea how to take them back down.

"You were talking, but you were holding back. Whatever you're thinking and feeling has you so scared and uncomfortable you won't say it out loud, which is crazy because you're the bravest person I've ever met." He turned onto his side so he could look at her. "Nothing you say to me will shock me or scare me or make me want to run. I can see that you very much want to run, and that's okay, just as long as you don't actually physically run for another two weeks."

Rachel let out a little laugh. "Don't worry, I'm not going anywhere. Couldn't even if I wanted to." She turned her head to look at him, considering if she should tell him everything she was thinking and feeling. "I've never done this before."

"Never done what before?"

"This. Like a relationship thing," Rachel said. She was hesitant to be too vulnerable.

"No, I've never done the relationship thing," Christopher corrected her. "You most definitely have."

"When?"

"Carter?"

"Oh." Rachel paused. Somehow she'd forgotten all about Carter. "That doesn't count."

"Why not?"

"It's not the same." Rachel looked at the ground. She didn't know how to explain that doing something out of convenience, comfort, or sheer boredom wasn't at all the same as what they were considering doing together. She had actual genuine feelings of love and affection for Christopher. Their souls were connected, entwined with each other in such a profound way she knew she could never put it into words. It was entirely different from the sort of love one had for their childhood best friend or first boyfriend. She scrunched up her face and tried to explain. "When you're fourteen, you don't know what you're thinking or feeling. You just do stuff and then shit happens and suddenly it's been twenty years, and yeah. So, it really doesn't count."

"What?" Christopher had no idea what she meant.

"I mean, we were friends, and he was there. I don't know. It just sort of happened. It wasn't like we had deep, meaningful conversations about life or anything."

"Are you forgetting that I've met Carter? I've seen you with him. The two of you definitely had a relationship, definitely talked about life and feelings."

Rachel shrugged. "It's not the same."

"Why?"

"Because I was never scared to lose him, so it doesn't count!" Rachel blurted out before she could stop herself.

"And you're scared to lose me?" Christopher asked.

Rachel looked away from him, rolling onto her back to stare at the sky before continuing. She crossed her arms over her stomach, each hand gripping the opposite elbow, and dug her fingernails into her arms. "You're my best friend. The only person I've ever fully trusted. I'd rather ignore all these other feelings and keep you as my best friend than risk ruining everything."

"I'm not going anywhere, Rachel. I told you that." Christopher glanced at her hands and sighed.

"We'll see," Rachel said sadly. "At some point, you're bound to get sick of it all."

"I've known you for over eleven years and I'm not sick of you yet," Christopher assured her.

"It's not the same. Being here. It's different. I'm different here. I don't–"

Rachel covered her face with her hands. "I can't handle being here. I feel stuck. If I'm working at Command full time, I'm going to lose my mind and it will hurt you and drive you insane and you will hate me and leave."

"Rachel, I've seen you do some pretty crazy shit. I don't think anything you do is going to be particularly shocking."

"Tip of the fucking iceberg," she muttered.

"And how do you know that I'm not as crazy as you are? Maybe I'm just as fucked up, just fucked up enough to handle it?"

Rachel laughed. "I've seen your personnel file, Christopher. All of your psych evals. I know. You don't thrive in chaos like I do. You tolerate it like a normal person when you have to. I need chaos to feel . . . anything."

Christopher had seen it so many times before, how pending disaster and chaos could calm her down and how everyday situations bored her to restlessness and panic. "We'll just have to come up with lots of activities. Go skydiving on your days off, play paintball, whatever you want. You're not going to be chained to a desk 24/7 or stuck in a house."

"Just . . . sometimes, the restlessness . . . you know? I can get sort of careless."

"Yeah, I know all about the drinking and driving and a whole host of other shit you pretend you don't do." Christopher poked her arm where her nails had left fresh red marks on her arm. "I know you, Rachel Ryker. You don't have quite as many secrets as you seem to think."

"Is that so?" Rachel asked, surprised

"Working at HQ, living in D.C. full time, never deploying again. Sure, it's going to be a big adjustment for both of us, but we've been through worse and we've overcome every challenge we've ever come up against together. This will be just like all the times before. You and me against the world. It's going to be amazing."

"How are you still such an optimist?" Rachel asked. "With everything we've done and everything we've seen, you're still convinced that the world is innately good and that everything is going to work itself out for the better."

"Aren't you the one always talking about karma and how the universe gives you what you deserve?" Christopher contested.

Rachel laughed. "You just made my point! You're an optimist, full of positivity," Rachel tried to clarify. Christopher looked at her, confused, so she continued. "Karma gives you what you deserve, yes. If you think I deserve good things, it implies that you believe I'm a good person deserving of good things. Hence, you're a crazy optimist."

"You are a good person," Christopher countered.

Rachel gave him a weak smile. He typically had a hard time seeing people's flaws. "I love that you believe that, Christopher."

"I don't believe it, Rachel. I know it. All the terrible, traumatic, fucked up things? That was war. That wasn't you. Those were things you had to do in order to do your job and stay alive. They don't make you who you are. You happen to be the most compassionate, empathetic, caring person probably to ever exist. You help everyone, put everyone's needs before your own. You're completely selfless. That's who you are. If you don't believe me, then I'll spend the rest of my life trying to prove it to you."

"Christopher," Rachel said. God, she wanted to kiss him, hug him, do all sorts of things she couldn't do to him. She looked into his eyes, trying to make her desire clear, trying to tell him with her eyes that she was his, even if she wasn't entirely sure she should be. There was no real reason for someone as wonderful and truly good and decent as Christopher Williams to want to be with someone as damaged as she was. As much as she wanted him, she knew that she'd only end up hurting him. Letting Christopher in, letting him choose her and choosing him back would be the most selfish thing she ever did.

Chapter 52:
JUNE 2020

THE DAYS PASSED, EVENTUALLY turning into weeks. They spent their days walking the trails around the ranch, going to the local gun range, and to the bar. Finally, eight weeks had come and gone since Rachel's surgery, and she could get back to regular physical activity, which was good since her fitness test was fast approaching. She woke up at 0500 excited and ready to go. She got out of bed, careful to not wake Christopher, and left a note on the kitchen table to let him know she'd gone out for a run.

She ran all the way to the meadow and back, a total of three miles in twenty-one minutes. Not fast enough to pass her test. She needed to be under a six minute mile, but not bad for her first run in eight weeks. She had ended her run at the lake and decided to give swimming a try. After taking off her shoes, she waded in and dove under the water. She knew the lake was about one hundred yards wide, so she needed to do five laps in under twelve minutes, which would be two minutes and forty seconds per lap. She started at a comfortable pace, checking if her body could handle it. *So far so good.* She swam to the opposite side of the lake and back and was tired. She checked her watch to see how fast she had been. Eight minutes. Not nearly fast enough.

She walked back up toward the cabin, determined to keep trying. This was only day one. She went over to the grass where she had tried several weeks before to start training again. She laid down and attempted a sit-up. No pain! She did another. She did sit-up after sit-up until it burned. Next, she tried a push-up. Easy! She did another and another until she couldn't anymore, then rolled over for another set of sit-ups. She alternated between the exercises until she couldn't push herself anymore and then walked back to the cabin.

Christopher was awake and in the kitchen with a fresh pot of coffee brewing.

"How'd it go?" he asked.

"Not great, but not terrible. I've got my work cut out for me."

Christopher nodded.

Rachel changed into dry clothes while she waited for the coffee and then sat down with Christopher at the kitchen table.

"I could do everything except pull-ups. I didn't try that yet. Nothing hurt, but I definitely can't do what I used to do," she said, a bit sad.

"You'll get there," Christopher reassured her. "It was your first time exercising in eight weeks."

"I know, I know, be patient." Rachel rolled her eyes.

"How far did you run?"

"Three miles in twenty-one minutes."

"Rache, I know you're more of a long-distance runner, but maybe focus on the one and a half miles. Be strategic," Christopher suggested.

Rachel pouted, hating the idea immediately. "Yeah, you're probably right. I'm going to have to get a top score if I'm going to make my point."

Christopher looked at her curiously. "I know you love being in combat," he started, "but do you honestly want to go back, or are you just doing this to prove something?"

Rachel shrugged. She wasn't sure. "I'm definitely trying to make a point. The Navy made the wrong call, and I see it as my duty to prove it to them. As for going back, there's nothing I would love more. But I don't know how I feel about going back without you."

"You'd miss me too much, wouldn't you?" Christopher teased.

"No, it's not that. I mean, yes, I would miss you, but it's not that exactly. I don't know. It would be weird to fight without you. I've had you right behind me for the past ten years, eleven if you count training. I mean, I'm sure it would be fine. I'd be safe with the rest of the team, obviously, but it's more fun with *you*."

Christopher smiled. He knew what she meant. "Both of us going back isn't an option, not if we . . . Or if you get pulled."

"I know."

"But I do get why you want to pass the test, why you need to make this point. The way they handled the situation was wrong. If it had been me or Matt or any of the guys, we would have collected our Purple Heart, gotten some extra paid medical leave to recover, and gone back."

"Exactly," Rachel said.

"You're going to pass the test. And that's not me being optimistic or overly positive. You're going to pass because no one works harder than you do," Christopher assured her.

Rachel and Christopher finished their coffee and had breakfast at the main house before going for a ride. Rachel was happy to be back in the saddle, and Breeze was just as fast as ever. They rode for two hours before lunch. After lunch, Christopher timed Rachel as she ran sprints on and off for an hour, trying to get her speed back. They ate dinner and then went on a long slow jog up the hill toward the ridge.

After a few days of moderate exercise, Rachel decided it was time to add hand-to-hand combat to their schedule. Jackie and Sara were fascinated and insisted on watching, sitting on the porch railing.

"You ready?" Rachel asked Christopher. She was dressed in her camouflage utility pants, combat boots, and a white tank top.

"Give me all you've got!" he answered.

They bumped fists and took their positions. Rachel landed a quick jab to his ribs. He threw an uppercut. She took a step back and gave him a swift kick to his stomach with her right leg and he grabbed her foot to stop her.

"Big mistake, Hawk!" Rachel said as she twisted. She reached her right arm down to the ground, putting all of her weight on it so she could spiral herself horizontally and kick the leg she had been standing on up into the air. Her boot slammed into Christopher's shoulder. He nearly lost his balance and dropped her leg.

Jackie and Sara laughed so hard they almost fell off the porch railing. Christopher recovered and went at Rachel, grabbing her and flipping her onto her back. She landed on the ground with a loud thud. Not to be bested, she twirled herself around and kicked him in the back of the knee, causing him to fall. They both got up. Rachel moved in with a jab-cross-uppercut combo, hitting Christopher as hard as she could without breaking any bones.

"Oh my god, Chris! I can't believe you're getting beaten up by a girl!" Jackie giggled.

"This is literally the best thing I've ever seen! We should have made popcorn for this!" Sara chimed in.

Just then, Rachel swung her leg around into a roundhouse kick, hitting Christopher right in the forehead.

"Fuck!" he yelled as he fell backward. He was bleeding badly.

"What the hell?" Rachel asked. "How did you not see that coming? You always dodge when I do that combo!"

Christopher grabbed his head. "I was distracted," he said, glaring at Jackie and Sara, who were trying to stifle their giggles now that he was hurt.

"I'll get the medic kit," Rachel said, running into the cabin. When she came back outside, Christopher was sitting on a chair on the porch, still holding his head and trying unsuccessfully to stop the bleeding. Rachel got to work cleaning the cut and pulled out a suture kit. "You need stitches. Probably three," she told him.

"Wait, wait, wait," Sara said. "You're going to stitch him up?"

"Yeah," Rachel and Christopher said in unison. They did this all the time.

"Isn't it better if I do it? I am a trained medical professional," Sara argued.

"You treat cows," Christopher said. "I think people are different."

"Still, you better let me do it since I'm here," she said.

Rachel shrugged and handed her the kit. "Certainly, Doctor Williams."

"Don't you have some sort of local anesthetic?" Sara asked, eyeing the medic kit.

"Don't need it," Rachel and Christopher both said.

Sara looked at them both like they were crazy and stitched up Christopher's head wound using exactly three stitches, just as Rachel had predicted, before covering it with a bandage.

The next two weeks continued much the same. Wake up, fitness test, breakfast, ride, lunch, yoga, fitness test, dinner, weight lifting, sleep. Rachel grew stronger and faster by the day as her test, and her court-martial case, quickly approached, but she was still nervous she hadn't had enough time to get back into shape and wouldn't pass.

Chapter 53:
JULY 2020

RACHEL FLEW TO DAM Neck Naval base on July 27th. After a long discussion with Christopher, he had finally conceded that it would be best if he stayed in Texas. The nature of their relationship had been questioned enough. The trial would likely go better if Christopher wasn't there, even if he insisted he was just there as a supportive teammate. He hadn't been called to testify, so there was no reason for him to be there. She had scheduled her fitness test for the next day to ensure that it would be complete and the results could be provided to her lawyer and defense counsel before court proceedings began on July 29th. She was nervous for the test but fairly confident she would pass. She just hoped she passed with a high enough score to really make her point.

Rachel's lawyer Kristen, the defense counsel, Admiral Eastwood, Admiral Leftwich, and the judge were all there. Any one of them would have been more than capable of administering the test, but for some reason, they all insisted on coming to watch.

Kristen could tell Rachel was nervous and pulled her aside. "You've got this, okay? Besides, the trial isn't hanging on this test. We can still win the trial even if you don't pass. You've had a month to train and obviously this is kind of crazy."

Rachel nodded and Admiral Eastwood approached them.

"Ryker, no matter what happens, you're still a SEAL. No one can take that away from you. Breathe, stay focused, stay out of your head. Don't get in your own way."

"Right." Rachel nodded again. "Give me five, okay?" They agreed, and she left to go hide in the bathroom and listen to a five minute meditation, hoping it would be enough to get her grounded and focused. It helped, but it wasn't enough. She needed Christopher.

Skylark to Hawk: *It's time!*
Hawk to Skylark: *You'll do great! One thing at a time.*

Rachel took a deep breath and went to rejoin everyone.

"Are you done wasting everyone's time?" Admiral Leftwich chided her.

Kristen flashed the judge a look, begging him to intervene. He did nothing.

"Alright, Ryker, you know the drill," Eastwood started. "Swimming, calisthenics, then running."

"Seriously?" Kristen raised an eyebrow. "Swimming first will make the rest of it more difficult."

"Exactly," Rachel, Eastwood, and Leftwich all said.

"Does she really have to be in uniform for this?" Kristen asked, staring at Rachel's utility pants, jacket, and combat boots.

"No, she's allowed to be in running shorts, a t-shirt, and sneakers, but she's crazy." Eastwood shrugged.

"If I were in combat, I'd be in uniform," Rachel pointed out. "It needs to be a realistic test."

"Yeah? You want a helmet and bulletproof vest too?" Eastwood teased.

Rachel tried not to laugh. He was well aware she would take off her vest and helmet in a heartbeat if they were slowing her down in combat. She took her spot by the edge of the pool, ready to dive in as soon as she got the signal. She took three deep breaths then heard the sharp screech of a whistle telling her to go. She was in the water instantly, her arms and legs powering her forward. She needed to do ten laps. The water was warmer and much cleaner than the lake at the ranch. That made it easier. Still, she knew she could do better. She focused on her muscles, raising one arm out of the water at a time, kicking with her legs, and suppressing her thoughts. Before she knew it, she was on lap ten. She was out of breath, but she had to finish. She thought of every man who had ever told her *no* and used her rage to fuel her.

"Seven minutes and fifteen seconds," Admiral Eastwood announced when her hand was on the edge of the pool and her head was above water. "Good job, Skylark."

"Fuck you. That's a terrible time," Rachel complained.

"For you, pre-surgery, yes," Eastwood chuckled. "Get your ass out of the water." Rachel put both palms on the edge of the pool ready to lift herself up. Eastwood shook his head and discretely motioned toward the steps. "Conserve your energy and buy yourself a break," he whispered. Rachel smiled and swam slowly to the ladder, happy to know he still had her back.

"Good job," Kristen whispered to her as she got ready for the calisthenics portion of the test.

"Yeah, this is the hard part though," Rachel whispered back.

"It's only hard if you think about how hard it is." Kristen winked.

"What?" Rachel squinted at her. Kristen flashed her phone toward Rachel so she could see the screen.

> Williams to Jones: *Tell Ryker it's only hard if she thinks about how hard it is. Remind her it's mostly mental. The only easy day was yesterday and she better not ring the fucking bell.*

Rachel smiled at the words of encouragement from Christopher, then took her spot on the ground. There was no way she was quitting. She elected to start with push-ups, knowing that was the most difficult. With two minutes on the clock, she got the signal to go. Her arms were burning, her core was tense, and all she could do was breathe through the pain and keep going. She could hear Christopher's voice in her head, telling her to push, reminding her how strong she was, encouraging her every step of the way. Her muscles were fatigued though, and she was about to give up when she heard the timer go off. She hadn't been counting. Hadn't wanted to know how horribly she'd been doing. She let herself fall to the ground and take a deep breath before looking up at everyone expectantly.

"Seventy-six," Eastwood stated. He was trying to hide the smile on his face. Admiral Leftwich was doing a much worse job of hiding his disappointment.

"Seventy-six?" Rachel repeated.

"Yeah, I'm not counting those last four."

Rachel burst out laughing and rolled onto her back.

"You don't want a break?" Kristen asked.

Rachel glared at everyone. "There are no breaks in combat."

"Okay." Kristen raised her eyebrows and pursed her lips, realizing just how crazy the SEALs were if the rest of them were at all like Rachel.

Eastwood started the timer for two minutes. Rachel did sit-up after sit-up, thinking about every woman she'd ever met on a base or at a training who had been looked down upon, treated differently, been asked to get coffee or take notes. Every story of sexual harassment or gender discrimination she'd ever heard. She was doing this for all of those women. Every woman in the military, every woman who aspired to be in the military, for future generations of girls who deserved a more equal playing field. Not that she'd be contributing to those future generations. *Don't think about that!* she scolded herself silently. Uterus or no uterus, she still had options if she ever decided she wanted kids. Not that she was planning on changing her mind, but now was not the time to think about that. She caught sight of the look on Kristen's face, determining she may be doing better than she thought. Eastwood's face was neutral, as always, unfortunately. The timer rang, and she stopped instantly.

"You needed to do fifty, Rachel." Kristen raised both eyebrows at her. "What the fuck is actually wrong with you?"

Rachel looked concerned for a moment until Eastwood laughed. "She's a fucking over achiever, Jones. Always has been."

"How many?" Rachel asked.

"Eighty-eight," the judge marveled.

"Eighty-eight that count?" Rachel looked at Eastwood.

"They all counted, and yes, you did eighty-eight. How many were you doing at home?" Eastwood asked.

"Not eighty-eight." Rachel's brow creased. Even she was shocked by her own performance. She got up and walked over to the pull-up bar, ready to go and feeling more confident. She knew she could do ten pull-ups, no problem. She jumped up, both hands on the bar. Her arms were burning, and she instantly wished she'd taken it easier on the push-ups. Oh well. She had to do ten. Twenty would be better. She went as fast as she could, engaging her core, using her shoulders and back as much as she could to relieve the weight on her arms. She couldn't see the timer, but she could count, and she did count. Five, ten. Ten was passing. Fifteen. She was running out of time and energy, but she was determined to do twenty pull-ups, even if it killed her, even if she could never use her arms again. *Pain is only temporary,* she thought to herself. The timer rang as her chin went over the bar for the twentieth time. She dropped to the ground and let out an exhausted sigh.

"Twenty pull-ups," Eastwood announced to everyone. "You ready to run, Skylark?"

"She's running five miles, right?" Admiral Leftwich asked.

"No, one and a half," Eastwood corrected.

"No, no, no. She's purporting that she can get sent back into combat with a Special Projects squadron," Leftwich protested. Everyone stared at Rachel.

"Fuck," she muttered to herself, looking at the ground. "What's my time limit, sir?"

"Thirty minutes," Leftwich told her.

"No problem, sir." Rachel nodded.

"Rachel, this is not what we agreed to," Kristen whispered to her as they walked to the track.

"It's fine, Kristen."

"It's not," she protested. "You are supposed to be doing the BUD/S entrance exam, not whatever this is."

"Welcome to my fucking life," Rachel muttered.

"I can object. Call it abuse of power, which it is."

"I can run five miles. Don't worry about it." Rachel sighed. "Maybe time the first one and a half miles separately, just in case."

"Alright," Kristen agreed.

Rachel did the math quickly in her head. Five miles in thirty minutes was a six minute mile. Should be a piece of cake. But she hadn't been running more than three miles at a time. Her speed wouldn't be a problem, but her endurance might be.

"You're allowed to take a ten minute break," the judge reminded her.

"No, it's fine." Rachel knew she'd just get in her own head about it. It was much better to get it over with and not think too hard about how Admiral Leftwich had changed the criteria halfway through the test when he saw how good she was doing. Not to mention the fact that the judge didn't seem to care.

"Alright, ready when you are," Eastwood said, stopwatch in hand. Rachel took a deep breath and took off sprinting. She pushed and pushed, lap after lap. The first mile and a half were easy enough. She saw Kristen hold up seven fingers as she passed by. That was good. That was passing for the regular fitness test. But she wasn't a regular SEAL. She cursed herself for not having seen this coming. She should have known she'd need to do more. Her legs carried her lap after lap as she sang to herself in her head. She had her running playlists all memorized and she let her brain glide back to the day she'd tried out for Special Projects. She'd run five miles in twenty-five minutes that day and gotten herself fast-tracked through the training. Normally she'd sing out loud while she did this run. But she needed to conserve her oxygen and let it all go to her lungs and muscles. Lap after lap flew by until she was on mile four. She was starting to get out of breath. "Time," she gasped as she passed Eastwood.

"Twenty-four. You're all good," he yelled back.

Rachel let out a sigh, knowing she would be cutting it close. She took a deep breath, refocused, and knew she had just under four laps to go. *Push. Push like your life depends on this, like someone else's life depends on this.* Adrenaline coursed through her veins as blood pumped to her legs. *Run like someone else's life depends on it.* She ran and ran until Eastwood yelled at her to stop.

"You lose count?" Eastwood teased.

"What?" Rachel slowed to a walk, hands on her hips as she tried to catch her breath.

"That's five miles, Skylark. You can be done. You're done. You passed."

"Time?" Rachel was completely out of breath.

"Twenty-nine minutes and fifty-eight seconds."

"Terrible," Rachel chided herself, but she had passed.

"Not good enough." Leftwich was beaming. "Good attempt, Ryker, but not good enough."

"She just had major abdominal surgery two months ago!" Eastwood protested.

Leftwich shook his head. "Not good enough. She should be able to do one hundred sit-ups and ninety push-ups. We haven't even talked about how much weight she can bench press or–"

"The agreement was to do the BUD/S entrance exam. Not the test to deploy with a Special Projects squadron," Kristen pointed out.

"Fine. If she wants to go through BUD/S again . . ." Leftwich shrugged.

Rachel put both hands on her hips and glared at him. "If you wanted me to pass the Special Projects test, why did you have me swim five hundred yards in the pool and not one mile in the ocean?" Rachel pointed out.

"Rachel, stop making it sound like you're volunteering to do more," Kristen cautioned.

"It wasn't good enough, Ryker," Leftwich insisted.

"Objection," Kristen yelled at the judge. "This is not what we agreed to and is also entirely unrealistic of expectations, given her medical history! She's had one month to train for this."

"Sustained," the judge agreed. "Ryker's performance was impressive. Impressive enough to deploy with a Special Projects squadron, no. But almost. We agreed she would be evaluated based on the BUD/S test, and she more than passed that. I'll see you all in court on Monday."

"You okay?" Kristen asked as she walked with Rachel to the female officer's housing.

"Nope," Rachel said. "I have to pretend that I am for a little bit longer though."

"I know." Kristen gave her a weak smile. "You should be proud of yourself,

Rachel. You did great."

"Not good enough." Rachel shook her head. "I passed. I barely passed. You know, I'm supposed to be in the top one percent. That . . ." She pointed behind her, toward the track as she walked. "That was the bare minimum to be considered eligible to be selected for a team."

"You just had major abdominal surgery," Kristen reminded her.

Rachel shook her head. "Not good enough."

The tears came the second Rachel was back in her room with the door closed. She slid down the door until she was sitting on the floor, then tucked her knees into her chest and dropped her face into her hands. She'd passed. Technically she'd passed. But it hadn't been good enough. Nothing she did was ever good enough. She pulled out her phone and instinctively pressed Christopher's name in her contact list.

"Rache? How'd it go?" Christopher asked excitedly. Then he heard her sobs. "Fuck. What happened? Did you pass?"

"It depends on who you ask."

"Tell me more."

Rachel proceeded to give him a rundown of everything that had happened.

Christopher was fuming before she'd gotten even halfway through the day. "I should have come with you."

"How would that have helped? That would just be more ammunition for them to use against me, and you know it."

"I'm so sorry this is happening, Rachel. I should have–"

"You should have what?" Her tone was sharper than she intended.

"I should have told the surgeon to repair your fucking uterus."

"I would have died."

"I know," Christopher agreed. "How the fuck can anyone expect you to pass the Special Projects test when you've had one month to train after not being allowed to do anything for two months? It's ridiculous! They do realize you're human right?"

"I don't get to be human. Women in the military don't get to be human. We have to be better. You know that."

"It's not right."

"It is what it is." Rachel sighed. "Eastwood told me regardless of what happens, I'm still a SEAL. I'll always be a SEAL."

"Well, that's true."

"I know. It's not enough though. I'm never enough."

"Stop being so hard on yourself. You did great and you are more than enough. Soon this will all be over."

"Then what? Everything goes back to normal?"

"We'll find a new normal, you and me. Everything's going to be amazing. You'll see."

Chapter 54:
JULY 2020

RACHEL SAT IN HOURS of meetings with HR representatives over the next couple of days, trying to get anyone to make an actual decision about whether she and Christopher could start a relationship without either of them being dishonorably discharged. She had the court-martial preliminary investigation into the charges Captain Simms had filed against her as solid evidence that nothing had happened between them, which was helpful, but the HR representatives still weren't willing to commit to an answer. After three days of meetings, affidavits, paperwork, and interviews, Rachel finally had their decision. She and Christopher needed to be the same rank when they got together to show there hadn't been any coercion, that she hadn't used her rank to make him do anything. The same went for her working at Command. If he wasn't retired, it put her in a position of power where she could influence him, give him direct orders. It was a sexual harassment lawsuit waiting to happen, according to HR. Christopher and Rachel needed to wait for both his promotion to captain and his retirement to become official before she could file more paperwork. If they promoted her before him, or if she started her new job before he was officially retired, then it would all be for nothing.

Kristen sat with her through most of the meetings, even though it technically wasn't her job, and Rachel was grateful for the company and the legal input.

"I have something for you," Kristen told her after their final meeting with HR. "I honestly don't know what to do with this, but I thought you would want to see it. I subpoenaed Leftwich's emails like you asked me to." She pulled a file out of her purse and handed it to Rachel.

"What the fuck am I looking at?" Rachel mumbled to herself as she skimmed through the file. "Leftwich seems intent on going to war with Iran..."

Kristen looked over her shoulder and flipped forward a few pages. "I thought this one was particularly interesting."

Rachel's eyes narrowed as she read an email chain between Leftwich, her father, and several other people. "They wanted to use that malware code to knock out power in all of Iran then . . . what?" Rachel furrowed her brow. "What's the play here?"

"Not sure, but your father stopped it, from what I can tell." Kristen showed her the next email. "If you go further back in the file to his phone records, there's phone calls with a few numbers I couldn't identify."

Rachel studied the page in question, scrunched up her face, then sat down right in the middle of the sidewalk. "The country codes are for Iraq and Syria," she told Kristen.

"Yeah, that's as far as I got."

Rachel pulled out her phone to compare the dates of the calls with dates in her calendar. "Maybe I'm crazy, but these calls line up with when my team was tracking Samir Al-Abadi."

"What are you saying?" Kristen's eyebrows knitted together with concern.

Rachel looked up at her. "I'm saying that while my team was hunting the person who has this code and the USB stick with the passwords to activate the code, Leftwich was calling someone in Iraq and Syria, which is where we were tracking Samir Al-Abadi."

"Someone on your team?" Kristen guessed.

"Nope. I can assure you, no one on my team would ever speak with him voluntarily." Rachel shook her head. "We kept missing Samir by days, sometimes hours or minutes. Almost like . . ." She closed her eyes, unable to say what she was thinking out loud.

"Almost like what?" Kristen wasn't following.

"Almost like someone was tipping him off, telling him to move, to run." She took a deep breath and looked at Kristen. "Samir hates Iran. If there was a way to get the U.S. to focus on Iran instead of ISIS . . ." She sighed. "My dad said there was no way for someone to get the USB with the passwords and activation codes without taking it from his house. Leftwich was at his house. I know I sound crazy."

"What do you want me to do with that file?" Kristen asked. "It's not exactly pertinent to your trial."

"Can I keep it?"

"What are you going to do with it?"

"You may not what to know." Rachel cringed.

"Your team can identify those phone numbers." Kristen nodded, understanding the SEALs would have access to better tools and technology than she did.

Rachel pressed her lips into a tight line. "They can try."

Rachel went back to her room and highlighted the mystery phone numbers. She left Post-its with a few notes, then packed up the file and sent it via currier to Daniel, hoping he could make better sense of it. She didn't mention her suspicions, knowing they were crazy and lacking foundation. Those phone calls were likely coincidence. If they weren't, then Daniel would reach the same conclusion she had all on his own.

Chapter 55:

JULY 2020

THE COURT CONVENED AS scheduled on Monday, July 20th. As it was a general court-martial, the panel was composed of a military judge and five members who would act as jurors. Rachel had demanded that at least one juror be female to help ensure she had a fair trial. She got her wish. Matt was called to testify since he had witnessed Rachel getting injured firsthand and had treated her.

"Lieutenant Commander Johnson, can you please describe the events leading up to Captain Ryker's injury in as much detail as possible, to the best of your recollection?" Kristen requested.

Matt gave them a full account of the mission, from breaching the compound to treating Rachel in the helicopter.

"Would you say that the mission was done according to established protocols and procedures?" Kristen asked.

"Yes, everything was completely textbook. Not a single rule or protocol was broken."

"Can you explain why Captain Ryker was the first to advance up the stairs, rather than someone else on the team?" Kristen prompted.

"Captain Ryker is always the first in and last out. She leads by example."

"And is it normal for you all to split up into pairs when doing that sort of work? Clearing rooms in a compound, I mean," Kristen asked.

"Yes, always. We do everything in pairs. Safety first."

Kristen nodded. "Can you please explain, from a medical standpoint, what happened?"

"Certainly," Matt started. He gave everyone a play-by-play of the medical treatment Rachel had received. "There were no complications from her surgery, no other organ damage. Everything went extremely well and she has since made a full recovery, according to her medical records and fitness test," he concluded.

"Objection!" the defense council screamed. "Lieutenant Commander Johnson is not qualified to make that determination."

"Sustained," the judge agreed, giving Matt a look of warning.

The defense was up next. "Lieutenant Commander Johnson, you testified that Captain Ryker sustained organ damage and even had an organ removed. Is that correct?"

"Yes, her uterus, an organ which she can easily live and fight without," Matt answered bluntly.

The judge gave Matt another admonishing look before the defense council could object again.

Matt ignored the judge entirely and kept talking. "All the other SEALs fight even though they don't have uteruses. While Captain Ryker does outperform all of us on most things, I find it hard to believe that any of her skills are due to her uterus, and I am entirely confident that having undergone a hysterectomy will not affect her ability to lead or serve in any way."

"Your Honor," the defense council said to the judge.

"Lieutenant Commander, I will find you in contempt of court," the judge warned.

"Your Honor, that is my medical opinion, which I believe I was asked to provide," Matt insisted as politely as he could manage.

"You say she outperforms the men," defense counsel started with a sly grin. "Wasn't one of your teammates killed in action due to Captain Ryker's inability to read a map?"

Matt scrunched up his face. "What are you talking about?"

"Aiden Bennet," the defense council clarified.

Matt winced. "Aiden ran straight into enemy fire to save the life of one of our intelligence assets. Maps had nothing to do with it."

"Aiden Bennet died a fucking hero and saved the lives of ten American aid workers who had been taken hostage," Rachel said. "How dare you bring that up here." Rachel's tone was icy cold, her eyes like daggers.

"Captain Ryker, while I'm inclined to agree with you, you're out of order," the judge scolded her.

Kristen clutched Rachel's forearm and squeezed hard, trying to get her to calm down. Matt was dismissed from the stand. He locked eyes with Rachel and gave her a reassuring nod as he walked past her.

Kristen proceeded to walk the court through the charges, citing Admiral Leftwich's emails to Rachel as evidence of his bias against women in general, and Rachel in particular.

"Your Honor, I would like to bring the court's attention to the document labeled prosecutorial evidence 1-75-10. This is an official letter from Admiral Leftwich to then Lieutenant Commander Ryker, informing her that she, despite graduating at the top of her class from SEAL training, would not be assigned to a SEAL team because, and I quote 'of the risk of irreparable harm which may befall a woman if she were to serve in that capacity.'" Kristen looked at Admiral Leftwich who had been sworn in to testify moments before.

"Sir, do you remember writing this letter?" Kristen asked him.

"Yes," he answered.

"And what, if you recall, did you mean by 'irreparable harm which may befall a woman?' Please Admiral, could you enlighten the court as to what type of harm a woman could suffer in combat that a man could not?"

"Sexual assault, rape, irreparable damage to the reproductive system. We saw an increase in birth defects after Vietnam due to women's exposure to Agent Orange, for example."

"And, to be clear, Admiral, you postulate that none of those things can happen to a male SEAL?"

"I wouldn't think so, no."

"Captain Ryker is more proficient in firearms and hand-to-hand combat than anyone else on her team, and her team is better than any of the other SEAL teams. I fail to see how she would be at increased risk of being assaulted. And as for the risk of irreparable harm to her reproductive organs, it's my understanding that you refused to assign her to a SEAL team unless she took certain precautions first?" Kristen paused to let Leftwich react before continuing. "I would like to present to the court prosecutorial evidence 1-76-19. This email has already been verified by the tech team to have originated from Admiral Leftwich on December 15, 2009 and was sent to then Lieutenant Commander Rachel Ryker. Admiral, could you please read this email out loud? Just the highlighted section is fine."

Leftwich read, "'It is my decision that you will be assigned to a command post and cannot be active in combat unless you agree to take precautions to guarantee your future reproductive health and potential for having a family.'"

"And what precautions specifically were you referring to, Admiral?" Kristen asked.

The Admiral refused to answer.

"Excuse me, Your Honor?" the female juror asked. "I understand the defendant's Fifth Amendment right not to self-incriminate, but I think it's pertinent to the case to have an answer."

"I agree," the judge said. "Captain Ryker, what did you take that statement to mean at the time?"

Rachel stood. "Your Honor, Admiral Leftwich informed me that the only way I could be assigned to a SEAL team would be if I froze my eggs."

The court was silent. Everyone stared at Rachel for several minutes before Kristen continued. "Admiral, have you ever requested that a male SEAL freeze his sperm?"

"No," he admitted.

It was the defense's turn again. Defense counsel started by trying to claim that the emails Kristen had presented were simply taken out of context and that

Rachel had misinterpreted everything, choosing to freeze her eggs herself, if she had in fact done so. He then tried to argue that Rachel's claims didn't constitute discrimination as she wasn't being treated unfairly, she was in fact being promoted.

"Reassigned," Kristen corrected. "Captain Ryker is being reassigned to a new position following her injury. A male SEAL would have been allowed to return to combat after making a full recovery, which, according to her fitness test results and medical records, she has."

"You have no proof that a male SEAL wouldn't have been reassigned to Command HQ," the defense counsel argued. "How many captains do you see, male or female, out running around in the desert with their team? Most of them are in command positions locally, regionally, or at one of the main command posts in Dam Neck, Coronado, or D.C."

Rachel rolled her eyes as she listened to the lawyers bicker back and forth. She knew this was going to come down to the juror's subjective interpretation of the definition of discrimination. She was going to need to do something to make her point.

"Most SEAL teams don't do what we do," Rachel said calmly. "It's not a fair comparison."

"Captain Ryker, you are out of order," the judge yelled at her.

"Your Honor," Rachel said, standing. "I think it's in the court's best interest to ensure counsel is making sound and reasonable arguments and comparisons. Special Projects is not your typical SEAL squadron. That is why we have higher ranked officers and more officers than the other teams. Defense counsel is trying to compare apples and oranges with shoddy logic and speculation!" Rachel made sure to raise her voice, knowing there would be consequences and hoping it would elicit the response she was after.

"Your Honor!" Admiral Leftwich exclaimed. "The girl is getting hysterical! This is precisely why it was determined that she be pulled from combat and reassigned. Her injury was clearly traumatic, and she's obviously unstable!"

Rachel fought hard to suppress her laughter. Her plan to bait Leftwich had worked. "Your Honor, if I may have one minute to speak please?" She was calm, cool, and collected as she asked this.

"Fine," the judge grumbled. "Speak, Captain Ryker."

"Thank you, Your Honor. I would like to point out the Admiral's choice of words. I raised my voice slightly, not as much as he did, and he claimed I was being hysterical. The word hysterical, or hysteria, comes from the Greek hysterikós, meaning *suffering in the womb*. The ancient Greeks believed symptoms of hysteria, emotional instability for example, were caused by a woman having a defective womb, a defective uterus. Given that my recent trauma resulted in a hysterectomy, I find the use of that word even more offensive than I did prior to being injured. The idea that women could have physical and psychological symptoms of distress caused by a defective womb is ridiculous, and I can assure you that every woman in this room is offended and horrified at Admiral Leftwich's choice of words. Although," she added, "I do feel the need to thank him for so eloquently making my point."

"Hold on," the defense council stood up. "Hysterectomies do result in hormonal imbalances. Her argument is entirely flawed."

"Only if the ovaries are removed as well, which in Captain Ryker's case, they were not," Kristen clarified.

"Thank you for sharing that with us, Captain Ryker, and for the clarification Lieutenant Commander Jones," the judge said, sounding irritated.

Rachel gave him a warm, friendly smile and sat down.

The trial lasted seven days before concluding for the jurors to deliberate. It took half of a day for them to reach a decision. Rachel tried not to be nervous. Kristen had done a fantastic job presenting their case, and she was confident that she would win.

"Has the jury reached a verdict?" the judge asked once they had reconvened.

"We have, Your Honor," the female juror responded. "We find the defendant, Admiral Leftwich, guilty on all counts of gender discrimination as listed in the statement of charges."

"Thank you to each of you for your service on this panel. You are all dismissed," the judge said. "Let's move on to sentencing."

Rachel held her breath as the judge proceeded. "Admiral Leftwich, you have a long record of service to the Navy and to the United States of America. Your service record is impressive, but this court has found you guilty. I request you submit your letter of resignation to me by the end of today. If you do not, you will be dishonorably discharged," the judge announced. "That being said, Captain Ryker, your talents are in fact needed at SEAL Command Headquarters, and you will be permanently reassigned there. If that is unacceptable to you, then you may medically retire with full pension and disability."

"Thank you, Your Honor. I will happily take my post at Command," Rachel said.

The day after the trial, Rachel called Admiral Eastwood and set up a meeting with him at SEAL Command HQ, where she was supposed to start working any day now. Eastwood had been the one to finally convince the Navy to admit her to SEAL training and had been the one to get her assigned to the Middle East Specialty Division. He had watched her and Christopher train together and fight together for the past eleven years, and now it was time to have a potentially awkward and difficult discussion. She was sitting in his office, across his desk from him, staring at the floor, not sure where she should start.

"Ryker, why are you being weird and not talking? You asked for this meeting, not me," Admiral Eastwood chastised her. "You know I have better things to do than to sit here and watch you pout about whatever it is you're pouting about, right?"

Rachel's head snapped up. She looked at him, finally daring to meet his eyes. "I can't start at Command yet."

"Why not? You've got big vacation plans or something?" Eastwood joked.

"No, I need to stay at the rank of Captain for a bit longer and not work here yet for . . . something," Rachel said, looking back down at the floor.

"Why?" Eastwood asked, irritated.

"It would just be a huge favor that I would really appreciate, that's all," Rachel said, meeting his eyes again.

Eastwood raised an eyebrow. "This has to do with Williams, doesn't it?"

Rachel averted her eyes from his, not wanting to say it out loud.

"Ryker, I'm not an idiot. You got injured. He put in his papers. I know he refused to leave your room the entire time you were in the hospital. Hell, I even know you've been staying with him!"

"I wasn't allowed to be discharged if I was going home by myself." Rachel pointed out.

"You had a few other options of where to go. Like I don't know, how about the guy you're legally married to? Or your parents?"

Rachel looked at the floor again.

"God, Ryker! Don't forget, I've been watching the two of you together for eleven fucking years. I'm not blind. I know nothing's happened. You're both too dedicated to your jobs for that. Besides, there was an investigation into that, wasn't there? I'm hoping—assuming—you've spoken with someone from human resources about this?" He tried to sound calmer.

"Yes sir," Rachel said.

"And?"

"And HR concluded that we have to be the same rank, I can't be working here because it puts me in a position of power apparently, and he has to be retired. And if all of that by some miracle lines up, then I can file another giant stack of paperwork and then maybe . . . I don't know. I don't even want to think about it until I know for certain that it's even possible."

Admiral Eastwood nodded. "Alright Ryker. I'll delay your promotion and your transfer and try to push through Williams' promotion and retirement, then make Johnson's promotion to team leader official. Shit, that's a lot of paperwork for me to do now and a lot of fucking strings to pull." He paused and looked at her. "You're sure this is what you want?"

"It's the only thing I've ever actually wanted in my entire life, other than being a SEAL." Rachel stared directly at him with a straight face so he knew she was serious and sure that this was exactly what needed to be done.

"Okay, Skylark. I'll get it done," he promised with a nod of his head. She had never asked for anything. Not for herself, anyway. She argued vehemently for her team, for all the teams, but had never, not once, made a personal request. She had hardly taken leave and was always the first one to volunteer for extra work, always putting her team and the rest of the squadron first. He really couldn't deny her this. Christopher had always been the same way. They were the two best, most dedicated SEALs he had ever worked with, and she hoped Eastwood felt they both deserved a shot at happiness.

When Rachel didn't budge, Eastwood asked, "Why are you still sitting here?" He glared at Rachel.

Rachel pulled a file out of her backpack. It was the one she'd gotten from Kristen and sent to Daniel, now complete with his conclusions. The dates of the phone calls Leftwich had made to the mystery numbers lined up perfectly with the dates the SEALs had hit each compound in Syria—always, it had seemed, right after Samir had left. Daniel had been able to uncover even more emails and texts than the ones Kristen originally had. The evidence was still circumstantial but damning enough that someone needed to investigate it officially.

She put the file on the desk in front of Eastwood and sighed. "We have credible evidence that Admiral Richard Leftwich was conspiring with Samir Al-Abadi to start a war with Iran. We're fairly certain he's the one who gave the USB to Samir. It's not conclusive, we can't prove it, but there's enough evidence to show it's likely what happened."

"First you accuse the man of gender discrimination, now treason?" Eastwood didn't sound happy at all.

"Read the file, sir." Rachel gave him a weak smile and left to go back to Christopher and the ranch.

Chapter 56:
AUGUST 2020

CHRISTOPHER AND RACHEL MADE their way up to the main house, tired and hungry from a day of swimming, riding, and running. As they entered the house, Bob called to Christopher from the living room and walked toward him with a letter in his hand. "This came for you after lunch, Chris. Looks important."

Christopher eyed the official Navy seal on the envelope and looked at Rachel, his eyes wide with anticipation. She of course already knew what was in the letter since they had informed her the day before that he was officially retiring, and she was no longer Christopher's boss. He tore the envelope open with such haste that Rachel couldn't help but laugh.

"Calm down! It'll be easier to read if it's not torn into pieces!" she ordered. But it was too late. The letter was opened, torn slightly, but not too damaged.

"Attention Captain Christopher Ryan Williams," Christopher read out loud. "When did I get promoted?"

Rachel gave him a wink. "Did I forget to tell you? Your pins and insignia are in your cabin."

Christopher kept reading. "The Navy thanks you for your fourteen years of service and dedication and hereby grants you medical retirement with full pension and disability, effective immediately." He looked at Rachel, excited to see her reaction.

"It's official then, I guess." Rachel smiled "No regrets?"

Christopher shook his head. A huge grin broke out on his face as he looked at her. "I'm hoping that makes the other thing official too."

Jackie laughed, knowing exactly what he was referring to. "I still don't believe you two that it hasn't happened before. I mean really, ten years wandering the desert, plus a year together for training? Surely you two must have gotten bored at some point."

"Sorry to disappoint Jackie, but no. I can assure you it never happened. We were definitely too busy to be bored, and the Navy has done a very thorough investigation checking out our story," Rachel replied matter-of-factly. Jackie shrugged before sitting down at the dinner table next to Sara.

"Well, congratulations, Christopher! And Rachel, I guess," Mary said. "I know I'll be more at ease knowing you two aren't going back into combat."

Rachel winced slightly at that, but only Christopher seemed to notice. He grabbed her hand and gave it a squeeze before joining his sisters at the table. He was well aware that being put on a desk was something Rachel was still struggling to accept and couldn't imagine her sitting still for eight hours a day. He'd had plenty of experience watching her fidget in her seat as they sat through courses, training workshops, and meetings, trying to fight the urge to get up and run around the room. Even when they were planning missions, a task she loved to do, she wandered around or would run in place, asking questions and making decisions as she did.

Rachel went into the kitchen to help Mary bring the food over and was overjoyed to see fried chicken and sweet potatoes were on today's menu. She carried two serving dishes over to the table before going back for two more. She loved being at the ranch. She never ate this well at home since she couldn't cook.

"Chris, what are you going to do now that you're retired?" Sara asked.

"What do you mean?" Christopher asked, genuinely confused by his sister's question.

"I mean, you're thirty-six years old and you're retired. You aren't going to stay here and live off your Navy pension the rest of your life, are you?" Sara clarified.

Christopher shrugged and looked at Rachel. "We'll see. I hadn't really thought about it," he lied. He had thought about it a great deal and had already decided he was moving with Rachel to D.C. What happened after that, he would figure out once he got there.

"I'm sure he'll come up with something," Rachel reassured everyone. "He's smart and has a lot of skills that could transfer to a lot of jobs. Give him time to figure out what he wants to do."

Mary cut Rachel off. "Grace first, then we can eat." The family all joined hands. Rachel took part reluctantly.

"What's everyone doing tomorrow?" Bob asked.

Christopher smiled down at the table then looked at Rachel. "What do you say, Rache, should we take the horses up the ridge tomorrow?" Christopher suggested.

"I'm always up for a ride." Rachel replied.

Rachel tossed and turned in her bed all night. She had a decision to make, and she couldn't make it, not rationally anyway, if she was in Christopher's bed. She missed him desperately and knew that must be a pretty clear sign of which direction her heart, or some part of her anyway, was leaning. Her brain was protesting vehemently with logic and reason and caution. She rarely denied her body's urges. If she wanted someone, she got them. But this was different. This could have terrible consequences she wasn't sure she was ready to face.

She'd done this before. Almost this exact thing, actually. She and Carter had been friends for years before they had gotten together, and their attempted romance had destroyed them in many ways. It had devastated their friendship and caused irreparable harm to both of them. She cared for Christopher so much more than she had for Carter. Christopher was like the missing piece of her soul, her other half. She knew the sex would be great. She wasn't worried about that. It was the relationship part that was the problem. The part neither of them had any actual experience with. Sure, she'd been with Carter for decades, technically, but that was a mostly supportive friendship that both of them had taken for granted, interlaced with intermittent periods of intense sex. That didn't really count as a real romantic relationship. It certainly hadn't been a stable or good relationship, even if she and Carter had both kept up the pretense that it had been. Neither of them wanted to admit how much they had actually hurt each other or how incapable of loving and caring for each other they had been. They had, of course, loved and cared for each other emotionally as best as they could, but neither of them knew how to actually act, how to show that love authentically, or how to accept love in return. Rachel had always run from love, just like she wanted to do now with Christopher. Carter had always tried to pull her in closer, clinging to her desperately and constantly pleading with her to do the one thing she couldn't—stay. She knew she wouldn't be able to live with herself if she hurt Christopher, and she didn't trust herself not to hurt him, even if she didn't want to, even if it wouldn't be on purpose. She let out a sigh and pulled out her phone.

> Skylark to Hawk: *I'm going to try to run.*
> Hawk to Skylark: *You're always running.*
> Skylark to Hawk: *From this specifically, I mean.*
> Hawk to Skylark: *I know. Which part are you afraid of?*
> Skylark to Hawk: *Oh, I'll do something to screw it up and hurt you. I can promise you that!*
> Hawk to Skylark: *Do your worst. I'm not going anywhere. Let me know when you decide what you want.*
> Skylark to Hawk: *I know what I want.*
> Hawk to Skylark: *Okay.*
> Skylark to Hawk: *I'm going to try to run all the time, though, so you know. Not on purpose or anything, but I'm going to do something stupid and fuck everything up and you're going to get hurt and I'm gonna be sitting here feeling stupid and guilty and terrible.*

Hawk to Skylark: *What are you going to do to fuck it up?*

Skylark to Hawk: *I don't know yet. It's not like I'm consciously planning anything.*

Hawk to Skylark: *How do you know I won't fuck it up before you do?*

Skylark to Hawk: *I don't.*

Hawk to Skylark: *I understand you're scared. It's okay to be scared. You wouldn't be scared if you didn't care, if this wasn't important to you. And if you care that much, then you're less likely to fuck it up.*

Skylark to Hawk: *Yeah… okay. Go back to sleep. I have to keep thinking about this.*

Hawk to Skylark: *Take all the time you need. I'm right here when you decide, regardless of what you decide.*

Chapter 57:
AUGUST 2020

THE NEXT DAY, RACHEL was standing beside Tundra, a large Bay Quarter Horse. Tundra was a slightly older mare, but Jackie assured her she was still fast as could be. "Hey girl, we're gonna go for a ride, okay?" Rachel whispered endearingly.

She loved working with the horses. It always brought her back to the few happy childhood memories she had of spending time with her horse, Anchor, and her Grandpa Jack. Riding had taught her to stay grounded, humble. It had taught her respect. Horses had an innate way of sensing someone's energy. She had to be calm around them, had to control her emotions and act from a place of kindness and empathy to get them to respond to her. It had taught her to be competitive too, though, and she had the belt buckles to prove it.

"Hey, Rodeo Queen, let's pick up the pace," Christopher called to Rachel, a bit of amusement in his voice.

Rachel continued talking to Tundra, stroking Tundra's face and neck, and did her best to ignore Christopher. Then she walked to the tack room and grabbed a curry comb, moving it in circles all over Tundra's body to lift the dirt buried deep in her hair. She used the hard brush next then followed with the soft brush, wiping every speck of dirt clean off Tundra's body, convincing herself this was just proper horse care. She wasn't procrastinating at all. Christopher just stared, watching her work, until their eyes met over Tundra's back.

"Come on, cowboy, get to work!" she ordered when she noticed he was just standing around and hadn't even started grooming Cash. Christopher smiled at her and hurriedly groomed Cash, not putting in nearly the effort Rachel had with Tundra. Rachel moved on to picking Tundra's hooves.

Jackie brought over a saddle, pad, and bridle for each of their horses, knowing exactly what each of them would need. Rachel placed the saddle pad and then the saddle over Tundra's back, tightening the girth as much as possible. She adjusted the stirrups to the correct length, noting that Jackie must have been the last one to use this saddle, before sliding the bridle over Tundra's head. Christopher worked efficiently beside her, following the same steps to get Cash ready to go.

Jackie helped Rachel attach the saddlebags, which contained a picnic lunch and bottled water, just as Christopher bridled Cash. Rachel slid her phone in with the other supplies and Christopher did the same.

They led the horses out of the barn and mounted them with ease. One of the few places either of them felt natural or normal, other than in combat, was on a horse. Christopher led the way up the trail with Rachel close behind him. She quickly caught up, and they rode side by side up the steep hill, walking at first to warm up the horses before breaking into a smooth but swift canter. It was about an hour ride up to the ridge. They started up the hill toward the south border of the ranch, making their way effortlessly up steep hills and crossing streams of water along the way. This wasn't the most direct route. There was a very clear trail wide enough for a pickup truck to drive on, but it was, according to Christopher, the most fun route. They listened calmly to the sound of the horses' hooves on the trail, twigs snapping underfoot as they rode along, keeping their thoughts to themselves. Neither of them had ever been this quiet for this long before. They were both acutely aware that something was about to happen that would change their lives forever, for better or worse.

Rachel was calm and self-assured. She contemplated the past eleven years as they rode and remembered the first time she really noticed Christopher during SEAL training. They had been there for a few days. Rachel had been the only female in the entire place, the first woman other than a Navy nurse to walk through the door, let alone attempt to complete the training. She had worked hard to prove herself just to get in, and she had to keep working hard, harder than any of the men, every single day to keep her place there. They worked in teams or pairs during training, learning to complete various tasks. Some of the instructors did their best to make things more difficult for her, some of her classmates too. But not Christopher. He treated her just like everyone else. She remembered the first time they really spoke; their first real conversation had happened on their third day there. She immediately found him attractive. Who wouldn't, with his square jaw, broad shoulders, and perfect body where every muscle was impeccably defined? Not to mention his gorgeous smile and bright blue eyes that reminded her of the ocean. She could easily drown in those eyes and she'd be perfectly okay with it. But she had known that if she was going to succeed there, she had to shut down her feelings entirely. No distractions.

She had carefully considered what consequences they would face if this happened. Unattached sex was one thing. One night stands on leave were the norm for them both. But this was different. This involved emotions and crossing a boundary that could never be uncrossed. She had reached the conclusion, finally, that no matter what arguments she made against the idea, that this was meant to be, like some sort of destiny. Almost like this was their reward for surviving everything they had been through together.

Rachel reigned in Tundra at the top of the ridge as Christopher motioned for Rachel to slow down. She stared out over the horizon at the miles of dense forest that backed up to Lake Tawakoni. This was one of the first places he had ever taken her on the ranch the first time she came to visit after Aiden died. It was Christopher's favorite spot, where the sea met the land and sky. Or in this case, a giant man-made lake, but close enough. She watched as Christopher dismounted and tied Cash up to the tree, allowing him enough lead to graze.

Rachel reached into her saddlebag before dismounting and slid a few condoms she'd gotten from Jackie into her back pocket, knowing she was still at risk of ectopic pregnancy, which could be fatal. They hadn't really talked about the need for birth control. They hadn't actually talked about sex at all, which was weird for them. They talked about everything. She assumed he wouldn't mind. For all the reckless shit they both did, they were pretty safety conscious as well.

She tied up Tundra near Cash and walked over to Christopher, who was standing under the large oak tree. They stood next to each other and admired the view, full of anticipation for a few minutes, before she took his hand. She leaned in close to him, shoulder to shoulder, and squeezed his hand tightly and held her breath. Her eyes grew wide with wonder as she took in the gorgeous view before them.

"I love you, Christopher Williams. I mean, I'm in love with you," Rachel stated confidently. It was the first time she had said it. He'd said it probably a hundred times, and she'd said she felt the same, but she'd never actually said those words out loud, at least not to him. But there was no denying it.

Christopher took her in his arms and kissed her softly on the forehead. He'd kissed her there before, jokingly of course, one time when she had a head laceration and was high on morphine, insisting someone kiss it and make it better. But this kiss, full of tenderness, full of love, was new.

They stood facing each other, his hands in the loose blonde curls she always had from wearing her hair twisted in a Navy regulation bun. He stared deep into her eyes. It was as if the world had stopped spinning and they were all that was left. They gazed into each other's souls as if they knew exactly what the other was thinking. Rachel kissed him on the lips, softly at first, as though she were testing it. Sparks danced through her entire body. She pulled away and looked at him questioningly, waiting for confirmation that she should continue. It felt good. She was surprised by how good and how comfortable it felt, like they should have been doing this all along, but wanted to confirm he felt it too before things went too far.

Christopher smiled down at Rachel and kissed her passionately, his tongue in her mouth, his hands on her waist, holding her as close as he dared as her arms circled around his neck. *Just go slow.* They couldn't go back to just friends, just Skylark and Hawk, after this. Maybe after a kiss, but that kiss had ignited something deep in Rachel's gut. There was no turning back. She ran her hands up the sides of his body and under his t-shirt, taking it off with so little effort and so much confidence, finally convinced this was right. Following her lead, Christopher took off her worn out Navy t-shirt, the same one she always wore.

Christopher's eyes scanned her body from head to toe. His eyes were bright, and the corner of his upper lip curled as he looked at her, as if for the first time. He'd seen her without her clothes on plenty of times before, either while helping Matt with medical checks when she'd gotten injured or as she took off her pants before going to sleep. But none of those times had been like this. It was different somehow. Suddenly she wasn't Skylark anymore, and he wasn't Hawk. A barrier had been eliminated in their minds. Rachel felt a rush of repressed thoughts and feelings as she stared up at him, watching his eyes dart up and down her body. She laid her palm on his bare chest and felt his warm skin and firm muscles. That spot, right over his heart—that's where she belonged. That's where she'd lay her head to fall asleep every night for the rest of her life, if it were up to her.

Christopher slid one hand into her back pocket, pressing her hips into him as his other hand made its way slowly up from her waist, over her ribcage, and to her breast. Rachel looked away, silently cursing herself for not packing better. She was wearing a navy-blue lace bra and a matching thong. It was cute, but not exactly sexy. She still hadn't made it home to Florida, though, so it would have to do. She wasn't typically insecure about this sort of thing, but she liked Christopher—loved him—and for the first time in her life she actually gave a shit about someone else's opinion of her.

Rachel took a steadying breath as Christopher's hands glided effortlessly over her body. She pressed her forehead to his, their noses touching and their warm breath mingling until his eyes closed and he kissed her again and again, over and over. He let his tongue intertwine with hers before he moved his lips down her neck and tangled his hands in her hair. That was it. He'd found some sort of magic button, and Rachel couldn't hold back anymore. Her hands were on him, undoing his belt like it was something she'd done every day of her life. *So much for going slow.* She pulled down his jeans and boxers as she gracefully dropped to her knees, pulling him into her mouth. Moments later, he gently pulled her head away, then knelt in the grass in front of her. He kissed her sweetly before laying down, pulling her onto her back next to him. He kissed her softly, from her forehead to her lips and down along her neck, his hand caressing her body and grazing over her breasts.

He kept kissing her up and down her upper body until she sat up. "Shoes." She pointed at her feet and made him stop so she could take off her boots. Then she laid back down in the soft grass and unbuttoned her jeans. She handed him one of the condoms she had put in her back pocket, giving Christopher a look that signaled she was ready for more. He slid off her jeans as she lifted her hips. He kissed her inner thigh once, then her new scar, then her stomach, working his way slowly and expertly up her body. He slid her left breast out of her bra, rubbing his thumb over her soft pink nipple a few times before taking it in his mouth. He cupped his hand under her head and pulled her up just enough to unhook her bra and slide it off.

"You are absolutely perfect," he murmured, staring at her.

Rachel let out a quiet laugh. Unlike him, she was far from perfect, but she was happy he was happy. *Enough of all this staring at each other!* Rachel's patience was running out. She didn't know what he was waiting for. She grabbed his arm and pulled him back down to her, kissing him more deeply and with more passion than she had ever imagined possible. Rachel's hands were firmly on his face. Her tongue dipped into his mouth, urging him to keep going. He slowly slid his hand down under her navy-blue lace underwear, and he felt her for the first time, exploring every inch of her—touching her, rubbing her gently, sliding one finger deep inside her, then two as she let out a deep moan. Then he moved down, kissing her everywhere. Trying to move slowly, he pulled her underwear until his mouth was on her, his tongue licking her while he slid two fingers in and out of her until she called out his name.

Christopher looked up at her from between her legs, never stopping what he was doing, and watched with delight as she touched her own breasts, playing with her nipples, which were now hard pink peaks. She arched her back and moaned with pleasure, so he kept going, working her into a frenzy of passion. Rachel felt a rush of warmth as her muscles contracted. It was euphoric. Her orgasm peaked and she started to come down from the high, but he kept going, giving her more and more until she pulled him up to her.

"I need you Christopher," she breathed.

Kissing her on the mouth, he hurriedly tore open the condom and slid it on before taking the opportunity to thrust himself into her for the first time. She arched her back, inhaling sharply, and opened her eyes just enough to look at him, assuring him she was okay. She begged him to keep going as he moved in and out of her slowly. She wrapped her legs around him, pulling him in closer, deeper inside of her, kissing him and moaning. She repeated his name over and over as he kissed her neck and her breasts, running his hands over her entire body as she did the same to him. Finally, her muscles tightened around him, signaling she was close. She kept tightening, arching, calling out. He pushed into her a little deeper, a little harder, a few more times, until neither of them could take it anymore and they both let go, finishing together.

Rachel pulled Christopher in for a kiss before he rolled her over so that she was on top, straddling him, kissing him, and looking down at him. She thought she'd died and gone to heaven, not believing it was real or that anything that wonderful could exist, certainly not for her. They laid there together under the tree, Christopher holding her on top of him while they kissed. She couldn't get enough and needed more of him. Great sex was what she expected and typically what she got, but this, with the emotional intimacy, was something else entirely. She slid her hand down, urging him to get hard. She knew he probably needed more time, but didn't care.

"You first," he said, rolling her onto her back again. He kissed her deeply, making his way back down her body. Kissing, licking, exploring every inch of her. Moving even more slowly than before. He brought her slowly almost to the point of orgasm before putting on a new condom and taking her with a bit more force than the first time. She kissed him, moaning his name and arching her back until she shifted her hips and rolled on top of him. She stared down at him, gyrating her hips slowly at first, then moving faster and harder against him. Her long, loose curls flowed over her shoulders, partially hiding her perfectly proportioned breasts but giving him a peak when she moved in just the right way. She started touching herself, adding to her own pleasure and his. Suddenly her muscles tensed around him again, and he exploded inside of her, both of them calling out, giving voice to their contentment.

They lay together in a state of bliss. Christopher's arm looped around Rachel as she rested her head on his chest. "You really do have to be the best at everything, don't you?" Christopher remarked.

"*We're* the best at everything," Rachel corrected as she let out a small giggle, delighted at the praise.

"I mean, seriously Rachel, this is like nothing I've experienced before," he told her.

Rachel smiled up at him sweetly, knowing they were just getting started. Knowing it would get even better than this. "Yeah, if it's this good with a condom, just think how it will be once I'm back on birth control and we don't need those anymore."

Christopher looked at her, confused. "Why do you need to be on birth control? I'm pretty sure the Navy surgeon sort of took care of that . . ."

"Ectopic pregnancy is still a risk," Rachel explained.

Christopher stared at her blankly. "I'm sure I'm supposed to know what that is, but maybe a quick refresher?"

"An ectopic pregnancy occurs when a fertilized egg implants and grows outside the main cavity of the uterus, usually in the fallopian tube." She looked at him, checking for understanding. Christopher nodded. "It's rare, but usually life threatening and hard to diagnose so . . ."

"Birth control," Christopher finished for her.

"Safety first!" she said with a wink.

"But you're sure?" Christopher asked Rachel.

"Sure, about what?"

"You don't have to go on birth control. I know there can be crazy side effects. Condoms are fine. It's entirely up to you. Your body, your choice," he said seriously.

"Kind of ruins the chances for spontaneity, don't you think? I mean, always be prepared and all that, but really, I'm going to keep a Costco sized box of condoms with me at all times?"

Christopher laughed, a clear image in his mind of Rachel wandering the streets of D.C. with a backpack full of condoms. "Not exactly Navy issued supplies!"

"The Navy issues condoms. You just have to go to the medic station on base with your leave orders," Rachel said, shocked that he didn't seem to know. "They hand them out for free. Did you really not know that? Have you been buying condoms this whole time with your own money?"

Christopher looked at her, mortified. "Oh my god, I'm not going to go to the medic station and ask the nurse for condoms!"

"Why not? It's preventive medicine. The last thing the Navy needs is a bunch of irresponsible sailors running around with chlamydia."

"Rachel, I spent the past fourteen years basically having no expenses since my basic housing allowance from the Navy goes to my parents since my mom is technically my landlord. The Navy pays for my phone, my health care . . . I think it's okay to pay for condoms."

Rachel shrugged. "Well, I guess it won't be a problem for much longer. I'll go to the doctor once I'm in D.C. and get a prescription."

"Once we're in D.C." Christopher corrected her.

"Once *we're* in D.C.?" she asked.

Christopher smirked. "Yeah, you didn't think you were going without me, did you?"

"Well, I didn't want to assume . . ." Rachel turned away from him, laying on her back to stare up at the bright blue cloudless sky. She let out a sigh. "Christopher, you can go anywhere and do anything. No more following orders, having the Navy send you around the world as they see fit. Really think about what you want. Leave me out of the equation. I'll be in D.C. because I don't have a choice about that, but you do." Rachel was so straightforward and unemotional with her speech that Christopher was taken aback.

"I've *been* thinking about it, Rachel. From the second I saw you collapse into Matt's arms, blood everywhere. I thought you were going to die. I was sure I was going to lose you, and I knew I couldn't bear it if that happened. Everything clicked in that second. You're it. You are all that matters to me.

My whole world. My everything. So, like it or not, I'm coming to D.C. with you. I've already decided." His voice was steady, unwavering, and sincere.

"Where are you going to live?" Rachel asked inquisitively.

"With you," Christopher stated as though it were obvious.

"And what are you going to do once you get to D.C.?" she asked.

A big smile crept over Christopher's face as he pulled her back on top of him. "This," he said, kissing her and moving his hands over her again. Feeling her breasts, grazing her nipples with his hands, then his mouth. "I'm going to do this as often as you'll let me."

Rachel laughed, brushing his hands away and sitting up, straddling him. "Christopher, I'm being serious. You know I'm going to be at HQ all the time. I may as well move in there. I don't think they'll let me bring you with me. Unless I can somehow convince the Navy, and then I don't know where I'll be." She looked sad.

Christopher gently squeezed her thigh and smiled up at her. "No matter what happens with your new job, I'll be at home, wherever we make it, ready to love you and support you and care for you always," he vowed.

Epilogue:
SEPTEMBER 2020

YASHFA KHAN WAS STANDING in her kitchen in Khost, Afghanistan. Her sister Yamna was crying in the other room, her nose bleeding and her face swelling from where their father had hit her. Things were bad and getting worse. The only small mercy was that the children were all asleep, tucked safely into bed. Their father had known, of course, somehow, that their husbands were away. Off at some sort of political meeting. That had been the problem. Their father had arranged marriages for them to men from good families. Proper families who supported the Taliban and whatever else their father found acceptable. Righteous, he called it. Not everyone thought like he did though. Not everyone bought into what their fathers wholeheartedly believed. Indoctrination wasn't working on her generation as well as he and his friends believed, and she was determined to ensure it didn't work on her children either. They deserved better, and her husband agreed.

Her sister was still bleeding, still crying, still horrified that their father had come by to take her son away with him—off to some training camp. She'd said no. Argued that her son was too young. He was thirteen. Old enough. Beyond old enough according to their father. He'd hit her and she'd hit back. He hadn't been expecting it. Hadn't had the slightest inkling that his youngest daughter—sweet, polite, people pleasing Yamna—knew how to throw a punch.

Yashfa smiled to herself at the thought of telling their father they'd befriended an American spy, or soldier, or whatever she'd been. Then she grimaced, knowing exactly what sort of retaliation their father would come at them with if he ever found out they had been friendly with Americans, let alone American soldiers.

Yashfa took a deep breath. She didn't know what to do. She needed help and there was only one person she knew who may be able and willing to stand up to their father, to put a stop to him once and for all. She'd promised once upon a time to make all the bad men disappear. Said it might take her years to do it, but that she would. Yashfa hadn't seen Rachel in nearly two years, hadn't spoken to her in a while either, but it was time to call in the favor.

Yashfa to Skylark: *Call me. I need help!*